DARE

BLOOD BROTHERS
BOOK FIVE

HEATHER LONG

*"Men are afraid that women will laugh at them. Women are afraid that men will kill them." - **Margaret Atwood**️*

This is for the girls.
Give 'em hell!

SERIES SO FAR

Burn
Lure
Own
Oath
Dare

FOREWORD

Dear Reader,

Welcome to the fifth and final book of the Blood Brothers series. This is a series that should be read in order so if you have not read the first four, please pause and begin there. If you are curious about where the Blood Brothers story came from, I shared some background on that in the foreword of *Burn*.

Previously in *Blood Brothers*: Grace and Bones boned after three books of edging, Bones is taken hostage, rescued, there was a foursome with Grace and the guys (except for Bones), and the hunt for Amorette resumes. For those wanting more than that TLDR, the previously goes something like this:

After several weeks in Braxton Harbor helping Doc—one of their former unit brothers—and his family, the team returns to the hunt for Grace's sister, Amorette. Training ramps back up, from hand-to-hand to weapons work, and Grace pushes herself hard. After an extended stretch of Bones wringing repeated orgasms from her, they finally cross the last threshold and become lovers in truth, the shift sparked by her emotional break during training. Bones helps her gather the shattered pieces of herself and put them back together.

A meeting with Declan O'Rourke unfolds exactly as expected: into an ambush. The setup ends with Bones in enemy hands while the rest of the team scrambles to find him and interrogates O'Rourke. Grace is haunted by fear for Bones—and by the gnawing thought that this might be her fault. Subjected to "torture" and "interrogation," Bones gives up nothing, focused solely on staying alive.

Once they locate him, the team launches the rescue, with Grace playing a pivotal role. O'Rourke infiltrates a museum gala with Grace on his arm while the others work the shadows. They gain access to the service corridors, and though Bones is a bloody wreck, he forces himself to his feet to take out anyone who threatens Grace as she hauls him out. They slip through a loading dock, use a service van to mask their escape. Later, they dump O'Rourke somewhere in the desert, having only let him survive because he did help with Bones. Good riddance, as far as they are concerned.

Back at Base in Montana, Bones begins to heal while they sort through the intel. The ambush and kidnapping turn out to have nothing to do with Grace; it all traces back to an old job the team took—one thread finally tied off.

With that behind them, they shift focus to Amorette's former law firm and its "senior" partner, Mark Sinclair. The trail leads to Virginia, where Grace shadows Sinclair into court and lets him see her. When he reacts as if he's seen a ghost, she knows they're on the right track. While Lunchbox tails Sinclair, Grace and the others head to his home in McLean.

Channeling "Amorette," Grace gets inside, noting a

deeply nervous housekeeper and the convenient absence of Sinclair's wife, who's "out of town." Upstairs in Sinclair's office, she's seconds from plugging in the flash drive so Alphabet can pull what they need—when movement behind her freezes her blood. She turns and finds herself face-to-face with the man who held her captive at the start of this entire odyssey. Terror clamps down like a vise.

And that, my fabulous reader, brings us to *Dare*, and the final descent into this dark adventure.

Please be aware this book contains content with dark themes and intense situations intended for mature audiences only, including but not limited to: sexual assault, dubious consent, physical violence, emotional and mental abuse, as well as kidnapping, stalking, manipulation, and other potentially triggering topics.

And now, as always, the housekeeping notes:

For those of you who have never read a why choose, or reverse harem before, first let me thank you for picking this up and giving it a shot. Second, the heroine will not make a choice in this book or any other between the guys in her life. It may take her a while to reach that conclusion, but it's the journey that drives it. There are many ways to frame this kind of relationship, currently why choose fits it very well.

I'll see you on the flip side.

xoxo

Heather

P.S. The dog doesn't die.

CHAPTER

ONE

GRACE

He smiled like he'd been expecting me.

For a second, the whole room went soundless — no hum in my comm, no air from the vents, no breath in my chest. Just that half-ruined face, the white of his blind eye catching the dim light like a coin on the bottom of a river.

The scent hit next. Not smoke, not cologne, but the phantom reek of oil and iron tangled in vicious knots with the memory of his hands. My fingers twitched, reaching for the weapon I didn't have. The bag was by the desk, six feet away, a thousand miles.

My brain knew the steps: pivot, distance, draw, strike.

My body forgot every single one.

It was like waking up inside a nightmare I'd already survived once. Muscles I'd trained to obey me just... refused. My knees locked. My breath stuttered. My heart was a hammer behind my ribs and every hit made my vision flare white around the edges.

He took another step. Slow. Deliberate. The way you move toward a frightened animal you think you still own.

"You look good," he said. His voice rasped like gravel in a glass. "Did you miss me?"

The words slid under my skin, finding all the old bruises that had never really healed.

I tried to answer, but my tongue was thick, my mouth dry. Somewhere, someone was shouting my name — *Bones? Voodoo?* — but it was like the sound came from underwater. The comm was still in my ear, and I couldn't make my hand rise to touch it.

He tilted his head, that smile widening just a little. "Still so quiet. I always liked that about you."

A flicker of movement — his hand lowering toward his side, not to draw a weapon, just to remind me who'd always had the power.

Something inside me cracked then. Not courage. Not even rage. Just the thin, splintering sound of the line between *then* and *now* snapping clean through.

I wanted to run. I wanted to scream. I wanted to remember how to fight.

Instead, I stood there, every nerve raw, and stared at the man I'd thought was gone forever. The one who had taken everything from me — and had the audacity to smile like he'd found a lost pet instead of a person.

He moved ever closer, the limp still there, subtle but real. His shadow reached me before he did.

"You didn't really think you could escape forever, did you?"

The tremor in my chest climbed my throat. My lips parted, but no sound came out.

The air was thick, cloying, like it had settled in my lungs without asking permission. I couldn't think. I couldn't breathe. My fingers curled into fists, nails biting into palms, but they didn't reach for anything. Not the desk, not the bag, not the flash drive. They might as well have been carved from stone.

Another step. That blind eye gleamed in the dim light, his scar catching shadows like it was alive. Every step he took made my stomach twist, like the ground itself was betraying me.

I remembered the way he'd touched me. Not just the physical, but the ownership, the hunger to make me small, pliable, obedient. And all at once, months of training, months of planning, months of knowing exactly how to disarm and escape... evaporated.

I was just a lost girl in his presence.

My knees shook. My heart was a jackhammer inside my chest, pounding out a rhythm I couldn't control. It didn't matter that I'd killed, snuck, lied, stolen, survived — none of it meant anything here. Not when he looked at me like I was exactly what he wanted. Like he still *owned* me in some private ledger only he could see.

I wanted to close my eyes. I wanted to shrink into the chair. I wanted to disappear. Every muscle in my body coiled tight, frozen between fight and flight, and yet unable to do either.

"Look at you," he murmured, slow, satisfied. "You're even more... beautiful."

The words weren't compliments. They weren't harmless. They were chains. Every syllable wrapped tighter around me, knotting the pit of my stomach. My mouth opened, closed, opened again. Soundless.

I could feel the sweat on my back, the cold of the office seeping through my blouse, my pulse hammering in my ears louder than his voice. The past and present collided, and I couldn't tell which was which. The months of planning, the team outside, the safe, the drive from

Alexandria... it all felt like a dream I had forgotten the ending to.

And then he smiled again. That same twisted curl, the kind that had haunted my nightmares.

"You've been a good little pet, haven't you?"

God. The word made my stomach twist even harder, coiling my intestines into a knot that burned with nausea. My hands trembled at my sides. My legs felt heavy, cemented to the floor.

I tried to tell myself I was still Grace. That I wasn't the scared girl who woke up in that horror show. That I had skills, weapons, allies.

But none of it reached me. Not now.

He moved closer. Slow. Certain. Watching me. Happy to see me scared. Happy to see me... *here.*

I could only breathe shallowly, heartbeat a drum of panic in my ears, and feel the raw, unfiltered terror that reminded me — he didn't need to strike me. His presence alone was enough to undo every hard-won inch of control I thought I had.

Yet, my feet seemed sunken into concrete. I was shackled in place like I wore that chain around my ankle again. All I could do was stand there, frozen, waiting for the next move, every instinct screaming at me to survive while my body refused to listen.

His hand moved again. Just a fraction of an inch this time, but in my world it was seismic. Every nerve ending in my skin screamed before he even touched me. My vision narrowed to him—the scar, the blind eye, the ghost of his smile—and the rest of the room became a soft blur.

I could feel the air shift as his fingers hovered over my arm, the faint brush of fabric sending sparks of panic up my spine. It was unreal. I wanted to jerk away, to shove him, to strike, to do *something*, but my body didn't belong to me anymore. My muscles twitched, useless, and my thoughts were a riot of broken memory fragments.

Waking up to that hell. The gut-wrenching cries of despair and pain. Skin slapping against skin. The odors of bodies, sex, and sweat. The sticky feeling of his release all over me. The suffocating smell of his cum staining the air.

Each memory collided with the present, folding around his hand as it descended toward me. It moved like slow water, inevitable and unstoppable.

The tip of his finger brushed my cheek. Just a touch, feather-light. I felt it in every cell. My stomach lurched, bile rising. My knees threatened to buckle, but I stayed upright, rooted to the floor by some cruel twist of fate.

His smile widened. "Still so tense... I like it."

I could feel the phantom of his hands where they'd held me before, the ownership, the violence, the control. My body responded—adrenaline, fear, nausea—a symphony of sensations I couldn't smother.

Everything slowed. My pulse was thunder in my ears. Every breath was deliberate, hot and rasping. My skin tingled, hairs on end. His hand brushed again, slightly firmer this time, and it was like fire on my veins, a lightning strike I couldn't escape.

Remember. Breathe. Move.

My mind tried, weakly, to summon the Grace I had spent the past several months becoming. The woman who could take him down, who could fight like hell, who could and *would* fight without choking on terror. But she seemed a distant memory and so alien from the one standing here as to be from a different galaxy.

I was small.

Scared.

Trapped.

In a nightmare all over again.

Had I ever actually escaped?

That scraped open another layer of horror, ripping me apart.

His hand lingered, cupping my cheek and filling my nostrils with the stale scent of tobacco. He'd been smoking. It was acrid. Made my eyes water. My nose run. I wanted to sob, but even my tears abandoned me.

"My beautiful pet," he said, possessive pride in his claim of ownership.

My stomach twisted into itself, nausea clawing up my throat. My vision tunneled even tighter. All I could see were his fingers, the scarred knuckle, the curve of his wrist, and nothing else existed.

His other hand moved closer. Slow. Casual. Watching me. Measuring. Enjoying. Even as that awareness I was frozen in the gravity of it, trapped between every instinct I had ever had and the pure, raw terror that had returned to claim me.

Fight. Run. Scre—

The words died before they formed. My tongue felt like sandpaper. My throat contracted. And all I could do was let him close that last inch, let him touch me fully, and endure the moment where control was no longer mine, where fear ruled everything.

Because if I didn't fight, it gave him no reason to hurt me. If I could control the interaction, then I wasn't a victim. Even as those thoughts played through my head, there was something deeply, intrinsically wrong with them.

That wasn't right.

The stroke of his rough thumb over the line of my cheekbone froze my soul in place. One milky eye and one narrowed eye seemed fixed on me. The taut band inside of me snapped and warmth spread along my legs. The stink of urine filled the room as the man dipped his head.

"Grace, status—" Bones' voice cracked through the comm.

The wrong sound at the wrong time. The dark man's good eye narrowed abruptly and his grip on my face turned brutal. He jerked my head to the side to see the earpiece. Pain lanced up my jaw where his fingers dug in, a white-hot flare that snapped through the fog. The shock of it pulled a sound out of me—a choked gasp that wasn't quite a scream.

He yanked my head sideways, the skin at my temple burning under his grip. "Who are you talking to?" His breath was hot against my ear.

Somewhere in the house, a door banged open. Not in my head. No, it was real. The thud reverberated through the floorboards. A muffled scream came from downstairs. A woman. There was a housekeeper. Then another crash, closer, the sharp splinter of wood giving way.

His head jerked toward the noise, and for the first time I saw something like confusion cut across his ruined face.

"Grace!" Bones again, louder now, raw. "We're in! Hold—"

The rest of it vanished under the crack of another door giving way downstairs and the echoing bark of Voodoo's voice.

The man snarled, fingers tightening until spots bloomed behind my eyes. "Who did you bring here?"

My pulse roared. Every sound blurred into one long, rising wave—boots on tile, shouted commands, the dull thud of something heavy hitting the floor below.

Then his hand left my face only to slam against my

shoulder, shoving me backward. My head hit the corner of the desk. Pain exploded, bright and electric. The world tilted; the edges of my vision went white, then red.

Instinct finally found me. My body lurched, unsteady, more reflex than reason. I stumbled sideways as he reached for me again, his curse lost in the noise of another crash—another door being kicked in. The sound was unmistakable as wood cracked and shuddered.

The air filled with chaos: footsteps pounding the hall, someone shouting "Clear!" The comm crackled against my ear, a thread of sound in the storm.

My legs wouldn't cooperate; they were rubber and fire at once. The copper taste of blood spread across my tongue where I'd bitten it. It was almost deja vu all over again. Only then, he'd dragged me out of the bedroom and into the utilitarian hallway with its bare concrete floors and walls.

He'd *run* like a rat, fleeing a sinking ship, hauling me with him. But pain. Pain and terror had locked me in place then too. I'd frozen. When the gunshots came—he'd fled.

Then...

He turned toward the door, muscles coiling, and for an instant he looked almost startled, as if he never thought to find himself the prey instead of predator.

Only, he'd been prey before. That reality floated up from the deep morass where it had sunk. When he jerked me upward, I didn't fight the roll of my stomach this time.

I threw up on him.

Every ounce of food and drink I'd had that day spewed out of me. Not that it had been much. It was mostly bile. It all burned, but he swore as he took it in the face and the chest. When he slapped me, I took the blow and stumbled sideways, but I didn't go down.

The voices on the comm were constant now. They were coming.

AB was talking to me. He was letting me know they were coming. The world that had slowed down to a painful crawl slammed into fast forward and I grabbed the first thing on the desk my fingers touched.

A hard marble paperweight.

I threw it.

Ignacio. That was his name.

It rushed back into the void along with sound and fury. His name was Ignacio. I threw the paperweight as the door to the office slammed with a hard kick.

One.

Two.

Then cracked under the fierceness of the blows, the wood splintering and the lock sheering away.

But I'd already grabbed the next thing off the desk and threw it even if I didn't need to do another damn thing. Ignacio was already dead, even if he didn't know it. And his death? It would be brutal as fuck. As he'd soon find out.

My guys were here.

TWO

GRACE

The door slammed behind me, and the world narrowed to the split second before disaster hit. Ignacio lunged, that same cruel, twisted smile stretched across his scarred face. My stomach pitched. My hands shook, my muscles frozen—but my eyes landed on the paperweight sitting heavy on the corner of the desk.

Instinct overrode fear. I grabbed it, hefted it, and hurled it as hard as I could. It smacked into Ignacio's temple with a satisfying crack. He staggered sideways, swearing, but didn't go down. My chest heaved, adrenaline lancing through every vein.

From the corner of my eye, a hidden door burst open and men poured in. Weapons raised, faces twisted in rage. My knees nearly buckled, but I threw myself behind the desk, grabbing the heaviest object within reach—a brass lamp. I swung it at the closest man as he lunged. The lamp smashed against his shoulder, sending him sprawling backward, arms flailing.

"Grace!" Bones' voice cut through the chaos, sharper now, urgent. "Hold—"

A second man dove toward me. Reflex finally caught up with my brain. I rolled to the side, dragging the desk chair partially between us, and grabbed a hefty book. The man's aim wavered; he stumbled as I threw it, and it clattered against his chest, knocking him off balance and giving Voodoo the opening to pin him to the floor.

Ignacio recovered from the first hit and lunged again, eyes wild, rage spilling over. I froze, a frozen statue of fear and nausea—but before he could reach me, Bones slammed into him from the side, twisting him off balance. My stomach dropped when I realized he might... no, he could kill him.

"Wait!" I gasped, voice trembling but sharp. "We can use him."

Bones' hand tightened on Ignacio's arm, and for the first time, he paused. Voodoo hesitated as well, their eyes flicking to me, questioning. I swallowed bile, forcing my voice steady. "Don't kill *him*."

Movement flickered from the corner of my eye and I twisted to see the last man lunging at me. I grabbed the ornate paperweight again, hurling it directly at his knees. He went down with a sharp yelp, scrambling to regain footing, but Voodoo was on him instantly.

"What about them?" Bones' voice was a shard of winter cutting through the room. His intonation was flat, precise, and utterly devoid of warmth, as if the question barely registered in the air around him.

"I don't care about them." Truth. Harsh. Implacable. I didn't know who they were and my attention was on Ignacio. Bones locked an arm around Ignacio's throat, strangling the man who struggled, clawing at his arm to no avail. Ignacio's eyes went wide, even his milky scarred one and I didn't look away as the fear and terror registered on that man's reddened face.

The grim satisfaction that flooded me in those seconds before the man lost consciousness was a kind of brutal wakeup call. But I didn't care. I wanted Ignacio to hurt. I wanted him afraid. The thump of Ignacio dropping as his expression went slack and Bones rendered him unconscious added another savage layer to the whole scene.

The next sounds were the cracking of necks. It wrenched my attention from the man now on the floor that Bones secured to the others in the room. Voodoo went through them one at a time. Eliminating them. I kept waiting for the revulsion to hit me, but it didn't. He removed their weapons once they were dead. No one left to come after us from behind.

Some distant part of my mind even registered why Voodoo used his hands rather than a weapon. No blood spatter. No DNA. Not that we'd be able to hide the signs of violence.

My legs shook, my blouse was damp, and my hands were slick with sweat. My chest heaved, every inhale tasting copper and panic. Bones' eyes flicked down; his gray gaze was sharper than steel, cold enough to cut, yet scorching in intensity. He seemed to take in everything about me—from my trembling hands to the flush creeping across my skin, reading me as if I were laid bare.

For just a heartbeat, his expression softened. Before, he'd always seemed so remote, so meticulously composed, without a hint of feeling. That wasn't him at all. It was a mask. The veneer of control, taut and precise, concealed a fire that could scorch and consume. Beneath it all was the violently passionate man I'd come to know and love. I'd never been so grateful to know he had that power—especially now, with Ignacio in our custody.

"Housekeeper secured," AB's voice cut through the comm. "Sweeping the house. Clear except for your room."

Bones exhaled sharply, then looked at Voodoo. "Back him up."

Voodoo brushed a knuckle down my cheek, soft but grounding. "Good job, Firecracker," he murmured before he disappeared through the broken door.

I forced a shaky nod, aware that the adrenaline was fading, leaving me raw and trembling—but alive. Alive, and with a tiny, burning spark of control that seemed to have evaporated with Ignacio's arrival.

The room finally settled into an eerie stillness, broken only by the ragged rhythm of my own breathing. Bones moved closer, silent but watchful, like a shadow that had softened its edges for me.

I sank to the floor, pressing my palms into the carpet, trying to steady the trembling that had taken root in my bones. Every inch of me felt raw, exposed, fragile. That's when the smell hit me. My stomach lurched. The wet heat at my thighs, the slick copper tang in the air. I'd pissed myself. The dampness on my blouse was my own vomit and it clung to me, smeared in some places.

I froze, a wave of panic overtaking the adrenaline, the brief triumph, everything. My hands flew to my face, my body shaking so violently that I could hear it in the quiet.

Bones knelt beside me before I could even move, calm as a mountain. His gray eyes locked onto mine, steady, assessing—but not judging. Not once had I felt anyone look at me like this before, and it made my chest tighten.

"Do you want to clean up?" he asked softly, his voice an anchor in the storm of my shame and fear.

When he lifted a hand to touch my face, I shook my head, voice a broken whisper. "No... I... I'm filthy." I shouldn't have let Voodoo touch me.

"Filthy," he echoed, carefully, almost like testing the word against the room, against me. This time, he reached for my hand. "Grace."

I flinched, yanking it back. "Don't touch me. I'm... I'm disgusting."

Bones didn't pull away. Instead, he tilted his head, still calm, still unflinching. "You're alive. That's what matters." His voice didn't scold. It didn't pity. It simply... held. I could feel the warmth of his hand hovering near mine, patient, steadying, as if just being in contact might anchor me back to myself.

"I... I—" I swallowed, the words catching in my throat, my trembling redoubling. My knees drew up instinctively, hiding, curling in on myself.

I let my breath hitch, a single tremor rippling through me, and my hands rose to rest atop his, letting the warmth of both anchor me even as the humiliation and the shaking surged. Bones' thumb brushed against my knuckles, methodical, steady, and I realized I was clinging to it—not just for support, but because it reminded me I hadn't failed completely. I hadn't been broken, not entirely.

I wasn't back in that warehouse. I wasn't chained, gasping for air, unable to protect myself. I wasn't there at all.

"You're safe now," Bones said, low and even. "No one can hurt you here. Not while I'm standing."

I wanted to believe him, wanted to stop trembling, wanted the room to stop spinning and the nausea to fade. But I let myself stay there, huddled, fragile, and alive. I couldn't see Ignacio, Bones blocked my view of him.

"Do you need to clear the house?" I asked, my voice still small, unsure.

Bones shook his head slightly. "Alphabet and Voodoo will handle the clear. You don't need to worry about it." His gaze didn't leave mine, steady and unflinching.

I hesitated, fumbling for what we were supposed to have been doing, then asked, "Do we need to search the office?"

He shrugged, an almost faint smile tugging at the corner of his lips. "It will keep."

My chest tightened. "I thought we were on a timetable," I pressed, finally meeting his gaze squarely.

"The only timetable we're on," he said, voice low, almost teasing, "is our own."

"But... the plan..." I argued, the words tumbling out even as my stomach knotted.

Bones didn't pull away. Instead, he continued to rub my knuckles in slow, deliberate circles. Each touch chipped away at the tension coiled in my limbs, bit by bit loosening my death grip on my knees.

"Plans change," he murmured, as if reading my mind.

"I... I—" I swallowed hard, the words catching in my throat. I didn't have another argument.

Bones didn't rush me. He let his touch anchor me, methodical, steady. His thumb brushed against my knuckles again, drawing my hands to rest atop his. The warmth radiating from him seeped through the tremor, and despite my retreat, it was like he held me.

"Still with me, Dollface?" The utter gentleness in his voice threatened to undo me.

"I think so," I whispered and shifted just slightly, letting my body lean toward him without realizing it. The pressure of his presence was grounding, the slow, deliberate touch of his hand a lifeline in the storm inside me. And though my mind raced, my chest heaved, and my legs still shook, there was a small, stubborn spark of control flickering inside me.

"Good." He eased to sit on the floor right there, not seeming even a little put off by how dirty I was. "Just going to sit here with you until you're ready to move." The explanation accompanied his careful movements, each one telegraphed to show me what he was going to do.

"Might take a while," I confessed, as much as I wish it wouldn't.

"We'll take as long as you need."

The words wrapped around me, fragile as they were, like a shield. I wanted to believe him. I wanted to stop trembling. I wanted the room, my body, my mind, to stop spinning. But I stayed huddled, fragile, and alive, letting myself feel the contrast between the chaos we'd survived and the quiet here, between my fear and the safety he offered.

We stayed that way for a long moment—just us, and the unconscious Ignacio at our feet, and the quiet that stretched around the aftermath of violence. But when I rasped, "Okay... okay," something in his shoulders eased by a fraction.

"Let's get you cleaned up," he said quietly.

The words made a hot spike of shame twist through my stomach all over again. I stiffened instantly. "I—I can't. I'm —" My breath hitched, and I swallowed hard, the burn of bile still bitter at the back of my throat. "I'm so gross."

Bones' eyes held mine, steady as gravity. "You're hurt. You fought. You survived." His voice didn't rise, didn't harden. It softened. A dangerous softness, because it saw everything. "That's not gross."

A tremor rolled through me so violently that my arms wrapped around my stomach before I even realized I'd moved. "But I—" My voice cracked. "You don't understand. I pissed myself. And I threw up. There's—" My breath stuttered. "It's on me. I can feel it."

He lifted our joined hands, brushing his thumb along my knuckles again in that same slow, deliberate circle that had kept me tethered through the last moments of hell. "Grace." His tone was a low command wrapped in velvet. "Look at me."

I forced my eyes upward. The intensity in his gaze—steady, immovable—made my lungs seize, but in a different way than Ignacio had. Bones' gaze held no ownership, no expectation, no hunger except the kind that meant he would burn the world down before he let anything else touch me.

"Nothing on you," he murmured, "diminishes you. Not this. Not anything he did."

My mouth parted, but no words came out. My voice had abandoned me again. Bones moved first, shifting closer—not touching more, not crowding, just moving into my space with the same quiet confidence he used approaching live explosives.

"Can you stand?" he asked.

I shook my head quickly, panic flaring sharp. "No—no, I —Bones, I can't get it on you. I smell. I'm—"

He didn't let me pull away. His fingers slipped beneath my hand and curled around it, firm, anchoring. "Grace. Look at me." I did. Barely. "You could be covered in blood and mud and ash," he said quietly, "and I'd still touch you."

My pulse stuttered, a shock of heat rolling up my spine before I could smother it. He wasn't flirting. He wasn't trying to soothe me. He was stating a fact as solid as the floor beneath me.

"You're shaken," he continued. "And you're allowed to be. But don't mistake that for weakness."

"But I—" My voice cracked again. "Bones, I'm disgusting."

"Not to me." The way he said it—leveled straight at me, voice low and steady—made something inside me unravel. My breath shuddered. My fingers tightened around his almost desperately.

For a long moment, he let that settle between us.

Then Bones shifted, rising to one knee. His hand slid from mine only so he could reach up and brush the hair back from my face—so gently it made tears burn behind my eyes.

"You can lean on me," he said. "Or I can carry you. Your choice."

The tears threatened harder. "I don't want to get anything on you."

He gave a slow, almost imperceptible shrug, his lips beginning to pull into a faint, devastating half-smile. "It washes off."

I let out a shaking breath that was almost a laugh. Almost.

Bones held out both hands this time, palms open—not pulling, not pushing. Waiting.

My body shook so hard I wasn't sure I'd be able to move. But I reached for him. Carefully. Slowly. As though the movement itself might crack me in half.

His fingers wrapped around mine, warm and steady, and he guided me upward, supporting my weight easily.

My legs almost gave out. Instantly, his arm slid around my waist.

"I've got you," he murmured, voice so close to my ear it sent a different kind of shiver down my spine.

I didn't protest this time. I couldn't. Something in me gave in—not to fear, but to safety. To him.

When I finally managed to whisper, "Where are we going?" Bones' grip tightened just slightly.

"To clean you up," he said. "Somewhere quiet. Somewhere safe."

Behind us, Ignacio lay unconscious on the floor. But Bones didn't look at him. He looked at me—at every tremble, every breath, every inch of shaking, messy humanity I was trying to hide.

"At our pace," he added softly. "Not his. Not the plan's. Ours."

My throat tightened. My fingers dug into his shirt and I let myself lean fully into his strength.

CHAPTER

THREE

BONES

Grace was shaking so hard I could feel the tremors through my arm, even with her barely leaning on me. Light contact. Bare minimum pressure. She was trying not to touch me more than she had to.

That wasn't going to work.

The guest room was clear. I swept it myself before I let her in. AB and Voodoo had the rest of the house. Her assailant was unconscious and zip-tied to a radiator in the office. Nothing was getting to her.

I walked her into the adjoining bathroom—clean tile, soft lighting, nothing sharp in sight. Neutral ground. A place that wouldn't trigger anything unless she projected it there herself.

Her breath started to hitch the second she caught sight of herself in the mirror. She froze. Went rigid. Like she expected the glass to judge her.

"Don't look at that," I said quietly.

She flinched at the sound of my voice. Not from fear—startle response. Too much adrenaline, too much shock running through a body running on fumes.

Her fingers clenched harder in my shirt. She tried to pull back. "Bones... I—I don't want you to see me like this."

I angled my body between her and the mirror. "Grace."

Just her name. Low. Solid. Something she could push against if she needed to.

She wouldn't meet my eyes. Her gaze was fixed somewhere around my collarbone, unfocused.

"I pissed myself," she whispered. "I threw up on myself. I'm—" Her breath cracked. "I'm disgusting."

Deep breath. I wrapped iron control around my responses. Grace didn't need my rage. Not yet. We'd get there, but she needed something far different. Maybe Voodoo might have been the better choice to look after her. But I wanted to take care of her right now.

Pain and shame were two very different responses. The first was just information. You could ignore it, override it, or just compartmentalize it under something survivable. The second? It just didn't work that way. Shame rewired the whole system if you let it.

"Grace," I murmured again, slower this time, "none of that matters."

Her breath came fast and shallow. "To you."

"To me," I said, "especially to me."

That got her attention. Her eyes flicked up—quick, uncertain.

She didn't pull away this time when I reached out and brushed my fingers along her forearm. Barely a touch. Just enough to remind her she was here, in the present, not back in that warehouse. Not in that room.

"Sit," I said, guiding her toward the closed toilet lid. Soft voice. Command underneath it. She listened more to tone than words right now.

She sat, elbows on her knees, fingers locked tight.

The shaking hadn't stopped. Her whole body looked like it was trying to outrun the memory of the last hour.

I grabbed a clean towel from the cabinet, ran warm water over one corner. Routine movement. Predictable. Safe. I wrung out the excess.

When I knelt in front of her, her eyes widened. "Bones, you don't have to—"

"I know what I have to do." I met her gaze. "And what I'm choosing to do."

Color rose on her neck. Embarrassment. Vulnerability. And something underneath all that—something she didn't have a name for yet.

Her voice was barely audible. "I don't want to get anything on you."

"Grace." The word came out softer than I intended. "*Nothing* on you scares me."

Her breath hitched.

I lifted the towel and touched it to her cheek—slow, deliberate. She made a small sound, too soft to classify. Not pain. Not fear. Something closer to relief.

"I don't want—" she tried again. "I don't want you to have to clean me."

"You think this bothers me?" I asked, gently wiping away the dried edge of vomit at the corner of her mouth.

Her lashes fluttered. She tried to pull back; I followed, keeping the touch steady, controlled.

"I'm dirty," she whispered. The shock was still visible in her blue eyes, her pupils huge.

"You fought," I corrected. "You survived. That's not dirty."

I kept working—jawline, temple, the edge of her neck. Every motion precise. No rush. No hesitation. I'd cleaned blood off teammates in worse conditions. I'd cleaned worse off myself.

But this wasn't about sanitation. This was about giving her back control, one inch at a time.

"Lift your chin," I said.

She did. Shaky. Trusting me in spite of herself.

Warm water caught the scars on my knuckles as I worked. She noticed. She always did. And when her gaze traced the line of my hand, something inside her steadied for half a second.

"That's it," I murmured.

Her breathing evened out by degrees. Not steady. Not calm. But no longer the edge of collapse.

When I finished with her face, I set the towel aside and reached for another. "We're going to take this slow. I'll talk through every step. You stop me if anything feels wrong."

She nodded, small and tight.

But when I reached for the first button on her blouse, her hand shot out and grabbed mine. Not to stop me—just to hold on.

Her grip was desperate. And warm. And shaking.

"I don't want to be alone," she said, voice breaking.

"You're not alone." I leaned in, close enough for her to feel the heat of my breath. "And I'm not going anywhere."

Her fingers curled tighter around mine.

Outside in the hallway, a distant floorboard creaked—Voodoo or Alphabet moving through the sweep.

I ignored it. The only threat that mattered was already unconscious. The only timeline that mattered was the one in this room.

"Bones...?" she whispered.

"Yeah."

Her eyes flicked to the door, then back to me. "Is Ignacio still—?"

"He's not waking up anytime soon," I said, pocketing the name Ignacio. "And he's not getting near you again."

Some of the tension drained from her shoulders.

"Good," she breathed. Then her eyes locked onto mine, sudden and sharp. "Don't let him die."

A request. No—an order wrapped in fear.

"We'll keep him breathing," I promised. "Until you're done with him."

Her pulse jumped at her throat. She didn't argue.

I reached for the buttons again. Slow. Careful. Prepared to stop if she so much as twitched wrong.

"Ready?" I asked.

Grace nodded once.

Steady.

Brave.

Shaking so hard she couldn't hide it.

I began to undo the first button.

Not touching more than necessary. Not pushing farther than she could handle.

But staying close enough that she could feel the heat of me—close enough she knew she wasn't doing this alone.

As the blouse loosened, inch by inch, I felt the shift.

Not sexual. Not yet. Something deeper. Trust with teeth. The kind that could wreck a man if he wasn't careful. The kind I'd already decided I wasn't going to run from.

Grace's fingers were still knotted around mine when I reached the second button of her blouse. They weren't holding me back—just holding on. Big difference. Her breathing hitched again when the damp fabric pulled away from her skin.

"It's okay," I said quietly. "You're okay."

Her eyes slid away, jaw tight like she was bracing for judgment. There wasn't any. I worked the buttons loose one at a time. Slow. Predictable. Talking her through every inch.

"You tell me to stop, I stop," I said. "You tell me to back off, I back off. You run the pace here."

She nodded, throat bobbing. "I don't like that you have to do this."

"Grace," I said, meeting her eyes because she needed that connection more than she needed modesty, "I've seen my teammates covered in blood, shit, and engine grease. I've cleaned worse off Voodoo at three a.m. while he insulted my entire family tree."

That made her lips twitch—barely, but it was movement in the right direction.

Her blouse slipped off one shoulder. She inhaled sharply, instinctively trying to cross her arms to hide—then stopped when she realized that contact only pressed the fabric against her.

She grimaced again.

"Hey," I murmured. "Look at me."

It took a moment, but she did.

"You're not broken," I said. "Not ruined. Not dirty. Your body did what bodies do under shock."

She swallowed hard, tears burning in her eyes but not falling. "I should've been stronger."

"You were," I said. "Stronger than you think. You're sitting here breathing—that's strength. You threw a goddamn paperweight at a man who clearly terrified you. That's strength."

Her breath shuddered. Her blouse slid the rest of the way down, and I caught it before it hit the floor. No need to let her see it again.

I moved to her skirt next, hands deliberate.

She stiffened.

"Grace," I said, keeping contact with her knuckles, "I want you to hear something."

She blinked at me, waiting. Fragile, furious with herself, and trying not to come apart.

"My first real firefight," I said, "I threw up."

Her eyes snapped to mine, startled. "You... what?"

I shrugged, deadpan. "All over my vest. And my boots. And Voodoo's boots. He still brings it up if he wants to win an argument."

A tiny breath escaped her. Almost a laugh. Almost.

"I mean," I added, "I hit the guy attacking me, but I'd already puked on myself. There's a photo. Alphabet found it. He pretends he's going to use it as blackmail bait."

Her grip eased a little. Color warmed her cheeks—something that wasn't shame this time.

"You?" she whispered. "You got sick?"

"Threat level, high," I said dryly. "Nausea, higher. Bodies do things under stress. Doesn't mean shit about who you are."

Her shoulders slowly—very slowly—unclenched.

I kept talking as my hands moved to the waistband of her skirt, giving her every chance to stop me. "I didn't feel strong then. Didn't feel capable. But I still did the job."

"And I...?" she asked, voice small.

"You did more than the job," I told her. "You survived a man who thinks he owns you. Then you threw things at every bastard who came for you. I call that an A-plus performance under pressure." I would keep telling her, over and over, until she heard it and believed me.

Her breath trembled, but her chin lifted. "Okay."

"Okay," I echoed. "I'm going to undo this now."

She nodded.

I unzipped the skirt. Fabric loosened. She didn't stop me. Didn't flinch. When I helped her to her feet, she just breathed. It was slow, if shaky, as I peeled the panties down with the skirt and when she stepped out of both. Her top and bra went next. I kept my eyes on her face the entire time. Not because I didn't want to look at her—I wanted to. God, I wanted to—but because she needed to see respect reflected back at her right now.

Once she was out of the soiled clothes, I wrapped a clean towel around her, tucking the ends in over her breasts gently.

"You're safe," I said again, softer. "And you're clean enough to move. We'll finish the rest in the shower once you're steady on your feet."

She nodded, leaning the slightest bit toward me. Not much. But enough that I shifted closer and braced a hand against the counter so she could lean if she needed.

I stood, gathering the ruined clothes, rolled them up, then pulled a bag out of one of the pouches on my belt. I sacked up the clothing. I wasn't leaving her clothes here. I also wasn't leaving them where she could see them. "I'm going to find you some fresh clothes. The housekeeper's closet probably has something neutral. Sit here. Don't move until I'm back."

She nodded again.

Before I could take a step, the comm crackled.

"Bones? Grace? Status check." Alphabet's voice. Tight. Edges controlled. He worried about us like other people worried about their own heartbeat.

I clicked my comm on. "We're good," I said, but she hadn't said anything and that was a tell more than anything else. "Grace is with me." He needed to know.

"Copy that," Alphabet said—but I could hear the tension. "Goblin and I are two rooms out. Bringing him in."

Grace straightened at that. Not panic—anticipation.

A moment later, the door creaked open and Goblin—the massive Staffy who loved Grace as he only ever had Alphabet—padded inside like he owned the place.

Grace made a tiny, broken noise as he went straight to her. Not sniffing. Not cautious. He walked up and pressed his big head against her thigh like he'd been waiting for this moment all day.

Her whole body softened. Shoulders dropped. Breath finally escaped her lungs in something close to relief.

Her fingers slid along his back. "Hey, baby," she whispered.

Goblin let out a low, rumbling woof, then licked her wrist, leaning harder into her.

Alphabet hovered in the doorway, eyes flicking from Grace to me, doing a silent assessment.

"She's good?" he asked, in a low voice that wouldn't carry. Nor would the doubt lacing the question.

"She will be," I said.

"I'll stand guard," Alphabet said. "Voodoo is keeping the housekeeper secured. The prisoner is still out."

"Find her some clothes first?"

"On it." Alphabet was gone on a soft step.

Grace buried her face in Goblin's neck for a long second. When she lifted her head, her eyes found mine—not panicked, not lost. Just present.

"I can stand," she whispered.

"You don't have to rush."

She shook her head, one hand still in Goblin's fur. "I want to."

I stepped forward, offered her my hand. No pressure. No demand.

She took it.

Her fingers were steadier this time.

When she stood, she leaned—just slightly, just enough—into my side. Goblin stuck close at her other leg, flanking her.

"Let's get you clean," I murmured.

Together—slow, steady—we moved toward the shower.

FOUR

ALPHABET

Voodoo handed her the mug before she'd even made it fully into the room, because of course he did. She looked... better. Not fine. No one with shadows that dark in their eyes was fine, but she was upright, showered, hair damp around her shoulders, and wrapped in a hoodie that made her look smaller than she already was. Pale, composed, but with a tremor hiding deep beneath the surface. A tremor I'd hoped the universe would never put back in her.

Goblin trotted in with her, tail wagging in a tight, almost anxious circle. I hadn't tried to make him leave her nor did he seem inclined. He was our best barometer for her emotional state. He had been since she joined us, and I was more than happy to share him.

Once she was in the kitchen, she sank down into a chair at the table. Goblin immediately settled his head against her thigh. She rested her free hand against his head, the tension bleeding out of her in slow, grudging increments. Smart dog. Smarter than all of us sometimes.

Bones watched her from near the counter, arms folded,

expression a little too carefully blank. Voodoo hovered by her other side, mug still half-raised like he was ready to intercept if she wobbled. I stayed behind the table where I'd spread out everything we'd collected—wallets, burner phones, a couple of cheap IDs, and one high-end encrypted comms device that was absolutely not cheap and absolutely not street-level muscle.

I'd been cataloging everything while Bones got her cleaned up. That meant I had enough half-formed theories to fill a whiteboard and no concrete conclusions I'd be willing to bet my prosthetic on.

Grace finally straightened, one hand braced lightly on Goblin's back as she finally took a drink from the cup of coffee Voodoo had given her.

"Thank you." Her voice was steady. Mostly.

"Anytime, Firecracker." He brushed a knuckle under her chin, everything about his contact soft, and careful.

I slid the encrypted comm unit toward Bones without saying a word. He met my gaze over Grace's shoulder; he'd already gone clinical again. Focused. Cold. He'd need to stay that way for what came next.

"We need intel," he said, voice low enough not to rattle her but sharp enough to cut steel. "Alphabet's cataloging the downed men. We still need to question the housekeeper before we deal with the other."

No one had to clarify who *the other* was.

Grace's fingers tightened around the mug. Just a flicker. But I saw it.

"We don't have to do anything right this second," Voodoo added. "You can just sit. Drink. Breathe."

She didn't *just* sit, she shifted her attention to the table in front of her, scanning the spread-out evidence. "Are those theirs?"

"Yep," I said. "Three IDs so fake they might as well have been printed at a high school computer lab. One that might be real but tied to a guy who doesn't technically exist. And this—" I tapped the encrypted unit with a fingertip. "This is government-grade. Or stolen from someone government-grade. That's the fun mystery."

Grace's throat bobbed. She was absorbing information, not flinching from it. That was something.

"What about the housekeeper?" she asked quietly.

Bones answered before I could. "We'll handle her."

Grace looked up sharply. "Meaning?"

"Meaning," Voodoo said smoothly, "we're not going to traumatize a civilian who might've been coerced. We'll be careful."

Which was the diplomatic way of saying, *Bones will interrogate her without terrifying her or letting her lie.*

And Grace understood exactly what we weren't saying. Her gaze went distant, vanishing somewhere we couldn't follow. A flicker of nausea crossed her expression—quick, but real.

My chest tightened. I hated that look on her. Hated it more than the swelling around my knee protesting that I'd been on the go too long.

Bones stepped closer, but not too close. "We'll take care of everything else. You don't need to worry about him."

Grace met his eyes and this time she didn't drop her gaze like she had earlier, wrapped in fear and humiliation and shock.

"What are you going to do with him?"

Bones didn't answer immediately. Which was answer enough.

"We're going to get information," he said simply.

Her jaw flexed. Her fingers tightened again on the mug. Goblin nudged her hip like he felt the spike of tension.

"And after that?" she pressed.

"That's not your burden," Bones said. Calm. Steady. Absolute.

Voodoo shot me a look that translated to, *We need to redirect before she digs into the part she won't like.*

"If I want it to be?" The question stopped me cold. The shadows had retreated and she was still sipping her coffee, but some color was returning to her cheeks.

"Do you want it to be?" Bones countered her question with one of his own without moderating his tone. Gracie had never backed down from him, even when he was at his most irritated. Now that she wasn't throwing things at him, it was still fun to watch.

"Yes," she said slowly and I straightened. "He was one of my captors at the warehouse...where I first woke up."

That had been my guess based on the fingerprint scan I'd run, but Ignacio Santo Juarez was a mid-level businessman who headed several import/export operations. It wasn't a stretch to realize he was a player in the trafficking operation that had scooped her up.

"Did he hurt you, Dollface?"

Voodoo's expression went grim. We all knew the answer. Her reaction had been the answer, but Bones wasn't making assumptions. More importantly, he was handing her back the power they'd taken from her.

Fierce Gracie had never stopped fighting. Voodoo had told me how they found her. Showed me the evidence of her fear and her physical reactions. I'd also seen the signs of how she fought back in the bruises on her assailants and the scattered objects from the desk flung around the room.

Our brilliant, fierce, impossible-to-contain woman

never gave up. She fought with everything she had and everything she was. That wounded creature I'd glimpsed in the bathroom was only the aftermath—she was already gathering up her pieces, rebuilding herself with the same stubborn fire that had carried her this far.

"Yes." Her answer was straightforward, direct. She didn't try to soften it or explain around it. "He was the one who had me set aside for him." Her gaze locked on Bones as his expression rippled. For as long as I'd known the captain, I'd also respected his will and ability to contain his emotions.

"Him?" A grim question.

She nodded once. "Him."

Bones blew out a breath. "You still want in?"

"I have to be in." Utterly implacable in her determination. "I want answers. I want to hear what he says." She drained the coffee. "I don't have to like it. But I have to hear it."

Instead of responding immediately, Bones glanced at Voodoo, their gazes locking for a pulse before he shifted it to me. Yeah, I got it. He wanted our opinions. Like Voodoo, I nodded.

She was correct. None of us had to like it, but she had more than earned the right to make this call.

"Then you will." He rubbed his jaw. "Want something to eat? Or more coffee?"

She shook her head. "Not sure I can eat right now. You should have some coffee though."

Normally, he'd have blown that off. But to my shock, a faint smile curved Bones' lips and he nodded. "A half cup," he said and I just stared.

"Gracie," I said in a stage whisper, snagging her attention, "the Bones whisperer."

It earned me an expected smack in the back of the head from Bones but Grace's sudden smile was more than worth it. Even better, the light that flickered back into her eyes. Satisfaction flooded me, but before I could say anything else, my phone rang.

I glanced at the caller ID. "It's me," I said, answering. "Go."

Lunchbox's low voice cut through the line. "Still on Sinclair. He's left the hotel and is now at a restaurant meeting four other men. I got photos for you. I'll send them through."

"Still taking his time, I see," I muttered as my phone began to vibrate, but I moved to the laptop to take the messages there so I could run the images.

"He seems very determined to not head home. Think he doesn't want to spend time with his houseguests?"

Couldn't blame him for those musings. Voodoo and I had debated a similar thought after I got a look at Juarez. "Maybe." I eyed the men in the photos. "These look like standard businessmen."

"Unless he's running with a different caliber of trash than we think he is, these are the types I'd expect to see with him." Lunchbox had a point. "How is she?"

"Hang on." I passed the phone to Grace. "It's Lunchbox."

She brightened a fraction as she took it. Her comm was out and when I glanced at Bones with raised brows, he patted his pocket. One nod.

"Okay," Gracie said in a soft voice, scratching Goblin's head the whole time in gentle short motions. "Yes." Another pause. "I'll be fine." This time she frowned. "No." Then again. "No." A sigh. "We'll finish here first then let Bones call it."

She blew out a long breath then lifted her gaze to Bones.

"Yes, he's right here." A hint of amusement. Barely there, but still there. "No, I thought I'd make him guess."

Voodoo's expression relaxed and some knot of tension in my gut let go. Yes, she was fighting her way back to us. Bones didn't rush her, just waited until she held the phone out to him.

The time we'd made him take to recover from his capture had paid off in other ways. The pair had developed their own language and Bones wasn't quite so remote and separate. All good things.

Bones took the phone from her, never looking away from her face until the receiver touched his ear. The shift was instantaneous—the faint warmth he'd let her see blinked out, replaced with that cool, clipped precision he wore like a second skin.

"Go," he said.

Lunchbox must've jumped straight in, because Bones' jaw ticked once, that tiny twitch he only made when he was thinking three moves ahead.

"When he wraps it, you shadow him out. If he doesn't wrap it—" Bones paused, listening, eyes narrowing. "One hour. If he's still sitting there bullshitting with his friends, bag him."

Voodoo let out a low whistle. "Clock's ticking."

Bones ended the call with a soft click, slipped the phone into his pocket, then looked at all of us.

"Housekeeper."

One word. A directive. And my cue.

I pushed away from the table. My leg protested—more a dull ache than a sharp one, but it was enough to make me adjust my gait as I led the way through the kitchen, past the laundry alcove, and toward the butler's pantry. The small room was tucked between the kitchen and the dining area, and when we'd secured her earlier, we'd moved anything sharp or heavy out of reach.

The housekeeper sat on the padded bench against the wall, blindfolded and with her hands tied behind her back. Not painfully—Voodoo had insisted on that—but firmly enough to keep her put. She was older, maybe mid-fifties, with a streak of gray through her dark hair and the ramrod posture of someone who'd spent decades serving people who thought "please" was optional.

The moment the door opened, she flinched. Her breathing hitched, rising in sharp, panicked bursts.

Then she started babbling.

Spanish poured out of her in a frantic stream—too fast, too panicked, too tangled for me to catch more than fragments of nouns and a few verbs. *Ayúdeme.* Something about *la esposa.* Something about *él.*

Grace startled me when she pushed past me carefully and crouched right in front of the woman. Her voice cut cleanly through the panic. The soft, calm, and steady tone stroked over my senses as if we all needed her to ease us.

"*No vamos a hacerte daño.*" She didn't rush her pronunciation, and I could follow her words easier. *We're not going to hurt you.* Good girl. Assure her.

The housekeeper froze mid-sob. Her head tilted sharply toward Grace, like the recognition of a woman's voice. Whether it was the fact that Grace was a young woman or that she'd been the attorney the housekeeper let in was what soothed her, I had no idea. Either way, the housekeeper's panic eased.

Grace kept going. Her accent was perfect, and so was her rhythm. Her gift with languages was so damn impressive. "*Necesitamos hacerte unas preguntas sobre Sinclair. Sobre los hombres que tenía aquí. Sobre las mujeres que pasaron por esta casa.*"

It took me a minute, but she was telling her what we needed to know. We had questions about Sinclair, about the men in the house and about the women who came through.

The housekeeper's breath hitched again. She turned her head blindly toward Grace, shoulders shaking.

"*No puedo...*" she whispered. *I can't.*

"Yes," Grace said in English, her voice warm and unyielding all at once. "You can."

Something in her gentle, if unyielding tone made the woman's chin wobble.

"They won't hurt you," Grace said, glancing back at the three of us. "We won't let them."

The woman's breath steadied—not completely, but enough that she wasn't moments from hyperventilating.

Bones shifted behind me, the smallest adjustment of his stance, but even blindfolded, she sensed him. A tremor ran down her spine like she'd felt a shadow move.

Grace reached out and took one of the housekeeper's bound hands, curling her fingers over hers in an offer of contact.

"We just need the truth," she said softly.

Voodoo leaned against the sideboard, arms folded, his expression unreadable but observant. He was watching Grace more than the housekeeper. I got it. We were all tracking the steadiness returning to her inch by inch.

"We're not here to punish you," Bones said finally, voice low, controlled, but stripped of any threat. He knew how to read a civilian's fear from ten paces away. "We're here to stop the men who would."

The housekeeper swallowed audibly, the sound loud in the small room.

I stepped forward and loosened the blindfold so it didn't cut into the side of her head. I didn't think she'd be able to see from beneath it, even if she tilted her head back. Still, this was a compromise. Less disorienting. Less terrifying.

Her breathing slowed.

Grace stayed right there with her, hand wrapped around the woman's, grounding her.

"Tell me," she said gently. "Start wherever you can."

In that gentle moment, the housekeeper broke. Relief swarming through her expression. Yet, in one harsh breath her sobs transformed from fear to release. How long had this woman been living under their iron thumb?

"We've got her," I murmured quietly to Bones and Voodoo. "Gracie's got her."

Bones didn't look away from Grace.

"I know." His voice was almost too soft to catch. "Let her lead."

Grace took a slow breath, squared her shoulders, and spoke again, steady, sure, and in control.

"Tell me everything."

FIVE

GRACE

"Can you tell me your name?" I asked after her sobs dwindled into soft, shaky breaths. The tile floor was cold against my knees, but I didn't move.

"Hannah," she said, still weepy. "Hannah Torres."

I held her bound hand between mine, repeating silently that she wasn't the one who should have been tied up today. But she was the one caught in the middle of something bigger and uglier than she'd ever wanted to see.

"It's okay," I whispered. "You're safe here."

Her breath hitched again. "*Mi familia... mis hijos... por favor...*"

"Don't worry," I assured her in a soft voice. "No one is going to hurt your family. I promise." Maybe I shouldn't make that oath, but Bones gave me point and no one disagreed with me earlier. "I need to hear it from you... tell us what you're afraid of."

Her head tilted toward my voice, even though the blindfold hid us from her. "They will hurt my children," she breathed. "If I talk. If I say anything wrong—"

"Who?" My voice didn't shake, even though something deep inside me recoiled at the familiarity of that kind of fear.

"I don't know their names," she whispered. "But they come here. Not through the front door." Her shoulders curled inward. "Never the front door."

I glanced back at Alphabet, who gave me the smallest nod. Yes—okay that matched what we knew so far.

"Do they have a key?" I asked.

"No." A breath. "There is a door. It was always locked before. *Siempre.* But after the Señora left..." Her voice tightened. "He told me not to go near it."

I smoothed my thumb over the back of her hand. "Hannah, when you say the Señora, you mean Mrs. Sinclair?"

"Yes." A soft choke. "She was kind. She... she helped me when my husband had his accident. She made sure we had insurance. She let me bring the children to the pool when she was home." Her voice wavered, a thready mixture of grief and guilt. "When she left on her trip, he said we couldn't stay in the cottage anymore. That I should only come twice a week and leave before dark."

Behind me, Bones shifted. A quiet, contained sound. Not approval.

"And you listened," I said gently. "Because you're doing what you need to do for your family."

A tiny nod.

"I asked if we could stay," she whispered. "I begged. But he said no. He said... I knew too much already."

Every hair on my arms lifted.

Under the blindfold, tears leaked down her cheeks.

"So you stayed," I said. "Even though you're scared."

"The money is good." Her lips trembled around the admission. "My husband cannot work now. His back... it is ruined. He cannot even lift our youngest without pain." A wet sniff. "We need the insurance, and Mrs. Sinclair arranged it so my insurance is paid out of my salary. The pay is still good, he didn't cut it back even if he trimmed the number of days." She swallowed hard. "So I come. I do as I'm told. I clean. I stay where they allow me."

"And barricade yourself in when you hear the men," I murmured.

She gave a tiny, broken laugh. "Sí. I go to the laundry room. The closet locks from the inside. They do not look for me."

God. I hated how well I understood that kind of survival.

"Hannah," I said, inching closer, "have you ever considered quitting?"

"Every day." The answer came out on a cracked breath. "But then I look at my husband, and my children, and I tell myself—*mañana*. Tomorrow. I will quit tomorrow."

"But now?" I asked gently.

Another tremor. "Now I think I must. He will know I was here when he comes back."

"He won't hurt you," I said, and my voice stayed firm even though my throat tightened. "We won't let him."

I didn't look at the men behind me, I didn't have to. Not when absolute agreement radiated through the room like heat. They were not fans of bullies. They may not think of themselves as heroes and maybe they weren't anything so prosaically labeled. Yet, they saved people.

That was more than enough for me.

I drew in a slow breath and asked the question that had been sitting like a stone in my stomach.

"Hannah... do you know where Mrs. Sinclair went?"

Silence. Heavy, terrible silence.

Her breath shuddered. Her fingers twitched in my hands.

"*No debo decir... no debo...*" I must not say.

"Hannah," I whispered. "Please. I'm not asking you to betray her. Just tell me if she's safe."

Another silence, even longer this time. More agonizing.

Finally, so softly I almost didn't hear it, she said, "I don't think she is coming back."

My heart lurched. "Why?"

She went rigid, as though she braced for a blow. "Because," she whispered, "Mr. Sinclair did something. Something that made the wrong people very angry."

Cold slid down my spine.

"What did he do?"

Her breath shook. "I don't know. I only heard pieces. Shouting through the walls. The men... the ones who use the door that is not the front... they said he made a mistake." She swallowed audibly. "A big one. And that they wanted their money back."

My lungs squeezed tight.

"And Mrs. Sinclair?" I asked. "What does she have to do with it?"

Another pause, and this one was filled with dread. She swallowed hard. "She was supposed to come home," Hannah whispered. "But she didn't. And the men said..." Her voice cracked. "They said she was the collateral now."

I didn't breathe. I couldn't.

Behind me, Bones said my name very quietly, like a warning and an anchor all at once.

But I didn't move. Couldn't.

I held Hannah's shaking hand and asked the question that felt like swallowing glass.

"What happened to her, Hannah?"

She broke.

Collapsed inward like her spine had given way.

"I don't know," she sobbed. "I don't know. But I think... I think they took her."

My stomach bottomed out.

Because suddenly, it clicked—Sinclair was more than likely behind Amorette's disappearance. He was involved with these men. His absolute pallor when he saw me had already confirmed that. But Hannah said he made a mistake and now these men had punished him. Punished him by taking his wife... But was the mistake Amorette? Or was it me?

Ignacio had wanted *me*. That had been clear. Not Amorette. Still... *Another* woman was missing now, even as this one shook from fear in front of me. How many had these people hurt? How many more would they hurt?

Behind me, Bones shifted again. The movement was enough for Hannah to stiffen again, as though she felt the air change. He didn't raise his voice, didn't loom, didn't do anything threatening. He didn't have to. Bones could project authority without lifting a damn finger.

"Hannah," he said, calm and steady. "I'm going to ask you a few questions. Grace will stay right here with you."

She nodded, trembling.

"Good," he murmured, tone precise but not unkind. "First—how often do these other men come? The ones who use the hidden door."

Hannah inhaled, shaky. "Sometimes once a week. Sometimes twice. Sometimes..." She flinched. "...sometimes every day. It depends."

"On what?" Bones asked.

"I don't know. I only know when I hear them. They walk heavy. They slam things. They speak fast—angry." A little shiver ran through her. "When they come, I stay far away."

"So no pattern you can track?" Bones pressed gently. "Weekends? Late nights? Early morning?"

She hesitated. "M-Mornings. Usually mornings. When they come at night, it is only two or three of them. But mornings..." Her breath quavered. "Mornings, I think there are many."

Morning activity might mean business. Deliveries, exchanges, planning. Maybe. Nights could be cleanup. My stomach soured.

Bones' voice cut through the rising haze. "Besides the door in the office—have you seen any other hidden doors? Panels? Locked rooms? Anything strange?"

Hannah shook her head immediately. "No. Only that one. But... but there is a room I am not allowed to clean. Always locked. He said he would handle it."

"Which room?" Bones asked.

"Upstairs," she whispered. "End of the hall. Across from the master bedroom. I have never been inside. Even the señora say that is his—space."

Alphabet's quiet curse was barely audible, but I heard it. Upstairs.

"Anything else?" Bones asked. "Anything you can think of that felt wrong or out of place? Anything Mrs. Sinclair said or did before she left?"

For the first time, Hannah's trembling slowed. She lifted her head a fraction, blindfold shifting.

"She... she cried."

My breath froze.

The guys behind me stilled—every one of them. Even Goblin, who had been sitting quietly next to me, seemed to freeze in place.

"Cried?" I asked softly. "When?"

"The night before she left." Hannah's voice broke on the words. "She called someone on the phone. She said... she said she was scared. Then she told me she'd be back in a week." Her chin quivered. "But she didn't take her big suitcase. Only a small one. Like she didn't want him to know she was going."

My pulse hammered.

"She left in the morning," Hannah continued, voice shaking again. "He drove her to the airport. And when he came back... he was different."

"How?" Bones asked quietly.

"He was... angry. Cold. Like he blamed me." Hannah swallowed. "He told me never to ask about her again. Never. And then the men started coming. More and more."

My mouth went dry.

Hannah hesitated, then whispered so faintly I almost missed it, "And one night... I heard them say *she* was a message."

I flinched.

Hannah bowed her head. "A message to him. I don't know for what, except that it must be bad. I only know she is gone."

My hand tightened around hers, gently but firmly. "You did everything you could. You survived. You kept your family safe. You're not responsible for what he did."

She sobbed once, a small, broken sound.

Bones exhaled—a slow, controlled release. Not anger at her. Anger at the situation. At Sinclair. At Ignacio. At everyone who had touched this.

He crouched then—not close enough to scare her, but enough to get to her level. His voice softened by degree.

"Hannah, listen to me."

She stilled.

"You're going to be safe. We're going to make sure of that. But I need one more thing from you."

"A-anything," she whispered.

"I am going to leave you with a phone number, I want you to memorize it but not put it in your phone. We're going to untie you and let you go home, but you need to walk out to your car and go, just like you would any other day. Don't look back, don't call anyone else, just go look after your family."

"Okay." Disbelief strung between both syllables.

"If you think of something later—anything at all—you call that number and you leave us a message. Even if it feels small. Even if it feels unimportant." He let a beat pass. "Sometimes the small things matter most."

She nodded, tears dripping off her cheeks. "I will. I will try."

"And Hannah?" Bones continued.

"Yes?"

"If anything happens and you need help, you call that number too."

Shock seemed to still her tears. "But I am..."

"A good person." His tone brooked no argument. There was no way not to believe him. "If you need help, you call. If you remember something, you call. Can you do that?"

"Si. Thank you."

I squeezed her hands again, my throat thick. "You did good," I murmured. "Really good."

Behind me, Voodoo quietly added, "Damn good."

Alphabet made a soft sound of agreement.

And Bones, the stubborn, intractable man, added, "You helped more than you know."

Hannah broke again, but this time it wasn't terror—it

was relief. As she cried, leaning forward until her forehead touched my shoulder, I held her as Voodoo slipped around me to free her wrists. Then he touched my shoulder and motioned to the door. We needed to withdraw.

I gave her a tight hug. Then Bones set a slip of paper on her lap with the number.

"Count to thirty," I told her. "Then take the blindfold off and go."

"Senorita," she said as I made it to the door. I glanced back at her and found her smoothing the piece of paper over and over, but she still wore the blindfold. "You are not the woman from the law office."

"No," I told her gently. "But I am here to find her."

A pause. "I will pray for you both. I will pray for Mrs. Sinclair too."

"Thank you," I whispered, then slipped out with Goblin trotting quietly behind me. It didn't take her long at all to leave. She didn't look back, not once. I watched as her car pulled down the long drive, then glanced at them. We still had Ignacio to deal with.

"Is she going to be all right?"

"I don't know, Dollface." Bones didn't sugarcoat it—he never did. "But she's safer now than she was this morning. We'll keep eyes on her, and the farther she is from this place, the better."

"I've got a lock on her phone and her address," Alphabet added from behind me. "I pinged a couple of guys I know. They'll keep a quiet perimeter on her and the family for a few days. Just in case Sinclair's friends get stupid."

My chest loosened. Just a fraction, but enough. I crossed to Alphabet and rose onto my toes to kiss him—quick, soft, an exhale of gratitude against his lips.

"Thank you."

He flashed that crooked grin of his. "Ma'am, I am but a humble employee following orders."

Voodoo barked a laugh. "Sure, Romeo. Okay, we've got, what? Maybe thirty minutes before Lunchbox bags our boy like it's Garbage Day." He glanced toward the ceiling. "So. Trash upstairs. Time to take it out?"

Three sets of eyes landed on me.

My stomach dipped. "I don't think I can take the lead on this one."

Alphabet laced his fingers through mine and tugged me a little closer. "You don't have to. Not even a little. Let Bones and Voodoo dismantle him. They'll consider it an afternoon hobby."

That absolutely should not have made a warm, molten swell curl in my chest, but there it was anyway.

"What will you be doing?" I asked.

He squeezed my hand. "Cuddling you and eating popcorn, obviously. Multitasking genius right here."

It was ridiculous. Completely ridiculous. And yet—

I laughed.

God, I actually laughed. After everything. It spilled out of me sharp and bright and shaky, but it was real.

"Okay," I said, drawing a steadying breath. "Let's get this party started."

SIX

VOODOO

We'd dragged Ignacio down to the basement because the concrete floor didn't care what got spilled on it. The old bulbs overhead buzzed with that sickly yellow glow that made everyone look jaundiced, but it was Grace I kept glancing at. Her skin was ash-pale, eyes hollowed from reliving what this man had done. She hugged her elbows like she was trying to hold herself together.

I wasn't a fan of torture—never had been. But I was less of a fan of watching Grace flinch every time Ignacio breathed.

We'd already zip-tied him to the chair, plastic biting into his wrists. Ignacio's shirt lay in a heap on the floor where Bones had cut it off. Without it, he looked small. Not weak—just suddenly mortal. Gooseflesh prickled up his arms in the damp chill.

Behind me, Bones paced, an unleashed predator ready to end Ignacio before this even began. Since I knew for a fact that he could stand motionless for hours without breaking a sweat, he was playing the part of psychological torturer. Worked for me.

"Bones," I warned. His fists were already balling up. The word and the tone were more for the show than because I wanted to actually keep Bones in check. He was already doing that by putting me in charge of the interrogation. If he handled it, Ignacio would be bloodied and unconscious before he could tell us a damn thing.

Alphabet crouched by the workbench, rummaging through the mess we'd improvised earlier. Wires. A battered dog shock collar I'd found in the garage. It was almost like Lunchbox was with us. Or maybe it had been his idea, he and Alphabet had been texting. That particular power pack had no business being attached to anything like a dog collar, but between them, they'd made it work.

Grace's voice came out thin. "You're going to talk." Her eyes never left Ignacio. "I don't care if you make it easy on yourself." That little gem almost made me smile. "In fact," she continued. "You should definitely resist as hard as you can."

Because it would hurt him so much more. Ah, my firecracker was a brilliant starburst ready to explode.

Ignacio lifted his chin, a sneer curling his lip. As shows of defiance went. It was pathetic, but he spat before he said. "You think you scare me, *pet*? I've—"

"No," I said, stepping into his line of sight, because if I let him finish the thought, I'd be the one killing him. Pet. He called her *pet*. Bastard was going to lose his tongue when he was done telling us what we needed to know. "You're already terrified. I can work with that."

The son of a bitch was the worst kind of bully. The kind that flexed his power over people smaller than him, physically weaker, or who held less control. His power stood atop a house of cards, wherein those beneath it were weaker, and he never tested himself against those of like size or ability.

Too bad for him, he was about to find out he'd been punching way above his weight class with Grace.

His scowl darkened as he glared up at me. Yet, look, he went mute when I met him stare for stare. Nothing about him frightened me. When I held out my hand, Alphabet moved.

Ignacio flinched when Alphabet put the collar in my hand. Not much—just a twitch—but enough to confirm every suspicion I'd had about how he'd act under pressure. The low, humorless and dark chuckle Bones let out was the thing of nightmares based on how our guest blanched.

"Low setting's a tap." Alphabet set the modified unit in my hand. "Medium setting, it's a little glitchy, sometimes goes low, sometimes high. High setting... don't use high unless you really mean it." There was a kind of brutal glee in the way Alphabet delivered the instructions. He kept his tone even and his cadence moderate as he listed off each one like this was basic tech support.

"Got it."

I was rather looking forward to high.

I slipped the collar around Ignacio's neck. Felt his pulse racing under my knuckles. He tried to mask it with a smirk, but his breath stuttered when the latch clicked shut. I gave it one tug to make sure it was secure, then turned to meet Grace's gaze.

"You don't have to be here for this." I kept it a murmur. I didn't expect her to go, and she had every right to be here. But there was nothing wrong with her choosing to leave either.

"I do," she said, trembling just once, then steadying

herself. "He took something from me. I want him to know what that feels like."

Ignacio's eyes darted to her as I returned my attention to him. For the first time since he woke up, I saw fear flare—raw and unmistakable.

Good.

I canted my head to the side. I could crouch, give him the illusion of power by putting his head above mine. But no, he was in a room with predators far more dangerous than he could ever imagine or pretend. It was time he learned what that meant.

The remote dangled loose between my fingers. "You'll talk eventually. The question is whether you do it while you still have control over your own reactions."

His mouth tightened.

"Let's start simple," I said. "What's your name?"

Sure, why not give all of us a little demonstration.

He spat at my feet.

I thumbed the remote, just a pulse—barely enough to make a dog yelp. Not that I'd *ever* use this on a dog, sick bastards. But very useful for questioning.

Ignacio's whole body jerked. Not violently—just enough that the zip-ties creaked and his breath hitched into silence. His eyes watered.

Patient, I asked, "Your name?"

Fear sharpened him like a knife, but stubbornness locked his jaw. Oh, good. He wanted to play chicken. When he firmed his lips, I gave him ten more seconds.

Then thumbed the remote.

Another jerk, this time, I caught the clack of his teeth and the choke as he inhaled his own spit. The harsh cough he released shook him.

I leaned in. "That was the lowest setting."

The man's dark eyes widened and the red decorating them seemed to worsen.

"Shall I ask you again?" Yes, this was a test.

This time, his stare broke first.

"Ignacio," he spat out, like the word burned his tongue.

"Good," I said softly. "See? Progress."

Bones hummed in approval behind me, low and predatory. Alphabet didn't even look up from whatever data he was already pulling on his tablet—because we all knew the name was just the warm-up.

"Now," I continued, "who paid you to take Grace?"

Ignacio's nostrils flared. He tried for bravado again, but even that came out frayed at the edges. "Nobody paid me."

I raised a brow. "Ignacio. We both know lying on the baseline question is just bad strategy."

His jaw clenched. Silence.

I sighed like I was disappointed in a particularly dense student. "You don't want to waste my time. Or hers." I tilted my head toward Grace.

If earlier she'd looked fragile, she didn't now. She'd gone still—cold still. A kind of focused quiet that made Ignacio swallow hard.

"Ask him again," she said.

I did. "Who paid you to take her?"

He worked his throat, but the only answer he managed was a glare—shaky, but aimed right at me, probably because he didn't dare look at Grace.

Right idea.

Wrong move.

I clicked the remote again. Medium setting.

The collar's response proved inconsistent—as Alphabet indicated—but that was half the point. The jolt hit Ignacio like a glitching live wire. His shoulders seized so hard the chair legs scraped. A strangled sound forced its way out of him, half grunt, half plea he tried to swallow.

Bones said, "Medium must've rolled high."

"Oops," Alphabet said blandly, not sounding apologetic at all.

Ignacio gasped like he was trying to remember how lungs worked. Sweat already slicked his hairline. His breathing stayed shallow, the way a man breathed when he wasn't sure his own body wouldn't betray him again.

"Who paid you?" I repeated.

"I told you—" His voice cracked. "No one paid me."

"Specifically?" I asked, rolling the remote between my fingers.

His gaze flicked to Grace again. Her trembling had stopped—not from fear, but from something colder, steadier. Resolve.

"I acted on my own," Ignacio snarled, desperation layering the defiance. "Wasn't hired by anyone, you hear me? Nobody put a gun to my head. Nobody promised me cash. I did it because I damn well wanted to. I'm the one with the power."

Grace inhaled sharply.

Bones stopped pacing.

Alphabet's tapping ceased mid-keystroke.

And Ignacio—poor bastard—realized too late he'd just confessed to the one version of events that guaranteed this wasn't ending cleanly for him. Particularly since we all knew he was lying.

Except...

I leaned in, letting him see the shift in my expression— the moment the line between interrogation and retribution blurred for all of us.

"Then," I murmured, "you've just made this very, very unfortunate for yourself."

Ignacio's breath snagged—just a flicker, but I caught it. He'd expected rage. Expected Bones to lunge or Grace to flinch. But calm—my calm—always rattled the weak-willed far more than anger.

Before he could scrape together a response, I added, "Tell me something, Ignacio. If you acted on your own... did you just decide to take Grace after your crew scooped her up? Because she wasn't the only one they grabbed."

His pupils dilated. A single, involuntary tick.

Got him.

"We know," I went on, quiet, steady, "her abduction was ordered. Someone paid for it. She wasn't random. So what I'm asking is simple, did you take advantage of the situation? Did you see her and decide to make her your personal project?"

Bones' boots stopped moving behind me, still and coiled to strike.

Grace didn't tremble. Didn't blink. Looking at her now, you'd never have recognized the sex kitten from all those ad campaigns as the same woman in this porcelain goddess with her flushed cheeks, bright eyes, and intractable will.

God, I loved her so damn much.

Ignacio started to shake his head, but not in denial. In panic.

"I—I didn't— That's not—" His breath hitched as he realized every direction he tried to run in, every version of his story, would only tighten the noose.

I let him flounder for a beat before stepping closer, lowering my head enough that he couldn't escape my stare but not enough to give him even a scrap of advantage. He still had to look *up* at me.

"You're lying," I said softly. "What's so damn insulting about it, is you're not even good at it."

He swallowed hard. "I'm telling you the truth," he whispered, voice cracking. "I wasn't paid. Not... not directly."

"So someone was paid," I clarified, then straightened.

He shut his eyes. "Yes. But not me."

Progress.

Grace exhaled, the sound sharp enough to cut.

Alphabet resumed typing, voice flat. "There it is."

Ignacio opened his eyes again, darting between us, realizing every shred of bravado he'd tried to wield had evaporated.

"I didn't pick her," he rushed on. "They grabbed everyone they were told to grab. I didn't—know she would be one until she arrived."

He cut another look up at me, and I stared at him. Waiting.

"Then...I wanted her so—I just... I just kept her."

A low, almost murderous sound escaped Bones. Somehow, I rather doubted it was that much of a show. This piece of infected puss had *hurt* her because he *wanted* her and just decided to *have* her.

"No," I said, holding up a hand, continuing the performance. "Let him finish."

Sweat soaked his hairline and ran down his skin. Fear had a way of wringing a man out. He sagged against the restraints, breath shaking. "I didn't pick her," he repeated, quieter this time, like saying it softer made it more believable. "I just took advantage of what fell into my lap. That's all."

That admission—not the words, but the intent—sent a

tremor through Grace that wasn't fear. It was memory. And rage.

I pivoted, enough to see Grace, to gauge her mood. As shaken as she was, the flush in her face was growing redder. When she met my gaze though, she just nodded. She could do this. Good. I spared the pulsating sack of shit in the chair a glance, the remote still dangling from my fingers. He watched it like it was a blade hovering over his throat.

"Thank you," I said. Ignacio jerked like I'd struck him. I'd be amused about that later. "Now we're getting somewhere."

Because now he'd confirmed what we already suspected.

Someone ordered the kidnapping. Ignacio had merely taken advantage of his position. He wasn't the mastermind —just a parasite who latched onto opportunity.

Ignacio blinked hard, as if that sliver of progress might save him. It wouldn't.

"So," I continued, "who gave the order? Who paid the bill?"

His breath stuttered. "It—it wasn't me. I told you. My crew—"

"No," I cut in, "I didn't ask who took the job. I asked who paid for it."

"I don't— it wasn't my role—" He squirmed, panic rising like a tide. "Talk to the others. They handled the arrangements. I just—"

I thumbed the remote.

The jolt wasn't violent, but it was *longer*—enough seconds that his scream tried to form but caught behind his teeth, coming out a strangled, garbled choke. His back arched. The zip-ties cut into his wrists as he writhed.

Alphabet actually winced at the duration; Bones looked like he wanted it to last longer.

I let go of the button.

Ignacio slumped forward, panting, sweat dripping off his brow. He glared up at me, eyes watering.

"*Hijo de puta,*" he spat, voice shaking with fury and pain.

I hit the button again.

A shorter pulse this time, but sharper, meaner. He jerked hard, almost tipping the chair, a broken bark of pain ripping from him.

I stepped closer, lowering my voice to something patient. Almost gentle. "We want a name."

Bones' boots creaked as he leaned forward, the sound alone promising violence. Grace didn't speak—didn't need to. Her silence was a blade.

Ignacio shook his head, breath hitching. "I—I don't know! I wasn't told—"

I angled the remote. "Ignacio. You're lying again."

"I'm not," he insisted, voice cracking. "I didn't handle the money. I didn't speak to the guy. That was Rudy's job. Or Domingo. I swear—"

He kept talking. Rambling. Listing random crew members, shifting blame from one ghost to another like he could exhaust us with names that didn't matter.

I cut him off with another shock—short, but unforgiving. He yelped, gasped, choked on air.

"Enough," I said. "We're not here for the grocery list of your little playgroup. We want the name of the person who ordered the grab."

He whimpered. Actually whimpered. "I don't know it."

I studied him.

No, despite his pleading, he still wasn't telling the

whole truth. As for this part? This part he might actually believe would save him.

It wouldn't.

I looked to Alphabet. "Give me the other one."

Alphabet's eyes lit with something like professional pride. He set the tablet aside and reached into the kit we'd scattered across the workbench. What he lifted wasn't a collar. It wasn't even finished-looking—more wires, more exposed metal, the kind of improvised cruelty that only brilliant problem-solvers under pressure could fabricate.

"This one," Alphabet said, handing it to me with a respectful nod, "is designed for… alternative placement." He demonstrated by creating a loop out of the cabling then miming how to close it. It would work quite well if we tied it around his balls.

Ignacio's breath froze. Completely froze.

Grace's eyes didn't move from Ignacio—not once.

I weighed the device in my hand. Cold metal. Coiled wiring. More intimate points of contact. More targeted pain.

"It's going to hurt," I told him plainly. "A lot more than the collar."

Ignacio's pulse hammered visibly in his throat. "No—no, please—wait, wait—"

"We are," I said, perfectly patient. "For a name."

He shook his head violently, straining against the restraints. "I don't know— I swear I don't— I never met the guy, I never talked to him— I only heard—"

I paused.

And the room went dead quiet.

Because *he'd said something*. Not much—but enough.

Grace leaned in, voice barely a whisper. "Heard what?"

Ignacio jerked like she'd slapped him, then squeezed his

eyes shut, as if not seeing us made us less real. "Just... rumors," he rasped. "Just a nickname."

Holding the new device loosely in my hand, I sighed. He really was going to make me ask. Fine. "What's the nickname, Ignacio?"

"I cannot tell you," he said, his wild gaze jerking to me. "I swear, I cannot. You don't understand—"

"Honeys," a familiar voice called from above before Lunchbox strode down the stairs, dragging a bound and unconscious Sinclair with him. "I'm home."

He flashed a grin when he came in and I kept an eye on Ignacio. His whole body tensed and his eyes widened when he saw Sinclair. What color he'd regained from his earlier writhing drained away once more.

"Did I miss anything?" Lunchbox asked as he dropped Sinclair in a lump and swept his gaze over all of us before honing in on Ignacio.

"He's about to tell us what we don't understand," I said and Lunchbox eyed him.

"We're listening."

The man's throat bobbed. Then he shook his head. "You're going to kill me anyway."

Well, he wasn't wrong. I held up the new device to Lunchbox. "You want the honors?"

"Got it." He took it and flicked out a knife, because the man still had his pants on. "Gracie, you might not want to watch this." Not that it slowed Lunchbox down and when Ignacio tried to struggle to get away, Lunchbox eyed him. "This is a sharp knife, keep struggling and you're going to bleed."

That froze him in place.

"I've already seen it," Grace said bluntly. "It's nothing to be intimidated by."

After making short work of the man's jeans, Lunchbox paused to eye his flaccid shaft. "Yeah, I can see that." When he gripped the man's dick, however, Ignacio started swearing and the stream of words were directed at Grace.

I didn't have to know all of them to hear the insults. Lunchbox twisted the man's cock until he broke off on a scream. Then without waiting, he looped the new device over the man's balls and pulled it tight so it was secure.

"Last chance," I told the weeping man who coughed and choked. "We tried this the easy way... now we're going to get rough."

"Fuck you!" Ignacio said, spittle flying from his lips. I pressed the button and the man's scream was brutal. I didn't let it go on for long though, but the smell was pretty bad. Someone should have said something about burning hair.

"Wrong answer."

CHAPTER

SEVEN

GRACE

T thought I was ready to watch Ignacio suffer.

I'd told myself I was. I'd repeated it in my head over and over while we dragged him downstairs—reminded myself of every moment he stole from me, every fear he carved into my bones. I thought feeling justified would make this easier.

It didn't.

Every sound in that basement scraped at nerves that were already bruised raw. The zap of electricity, the stifled gasps, the way the air shifted right before Voodoo pressed the button—all of it mixed into a nauseating cocktail I tasted on the back of my tongue. And the smell...

God, I wasn't prepared for that. Sweat, adrenaline, damp concrete, and something sharp and metallic that made my stomach twist until I had to brace a hand against my thigh to keep from doubling over.

I kept my face blank. Eyes forward. Breathing even.

My whole life had been choices made under pressure. Someone always wanted something from me—my talent, my charm, my image, my silence. Every deal, every performance, every false smile was a negotiation of what I was willing to give. And Ignacio... Ignacio was just the darkest twist on a pattern I'd spent years pretending I wasn't trapped in.

He saw me and decided he had the right to take whatever he wanted.

No warning. No care. No humanity.

He was the embodiment of every nightmare I'd swallowed and every compromise I'd made to stay afloat. Yet watching him jerk in that chair didn't erase anything he'd done. It didn't make me feel powerful. It didn't even make me feel safe.

It just made me feel hollow.

Like there were only so many pieces of myself I could carve away in the name of survival before I had nothing left worth saving. That sacrifice with Ignacio all those months back had helped to save me ultimately, I could live with that no matter how much he made my skin crawl *now*.

Voodoo was steady. Too steady. His voice was a low anchor in the storm, calm where Bones seethed like a bottled storm, and AB held himself apart. Yet even his clinical distance seemed a facade whenever I caught the anger blazing in his eyes.

Watching Voodoo work—measured, controlled, relentless—was its own kind of disorienting. He took no real joy in this. He would probably be happier if we could just end him and be done with it. At the same time, he hated what Ignacio had done to me more.

That knowledge both warmed and terrified me. Legend's arrival was a lifeline I didn't necessarily need, yet made staying above water that much easier. That he dragged an unconscious Sinclair with him...

My sister's former boss. The man who might know

exactly who Ignacio's "rumored" benefactor actually was. The man we'd needed since the moment this nightmare began and if only I'd realized it *sooner*.

Somewhere inside, a spark lit—small but real. Relief. Maybe even hope.

Legend had joined Voodoo after he deposited his burden, but he cut a quick look at me, warmth filling his eyes as he gave me a once over. Funnily enough, I'd been giving him a similar inspection. Wanted to make sure he was okay. "Hey, Gracie," he mouthed the words, winking once. "Miss me?"

I didn't trust myself to speak, so I nodded once.

But Ignacio whimpered at the sight of new faces, and the moment shattered. The torture wasn't done. The answers weren't complete. And the smell—the awful, cloying mix of fear and sweat and scorched air—hit me again, harder this time.

I forced the bile back down.

We needed the truth. All of it.

I could fall apart later.

So I stayed. I locked my reactions down. It was when I fixed my eyes on Ignacio once more, that realized his attention had gone to Sinclair. Fear, genuine fear, not pain-laced fear or begging-laced fear flooded his face.

Fear and defeat.

Had he just realized there was only one way out of this situation for him? A vicious part of me did a little fistbump.

Good.

Because maybe now—finally—he'd talk.

Ignacio's lips moved first—barely a twitch, like his mouth was trying to form a word before his brain could catch up. Whatever he tried to say came out as a raw, broken scrape of sound. I didn't catch it. No one did.

He swallowed. Tried again.

"—fanta." Barely more than a gasp. Garbled. Wet around the edges.

Voodoo took one slow step closer. Calm. Controlled. Deadly.

"Repeat it," he ordered, voice soft as a closing door. "Clearly."

Ignacio's eyes darted to Sinclair again—unconscious, slumped, completely unaware of the havoc his mere presence had wrought. Breathing shallow, Ignacio shook his head once, sharply, as if trying to refuse the word instead of the instruction.

Voodoo lifted the remote just a fraction.

Ignacio broke.

"Infanta," he choked out.

The word cracked through the basement like a gunshot.

Bones froze. Alphabet looked up so fast his chair squealed against the floor. Legend's easy slouch straightened into something sharp.

My stomach gave a sickening twist. I didn't know the meaning, not exactly, but something in the way Ignacio said it—half terror, half surrender—hit me like a cold hand on the back of my neck.

Voodoo didn't move. Didn't react outwardly. But something in the line of his shoulders changed, a subtle tightening, like a string pulled taut.

"Infanta," Ignacio repeated, quieter now, like saying it too loud might summon whatever nightmare the name belonged to.

"Who is that?" Bones growled, stepping forward, barely leashed violence rolling off him in waves.

Ignacio winced like even the question hurt. "A name,"

he whispered. "A title. I don't—I don't know which. That's all I heard."

"A nickname, then," Alphabet said, tone clipped, already typing one-handed. His eyes had gone flat in that dangerous, calculating way.

"It's all I know," Ignacio insisted quickly, desperately. "I swear. I wasn't told more. I wasn't—"

His voice cracked on the last word. Broke apart like something inside him finally understood he'd already signed his own death sentence.

Voodoo lowered the remote, just slightly. Not a reprieve, not really. More like a pause. A moment to weigh the truth or the lie in Ignacio's words.

I gripped my hands together, digging my fingers into the flesh of each as if that little bite of pain would keep me grounded and present. The scent of scorched hair lingered, thick and nauseating. My stomach rioted again, and I clenched my teeth until the wave passed.

Infanta.

That was a name given to the female offspring of a monarch, but not an heir. Not quite a princess, yet also a princess. That didn't make any sense.

Around me, the guys shot each other speaking looks, communicating more with their eyes and expressions than most people did with their words. Some of it, I even understood. Legend hadn't been here long enough to read Ignacio so he waited for Voodoo's verdict. Bones wanted verification before they ended him.

AB? His fingers flew over his laptop, always digging for more intelligence. But what was he going to turn on just searching *Infanta* unless it was some codename for another black ops program or dangerous operative. What were the chances of that? Really?

I didn't speak. Didn't move. Didn't let myself feel the flood of dread, fury, or the sick twist of vindication unfurling through me.

But if I was reading Ignacio right, and I was pretty sure I was, then *Infanta* wasn't just a clue, it was a key. We just needed to know where to look.

One more goddamn mystery.

Voodoo didn't waste the opening Ignacio had given.

A spare few moments after "Infanta" settled like poison in the air, Voodoo closed the distance once more until he was close enough that Ignacio shrank back even though he had nowhere to go.

"Where did you hear the name?" Voodoo asked.

Ignacio's breath stuttered. "I—I don't know—just... people talking."

"When?"

"During... pickups. Sometimes."

"Who said it?"

"I don't—someone from the docks—maybe—"

"What was your plan for Grace when you tried to escape with her?"

Ignacio flinched so hard the chair scraped. "I—nothing —I wasn't—"

"Answer the question."

"N-no plan, I swear—just—keep her..."

"Keep her?" Voodoo pressed.

"Keep her, my pet. She's beautiful, she feels beautiful when she rides your cock, she's so perfect and I wanted to keep her forever." He wet his lips, not looking at me as if he didn't dare. "The buyers would not notice, and if they did..."

Something inside of me went cold.

He didn't even have a plan. Just impulse. Just want. He played the power broker because he just wanted me.

"If the buyers were upset," Voodoo prompted, "what would have happened?"

Ignacio sagged. "They… would handle it." Me. They would handle him. Though he didn't say that aloud.

Not once did Voodoo let the answers just linger, from one question to the next, he pushed him. "How did you and your men get your tasks?"

"Phone. Burner phones. Always changing."

"Who gave the orders?"

A helpless shake of his head. "Never saw him. Never heard his real voice."

Voodoo's expression didn't flicker. His voice stayed maddeningly steady.

"Where were the orders sent from?"

"Different numbers. Sometimes texts. Sometimes calls. Sometimes a middleman at the port."

"Which port manager?"

Ignacio mumbled a name—one Alphabet immediately typed, only to shake his head a second later. "He died six months ago," AB muttered. "Not helpful."

"When were you given destinations?"

"Last minute," Ignacio whispered. "Always. They changed all the time. Pickups changed. Drop points changed. Nothing stayed the same."

"Why?" Voodoo asked.

"Competition? Malice? Stupidity?" Ignacio let out a choked laugh—half misery, half hysteria. "Because they didn't trust us. Because we weren't important. We were just… hands. Labor. Disposable."

His eyes darted to me once more and I refused to look away.

"Define your role," Voodoo said.

Ignacio swallowed hard. "The pickup. The allocation.

Then prepping the cargo for transport."

Cargo.

Prepping the cargo. They were raping those women, brutalizing them, and they were just *prepping the cargo for transport.*

Sickness surged again. I kept my breathing even by sheer force. A hand settled against my lower back, the touch almost ghost light, yet the warmth of Bones' contact seared me through my shirt.

"After that?" Voodoo asked.

Ignacio's voice cracked. "I got paid. In cash. Always cash. *Always* on delivery. No delivery, no payment. No transfers. No names. Then I waited for the next order."

"That's it?"

"That's it," Ignacio whispered. "I didn't have any control. None. You have to believe me."

Silence rippled through the basement, tight and sharp.

Voodoo looked at him for a long moment, then angled his head slightly, eyes flicking to Sinclair's unconscious body.

"All right," Voodoo said, tone shifting—not more aggressive, but more precise. Surgical.

"One last question."

Ignacio froze.

"What is the connection," Voodoo asked, "between all of this... and Sinclair?"

Every cell in Ignacio's body seemed to seize with terror.

And the look on his face told me he knew. He absolutely knew. Even if he didn't want to say it.

Realization hit me with sickening clarity. "He was the middleman."

All eyes snapped to me.

"It wasn't the port manager who paid you the cash," I

clarified. "It was Sinclair—maybe not always him, but you knew him enough to know he was the one who paid you."

Ignacio's flinch was answer enough. He didn't speak. Didn't deny it. His breath hitched and his shoulders shook.

I took a step forward, then another. Voodoo and Legend both shifted, letting me narrow the gap without moving out from between me and the man shaking in the chair. Keeping my arms folded, I studied Ignacio.

"What happened when you lost your delivery?" Because they had, hadn't they? When the warehouse we'd been in had been attacked? He'd run.

A shake of his head, a violent refusal, but Ignacio kept his lips pressed tight.

"You lost us," I said, reminding him. "That day is sketchy, but you dragged me up from the foot of the bed, you had my chain."

It was weird how those memory flashes cut in and out, so close I could feel the way his fingers had bitten into my skin and how clammy I'd been. Yet distant enough that it didn't suffocate me.

"There was shouting and gunshots, you dragged me into the hall. We were going to run away—well you were— you wanted to escape, but I froze." The fear had choked me then.

Freeze. Fight. Flight.

I'd frozen.

The gunshots had come closer. Then...

"You left me," I said slowly. "To save your own ass, you just left me and the man who chased you knocked me into the wall." Maybe. That part was very fuzzy. After, I'd woken in the truck far away from Ignacio, the warehouse, and the rest of the "cargo."

Ignacio's throat bobbed as if he fought to swallow.

"So what happened when you didn't show up with your prepared cargo?" Just saying the cold, dehumanized words made bile rise in my throat.

One second.

Two.

Three.

Voodoo pressed the button and Ignacio shook so violently the chair went sideways and he slammed into the concrete floor. The stink of burning hair wreathed the whole damn room. Hair, sweat, and now urine. The man had pissed himself.

In some small way, that felt like a victory. He'd made me feel that way. Now he would understand how it felt.

Hollow victory or not, I'd take it.

"Answer her question," Voodoo ordered, and the coldness in his tone turned the air frosty. "*Now.*"

Ignacio looked trapped, his chest rising and falling too fast.

Caught between the fear of lying and the terror of telling the truth. It took three more shocks and Ignacio actually sobbing before he said, "I didn't go!"

"I ran," he babbled. "They would have killed me. Cargo is valuable. They slaughtered most of my men. Killed them." His tears weren't faked nor were his wracking cries. "I stayed away. The ones who came, they were competitors. They came for what was taken from them. There were others hunting for me—Europeans."

That actually made him look mystified for a moment.

"They had questions, questions about you." He looked up at me from where he lay on the floor, trembling. "I barely made it out alive. Then I came here."

"Why here?" Legend asked and Ignacio jerked, as if he'd forgotten that he was here.

"Because Sinclair has money, has access, he is also in trouble. We could help each other." Eyes closing, the man sucked in one ragged breath after another, as though he could barely stand to say the words. Or maybe the truth just hurt him.

Good.

"Did he?" I asked, not willing to wait for him to get a grip.

"Not yet," Ignacio admitted, then he looked up at me with his bloodshot and defeated eyes. "Then I saw you in his office and thought he must have fixed it... You were here. You would be mine again."

For the first time since I'd stepped into the basement, the nausea wasn't from the smell or the memories or the pain in the air. It was from disgust.

"I was never yours," I told him. "When this is done, I'm never going to think of you again. Just passing road kill on the highway of my life."

The silence stretched and Voodoo glanced at me. Did I have any more questions?

"Only one," I answered, then blew out a breath. "Were you the one who also took my sister?"

The utter blankness in Ignacio's expression was the answer. He didn't know about Amorette. She had been taken. Likely by people just like this son of a bitch. More cargo to be prepared. My stomach bottomed out and I barely kept the urge to vomit again in check.

Barely.

So, that just left us with Sinclair.

The guys asked him a few more questions, his answers didn't change and he didn't reveal anything new. The fact he didn't even fight answering or try to evade gave his words an element of truth.

As if satisfied, Voodoo glanced at each of us in turn. One by one the guys shook their heads and when he checked with me, I shook mine too. I didn't have any more questions.

"Do you want to do it?" Bones asked, his lips next to my ear in a dark and sensuous caress. He was putting Ignacio's life in my hands, literally. The man was going to die, it didn't really matter which one of us pulled the trigger. But they were giving it to me if I wanted it.

Did I?

EIGHT

LUNCHBOX

Grace didn't answer Bones. Not out loud.

But the look on her face—God, that look—hit me harder than any punch I'd ever taken. Shock, grief, fury, all braided so tight she didn't seem to know which thread to follow first. I'd seen her angry. I'd seen her stubborn. I'd seen her broken and still pushing forward.

But I had never seen her look...*lost.*

The second Ignacio said he'd never heard of her sister? It was like watching the last tether holding her world together snap clean in half.

I felt it. In my chest. In my damn teeth. I wanted to tear the bastard apart just for that flicker of devastation in her eyes.

But Bones was right. This wasn't our call.

If Grace wanted Ignacio dead, we'd do it. If she wanted time—he'd breathe as long as she allowed it. If she wanted us to march him straight to hell, we'd carry him there ourselves.

But we weren't taking that choice from her.

Not this one. Not after everything else that was stripped from her without consent.

I swallowed the burn in my throat and took a slow breath—because if I didn't check myself now, I'd end him before she even spoke.

Sinclair groaned behind me.

Right.

The other bastard in the room.

I turned just in time to see him flinch awake, blinking through the fog of being drugged, dragged, and dumped on his own basement floor. As satisfying as it might have been, I hadn't dropped him on his head. We still needed him to answer questions.

He was, however, bound at the ankles and wrists. I'd also removed all of his devices—four phones and two digital tablets, not to mention a laptop. They were all powered down and in a case to block signals until Alphabet was ready.

Sinclair looked confused for about half a second.

Then he saw Grace.

Then Ignacio.

Then all of *us*.

Reality seemed to bleed in slowly, coloring his world from groggy to oh fuck. It was almost entertaining to watch. He blanched, then struggled and discovered that he couldn't move.

The gag was also firmly in place, so it muffled whatever creative verbal response he might have had. The sound he made climbed and cracked like a hormonal teenager.

I almost laughed. Not because it was funny—but because the timing couldn't have been worse for him.

Grace stiffened, brittle as glass. She'd been searching for her sister since the beginning of this damn odyssey, clinging to any thread that might lead us to Amorette. After waiting for months and wading through threat after threat, we now had Sinclair for her.

He was lying there, alive, uninjured—so far—and very conscious. If that didn't twist something inside of her, I'd be shocked.

We all knew it. Felt it.

Voodoo shifted his stance, putting himself between Grace and Ignacio once again. Bones stayed firmly planted next to her, as much ready to shield her as to back her play. Alphabet kept a watchful eye on both as the tension in the room shifted and swirled around our pair of prisoners.

For his part, Sinclair's struggles redoubled and he tried to kick out with his bound legs. Pathetic as the attempt was, we weren't quite done with Ignacio yet. I planted a boot on Sinclair's chest, leaning my weight into it and watched his eyes widen as he exhaled harshly through his nose.

I kept the pressure up until his face reddened. Outrage transformed into fear and no small amount of loathing. Guess we weren't going to be best friends. No loss. "You're home, Sinclair and as you can see, we're a little busy, so you need to wait your turn."

The jerk of his body didn't even threaten to dislodge me. Instead, it just invited me to lean in even harder. I had my temper fully in check. That was one of the reasons Ignacio was still breathing—for now.

"We're well past polite invitations," I informed him. "You had an opportunity to open a line of dialogue. You declined. Now, if you make me knock your ass out, I'm going to be annoyed."

The man had the good sense to look worried.

"Good, you understand. Now, sit tight and be quiet

while we finish with the other piece of shit in the room." One more little press with my foot and a distinct oof of sound escaped him. Then, and only then, did I lift the weight off and glance back to where everyone else was waiting.

"I think he's good to wait now."

While Voodoo didn't roll his eyes, I could practically feel his need to do it. My attention slid back to Grace, as always. She continued to stare at Ignacio. Something in her expression shifted. Not softer. Not colder. Just—resolute.

She was making her decision.

I wasn't the only one who saw it because panic slithered across Ignacio's face where he still lay on the floor. He shot a look at Sinclair, who began to struggle once more. Oh, the noose was tightening and they both knew it.

The smell of desperation and fear in the afternoon—a lovely bouquet, though the notes of fresh urine was kind of ruining it. One of them just pissed themselves but after what Alphabet let me know, I was fine with their brand of inflicted terror coming home to roost.

Sinclair let out another series of muffled demands, but the syllables were impossible to decipher. Ignacio was under no such impediments.

"Pet—"

The so-called endearment had me seeing red, but she lifted one hand in a small yet trembling movement and cut him off like she'd just slapped him.

Voodoo turned to her next. "We don't move forward without you," he said quietly. "So... what do you want?"

Ignacio tensed. Sinclair panted harshly, the whistle of air in and out of his nose almost too loud in the space. None of us moved as we waited. Whatever she chose, that was the direction we were going. No hesitation. No second-guessing.

Curling her fingers against her thigh, Grace swung her gaze to where Sinclair lay. "I want answers," she said in a voice that didn't waver, not once. "And he has them."

Far from being relieved to no longer be in her sights, Ignacio snapped a glance to Sinclair. "He will lie!" Ignacio tried to struggle to right his chair, but all he managed to do was flop. "He doesn't know how to do anything but lie. He traded his wife for his lies already..."

Sinclair snarled at Ignacio as Voodoo and I dragged the damn attorney upright. But I pulled out a knife after we dropped him onto the chair. That got all of Sinclair's attention and Ignacio went silent abruptly.

Not really worried about cutting the attorney, I slid the knife between the gag and his cheek. Slicing the cloth, I freed him from the gag. He would need to be able to talk in order to answer questions.

That done, I glanced from Ignacio to Sinclair then to Voodoo. "You already have thoughts on this?"

"Hmm." Like me, he glanced at Ignacio for a beat. The man was still wearing his pair of shock collars. "Not particularly. You?"

"Maybe." I slanted a look at Grace. "You just want answers, Gracie or do you want them asked in a specific way?"

"Just answers," she said. "You can ask them however you want."

My girl. I flashed her a grin and a hint of a smile curved her lips, rewarding me for the effort. "Two minutes."

"Just ask the questions," Sinclair said as I did a scan of the basement. It was relatively well organized. There was even a stack of additional chairs and other items that could be moved up for parties.

It took me a minute, but the Queen Anne dining room chairs were perfect.

"Grace," Sinclair said, twisting to look at her. "You're her sister."

I was on my way back with the chair when Sinclair tried to lunge toward her, not that Voodoo let him move.

"Of course, you're her sister. I knew she had a twin. They—" He cut off abruptly and I gave him a brief look before I began to use the knife to cut through the fabric seat, carving a hole in the center.

"Oh," Alphabet said with a slow grin. "Double-O seven?"

I inclined my head. "I've been wanting to try it, no time like the present. It's also effective."

"Gonna need to strip him," Voodoo mused and Sinclair let out a shriek. I paused mid cut to see Bones had joined them with a knife of his own.

He didn't bother to warn Sinclair not to struggle, he just sliced the man's clothes off. The number of cuts Sinclair got —well that was on him. Grace stood like a statue for the entire time as we worked, her arms were folded, her expression distant. She'd changed from her business clothes and wore sweats, a t-shirt, and a hoodie now. Her damp hair was curling at the ends, though she'd pulled most of it back into a ponytail.

No cosmetics hid the shadows smudging the underside of her eyes nor did it change how stark her bright blue eyes were against her pale face and dark hair. Still, she remained absolutely stunning. Now probably wasn't the best time to tell her that, but I planned to make sure she knew sooner rather than later.

Once I had the chair ready, I moved it over for the guys to sit Sinclair's bare ass down. The hole let the man's balls fall out the underside and the chair had the right height, but we'd need to test my swing.

"Got the rope," Alphabet said as I took over from Bones and helped Voodoo secure Sinclair.

"This is illegal," Sinclair said abruptly. "This is torture. It's a war crime."

I paused to meet his gaze. "If you were a prisoner of war, maybe. You're not."

"It's still illegal."

"So is selling people," Voodoo told him as he tightened one zip-tie brutally. "So is paying cash to facilitate the kidnapping and transportation of victims out of the country."

I jerked the last zip-tie around the man's ankle to make sure he couldn't get away from the chair leg. "Secure."

Voodoo nodded. "Secure."

"You can't do this," Sinclair yelled, and the chair hopped a little as he struggled. "You can go to jail for this."

Yeah, that didn't even deserve an answer. When Sinclair swung his gaze to Grace, she didn't even flinch.

"You *could* go to jail. End up locked up for the rest of your life, for what? These criminals?" He shook his head abruptly. "I'm a good attorney, I can take care of this, any charges, set you up and make sure you're fine."

Grace raised her brows.

As if seeing an opening, he leaned forward. "I am very wealthy. I have a lot more power than you can imagine and I can give you whatever you want."

I took the heavy rope from Alphabet and tested the heft, and the knot he'd made at the end. I added a second one to it. I wanted it to have a really good swing.

"Anything I want?" The soft question had Sinclair pouncing. He didn't see the trap.

He would.

"Yes," Sinclair swore. "Anything. Just name it."

"I want my sister, you son of a bitch. What did you do with her?"

His face blanched. That was the first honest reaction he'd had since waking up.

"I—I don't know," Sinclair stammered, throat bobbing hard. "Grace, I swear to you, I don't—"

"Wrong answer," she said.

Quiet. Flat. Deadly.

Bones exhaled like he'd been waiting for those exact two words.

I didn't hesitate.

The rope cut through the air with a sound that always made men flinch—sharp, fast, inevitable.

I didn't focus on where the knots landed, I didn't have to. Sinclair's whole body told the story.

His scream tore out of him raw, strangled, like it dragged pieces of his lungs with it. The chair rattled against the concrete from the force of his involuntary convulsion. He jerked so hard the zip-ties bit deeper into his skin— blood welling in thin, angry lines.

He gasped.

Once.

Twice.

Like he couldn't figure out how to breathe around the pain.

I didn't bother offering him time to recover. The rope was still warm in my hand.

Voodoo stepped closer, voice low and controlled. "Grace asked a question."

Sinclair's eyes were wide, terrified, already wet at the corners, not from emotion. From sheer, blinding pain.

"I don't—" he choked again, frantic. "I don't know where she is! I wasn't—I wasn't part of that! I wasn't—she wasn't—"

"Stop," Voodoo said.

Sinclair stopped.

Grace's expression didn't change. No triumph. No relief. Just a cold, carved-out steadiness.

"Try again," she told him.

"I don't—Grace, please—"

I swung.

He shrieked, higher this time, the sound bouncing off the basement walls like something alive and desperate to escape. His legs shook. His hands clenched white around the arms of the chair. Sweat burst across his face in a sudden sheen.

"What did you do with her?" Grace repeated.

"I didn't take her!" Sinclair gasped, voice hoarse and cracking. "I didn't—I never—! I only delivered payments, I only—Jesus—God— please—"

Bones leaned down, voice a low rumble next to Sinclair's ear. "You want to live? Stop talking about what you *didn't* do. Start talking about what you *did*."

Sinclair sobbed once—a pathetic, wet sound that scraped raw across my nerves.

"I was the middleman!" he blurted out sobbing. "I passed along cash, instructions— I don't—I don't choose targets, I don't pick up, I never see them again— I don't know where they go—"

Grace's jaw flexed. Barely. But I saw it.

Then she started walking.

Slowly—*deliberately*—she moved forward. Sweatpants,

hoodie, damp hair... none of it mattered. Grace walked like she was wearing a runway, a camera, and an entire industry beneath her heels. I'd seen her glide like this in commercials, in campaign shoots, in fashion shows where she was dressed in enough designer fabric to bankrupt a small country.

But this wasn't that Grace.

This was the distilled version—stripped of gloss, stripped of safety nets, stripped of every performance anyone had ever demanded from her.

Raw.

Perfect.

Dangerous.

She stopped in front of Sinclair, and the bastard broke. Tears smeared down his face before she even bent toward him.

Grace didn't touch him. Didn't need to. She lowered herself just enough that her eyes lined up exactly with his.

Sinclair went sheet-white.

"You're lying."

He flinched. Hard. Like the word itself hit him with the same force as the rope.

Grace straightened, gaze cutting to me.

"Again?" I asked.

She nodded once.

I reached for her hand—not to comfort, not to lead, just to move her aside so she didn't get clipped when I swung. She let me. Trusted me.

"N—!" Sinclair tried to scream.

The knot met flesh.

He jerked, strangled noise caught in his throat.

"Again," Grace said, voice soft as a prayer and twice as lethal.

"Whatever the lady wants."

I swung.

It landed.

He bucked.

I swung again.

And this time—

Sinclair shattered. His whole body seized and he vomited, helpless and heaving, the chair rattling under him. Pain didn't just hit him; it hollowed him out. His sobs tore free—ugly, raw, animal sounds.

"She was getting in the way," he choked. "She was going to ruin everything."

No one moved. No one spoke.

"She wouldn't listen to reason," he sobbed. "Goddamn crusader. She didn't understand how the world worked— we had too much money tied up in everything."

Grace wasn't breathing.

Sinclair finally forced his swollen eyes open, bloodshot and wild. "So I had them deal with her," he whispered. "I didn't care what they did or how. Just told them to make the problem go away."

Grace didn't explode. Didn't break. Didn't even blink.

She just stood there—so still the air felt afraid to move around her.

"Who are *they*?" she asked.

Her voice wasn't raised or sharp. It was soft. Controlled. Polished to a razor so fine Sinclair didn't realize he was bleeding on it.

Sinclair swallowed, throat convulsing. "I—I can't tell you that."

Grace's stare didn't waver.

"They're dangerous people," he rushed on, words spilling out too fast, too terrified. "You don't understand. It doesn't matter what you do to me—they'll do worse. They don't forgive. They don't forget. They—"

"Well," Grace said, cutting him off with the same tone she might use to remark on the weather, "I guess we can find out."

Sinclair froze.

"What?" he whispered. "F-Find out what?"

Grace tilted her head, just slightly, gaze steady enough to pin him to the chair harder than the zip-ties ever could.

"Whether what *you* can imagine," she said, "or what *we* can imagine... is worse."

Sinclair's breath hitched, just once, before another sob tore out of him.

For the first time since the interrogation began, he looked genuinely, viscerally afraid.

Not of the rope. Not of the pain. Not of any of us.

He was afraid of *Grace,* finally understanding far too damn late that he wasn't dealing with a victim anymore.

He was dealing with the reckoning.

NINE

GRACE

Sinclair fell apart faster than I expected.

The moment he realized I wasn't bluffing—that I wasn't trembling or panicking or begging—his whole being seemed to liquefy with terror.

He folded into himself, shoulders curling, breath hitching in frantic little gasps that sounded almost child-like. Sweat slicked his face. Tears and snot smeared together. He looked like a man unraveling one thread at a time, helpless to stop his own disintegration.

And still I felt... nothing.

Not satisfaction. Not triumph. Not relief.

Just cold, steady purpose.

Behind him, Voodoo checked the second shock collar AB was pulling together. It was a job Legend usually did, but Legend was handling this side of things. AB was a miracle worker and a menace in equal measure, he'd barely blinked when Voodoo told him to prep another unit. He'd just nodded, rummaged, and started fiddling with wires like he was assembling a toy instead of a torture device.

Legend swung the rope again.

The sound it made cutting the air always came a second before the thud. Always just long enough to let Sinclair anticipate the pain.

He screamed. Or tried to. It came out broken.

Legend didn't look at me, but he didn't have to. I felt him beside me—solid, grounded, radiating this strange mix of fury on my behalf and discipline I hadn't known he possessed. He wasn't doing this because he enjoyed it.

He was doing it because I wanted answers.

And he trusted me to decide when we stopped.

Another swing. Another impact I didn't need to see.

Sinclair sobbed harder, his whole body buckling in the chair, his bare skin blotching red and white with shock. His feet kicked uselessly against the floor. The zip-ties around his ankles held.

Voodoo snapped the fully charged collar in place around Sinclair's throat, the click sharp enough that Sinclair jerked like he'd been hit again.

"No," he sobbed, voice shredded. "No, no, please, please—"

Legend lifted the rope again.

Sinclair broke.

"It's—" he gasped, coughing on the words, "it's not one group—please—stop—"

Legend didn't lower the rope.

He waited.

We all waited.

Sinclair's chest heaved. His eyes squeezed shut in agony or shame—I wasn't sure which.

"It's a cabal," he spat, the word choking him. "South America. Not— not just one cartel."

Voodoo's expression sharpened. Bones went still as stone. AB laser focused.

Sinclair swallowed hard, shaking violently. "Three. Three cartels. They hired me—independently. Not supposed to pool resources. Product. People." He gagged, swallowed again. "But it's how I made my best money—by combining shipments. Higher value. Less oversight. Bigger cut."

Each word dropped like another stone in the pit of my stomach.

A cabal. Not a single monster. A hydra—with more heads than we could count.

"Your sister—" Sinclair wheezed, "—she was going to ruin everything. She wouldn't *stop* digging. Goddamn idealist, but she was going to make my life hell. The deeper she went, she got too close. I had to make her stop, make it go away. Or they would have erased me."

A coldness crept through my chest, but this one wasn't the controlled, purposeful kind.

This one hurt.

Legend stepped closer to me, not touching, not speaking—just there. A shadow at my side, an anchor I didn't know I needed.

I kept my voice steady. Steadier than the rest of me. "Who did you call?"

Sinclair shook his head violently, as far as the collar allowed. "I don't know their names. I never meet them. I only— only pass along the instructions. Cash. Coordinates. Pickup times. I swear to God, Grace, I don't know their identities. Except..."

Legend's fist clenched around the rope. Bones muttered something that sounded like a promise of murder. Voodoo's jaw locked.

I didn't flinch.

"Except?" I prodded him.

But inside—inside I felt something sharp and old and familiar tear open.

Tears and sweat seemed to drip off his face as he hung there then he raised his gaze to mine. "She is called Infanta. It's not her name, I know that much. It's just her code, a way for me to know it's her. She—found out about my operation."

"And used it to blackmail you?" That seemed to fit everything else we'd been dealing with.

"Yes, I would just tell her what was coming or what was ordered. It was all happening anyway." He tried to shrug it off like it didn't matter, but he couldn't stop his grimace or the way his muscles jerked and danced. "So I got paid twice. They didn't know about the European connection, and if there was ever an issue with payment, I could just shift the cargo to a different cartel."

"How nice for you." Thankfully, he didn't act like I was serious. I wasn't sure if I could deal with that.

"She paid for information, sometimes for me to slip other things in. I didn't have to acquire it. I was always just the broker, the money manager, that was it." Defeat hung around him. Not enough.

Nowhere near enough.

"So you contacted this Infanta?" Bones asked, his cold tone a snap that landed another blow on Sinclair.

Sinclair looked at him then at me, misery in his eyes. "Yes."

"What did you tell her?" I wanted the words. "And is she still alive?"

"I don't know about the second," he said and his eyes went wide. "I really don't know. She disappeared. One day she was there, the next she was gone. We took care of any questions at the office and then let it go. It was so much easier than I thought it would be."

The son of a bitch had the audacity to sound amazed by the simplicity of it all. He made my sister disappear and he was impressed by how *easy* it was.

I *hated* him so much.

"So no, I don't know. I assume she went out with one of our shipments. We had three that week."

Three.

That week.

Three shipments. Three cartels. A cabal moving human lives around like cargo and this whimpering disgrace of a man who traded those lives like they were just numbers on a board.

And Amorette had stumbled into their spotlight. Her grit and determination had put her into this man's crosshairs and he turned that spotlight onto her to stop her. He couldn't even fight his own battles cause my sister would have kicked his ass.

But no, she hadn't stood a chance.

But I wasn't letting that be the end of her story. Not when I had the truth in front of me. Not when Sinclair still had more to give.

I stepped closer.

"We're not done," I told him.

The way Sinclair whimpered at those three simple words gave me no joy.

"How did you contact her?" I asked. "Infanta." The name scraped out of my throat like broken glass. "How did you reach her?"

Sinclair jolted, shaking his head before the words even formed. "I—I didn't! Not directly. It was always different— different phones, different couriers, burner emails, coded drops—never the same twice. They didn't trust anyone to have a pattern."

"Remember," I said.

His panic spiked, eyes rolling white. "I *can't*—I'm telling you, I can't—there were too many—"

"Every single one," I told him. "Start listing them."

Before he could wheeze out another plea, a sharp buzz broke through the room.

Ignacio convulsed in his chair, strangled on a curse as both shock collars fired. The jolt ripped through him hard enough that his heels scraped against the floor.

I didn't look away from Sinclair, but I saw it in the corner of my eye—Voodoo lowering the remote, face unreadable.

"Don't move," he told Ignacio, voice almost bored. "It would be better for you not to draw our attention."

Ignacio froze, panting shallowly, sweat running in rivulets down his temple.

Sinclair watched the whole thing. Watched Ignacio thrash. Watched him go limp against the restraints. And Sinclair started to sweat harder—thick beads rolling down his face like he was melting from the inside out.

Legend stepped forward, rope still dangling from his hand, and nodded once at AB.

"Go," Legend said.

AB didn't need more. He launched into questioning like a surgeon dissecting a corpse—precise, merciless.

"What method first?" AB asked. "Earliest point of contact. How did they recruit you?"

"I wasn't—I didn't— they approached my firm, not me personally—"

"Bullshit," Legend snapped. "You just admitted you

were already working with them when Grace's sister started digging."

Sinclair flinched. "I—fine—fine—there was a drop box in Miami. At first. Cash-in, instructions-out. Happy?"

"Next," AB demanded. "Phones. Codes. Names. Every intermediary. Every hotel. Every flight. No skipping."

They tore him apart. Piece by piece. Contradiction by contradiction.

Sinclair answered too fast sometimes—too defensive other times. Legend called him out, AB dissected every excuse, Voodoo watched for lies like weighing each answer as if he needed to test it for veracity. Maybe he was.

Bones left them to it, he'd moved to stand with me and when he slid an arm around me and rested a hand on my hip, I leaned back into him. The shaking was still there, inside my skin. I shivered and trembled below the ice. Like a rock, steady and true, Bones stayed with me. He didn't take over or redirect. If anything, he seemed to be waiting for a word whether it was from the guys or from me, I wasn't sure.

But it wasn't until Legend asked, "When was the last time you heard from them?" that something in Sinclair shifted.

"A month ago," he whispered. "Before... before everything with my wife."

The mention of her hit me like a gut punch. His *wife*.

HIS WIFE WHO'D DISAPPEARED, leaving bloody sheets and a story no one believed.

Legend's eyes narrowed. AB paused mid-scroll.

Sinclair hugged himself, chest shaking. "They said— they said she'd gotten too curious. That she'd asked questions about my travel schedule. My clients. My—my files. They said she needed to be removed for her own good."

He said it like he expected sympathy. Like he was the one who'd been wronged.

And suddenly something ugly and sharp twisted through me.

How many people had he sacrificed? How many lives had he fed into this machine because it was easier for him? More profitable?

And if he'd let them erase his wife—

The realization hit me like the floor dropped out beneath my feet.

"Wait," I said, the word cracking through the room.

All four men froze.

I straightened, leaving the shelter of Bones' embrace to move closer to Sinclair. Everything inside me just burned. We'd thought they took his wife to punish him, but it sounded more like they were cleaning up his mess.

"Was Amorette the first time you asked them to clean up something for you?"

Sinclair didn't hesitate. Didn't even think. "No."

The instant the word left his mouth, he knew—*he knew*—he'd damned himself.

Because all that earlier shock, all the surprise, all the denial. Lies. He'd done this before. More than once. My nails bit into my palms.

Legend's rope went taut in his hand. Bones lifted his chin slowly. Voodoo's eyes went cold enough to frost steel. So, it didn't surprise me that he'd lied.

"I am so tired of being lied to," I said, and blew out a breath as I turned away from Sinclair, away from Ignacio, away from all of it.

Bones was right there, his gray eyes fierce as he met my

gaze. I saw the question right there, what did I want? How could they fix this for me? They all wanted to do it. It was there in Voodoo's questioning, in Legend collecting Sinclair and torturing him, in AB tearing it all apart.

"Can you handle getting the rest of what they know out of them?"

I was just tired. So tired.

Soft fingers cupping my chin. "Don't leave the house?" It was a quiet request from Bones. I nodded once.

"Just going up to sit with Goblin." We'd made him stay upstairs for all of this. He'd let us know if a threat was coming, and he also didn't need to be down here in this mess.

"You want one of us with you?" The fact he even asked made me smile.

I wanted all of them with me, but... "I need a few," I admitted. I needed to get the smell of burnt hair out of my nose, the memory of groping fingers, and the filthy lies perpetuated by Sinclair.

A soft stroke of his fingers down my cheek. "Alphabet will come up as soon as we have the last data point." It was a decision and Bones was making it. I'd handed the control back to him and he picked up the baton easily. He brushed a kiss to my lips, soft like a butterfly's wings branding itself to my soul.

"Sounds like a plan. If you need me..."

He nodded, not dismissing my offer in the slightest. One by one, I passed the guys, a brush of my fingers to Voodoo's arm, a pat of Legend's ass—that earned me a swift grin—and a squeeze of AB's hand.

Mouthing, "I'll be there in a few," AB returned my grip, and then I headed up the stairs.

"Wait!" A shock cry came from Ignacio and another

from Sinclair. My leaving seemed to have jolted something in them. Maybe they realized that without me there, the guys would not keep anything resembling gloves on. They'd been holding back, letting me make the decisions.

As I stepped out of the basement and into the light, their shrieks followed me before the door closed and cut them off. Goblin glanced up from where he waited, tail thumping and I went straight over to sink on the floor next to him. When he wiggled into my arms, I hugged him, careful not to squeeze too tight.

"We're going to find her," I whispered against him. "We have to."

We hadn't come this far to lose now.

TEN

BONES

The moment Grace's footsteps faded up the stairs and the door closed at the top, the shift in the room was instant and sharp. A sensation of your ears popping as you adjusted to the new pressure, only this was more intense.

Both Sinclair and Ignacio felt it too.

They'd been watching her the whole time, clinging to her presence like she was some kind of shield. And maybe she had been. Not because she was soft, Grace had steel in her blood, but because *we* were softer with her in the room.

The second the basement door clicked shut overhead, Ignacio let out a high, strangled noise. Sinclair wasn't any better; he jerked so hard the chair scraped across the concrete.

Legend let out a low whistle. "Well. They finally figured it out."

"They finally figured *her* out," I corrected.

Voodoo met my gaze, the corner of his mouth ticking up just enough to acknowledge the truth. "She trusts us to do what we need to do." She also didn't want to watch the rest.

She didn't need to.

Possessing all the poise her name implied, she had stood up to the task brilliantly. But her heart hurt so damn much and listening to the lies these men kept trying to feed us in lieu of what she wanted to know had to hurt. So yes, she was trusting us to finish the mission by any means necessary.

Unfortunately for this pair of selfish assholes, we still possessed a great many "means."

Alphabet straightened beside the table, his laptop was open. We would confirm every single data point they offered. Right now, we needed the identities of these so-called cabals, and what trail her sister had been on that made her a "problem."

Ignacio yanked at his restraints, breath coming in wild, panicked bursts. "W-wait—wait—please—don't—don't—she—she—she wants answers—not this—"

"She still wants answers," Voodoo said mildly, picking up the second shock device and checking the contacts. "We're just done wasting her time."

Sinclair trembled so hard the Queen Anne chair vibrated under him. "You can't—You can't do this—She—She said—she said—"

Lunchbox barked a laugh. "Man, Grace didn't say shit about keeping you breathing."

He swung the rope lightly against his leg, testing the balance again. The faint smack of the weighted knots made Sinclair flinch even as Ignacio whined in the back of his throat.

I checked them both—automatic habit. Assess the threats.

Assess the leverage. Assess how close they were to breaking.

Sinclair was dangling by a fraying thread. Ignacio was already past the point of dignity.

Good.

Because tired as she was, Grace had left us with one request, *"Can you handle getting the rest of what they know out of them?"*

"Alright," I said, stepping closer to Sinclair until my shadow hit him full-on. "Grace asked for everything. We're not stopping until we have the names, the routes, the drop points, and every last person involved in Amorette's disappearance."

Sinclair's teeth clicked together as he tried to swallow. "I—I told you about the cabal—three cartels—I already said—"

"That was the appetizer," Lunchbox cut in. "We're moving on to the main course."

Sinclair shook his head so hard spit flew. "No—no—please—listen—I can't—I can't give you anything else—they'll—they'll kill me—they'll slaughter everyone I know—"

Voodoo didn't even look up from adjusting the voltage. "If you think they're your bigger problem right now, you haven't been paying attention."

Ignacio sobbed at that—and that sound, sharp and pathetic, made Sinclair's eyes snap toward him. The two men locked on each other for the first time since Grace had walked out.

Ignacio's fear fed Sinclair's. Sinclair's terror fed Ignacio's.

Predator and prey didn't matter anymore. They were both prey. Far too late to really help them, they finally understood exactly who the predators were.

It was almost pathetic. Normally, I took no pleasure in

inflicting pain. It was a means to an end. These two, however, had told lie after lie in an effort to drag out *Grace's* pain. They were the type of men who abused the power they had, and in Ignacio's case, he'd *truly* abused Grace. I hadn't forgotten her reaction or his comment about how she looked and felt on his cock.

After resetting both targets and their chairs, Lunchbox and Voodoo took watchful positions while Alphabet waited. I was taking over the interrogation from here. My patience was not infinite and it had snapped the moment I'd seen the stark loss and terror in Grace's eyes.

These two were very much responsible for both the terror *and* the loss.

"Ready when you are," Lunchbox said, rolling his shoulders. He moved behind Sinclair to give me a clear view even as Voodoo shifted to stand behind Ignacio. It was almost comical how being surrounded increased the pressure on them. They didn't know where to look, because to see one of us they had to turn their backs on the others.

"Same," Voodoo concurred, remote dangling in his hand.

I took a breath, slow and centering. Grace's scent still clung to my shirt—a faint trace of the shampoo she'd used upstairs, herbs and something warm and clean.

Her fatigue. Her grief. Her hope.

I was carrying all of it now.

"Sinclair," I said, focusing on him. "We're going to start at the beginning. What was Amorette investigating that got her on their radar?"

"I can't—"

I didn't even let him finish the answer before flicking a glance at Lunchbox. The other man swung. The rope struck with a sick, meaty thud. Sinclair screamed.

Ignacio jerked, the sweat rolling off him waves now.

"Try again," I instructed Sinclair.

"You don't—"

Another glance at Lunchbox. Another swing. Another scream.

When the man's sobs slowed, I cocked my head to the side. "Let me correct a misapprehension you seem to be suffering from." I raised one finger. "I ask a question. You tell us the truth. If you fail to answer or try to prevaricate, then you suffer. We have the rest of the day and all of the night, Sinclair. Think about that before you answer my next question. We'll start with, do you understand?"

"Yes," came out broken and weepy.

"Excellent. Are you prepared to answer my questions now?"

Another ragged breath. "Yes."

"Good." I didn't even blink. "What was Amorette investigating that got her on their radar?"

"Nothing," the man said, but it came out a garbled confession. That was what I had thought. This man seemed to be incapable of the truth.

"Then how did she get on their radar?"

His gasps for air made the words come out on a choking sound. "I told them." Even as the words left his lips, he braced, expecting another blow. It didn't come.

"Good," I said. Now we were getting somewhere. "Next question."

From there, we kept going. He made it to a third question before he tried to lie again. Every lie got a blow. Every truth bought him a few seconds of recovery.

The panic spiked so high the room vibrated with it. Ignacio shook so violently the collar jangled. Sinclair hiccupped sobs between words, his voice dissolving into a slurry of fear.

Finally, he choked out a string of numbers. "T-They—they switch codes every time—the last one was—was six-three-blackbird—two-four-seven—rhinestone—oh God—oh God—"

Alphabet was already typing, dissecting, cross-referencing. "Good. Keep going."

Sinclair nodded frantically, drool mixing with tears on his chin. "I—I'm doing it—I'm doing it, please—don't hurt me—"

I leaned in.

"You're still breathing," I said. "That's more than your victims got."

He curled inward, shoulders heaving.

"Let's continue..." I fired off the next wave of questions. Some got straightforward answers, others got whimpered *"I don't knows"* accompanied by waves of begging and the stench of sweat and fear.

Some of the answers he really didn't have. But the most disgusting one of all was the fact that Amorette Black had been targeted for one reason and one reason alone.

She overheard this shitstain on a phone call and Sinclair wasn't sure how much she overheard.

"She—she was always such a crusader. If she understood—once she figured it out—she wouldn't let it go—"

"But you don't know what she knew or didn't, do you?" I had the answer, that was just more of my disgust showing. "You dropped her into human trafficking to cover your own ass."

Unsurprising and yet the man's cowardice turned my stomach.

"I had to protect myself."

Protect. Himself.

"And Grace?"

A blank look crossed the attorney's face. He opened his mouth then closed it again. I waited.

"I don't—know?" It sounded more like a question than an answer. "I may ha—I did tell them she had a sister. A twin. But—I didn't ask them to take her."

Guilt hung off every syllable. Grace had been wanted. He just provided them an excuse. Or an opportunity. Maybe she'd already been slated because of the European connection. Maybe it was all some macabre coincidence.

Maybe we'd never have the real answer. It was enough to know they'd taken her and he was involved, however much it had been on the periphery. At the end of the day, he was responsible for what had happened to her sister. That, we would never forgive.

He all but sagged in relief when Lunchbox didn't swing the rope again. I let him have his few second reprieve. But that was all it was. A reprieve.

"Let's discuss the cartels that you worked with…" I said, then switched the questions between the two of them, rapid fire, not letting them pause to think or anticipate. Maybe Ignacio only worked as ground transport here, or maybe he was just another middleman. Sometimes they didn't know what they knew.

We could work with the information.

Ignacio started talking first—too fast, too desperate— words tumbling out like he was trying to outrun his own terror.

"I—I know ship numbers," he stammered, eyes wild. "And containers—specific ones—ones they flagged for pickup or offload—please—please—if I give you those—"

"You're bargaining?" Voodoo asked, voice low, almost amused. "Right now?"

Ignacio swallowed hard. "I—I know things—real things—containers, manifests, routes. I can give you those. I swear, I swear—"

He jerked violently as the collar rubbed against his throat, whether from fear or instinct, I didn't care.

"Tell Alphabet everything," I said. "Every container number. Every ship name. Every route designation you ever handled."

Ignacio gasped. "I—I don't remember all of them—"

Voodoo clicked the remote. A sharp pop of electricity.

Ignacio screamed.

"Try again," I said, perfectly calm.

He rattled off a dozen numbers so fast Alphabet had to snap his fingers for him to slow down. Once we had the first list logged, we swung our attention to Sinclair.

"Your turn," I said, tone deceptively polite. "Cartel contacts. Direct ones."

Sinclair's eyes rolled up for a second, then he shook his head violently. "I only—I only spoke to one—no, two—two from the Sarmiento line—one from La Madrina—one—fuck, fuck—one from the Castillo syndicate—"

"Names," Lunchbox demanded.

Sinclair's chest hitched. "I didn't—I didn't keep track—I told you—I *told you*—I didn't want to know—didn't want to remember—that way I couldn't give anything up—"

"That was stupid," I said. "You should've kept track."

"I didn't!" he cried. "I didn't—I swear—some were faceless—I only saw a few—"

Lunchbox swung the rope lightly against his palm in a reminder.

Sinclair crumpled. Again.

"Five!" he blurted. "Five—I can give you five—I remember five—just five—please—please—don't—don't—"

"Names," Alphabet repeated, fingers poised over the keyboard.

Sinclair spat them out like rotten teeth he couldn't swallow fast enough.

"Marcos Sarmiento or de Sarjiento—maybe La De Sargento. I just called him Marcos."

He tried to wet his lips and his throat bobbed almost painfully.

"Phillip Rojas—de Roja—red. It was like red hat or red fish. I didn't—maybe Felipe—no, Phillip. He had a very strong British accent. Spanish last name, British accent."

Sinclair squeezed his eyes shut, it was like he was willing himself to remember.

"San—Zan—Xander—something. He sounds German—no more South African than German. Maybe. Zander Visser." He gasped out the last two syllables like he'd run a marathon to get to them.

The next two names came out even more garbled, but it was a starting point.

"Mykel—Michael—Mikael—*something* like that—I don't—God, I don't remember—just *Mykal,* okay?"

"Jochem—Jorchan—Jon—something Russian, definitely Eastern European."

"That's four and a half," Lunchbox said. "And Russian is not the same as Eastern European."

Sinclair sobbed. "I don't—I can't—most of the time I only ever had a first name. You have to understand, I didn't *want* to know their names. I didn't want to know too much."

"Just enough to make money," I said, not an ounce of

sympathy within me. I glanced at Alphabet and he gave a mild shrug. We could work with it.

I turned toward Ignacio. His breathing had gone ragged, panic rising like steam off his skin.

"You," I said, stepping closer. "What do you know about these five?"

"I—I only—only heard of two," he gasped. "Marcos and Joaquin. They—they were the ones who handled the *shipments*—they were—"

Joaquin or Jochem? Was it the pain that was shredding the names or did they really not pay that much attention?

Voodoo stepped closer, remote angled lazily in his fingers.

"Don't lie," he warned softly. "I'll know."

Ignacio whimpered. "I'm not—I swear—I'm not—I only dealt with the handlers—ground-level—never the bosses—I swear—I swear—"

The collar around his throat beeped a warning tone as Voodoo adjusted the contact sensitivity.

Ignacio froze like an animal smelling the knife.

"Then tell me something useful," I said. "Something *real.*"

"I—I can give you the containers they used for special cargo," Ignacio blurted out. "The ones with double-backs, false floors, temperature control—ones that don't get random inspections—I can—I can—there were three main ones they trusted—"

He rattled them off. Named ports. Named long-shoremen who were on the take. Alphabet typed.

Lunchbox stalked a slow circle behind him, rope tapping rhythmically against his palm.

Sinclair stared at Ignacio with pure terror—because

Ignacio was too willing to talk now. Too desperate. Too loud.

Apparently, the attorney was figuring out that if Ignacio talked, Sinclair's value dropped.

Good.

I leaned forward, bracing my hands on my knees so I could meet Sinclair's eyes directly. He flinched back like I'd swung the rope myself.

"Now," I said quietly. "Tell me how you contacted these people. Every method. Every drop point. Every burner. Every code. Every middleman. All of it."

He shook his head frantically. "I can't—it was always different—always—different cars—different phones—different buildings—they—they'd tell me to show up somewhere and—and a phone would be there or—or a person already waiting—or a voice through a grate—I don't know—I don't—"

"You can remember," I said.

"I *can't!*"

"You can." I straightened, looking at both of them. "And you will."

Sinclair screamed—not from pain yet, but from the panic spiraling out of him like his ribs couldn't contain it.

"Remember *every single one,*" I said.

He opened his mouth to argue, but from the corner of my eye, I saw Voodoo press the button.

Ignacio's scream tore through the basement. Full-body convulsion. Chair legs skidding. Foam flecking the corner of his mouth.

"Don't move," Voodoo told him calmly. "It would be better for you not to draw our attention."

Sinclair's sweat doubled instantly. He shook so hard the

chair rocked under him. He didn't even try to hide the panic now.

"Keep talking, Sinclair," Alphabet said as he approached him with the laptop, voice cool and clipped. "Because we're about to audit every part of your life. Let's start with the last time you heard from them."

He answered. Rapid-fire. Half-useful, half garbage.

Lunchbox slammed him with follow-up questions. We measured their answers against each other's reaction. Cross-checked the lies and tore apart the details. The location of his safe upstairs and what might be in it. The combination was the easiest bit.

Ignacio named everyone from his grade school instructors to his other bosses. Unsurprisingly, he was a handler for more than one supplier and that was news to Sinclair. It might almost be funny if we were talking about anything else.

That said, none of this was funny. It was horrific, disgusting, and tragic. I'd fought real wars with real consequences and these two had taken to commodifying people as products. The utter dehumanization of it all left me cold.

Two hours of hammering later, we had everything we were going to get out of them. There was no more blood to squeeze from this set of stones. I swept my glance around to each of the guys, eyebrows raised.

Lunchbox nodded once, never taking his gaze off Sinclair.

Voodoo twirled the remote around one finger as he nodded as well.

Alphabet gave me a swift bob of his head, his fingers flying over the keyboard as he continued to work on the details.

We were done.

"Unhook him," I told Voodoo as I motioned to Ignacio. He let out a sobbing gasp of relief, that choked just moments later as I headed for him with a knife.

I ignored his screams and his pleas just as he had ignored them in every person he'd transported. I removed the dick he'd been so proud of and shoved it down his throat before I strangled him.

Sinclair I left for Voodoo and Lunchbox. They carved out two pounds of flesh from him before they ended it.

Two pounds, one for each of the twins.

In the aftermath, Alphabet leaned back and met my gaze. "We might not have enough." Too many holes. Too many open questions.

"I know." But I refused to disappoint her again. "We make it work."

Grace needed to know. If it took the rest of our lives, we would get her what she needed to know.

ELEVEN

GRACE

The next twenty-four hours blurred, smeared, and folded in on themselves like pages of a book that had been rained on and left out to dry crooked.

I didn't remember leaving Sinclair's basement.

I didn't remember the drive.

I didn't remember the transfer through an underground garage, or the elevator, or the coded door that hissed open like something out of a spy movie.

I remembered Goblin's warm flank pressed against my leg.

I remembered Bones' hand on the small of my back anytime my steps slowed.

I remembered Legend's voice—low and steady—telling me we were almost there.

Then we arrived at a safe house. Another one.

This one near the District, tucked between a row of narrow brick townhomes that blended so well I wouldn't have noticed it if AB hadn't opened the door with a loud, "Welcome to the nation's capital, kiddos, please remove your shoes, weapons optional."

He was trying to make me smile.

It worked. Barely.

The place was...anonymous. Clean lines, bare floors, neutral colors. The kind of temporary shelter where nothing personal was meant to remain. No pictures. No memories. No ghosts.

I dropped onto the couch before any of them could herd me anywhere else. Goblin climbed up beside me, shoved his nose under my arm, and sighed with all the weight of the world.

"Yeah," I whispered to him. "Me too."

Across the room, Alphabet had already commandeered the dining table. Three laptops open, phone plugged in, tablet connected, cords like veins spreading out in every direction. The digital heartbeat of the entire mess pulsed beneath his fingers.

He didn't look up as he spoke. "Sinclair's five names are garbage in isolation, but when you run them against shipping manifests, port clearances, and the last twelve to eighteen months of diverted cargos? We've got movement. Not a full trail. But movement."

Legend slumped into an armchair opposite me, rope burns still on his hands. "Means we're not dead in the water."

Voodoo paced. He'd been pacing since we arrived—tight, contained circles like a lion searching for a threat it could already smell but not yet see. "Movement isn't enough. We need a direction, and we need to know whether following it keeps Grace in play or puts her in the crosshairs."

Bones stood behind the couch, both hands resting lightly on the back near my shoulders without actually touching me. His closeness alone was comfort.

I let out a breath that felt like it dragged broken glass out of my chest.

"So what are we doing?" My voice sounded steadier than I felt. "Going back to Montana? Staying here? Hunting for the next lead?"

AB finally tore his eyes from the screens, gaze sweeping the room before landing on me. "We're triangulating. Every name, every container ID, every port switch Ignacio babbled, every code Sinclair vomited up—we're stitching it together. By tonight, I'll know which cabal branch is most active and where the shipments converged. And from that, we can figure out the most likely vector Amorette was funneled into."

My stomach hollowed. Hearing her name still felt like stepping off a cliff.

Legend leaned forward, elbows on knees. "Montana gives us home turf. Resources. More privacy. But we lose proximity to the East Coast ports." He jerked a thumb at AB. "And Mr. Wi-Fi Overdose here gets cranky when the bandwidth sucks."

Alphabet lifted one finger from the keyboard. "Correction, I get homicidal when the bandwidth sucks."

Bones ignored both of them. His voice lowered. "Grace."

Just my name. But full of weight. "We follow your lead. If you need home—real home—we go. If you want us to keep pushing here, we stay."

Home.

Their place had become home at some point over the past several months. As much as we'd traveled, and all the safe houses, they brought part of that home with them. They were my home.

The word punched something deep in my ribcage. I wanted it. God, I wanted the pine air, the mountains, the quiet. I wanted my bed or theirs. I wanted to sleep without seeing Sinclair's face or hearing Ignacio sob.

But Amorette wouldn't be in Montana.

Time kept slipping away.

"I don't want to run from this," I said, fingers curling against Goblin's fur. "I'm tired. I'm...exhausted. But we're close. Closer than we've been since this started. I can feel it."

Legend nodded slowly, something like pride flickering in his eyes. "Then we stay until Alphabet gets the next solid lead."

AB lifted a hand. "I can get you that by tonight. Tomorrow at the latest." He grunted. "Okay, forty-eight hours tops. I want to make sure I drill down far enough that we don't miss anything."

Voodoo finally stopped pacing. "Then we prep. Weapons. Extractions. Evac contingencies. Because the second we tug one wrong strand of that cabal web, they're going to feel it. Might already know Sinclair's missing."

A tremor slipped down my spine.

"Does it matter?" I asked.

Bones came around the couch and sank beside me, letting his shoulder brush mine in silent answer.

He was right.

It didn't matter.

We weren't stopping.

Not until we found Amorette.

Bones raised his arm.

It was such a small gesture—barely more than a quiet invitation—but my body moved before my mind caught up. I leaned into him, curling into the curve of his chest as though that was the place I'd been meant to fit all along.

He didn't say anything at first. Just held me, his warmth

sinking into my skin, into me, into the hollowed-out spaces where adrenaline had finally burned itself out. We'd all showered and changed back at Sinclair's house before we left it behind—somewhere in the fog, I remembered that. The soap, the steam, the scrape of a towel across my skin. Washing off the sweat and fear and the stink of the basement.

But none of it touched the tiredness.

"Do you want to rest?" Bones asked quietly, his breath stirring the top of my hair.

"I don't..." My fingers curled in Goblin's fur again. "I don't know what I want."

That earned me the full attention of the room.

Legend's head lifted immediately, all that mischief he wore like armor snapping off his face as if someone had flipped a switch. Voodoo paused mid-swipe over whatever tactical list he was building on his phone. Even AB's typing cut off mid-click, his hands suspended over his keys.

For a heartbeat, nobody breathed.

Then Legend said, abruptly and with the weight of absolute certainty, "Food."

All of us looked at him.

He lifted his chin. "No joke. That's what we need. She needs to eat. We all do. And we need a beat. Just us. Nothing heavy. Clear the mental palate before we start wrestling with the next monster."

Voodoo's thumb tapped once against his thigh. "Agreed. Low blood sugar and high stress is a shit combination."

AB rolled his chair back from the table. "I can pause. Algorithms won't implode if I take thirty minutes. I have plenty of searches that can run while we break." He pointed to the screen without looking at it. "I already know where to pick the threads up."

Legend rubbed a hand over his jaw. "So. Options. We can cook here. Or we can pick up from that little place three blocks over—the one with the day-old pastries and the weirdly excellent sandwiches."

Voodoo snorted. "The café with the chairs that collapse when you breathe too hard."

"They fixed the chairs," Legend shot back. "Their grilled cheese is god-tier, don't even lie."

Bones glanced down at me. "Dollface? Any preferences?"

I didn't. But the normalcy of them debating sandwiches and collapsing chairs and delivery apps felt like a rope thrown to a drowning swimmer. Something to hold onto.

"I...maybe something simple?" My throat felt tight. "Warm."

"Soup," Voodoo said.

"Grilled cheese," Legend insisted.

"Both," AB decided. "I'll place the order. You—" he pointed at Legend, "—go pick it up. You look like you need to move before you start climbing the walls."

Legend blinked, then flashed a crooked grin. "True enough. I'll be back in fifteen."

"Take Goblin with you. He's been a trooper, but he could use a good walk too."

Bones pressed a kiss into my hair—soft, grounding. "We'll keep it light. Just food. No questions, no planning until you say otherwise."

For the first time in hours—maybe days—I felt something like steady ground forming under my feet again.

Not peace. Not safety. But something close to breathing.

Because even as the world kept spinning and the horror kept unfolding… I wasn't alone in it.

Not for one breath. Not for one step.

"Okay," I whispered. "Food sounds good."

Legend was already grabbing his keys. "Come on, buddy. Field trip."

Goblin perked up from where he'd curled up against me. Legend grinned and crouched. With a soft huff, Goblin nudged my hand as if asking if I minded and I stroked him between his ears.

"Go on, a walk sounds good." That earned me a wet kiss to my cheek before he hopped down and trotted over to Legend. Once he had the leash snapped on, they were out the door. The house exhaled into a quieter silence.

Voodoo slid his phone into his pocket and tilted his head at me. "Do you want to watch a movie?"

I blinked at him. "A… movie?"

His brows lifted, amused. "Yes, Grace. Moving pictures. Story. Usually accompanied by popcorn."

"That sounds—" I tried to find the right word. "—wildly normal."

Bones huffed a low laugh beside me, rubbing slow, warm circles on my arm. Voodoo shrugged lightly, leaning a hip against the table.

"Well," he said, "we could play cards instead. Something simple. Poker?"

Poker.

Poker after everything I'd just seen.

Poker instead of screaming, or panicking, or burying myself under the weight of it all.

The absurdity tugged the corner of my mouth upward. Barely—but it was there.

"Poker, huh?" I asked. "Are we playing for stakes?"

Bones' fingers stilled, then resumed their gentle motion. Voodoo's lips twisted into something that lived between a smirk and genuine warmth.

He pushed off the table with easy precision. "That depends," he said. "How badly are you planning to beat us?"

And for the first time today—I felt the slope of a smile tugging at me. Not full. Not bright. But real.

"You don't even know if I'm that good at it."

AB snorted from the counter. "Please. You have the best poker face I've ever seen. You make *statues* look expressive."

Bones rumbled a low agreement. "I've seen you deal with arms dealers and bakers with the same collected calm. You rescued me at the museum without a twitch. That's championship-level control right there."

Voodoo folded his arms, smirking. "Yeah, Grace. If that wasn't a poker face, nothing is."

Heat flickered in my chest—small, startled, but warm.

I tried for modesty, but the corners of my mouth betrayed me, lifting despite the weight of everything pressing against my ribs.

"Honestly," I said, shrugging lightly, "I'm not bad at it."

"Not bad?" Bones echoed, nudging my knee with his own. "You're terrifying at it."

I huffed out something close to a laugh. "Fine. But I'm better when we're actually playing for stakes."

Voodoo raised a brow. "Oh? Planning on taking all our money?"

"Money's boring," I shot back. "Besides... you guys need a break too."

AB snapped his laptop shut. "Hear that? The lady wants stakes and a break. Someone get the cards."

And for the first time in hours, between trauma and fear

and grief and the razor-edged hunger for answers, I felt myself exhale something that wasn't pain.

A smile. Real. Small. But mine.

"Cards are easy," Voodoo said. "We always keep some at various stops." He disappeared down the hall and when he came back, he had three decks with him. "Stakes... may prove a little challenging?"

"Do we need physical stakes?" AB mused aloud moving over to join us on the sofa. When he sat next to me, he stretched his legs out and there was a kind of slow sigh that escaped him. We were all aching in different ways. "Or just the idea of them?"

By the time Legend returned—with Goblin trotting proudly at his heels and bags of food swinging from both hands—we'd turned the dining area into something that almost resembled normal life.

Almost.

The circular table was pulled into the center of the room. Five mismatched chairs around it. Bones had cleared enough space that the whole setup looked intentional instead of desperate.

Legend stopped in the doorway, blinked once, then grinned. "Well, damn. I leave for twenty minutes and you degenerates turn this place into a Vegas side room."

Bones lifted the deck, letting the cards slap together in a clean, deadly shuffle. "Sit down, Lunchbox. You're in for the next hand."

"Sweet," he said, dropping the bags on the counter. Goblin trotted over to me, nudging my knee until I scratched behind his ears. "What are we playing for? Money? Bragging rights? Organs?"

"Clothes," AB said cheerfully, digging through the food. "And promises."

Legend went still. Then slowly, very slowly, his grin widened. "Clothes and promises. Okay. This I like."

I held up a hand before anyone got too excited. "One promise per day. Max."

Four pairs of male eyes cut toward me. Bones raised a brow. Voodoo paused mid-drink prep. AB froze with a spoon halfway to his mouth. Legend looked personally offended.

"One per day?" Legend echoed. "Gracie, sweetheart, we're gonna win you by the hour."

"You think so?" I countered, arching a brow.

Bones let out a low whistle. "She's confident."

"Confident?" AB snorted. "She's plotting our destruction."

I shrugged, the tiniest tug of amusement pulling at my lips. "I'm just saying... the odds might not be in your favor."

Legend set out the food—sandwiches, fries, soup, and something spicy AB immediately claimed—and dropped into the chair beside me. "You're talking big for someone who hasn't played us yet."

"Oh, I've played you," I said lightly. "You just didn't notice."

Voodoo returned with drinks—beer for the guys, sparkling wine for me, because he noticed things—and set them down. The fact Voodoo had taken the time to step out and grab drinks was sweet. "Alright. House rules, lose a hand, lose a layer."

AB raised his bottle. "Win a hand, earn a promise."

Legend bumped his shoulder against mine. "You ready for this, Gracie?"

I looked around at them—these men who had torn men down for me today and they'd do it again tomorrow and the day after that if I needed it—and felt something warm settle under my ribs.

They needed this.

God, so did I.

I nodded, settling into my chair. "Deal the cards, boys."

Just like that, for the first time since Bones had been taken, the air around us eased—not because the danger was gone, but because, for this moment, we let ourselves breathe.

TWELVE

ALPHABET

Caffeine made my pulse hum like malfunctioning wiring. Four cans of whatever energy sludge Lunchbox had stocked in the fridge were probably a sign I needed an intervention, but right now they were the reason we finally had movement.

Real movement.

My hands still shook a little as I braced one on the doorframe of the upstairs bedroom. I'd meant to knock. I really had. But the second everything clicked into place—the moment the name finally matched—I forgot all about etiquette.

"Hey," I hissed, pushing the door open with my shoulder. "Hey, wake up—guys, seriously, wake up."

In the low gray morning light, all three of them were a tangle of limbs on the too-small bed. Grace flat on her stomach, cheek pressed against Bones' shoulder; Bones curled protectively around her; Voodoo sprawled behind her, one arm draped over her waist like he'd anchored both of them through the night.

Three sets of instincts came online in the same instant.

Bones' eyes snapped open first—sharp, feral. Voodoo's hand went straight under the pillow for the knife he liked to sleep with. Grace jerked, inhaled hard, then blinked up at me in bleary confusion.

I lifted both hands. "Not a threat. Just me. Hi. Good morning. I need your brains."

Bones pushed up on one elbow. "Alphabet, you better be dying or this better be about her sister."

"It is," I said, too fast. Okay, maybe I was vibrating a little. "The second one. Definitely the second one."

That got everyone awake fast.

Grace pushed her hair back, sitting up between them as Voodoo rubbed a hand down his face. "AB... breathe," she murmured.

"Breathing later. Information now." I dragged my laptop case off my shoulder and set it on the foot of the bed. "I found the match. One of Sinclair's garbled names? It finally hit. Marcos Sarmiento. Or de Sarjiento. Or the alias 'La De Sargento.' One guy, three variations. Same signature style, same work patterns."

Voodoo frowned. "Sarmiento... rings a bell."

Bones grunted. "South American broker. The kind who handles deals between groups who don't like each other."

"Correct," I said, pleased he'd saved me ten seconds of exposition. "And more importantly, he's tied to a shell corporation that maintains a private port in Delaware. Harborstone Logistics."

Grace's eyes sharpened. She shifted forward, knees under her, the exhaustion dropping away like a shed skin. "What kind of ties?"

"Ownership. Operational control. And as of last month? One of Ignacio's listed container IDs was processed through that port under a fake agricultural manifest."

Bones muttered a low curse. Voodoo went still, like he was cataloguing every implication.

Grace's voice dropped to a whisper. "He trafficked through that port."

"Yes." I flicked open the laptop. The screen lit the room in pale blue. "If Amorette was passed out through the States—which she had to be, she started here, but if they didn't move her up to Canada or down to the Caribbean, then the supply chain would start there—Sarmiento would have known. Maybe even overseen."

I paused a beat.

"That made more sense in my head than aloud, but I managed to tie a name, a container number, and the private port. This is a solid lead." Maybe I needed more caffeine.

Behind me, someone yawned.

Lunchbox filled the doorway, hair damp from a shower, wearing gym shorts and a shirt he definitely hadn't put on for modesty reasons. Goblin pushed past him into the room to nose at Grace's hand.

Lunchbox squinted. "Why is everyone awake? It's barely six."

"Because Alphabet is buzzing like a neon sign," Voodoo said dryly.

"Because Alphabet found the name match," Bones corrected.

Lunchbox perked up, fully alert in an instant. "Which name?"

I pointed at the screen. "Marcos Sarmiento. Or de Sarjiento. Or La De Sargento. He's tied to a private port in Delaware that processed one of Ignacio's containers."

He blinked at me. "...And you were going to lead with 'good morning'?"

"I *did* lead with good morning. In my head." I waved a hand. "Point is—we have a direction."

Grace looked between us, something fierce slowly building in her eyes chasing away her sleepy expression. "Are we going?"

"That's the next question," I said. "But... yeah. I think we should."

Voodoo cracked his neck. "We need intel before we walk into that hornet's nest."

Bones nodded, his hand finding Grace's knee. "But we're not letting this sit." He pulled her to him and gave her a kiss that threatened to scorch the whole room. Her cheeks flushed and her lips were a little swollen. "Go shower, Dollface."

Before any of us could offer to join her, however, Bones pinned us with a gaze.

"She showers by herself, we need everyone focused. Showers. Lunchbox, food and start the pack up. Voodoo—"

Already standing, Voodoo helped Grace off the bed before he gave her a good morning kiss of his own, then said, "I'll get our transpo sorted out and lock in the location."

Breathless but looking a little shaky around the edges, Grace came right to me and I wrapped her up in my arms. Tucking my face down against her hair, I took a deep breath.

Two days. Just over fifty-three hours of tearing the data apart, longer than I'd liked, but still good based on what I had to work with, but we had a lead. Her arms tightened and I inhaled the sweetness of her scent. She steadied my jitteriness.

"Thank you," she whispered and I leaned back to meet her gaze.

"You never have to thank me." Ever. "I just wish I could have gotten you this information sooner."

"Well, if you had it any sooner, you'd have been waking us at four instead of six." It was a light comment, a teasing one. One meant to make me play with her, and it worked.

"Go on," I told her. "Shower. I'll put together the briefing so you have everything."

"Okay." When she pushed up on her toes, I lowered my head obediently so she could kiss me. I savored the closeness, drinking in her simple presence before she darted into the bathroom.

No one moved until the bathroom door shut and the water kicked on—sharp rush, muffled by tile. The second it did, Bones rose from the bed like someone had flipped a switch. He pinned me with that steady, surgical stare of his.

"How solid is this?"

"Pretty damn solid." My caffeine buzz dimmed under the weight of the moment. "And it gets better. Based on travel indicators and financial pings, Sarmiento's in country. Right now. He should still be in Delaware."

Voodoo's posture shifted—a predator scenting fresh blood.

I pushed on. "There's been zero chatter about Sinclair going dark. No alerts. No escalation. Nothing tying back to us. So for once? We might actually have surprise on our side."

A rare beat of silence settled.

Getting ahead of the problem instead of chasing it like idiots through fire—that was new. It felt good. Dangerous, but good.

Bones didn't waste a beat. "Shower. Food. Then you sleep in the car." The last part landed like a gavel, aimed square at me.

I flinched. "Sleep... in the car?"

He sliced a hand through the air, precise and final. "You haven't slept in two days. Napping at the keyboard while waiting on a search ping isn't rest. You sleep in the car, or you stay here and remote in. Your choice—but the car's the safer bet."

The implacable set of his jaw told me exactly how that fight would end before it started. I gritted my teeth and muttered an agreement.

"I'll... uh, walk Goblin?" I asked, stalling.

Bones gave me a single look. "I'll take care of it. Get your gear ready, then eat after the shower."

Lucky for me, there were two showers in the safe house. Lunchbox was already ducking downstairs to make food. I slipped into the empty room, the faint hum of pipes greeting me.

As the water hit, I caught Bones' voice from the other room. "Cut him off."

I rolled my eyes. Energy drinks? Please. I didn't need the fake stuff when I was already juiced up on a lead this hot.

By the time I stepped out, the smell of cooking had already started to pull me back into motion. Two days of running, two days of little sleep—but finally, finally, the hunt was starting to feel like something we could actually get ahead of.

By the time we loaded the SUV and climbed in, the early morning chaos of rush hour traffic had the Beltway in knots. It was as good an excuse as any to take the time to sleep. I had search programs running that would ping me on other data, but it could wait—for now.

As it was, I stretched out on the third row seat as much as I could, tucked my head down and folded my arms then went to sleep. Sleep was a discipline as much as anything else. Threading through traffic was as good a time as any. A hand on my shoulder stirred me from patchy sleep.

It was nearly ten. The roads clogged with commuters and delivery trucks had given me more time than I expected to actually rest. My eyes gritty, jaw unshaven, but my body finally feeling like it'd caught up enough to function. Grace passed me a bottle of water and gave me a smile that immediately improved my day.

She sat on the middle seat with Voodoo and Goblin. Her hair, braided into one long tail, fell over one shoulder. Her bright blue eyes were alert, but the shadows that smudged the skin beneath them remained. I didn't think we were going to get rid of those until we finished the mission. The quiet intensity in her reminded me exactly why we were chasing this lead.

I sat up, back creaking a little and my neck popping. I downed about half of the water bottle as I scanned the area, taking in the route, the cars, the weather, everything.

Up front, Bones navigated the traffic with his usual precision, calm as the city churned around us. Lunchbox sat beside him, eyes flicking between the tablet and the road, as he and Voodoo ran routes and contingencies in a quiet hum of conversation that I was so used to hearing, I didn't even register it until I was awake.

I rubbed at my stubble, flexed my shoulders, and drained the water before taking the pair of protein bars Grace passed back to me, along with another bottle of water.

"You are the best," I murmured as she handed over the

pain relievers. The low-grade headache was manageable, but the ache in my leg wouldn't be if I didn't take care of it.

"I know," she replied softly. I popped three pills, washed them down with the water, and tore into the bars. For the first time in a while, I felt almost human—or at least a reasonable facsimile.

Bones glanced in the rearview mirror, voice calm but sharp. "Port's coming up. GPS says we're close. Ready to move?"

I nodded, letting the last bit of alertness settle in. "Good to go. What's the plan?"

He leaned back just slightly, eyes narrowing as he began to read me in, like he was layering the pieces in his head. "We're not chasing anymore. We're here to control the play, not react to it. For once, we get the jump on these jerks."

I allowed a small, satisfied exhale. The sun caught the dashboard, glinting across Grace's face in the backseat. We had a lead, daylight on our side, and, for the first time in a long time, it felt like we were the ones dictating the hunt.

THIRTEEN

GRACE

The port looked ordinary. That was the first thing that struck me.

Just rows of corrugated steel containers in dull colors, cranes moving like patient metal giants, trucks weaving through lanes painted with peeling lines—nothing that screamed *monsters operate here*. Nothing that hinted at the kind of nightmare my sister had been swallowed by.

But the guys didn't trust ordinary. Neither did I.

Bones drove slow as we looped around the perimeter roads—sweeping each access point, the chain-link fences, the double gates, the security booths. Voodoo took photos from low angles with his phone. Legend muttered observations under his breath, and AB kept tapping on his tablet, cross-referencing what he saw outside with the digital breadcrumbs he'd collected.

Goblin, head in my lap, watched it all in silent, canine judgment.

We took a short foray to a park to let Goblin walk. I took "point" on the task with AB so he could stretch his legs, and the others went two blocks down for coffee and food. By the time they returned, I had most of the kinks out of my back and Goblin was in a better mood.

When Bones finally pulled into a plain, beige-and-brown highway hotel a mile down from the port, I felt the tension in the SUV shift. We weren't pouncing yet—we were staging.

The lobby smelled faintly of burned coffee and industrial carpet cleaner. Legend handled the check-in with a casual charm that made the clerk forget to blink, and minutes later, the five of us crammed into a single room with two beds and an extra rolling chair.

Voodoo locked the door behind us. Bones closed the curtains. Goblin sniffed the floor like he was sweeping for landmines.

Legend tossed the keycard on the dresser. "Alright. Recon review."

We gathered around the small circular table while AB set up at the room's desk, his laptops and drives clicking into place like he was assembling a portable command center.

I wasn't quite ready to eat even if they picked up sandwiches, including a ham and swiss croissant for me. Though, after France, that sandwich looked terribly sad in its plastic wrap. So I left that in the bag and claimed my coffee.

"Alright," I said, sipping the flat white while they began their breakdown. "What can I do to help?"

Bones looked at me first. Always him. Always that quiet, anchoring weight in his gray eyes.

"That depends," he said slowly. "Do you want to be on-site? Or stay here and back us up?"

My heartbeat lifted in my chest, not from fear—something heavier. "Define 'on-site.'"

Voodoo leaned back in the rolling chair. "On-site means you're physically with us. Potential eyes-on with Sarmiento's crew. Possible proximity to danger. Not necessarily engaging—just shadowing us."

Legend added, "Staying means you watch feeds AB sets up. You run comms with us, call out any shifts in traffic, security patrols, container movement, or anything weird we can't see from the ground."

I swallowed once. "What are the goals?"

"Threefold," Bones said, holding up fingers.

"One—locate Sarmiento, confirm he's actually here and not just using this port as a drop point."

"Two—identify his crew. Anyone connected. Anyone loyal. Faces, habits, routine."

"Three—figure out the physical layout of his operation. What containers he uses. Who he pays. How they move cargo."

Legend cracked his neck. "Four—don't get caught."

"That too," Bones said dryly.

I exhaled slowly, sorting through the buzzing static in my head. "So if I go with you, I'm—what? A spotter?"

"More than that," Voodoo said, voice calm but threaded with warning. "But less than front-line. You'd be eyes and instincts. You know what this looks like from the inside, Grace. We don't."

Legend's voice softened. "But if staying feels safer, no one will hold it against you. You've already done more than most people could stomach."

"To keep us all honest," AB added. "We don't know if you were meant for this port. We can presuppose you didn't make it this far and that somehow you ended up more than halfway across the country..." But the way he spread his hands said that was all up for debate.

Goblin nudged my knee, like he was voting too.

I looked between them—four men willing to put themselves in the line of fire for me. For Amorette. For truth.

Whichever choice I made, they'd adjust without hesitation. They weren't trying to keep me small. They were trying to keep me *alive*. But they were also letting me choose.

I set my coffee down, fingers tapping lightly against the paper cup while the room waited on my answer—four lethal men and one extremely opinionated dog.

"If you can use me there, then I'd like to be on-site," I said finally. They were giving me the choice, but they were also the professionals. "If Sarmiento or any of his crew are here, I want to see it. I want to see *them*. I need to know..."

I turned it over in my head, I needed to know a lot but what specifically did I need to know there?

"I need to know if I recognize any of them. I may not, it may be nothing."

"It may be something, too," Voodoo said. "We get it, Firecracker."

Bones didn't smile, but something in his posture eased, subtle as a breath. "Then we tailor it to that. Controlled exposure. You don't separate from any of us. If we say move, you move. If we say get down, you get down. That's the whole deal."

"Copy that," I said, lifting a shoulder.

Legend's mouth curved into something warm and crooked. "We'll run it like a low-key recon circuit. Walking the public-access areas first—tourist edges, lots of traffic, nothing suspicious. Just a couple and their friends checking out the port."

"Couple?" I echoed.

Voodoo gave a shameless shrug. "Optics. People look twice at four guys in tactical boots casing a commercial dock. They don't look twice at a woman and her boyfriend walking hand-in-hand with a few friends trailing behind them like overgrown ducklings."

AB didn't even glance up. "I'm not a duckling."

"No," Legend said solemnly. "You're the angry mallard who steals French fries."

AB flicked a pen cap at him.

Despite myself, I smiled.

Bones refocused us before the banter could take off. "We'll rotate positions. Grace with Lunchbox first, Voodoo second, me third. Alphabet stays here with remote feeds and a line of sight on our exits. Once we get the lay of the land, we escalate to a closer sweep."

"And if I see someone I recognize?" I asked, heat already creeping up the back of my neck.

Bones didn't miss a beat. "You tell one of us. Quietly."

Then, softer, "You do *not* approach. Not alone. Not first."

My throat tightened, because he wasn't patronizing me. He was worrying in that razor-edged, tactical way of his—silent calculations behind gray eyes.

Legend pushed the sad croissant toward me anyway. "Eat something. Even a bite. Running on fumes only works in movies."

I tore off a corner, just to satisfy him. It tasted like plastic-wrapped disappointment, but he still looked pleased that I ate it.

"Once we decide to go in," Voodoo said, leaning forward, elbows braced on his knees, "we'll move as a unit—even when we're split. You track with one of us. Goblin too."

Goblin huffed like this was obvious.

AB finally turned away from his monitors. "If there's a smuggling route tied to Sarmiento, I'll pick it up. If there's chatter he's on-site, I'll hear it. If there's a sudden movement of unregistered containers—hello, red flag."

"Good," I murmured, adrenaline beginning a slow simmer under my skin.

The guys shifted subtly, that collective awareness I'd come to recognize—all of them feeling the same invisible turning of gears.

We were getting closer.

We weren't stumbling blind anymore.

We had a location, a name with weight, a direction.

"Then what's next?" I asked quietly.

Bones pushed back his chair, unfolding to his full height with that military precision that always made people step aside without knowing why.

"We gear up," he said.

"We go in," Legend added.

"We watch everyone," Voodoo finished.

"And we don't stop," AB said, "until we have a trail."

I drew in a slow breath.

"Good," I whispered.

Because under all the fear, grief, and exhaustion, a single truth was burning, we were hunting again.

Voodoo drummed his fingers against his thigh, eyes narrowing thoughtfully as he studied me. "One more thing," he said. "Did you bring anything in... I don't know... touristy chic?"

I blinked. "Touristy chic?"

Legend snorted. "Translation, something that says 'I am innocent, non-threatening, and definitely not here to watch organized crime.'"

I spread my hands. "Does such a thing exist in my wardrobe?"

Bones answered without missing a beat. "No."

Voodoo clapped his hands once, decisive. "Alright then. We'll fix it."

Which was how, twenty-five minutes later, I found myself stepping out of the SUV at the port's public-access promenade wearing a *Delaware* sweatshirt three sizes too big, a navy baseball cap with a crab on it, and sunglasses so large they bordered on parody.

"This is ridiculous," I muttered, pushing the brim of the hat up.

"No," Voodoo corrected solemnly, adjusting the strap of his own camera bag, "this is camouflage."

Legend walked past in a tacky "BIDEN COUNTRY" t-shirt and jeans, sipping iced coffee like he was preparing to review a food truck festival. "Honestly?" he said. "You look extremely normie. Can't even see the murder in your eyes."

Bones wore jeans, a hoodie, and a backpack—standard under-the-radar dad-on-a-day-trip gear. On him, it looked like a tactical uniform pretending to be civilian clothes. Goblin trotted happily beside him in a bright blue *SERVICE ANIMAL* vest, which was probably the only legitimate accessory among all of us.

Even AB, who had remained at the hotel but insisted on blending in for safety, was currently wearing a local minor-league baseball cap and sending us live updates like a retired accountant moonlighting as an intel analyst.

I stared at my reflection in the SUV window—hat, sunglasses, sweatshirt.

I really did look like a tourist.

A tired tourist.

A grieving tourist.

A tourist hunting human traffickers.

"Okay," I said, exhaling a laugh despite myself. "Fine. I look like someone here to buy saltwater taffy and take pictures of boats."

Voodoo grinned like he'd just won a prize. "Exactly. Perfect."

Bones fell into step beside me, shoulder brushing mine. "Stay close. First pass is wide-angle. Public spaces only."

Legend led the way toward the boardwalk overlook. Voodoo angled off to take fake photos of the harbor. Goblin sniffed every post like he was conducting his own investigation.

And as I adjusted my ridiculous crab hat again, it struck me, we really did look like tourists.

Lethal tourists.

Determined tourists.

Tourists hunting a predator across state lines.

And the strangest part? For once, the monsters wouldn't see us coming.

The Atlantic wind cut straight through my oversized *Delaware* sweatshirt, sharp enough to sting. It whipped the edges of the pier flags, sent salt spray climbing the air, and made Legend's iced coffee a questionable life choice.

Despite the cold, a handful of tourists wandered the public overlook—families pointing at container ships, a pair of retired birdwatchers with binoculars, two teenagers taking selfies beneath the "PORT OF DELAWARE" sign.

Completely average.

Completely harmless.

Completely misleading.

Voodoo lifted his camera again, angling it toward the cranes. The shutter clicks were soft beneath the wind, but I knew AB was getting every image in real time—zoomed, filtered, cross-referenced, and compared to satellite data.

In my left ear, AB's quiet voice buzzed through the comms. "Blue-liveried cranes on Pier C are consistent with the container transfers from three of our flagged manifests. If Sarmiento is here, that's where he would be staging the movements."

Bones murmured under his breath, "Pier C is three hundred yards to our right."

Legend followed my gaze, sipping his slush of melting coffee. "Which means we take our time."

So we did.

We walked like tourists—casual, curious, slightly cold. Goblin sniffed the boardwalk planks, stopped to investigate a patch of old salt dried into a pattern only he understood, then continued his slow march.

I tried to mirror everyone's nonchalance, but it felt like wearing someone else's skin. Too loose. Too soft. Too wrong.

AB's voice came again, quiet but alert. "Security rotation just shifted. The guy in the bright orange vest is new. He's walking fast."

Bones' eyes flicked without moving his head. "Direction?"

"Toward the Pier C guardhouse."

Legend muttered, "Convenient."

We paused at the overlook railing, pretending to admire the cargo ships. They towered above the water, hulking metal beasts belching cold steam into the sky.

"Okay," AB continued. "Update, two private vehicles entered through the south gate without stopping. No port markings. Not unusual, but they drove straight toward the restricted side of Pier C."

Voodoo's camera clicked, clicked, clicked. "Got their plates. AB?"

"Recording."

The wind gusted hard, rocking the boardwalk under us. I shivered and Bones angled himself between me and the ocean like he could shield me from the air itself.

Still—everything looked normal. Dockworkers in reflective vests. Stacked containers. A local couple taking pictures. Tourists chatting about where to get fresh lobster.

Nothing screamed cartel. Nothing screamed human trafficking. Nothing screamed my life is about to split open—

Until—

"Grace," AB said suddenly, tone shifting from commentary to razor focus, "look left, two o'clock, by the chain-link fence."

I turned casually, heartbeat stalling.

A man was standing there.

Lean. Mid-thirties. Worn jacket. Hands in pockets.

Watching us.

Not the ocean.

Not the ships.

Us.

The worst part wasn't his stare.

It was the way he looked away so quickly—too quickly —and pretended to light a cigarette he didn't actually light.

My mouth went dry.

Bones was already moving closer to me, not touching, but anchoring. Legend shifted to the other side, posture loose but ready. Voodoo lowered his camera as if adjusting the settings, lens angled toward the man.

AB spoke in my ear. "He matches the description of one of Sarmiento's ground spotters from the Reynosa hub."

The boardwalk suddenly felt too open. Too exposed. Too ordinary to trust.

Wind slammed into my hat. Goblin pressed against my leg, alert and still.

"Alright," Bones murmured, voice pitched low. "We've got our first shadow."

And just like that—

Normal was gone.

FOURTEEN

VOODOO

The moment Alphabet confirmed the guy by the chain-link fence, the air around us tightened—subtle, just enough that anyone watching would chalk it up to the cold wind coming off the water. But I felt it. All of us did.

I lowered my camera, let the strap slide across my chest, and breathed out slow. "Spotter," I murmured, barely moving my lips.

Bones shifted a half-step closer to Grace, shielding her from the angle of the man's line of sight without making it look like shielding. Lunchbox drifted outward, lazy-like, the way he always did before he decided whether someone needed to be punched, followed, or quietly moved off the map.

The guy tried to look casual—leaning a shoulder into the chain-link, fumbling with a cigarette he didn't bother to light. He wasn't good at pretending. That was useful. The ones who were good at pretending were harder to flush out.

Sandwiched somewhere between Bones' protective gravity and Lunchbox's quiet violence, Grace kept her sunglasses angled toward the container field. But I saw her jaw tighten beneath the brim of that ridiculous crab hat.

"Okay," Alphabet said in our ears, voice tight with the static of distance and adrenaline. "We can use this. He clocked you, but he's unsure. I expect he'll follow a usual pattern before he escalates."

Pattern. Right. These spotters were creatures of habit. Small ranges. Predictable loops. They stuck to whatever corner they were assigned and phoned home when something felt wrong.

Which meant if we tugged the wrong thread, he'd alert Sarmiento's people before we got anywhere close to them.

We needed to isolate him. Quietly. And we needed access.

I scanned the pier again, camera raised like I was framing a shot of the cranes.

"Control room's on the upper deck of the admin building," I murmured. "North side. Restricted but nothing we can't walk through with the right stride."

Lunchbox hummed under his breath, the sound of a man who'd already mapped three ways in and four ways out. "We splitting?"

Maybe. Probably. I didn't love it, but Alphabet's flash drive wasn't a suggestion—it was our best chance at seeing what containers were incoming, outgoing, mislabeled, hidden, or straight-up ghost entries. The port tracked everything. Or at least pretended to. It had to in order to hide the ones they wanted hidden in the first place. If Sarmiento was using a pipeline through here, there'd be digital scars. We just needed a vein to tap.

Bones didn't look my way, but I felt him thinking, weighing, grinding through the risk factors like teeth on stone.

Grace glanced at him first then at me, barely a tilt of her chin. "What's the play?"

I bumped the camera bag higher against my shoulder. "Two options," I said quietly, locking gazes with Bones briefly. "Option A, we keep moving as a group and hope Spotter Man gets bored. Downside? We lose the window to slip into admin before security rotation resets."

Lunchbox snorted softly. "And Option B?"

"Option B," I said, "I peel off, hook into the control room, run AB's drive, and walk out before anyone realizes the system hiccuped."

Grace stared. "Alone?"

"Not alone," Bones said, nodding once before he turned and scanned the area like he was trying to decide what to do. "Shadowed."

In other words, he'd trail at a distance, invisible backup. Good. Necessary. But Grace didn't look convinced.

I kept my voice low. "The control room's small. One or two operators. If I walk in looking like a bored photographer who got lost, I can plant Alphabet's drive in under ninety seconds."

"And if the wrong person is in there?" Grace asked. Honestly, there was a fist of pride in my chest for how swiftly she had taken to analyzing even the most moderate of action plans.

"Then I'll improvise something humiliating," I said. "Nothing gets you out of a tight spot like embarrassing yourself convincingly."

Lunchbox coughed a laugh. Bones didn't.

Alphabet piped up, "Timing is ideal now. You've got a four-minute window before the next guard runs his dock loop. There's a back stairwell they don't monitor. If Voodoo moves, he should move now."

Wind rattled the boardwalk railing. The spotter was still watching us from behind the fake cigarette, pretending he wasn't.

Bones' jaw flexed. "Lunchbox, keep Grace in the crowd. Don't let her out of sight."

Lunchbox gave a lazy salute with his iced coffee. "Babysitting mode engaged."

Grace rolled her eyes behind her sunglasses, but I saw the tension in her throat, the tight hold she had on Goblin's vest strap. Not even a murmur of protest that she didn't need a guard or that she would buck the plans. Still...

I leaned in just enough for her to hear me. "He's a spotter, not a hitter. If he makes a move, Bones will be on him before he takes a second breath."

She didn't smile, but some of the fear shifted, compressed into something sharper.

Resolve.

"Go," she whispered. Her confidence stormed through me and bolstered my own. The lady had given me the order so... I went.

I pivoted away from the group, camera swinging, posture loose. Tourist on a day trip. Took a few meaningless photos of cranes, water, the sky. Then I drifted toward the north side of the promenade, slipping between two families arguing about clam chowder.

Bones split off behind me, far enough to look like we weren't together anymore. Close enough that if I vanished behind a cargo hauler he'd rip the world in half to find me.

Alphabet's voice guided me. "Straight ahead, Voodoo. Past the blue information kiosk. The stairwell door is tucked behind the vending machine. No camera on the hinge side."

Perfect.

I crossed the boardwalk, the wind slicing at my jacket. The admin building rose just ahead—gray concrete, tinted windows, the kind of architecture designed by someone deeply committed to misery.

The spotter didn't follow.

Not yet.

Good. One problem at a time.

"Opening the stairwell," I murmured.

"Copy," Alphabet said.

I tugged the door. It gave.

Empty.

I slipped inside and let it close behind me, the sound swallowed by concrete walls and humming fluorescent lights.

Showtime.

And if the spotter had friends? If this place wasn't as ordinary as it pretended to be?

Then this was the moment everything cracked open.

The stairwell smelled like dust and rusted metal—the kind of place janitors avoided and security forgot existed. Perfect. I took the steps two at a time, listening for footsteps above or below. Nothing. Just the thrum of HVAC and the distant bellow of cargo haulers outside.

Alphabet guided me soft in my ear. "Top of the stairs. Door opens into the west end of the control room. Two workstations, one break table. No heat signatures on the thermal ping from twenty seconds ago."

"Copy."

Thermal ping, my ass—he was probably using a hacked port building blueprint from 2004 and vibes. But Alphabet's vibes were usually terrifyingly accurate.

At the top landing, I cracked the metal door open an inch.

Voices.

Two of them.

Close.

My pulse ticked once, not out of fear—just calibrating.

Alphabet hissed, "That's new. Hold."

The voices came clearer through the crack. One male. One female. Both bored. Both complaining about the morning cold and whose turn it was to refill the sugar packets.

Civilian port workers. Not cartel. Not security.

I could work with bored.

I pushed the door open like a man who absolutely belonged there.

The woman glanced up from her coffee. The man was elbow-deep in a vending machine, trying to shake loose a stuck bag of chips. Neither looked alarmed. Good.

"Oh—hey," the woman said. "Can we help you?"

I plastered on my best sheepish grin. "Uh... yeah. I'm supposed to drop off disks from the visitor center. Some... PR thing." I patted my camera bag. "They told me someone up here handles the media archive?"

Total bullshit. Delivered with confidence.

Her eyes softened with the weariness of someone underpaid and overworked. She pointed to a dusty corner desk with a half-dead desktop tower humming beside it. "That's Thompson's workstation. He's out sick. You can probably just leave the files there."

"Perfect," I said, walking like a man who had absolutely no intention of doing such a thing.

As soon as their attention drifted back to their own misery, I slipped into Thompson's chair and pulled the flash drive from my pocket.

The USB ports looked like they hadn't been cleaned

since the Bush administration. I shoved the drive in anyway.

Alphabet chimed immediately, sounding like a kid on Christmas morning. "I'm in."

I watched the screen as windows blinked open—system maps, container logs, assignment rotations. All the port's digital veins laid bare.

"Good news," Alphabet murmured. "One of the inbound manifests for today include a flagged container ID we got from Ignacio. There's definitely a trail here."

My stomach tightened. "Where?"

"Pier C."

Of course.

I flicked my eyes to the glass wall. Through it, I could see across the yard—cranes, trucks, and the layered steel labyrinth of containers. Somewhere in that grid was a path Sarmiento had walked.

The woman refilling her coffee glanced over. "Everything alright?"

I needed to redirect attention. Fast.

So I did the only thing that came naturally to me when under pressure—

I opened one of Thompson's media folders and double-clicked the first file I saw.

And immediately regretted it.

An audio file blasted from the speakers—obnoxiously loud, tinny, and unmistakably...

"Oh my god," the female operator choked.

The male operator turned around so fast he hit the vending machine.

Alphabet sputtered in my ear. "Voodoo—what the— what is that?"

What *that* was...

Was a heavily auto-tuned, off-key recording of someone screaming the lyrics to "Total Eclipse of the Heart" in a falsetto that could legally be classified as a weapon.

I slapped the volume down, but the damage was done.

Both operators were staring at me like I'd just confessed to murder.

I cleared my throat. "Thompson's... uh... side project. Didn't expect that."

The woman snorted. The man cackled. "Dude, Thompson's gonna die when I tell him we finally found his karaoke folder."

Their attention drifted again, amused now instead of suspicious.

Good. Humiliation successful.

"Alphabet," I whispered. "You got what you need?"

"Got everything," he said. "And Voodoo?"

"Yeah?"

"You realize you just assaulted everyone in a twenty-foot radius."

"Occupational hazard."

I removed the flash drive, slid it back into my pocket, and stood.

Time to leave.

I gave a friendly nod to the operators. "All set. Sorry for the... musical interlude."

"Man," the guy wheezed, "that was incredible."

"I'm gonna have that song stuck in my head all day," the woman groaned.

I stepped into the stairwell and let the door close behind me.

Alphabet's tone sharpened. "Heads up. The spotter is moving. He's breaking from his post."

Of course he was. Bones, Grace, and Lunchbox were still

out there. The spotter seeing me peel off probably shifted his calculus.

"I have him," Bones said through the comms, low and tight. "He's heading toward Grace."

Of course the prick was. The stairwell vibrated under my shoes as I started down fast. Three steps at a time.

"On my way," I said.

Then this wasn't just recon anymore.

The hunt was changing shape.

Again.

I hit the bottom of the stairwell and shouldered out into the wind, boots slapping the boardwalk hard enough that a couple tourists looked over. Didn't matter. Subtlety wasn't a priority.

"Lunchbox, status," Bones demanded in my ear.

Lunchbox's voice came back lazy if you didn't recognize the current of tension running underneath, taut as tripwire.

"He's cutting us off," Lunchbox said. "Not a fan of our little sightseeing tour, apparently."

"Distance?" I asked, lengthening my stride.

"Forty feet and closing," Lunchbox said. "Grace is playing it cool."

"Totally faking it," Grace admitted with only a hint of humor. "I'm freaking out on the inside."

A grin curved my lips almost involuntarily. That woman... *Our* woman. I didn't care how many of these bastards we had to take apart, but I really wanted the threat to her eliminated. Period.

The pier stretched in front of me—tourists, benches, informational plaques about maritime trade. And at the far side, near the railing:

Grace, holding Goblin's leash in a tight fist. Lunchbox at her left, posture loose but eyes sharp. The spotter moving toward them with a slow, deliberate angle—crossing the space like he owned it.

I felt my pulse pick up, not fast—just hard. Focus tightening down to a single point.

"Don't intercept yet," Bones said. "Let him commit."

Of course Bones was a stone wall even now. Let him commit. Let him make the mistake.

I slid into the crowd, threading past a family with strollers. The wind caught my hat and whipped it sideways, but I didn't stop to fix it.

"Lunchbox," I murmured, "pull her three steps left. That gives Bones cover from the kiosk."

"On it."

I watched the shift play out in a beautifully natural progression. Lunchbox "accidentally" angled himself so Grace and Goblin drifted left—still looking like tourists, but now perfectly aligned with Bones' approach vector. Bones materialized from behind a cluster of informational displays, blending into the foot traffic like he'd been born in it.

It was choreography. Dangerous, invisible choreography.

The spotter didn't see a damn thing. Yet, he reached them—too close.

Grace stiffened, just a fraction. Goblin planted himself in front of her leg, hackles whispering upward beneath his vest.

The spotter lifted his chin at them, eyes hidden below the brim of a greasy ballcap. "Excuse me," he said, voice too smooth to be casual.

Lunchbox didn't blink. "What's up, man?"

"You folks lost?" the spotter asked. "This area isn't for visitors. Security only."

Lunchbox smiled like a wolf on vacation. "Pretty sure the sign back there said 'public access,' bud."

The man's gaze flicked to Grace. Not her hat. Not her sweatshirt.

Her.

My blood heated.

Grace kept her sunglasses angled down, voice steady. "We're just walking our dog."

A lie. A good one.

Goblin leaned forward just slightly, reading the man like prey.

The spotter zeroed in on that, eyes narrowing—but not at the dog.

At her hand.

Her right hand.

Where her sleeve had ridden up just enough for him to see what? The faint scars from restraints. They were there. Faded, but not invisible.

My chest went cold.

He recognized something. Or thought he did.

Bones' voice cut through the comms, sharp as a blade. "Voodoo."

"On your right," I said.

We hit the edges of the confrontation at the same time—

Bones from the blind side. Me from the flow of foot traffic behind the spotter.

Lunchbox straightened, energy shifting. Grace didn't move, but her fingers flexed once on Goblin's harness.

The spotter stepped a half inch closer to her—too close—and I saw Bones' jaw lock like he was grinding stone between his teeth.

"Sir," the spotter said, still speaking to Lunchbox but

looking at Grace. "I'm going to have to ask you to come with me to security."

"Nope," Lunchbox said pleasantly. "That's not happening."

The man's left hand slid into his jacket pocket.

Bones murmured, almost soundless, "Weapon."

My muscles fired.

I stepped forward at the same moment Bones closed in from the opposite flank, our approaches tight enough to squeeze the spotter into a wedge he didn't realize existed until it was too late.

But Grace—Grace got there first and Goblin growled—low, primal, a warning with teeth. The sound froze the spotter.

Bones' hand clamped around the man's forearm from the right, iron-hard. I grabbed the jacket fabric at the collar from behind, jerking him back just enough to disrupt his balance.

Lunchbox planted himself between the man and Grace, voice still a calm summer breeze over a field of landmines. "Hands where I can see them, amigo."

The spotter panicked—tried to yank his hand free, but Bones' grip didn't budge.

I leaned in close to the man's ear, voice low and warm. "Bad move."

He froze.

His hand emerged from his pocket—not with a weapon, but a radio. A tiny one. Disposable. Already half-pressed from the motion he'd started.

He hadn't pulled it to call security. He'd pulled it to call *them.*

Bones ripped it from his grip before he could speak into it. Lunchbox casually tipped it off the pier into the water.

Grace exhaled once—soundless. But her eyes behind her sunglasses were burning.

We had him. Which was good, but we also had an issue. He'd tried to report her.

And that meant Sarmiento's people weren't just here.

They were watching.

I tightened my grip on the man's collar, lowering my voice. "We're going to take a walk," I told him. "Somewhere quiet."

Bones met my eyes and nodded once. Lunchbox cracked his neck, ready. Grace didn't move—but Goblin did, stepping back to heel at her side like he knew the choreography too.

Alphabet's voice broke through the comms again, breathless with urgency.

"Guys—you need to clear the boardwalk now. I've got movement at Pier C. Not workers. Not security. You've got incoming."

Of course we did.

The hunt wasn't just changing shape.

It was about to hit back.

FIFTEEN

GRACE

The moment AB said *incoming*, the air around us snapped tight like someone had cinched the world one notch smaller. Lunchbox shifted his stance. Bones' grip on the spotter became something carved out of iron. Goblin pressed against my leg—silent, focused, all business.

And I?

I was doing my best not to show that my knees felt like someone had swapped them for wet cardboard.

"We move," Bones said. No raise in volume. No worry. Just a simple declaration everyone obeyed—even me. We all fell into step as soon as he finished the second syllable. Well, Spotter McSpotterson didn't. Not on purpose, anyway. Bones jerked him forward by the arm and his feet scrambled to follow.

"Grace," Bones added, "with me."

There was no room for argument. Not from him, not from me. I kept my hand on Goblin's harness and followed as they cut us off the boardwalk and down a narrow maintenance path that ran between the admin building and a long line of recycling dumpsters. The tourists faded behind us, swallowed by distance and the roar of the cranes.

My pulse thudded in my throat.

Voodoo dropped back just long enough to brush his fingers against mine—a single second, quick, grounding, before he passed in front of me again to take point.

"Eyes up," Legend murmured from behind. "Grace, don't look at the ground. Watch shadows. Corners. Head on a swivel."

"I wished that helped more," I whispered.

"Not trying to help," he replied, all teeth. "Trying to keep you alive."

Fair.

Bones hauled the spotter down the side path with the efficiency of someone dragging a bag of laundry, except this bag was sweating and breathing fast and trying really hard not to stumble. The guy didn't seem like he was a fighter—not a real one. He was wiry, jittery, dangerous in the way of someone who carried a gun he didn't really know how to use. His eyes flicked everywhere except at us, and I saw the moment he realized he wasn't getting rescued by whatever team he'd hoped was nearby.

"Please," he whispered, voice cracking. "You don't understand—"

Legend snorted. "Buddy, *we* don't understand? You tried to report her."

His head snapped toward me, desperation flaring. "I didn't—I wasn't—"

"Save it," Voodoo said. Calm. Cold. "Where we're going? Talking is optional."

I swallowed. *My* voice would've shaken too if I tried to speak, so I didn't.

Bones finally slowed as we reached the back edge of the

admin building where a chain-link gate stood half-obscured behind a dumpster and a maintenance truck. A faded sign hung crooked on the fence:

AUTHORIZED PERSONNEL ONLY – UTILITY ACCESS

Voodoo popped the lock like it was an inconvenience more than an obstacle and shoved the gate open. Bones guided the spotter inside, then glanced at me.

"Grace. In."

I stepped past the dumpster wall and entered a narrow gravel alley that ran between two electrical sheds—the kind of place no tourist would wander, no worker would bother checking unless a circuit blew.

Goblin stayed glued to my knee, alert, tail stiff.

Once we were all inside, Voodoo closed the gate behind us and tucked the busted lock back into place to make it *look* shut.

Bones pushed the spotter to his knees on the gravel. Not hard. Not gentle. Just unavoidable.

The man winced. "I wasn't—I wasn't going to hurt anyone—"

"You were going to talk into that radio," Bones said, crouching eye-level. "That's enough."

The spotter swallowed and stared at the ground. Sweat dripped from his temple even though the wind was cold.

Voodoo stood on the other side of him, camera bag slung across his chest, eyes sharp and bright in that unnerving way he got when he was running all the possibilities. "Grace," he said gently, "you okay?"

I wanted to say *yes*. I wanted it to sound steady.

"Yeah," I said. It didn't.

The truth was clawing up my throat. The man had seen *something*. He'd *recognized* something. He tried to report *me*.

Bones must have read it in my face. He always did. "He doesn't get another look at you," Bones said, voice low enough the threat seemed to vibrate within it. "Not one."

That helped. More than I expected.

"Alphabet," Lunchbox said, tapping his earpiece, "talk to us."

AB's voice came through thin, breathless. "Team of four—maybe five—moving out of Pier C now. Fast. Not subtle. They're looking for the spotter. And probably whoever was with him."

"ETA?" Voodoo asked.

"Two minutes, tops. You need to relocate or dig in."

Bones looked at Voodoo. Voodoo looked at Bones. Some silent calculus passed between them.

"We extract the spotter first," Bones said. "We can't have him screaming when they fan out. Or recognizing Grace again."

The guy jolted upright. "I won't say anything—just let me go—"

Legend squatted behind him and clamped a massive hand around the back of his neck, not squeezing, just controlling. "Man, don't beg. It's awkward for everyone."

I exhaled slowly, trying to anchor myself. Goblin pressed against me, sensing the tremor I didn't realize I'd let slip.

Voodoo stepped close to me—not touching, but near enough that his warmth cut through the wind. His voice dropped so only I could hear. "He's scared because he should be. But we're not hurting him, okay? We just can't let him make our lives harder."

My chest eased. A little.

The spotter looked between the four of us, eyes darting like a trapped animal. "Where are you taking me?"

Bones answered simply. "Somewhere quiet."

Not threatening. Not reassuring.

Just true.

Voodoo jerked his chin at Legend. "Bag him."

Legend pulled a spare beanie from his jacket pocket—it looked like something he'd either stolen or knitted himself—honestly, if one of them turned out to knit it really wouldn't shock me—and yanked it down over the man's eyes. Darkness. Panic. A stifled sound.

Bones stood, hauled the guy to his feet again with one hand, and looked at me.

"Stay between me and Voodoo," he ordered. "Lunchbox rear."

"I'm not helpless," I murmured, though I still moved instantly into place.

"Never said you were," Bones said. "But you're ours and you're protected."

Those words hit a very stupid, embarrassing place in me. Particularly from Bones, because my boney boy had held himself back for so damn long.

No time for that.

AB's voice crackled back in. "They're splitting—two taking the west dock, two moving toward the admin building. One holding back by Pier C like a coordinator."

"Then we move now," Bones said.

Voodoo gave him a curt nod. "Utility corridor to the service road. Then behind the seawall."

"Copy."

We started moving—quick, controlled, silent. The spotter stumbled blindly between Bones and Legend while Voodoo kept an eye on every exit point like he'd memorized the place weeks ago instead of *today*. Goblin flowed at my heel like smoke.

My heart pounded hard enough it felt like my ribs were vibrating.

Up ahead, Voodoo lifted a hand—a silent stop signal.

We all froze.

Footsteps.

Not ours.

Close.

Coming down the other end of the alley.

Bones turned, grabbed the spotter, and shoved him tight against the wall, one hand clamped over his mouth over the beanie. Legend braced beside them, ready to quiet the man if he panicked.

Voodoo drifted backward until he was inches from me, positioning himself between me and the approaching shadows.

He didn't even look back. He just said, low and calm, "I've got you."

And I believed him. I believed all of them. The footsteps drew nearer, slow and searching. We held our breath.

The hunt had found the trail. Unsurprisingly, we were the trail. The footsteps came closer. Slow. Careful. Someone sweeping the alley like they expected rats. Or bodies.

Voodoo's body blocked half my field of view, but not his peripheral awareness—he kept his weight on the balls of his feet, shoulders angled, hand near his camera bag like the thing doubled as a weapon. Legend tensed behind me, and based on his whitened knuckles, Bones' grip on the spotter's mouth tightened.

Then—

The footsteps stopped.

A man's voice—low, irritated—muttered something in Spanish I didn't fully catch, but between what words I did hear and the tone, it was most likely, *Where the hell is he?*

A second voice answered from somewhere farther down the dock, it was clearer if barely audible but still in Spanish. *He stopped responding. Sweep wide.*

My stomach dropped.

They were hunting their missing spotter.

Bones' lips moved in a faint whisper we could hear through the comm, "Two inbound. One ahead, one right."

Voodoo's posture shifted—so small I don't think I would have noticed it before, but I did now. I knew him, how he moved, how they all moved. I'd learned the difference between soft tension and lethal readiness.

He was ready.

"Grace," he breathed without turning, "when we move, follow me. Don't stop."

I nodded, then said, "I will," in the barest whisper I could manage because he wasn't looking at me. I didn't realize until that second that my hands were shaking.

Which was when the first man stepped into view.

Tall. Broad. Gray tactical jacket. One hand in his pocket like a guy walking to grab lunch. As casual as he was trying to appear, it registered as wrong. Not just because of the way predators moved before they struck, but also *where* we were.

He scanned the alley.

His gaze was about to land on Bones. On the blindfolded spotter. On us.

Bones moved first.

He exploded sideways off the wall, one hand grabbing the man's wrist while his other slammed into the base of the man's skull. Fast. Brutal. Quiet.

The man sagged before he could make a sound.

Bones caught him, lowered him to the gravel, and dragged him into the shadow of the dumpster.

My breath caught.

Then the second man rounded the corner.

This time we weren't in position.

"Contact—rear!" AB snapped in my ear. "He's fast. He—"

But he was already here.

He barreled toward us down the other end of the alley, not subtle at all—charging like someone who'd gotten the order to kill anything that moved.

Legend stepped forward, broad shoulders blocking him from me. "Stay back," he murmured.

Goblin's body coiled, muscles taut, teeth bared.

Bones couldn't intercept this one—he still had the unconscious man slung half-hidden behind him. And the spotter was pinned between us and the threat.

Voodoo made the split-second call.

"Lunchbox," he said sharply. "Left side. Funnel him."

Legend stepped left without hesitation, forcing the charging man to adjust his angle by instinct—straight into Voodoo's attack line.

Voodoo moved.

I loved to see them fight. It was always faster than I expected, like they broke physics in half on the way to hitting someone.

This time he ducked low under the guy's swinging arm, pivoted, and hooked the attacker's knee with his own. The man stumbled forward—off-balance.

Voodoo struck him across the ear with something metal from his camera bag—once, twice—enough to disorient but not kill.

The man reeled.

But he didn't go down.

He swung blind, a wild arc of muscle and panic that

would've smashed into Voodoo's skull if the world hadn't slowed around me.

I moved before thinking and grabbed Voodoo's jacket and yanked. His body jerked back, the guy's fist slicing through the air where Voodoo's head had been a second earlier.

My heart hammered against my ribs.

Voodoo twisted, shock flashing across his face for a fraction of a second—shock, then something hotter, deeper. But he used the opening.

He jammed his elbow into the man's throat. The guy dropped like someone had cut the power to his spine.

Bones stepped in immediately, catching the attacker and dragging him beside the first. Legend covered the far end of the alley, shoulders filling the entire width like a barricade.

Goblin finally eased off his snarl.

"Grace," Voodoo breathed, turning toward me, "that was—"

"Lucky," I said, though my legs felt unsteady.

He didn't correct me. He didn't need to. The look he gave me said enough.

We didn't have time to linger.

Bones stood fully, wiping his knuckles on his jeans like he'd brushed dust off. "Move. Now."

We fell back into formation—Bones dragging one unconscious man behind him, Legend hauling the other by the collar, Voodoo beside me with the spotter shoved between us like a shield he didn't trust.

"Alphabet," Bones said as we moved, "route."

"Go straight," AB replied. "Service road is clear for the next twenty seconds. I've got three heat signatures sweeping the west dock but they haven't reached your lane yet."

"Copy."

We broke out of the utility corridor and moved fast across the service road behind the seawall. My lungs pulled cold air in too quickly; my feet felt too light, too loud. Goblin jogged at my heel, glancing up at me every few strides like he was checking my pulse.

Voodoo stayed glued to my side like a second shadow.

When we finally ducked into the narrow stretch of brush behind a row of stacked shipping containers, Bones and Legend dumped the unconscious men beside an overturned pallet. The spotter was shoved to his knees again, still blindfolded.

We were out of direct sight. Hidden—for now.

My heartbeat finally started to settle.

Bones faced me first, then hauled me to him for a fierce kiss. "You did good, Dollface."

I shook my head, still breathless. "I just—pulled him out of the way."

"Exactly," Legend said with his crooked half-grin, hooking me right out of Bones' arms to press his own kiss to my lips. "Which means he gets to keep that pretty brain of his. So yeah. Good."

Voodoo watched me intently and as soon as Legend's grip loosened, he pulled me into him until our chests touched. He cupped my jaw with one hand, gentle, grounding.

"Firecracker," he said softly, eyes scanning me like he needed to confirm every cell, "you saved me."

That hit somewhere deep. Deeper than I expected. Somewhere that ached and glowed at the same time.

But before I could say anything—

Before the moment could settle—

A memory punched through the adrenaline like a fist wrapped in ice.

A huge warehouse.

Women screaming.

Sobbing.

My head ached, my wrists...

I blinked hard.

The alley was back.

The seawall.

Bones.

Lunchbox.

Voodoo's hands on me. My breath shook once and they noticed.

"Hey." His voice dropped, soft as a secret. "You're here. You're with us."

I nodded. It wasn't a strong nod. It was enough.

Bones didn't interrupt. He just scanned the perimeter, jaw tight like he'd fight the whole pier himself if I needed thirty extra seconds.

"Guys," AB said suddenly, sharp and urgent, "you need to move deeper. They found the radio. They know the spotter's missing."

Bones straightened. Voodoo released me but stayed close.

We weren't done.

Not safe.

Not yet.

But we had the spotter.

We had two of his backup team.

And we were still standing.

That meant we were ahead.

For now.

Bones jerked his chin toward the darker stretch between container stacks. "We move. Keep it tight. Grace, you stay between me and Voodoo. Lunchbox, rear."

I wiped my palms on my jeans, exhaled once, and stepped back into formation.

Goblin nudged my hand with his nose.

Voodoo brushed my shoulder with his fingertips.

Bones checked the next corner for movement.

Then we moved deeper into the container maze, following AB's instructions. We navigated through a world carved into narrow steel canyons. Colors blurred—faded blues, chipped reds, shipping logos half-peeled. Goblin's nails clicked on the concrete, the only sound besides our controlled breathing.

Bones didn't stop until we reached an alcove formed by three containers pressed tight and a fourth pulled half a foot off its frame. A hidden square of shadow. No camera lines. No foot traffic. No workers.

"This," Bones said, sweeping the area with a glance, "will do."

Legend dropped the unconscious men beside the far wall, then propped them in positions that looked almost casual—like they'd fallen asleep on the job. He checked their pulses, quick and efficient.

"They'll be out a while," he reported. "One's gonna have a headache the size of Miami, but he'll live."

Voodoo set the spotter on a crate in the center of the space. The guy stumbled, blindfold still on, breathing sharp.

I stayed near the entrance with Goblin while Bones secured the perimeter—checking angles, shadow lines, reflective metal, anything that could give us away. After thirty seconds, he nodded once.

"Secure."

As secure as a port filled with cartel watchers could be I supposed. Fortunately, I'd wager my guys against theirs every day of the week.

Legend tugged the blindfold off the spotter's head. The man blinked wildly at the sudden light, eyes darting between us, landing on me last.

He flinched.

Voodoo had already seen it. So had Bones. Legend, too.

I didn't know whether the flinch was guilt, fear, recognition, or habit. I just knew I hated it.

Bones crouched in front of him—not touching, just occupying his entire horizon. Calm. Heavy. I'd once watched Bones stop a guy's swing with a glare *before* he laid the man out with his fist. This was that, but weaponized.

"What's your name?" Bones asked.

The man's throat bobbed. "Luis."

"Luis," Bones repeated. "We're going to ask you some questions. Your answers determine what happens next. Understand?"

Luis nodded quickly. "I didn't call them. I swear—"

"You tried," Legend said. "Intent counts."

"I wasn't sure," Luis said in a rush. "I thought she—" His eyes flicked to me again. "I recognized—"

Bones' voice dropped to something raw. "Don't look at her."

Luis's gaze snapped down to his shoes.

My pulse spiked, but Voodoo stepped closer to me, not touching, but present enough that my body understood *safe*. Goblin leaned against my leg like he was trying to glue me to the ground.

"Alphabet," Voodoo murmured into the comm, "status."

AB's voice was tense, fingers audible on a keyboard miles away. "Working. The manifest trails aren't clean—someone scrubbed the container logs retroactively. I'm digging through hardware-level timestamps now. Keep him contained. I need ten minutes."

Bones gave a short nod. "You have it."

Legend cracked his knuckles, suggesting he was bored rather than angry. Not sure what would be worse for Luis. Not sure I cared either.

Bones kept his focus anchored on the man. "Who are you reporting to?"

Luis swallowed. "I—I don't know their names. I get paid through dead drops. They don't talk to me."

"Specifics," Bones said.

Luis shook his head. "I mean it. I'm not— I'm not high enough for names."

"Then why did they place you here?" Voodoo asked.

Luis hesitated.

It was Legend who crouched beside him slowly, arms braced on his knees this time. "Think carefully. If you lie, Bones knows. He'll hear it."

Luis's breath rattled.

"They put me close because I have a good memory and sometimes I recognize faces," he whispered finally. "People they're looking for. People who tried to run."

Run.

My stomach flipped.

"Who did you think she was?" Voodoo asked softly.

Luis's eyes darted between Bones and Legend before settling near Voodoo's boots. Anywhere but my face.

"I don't know. A rumor, maybe." He swallowed hard. "Someone said they lost someone months ago. A girl. From a warehouse. They look for her everywhere now."

My spine went rigid.

Voodoo's breath caught—barely. Bones shifted his weight toward me a single inch, subtle but protective.

"They have a name for her?" Bones asked.

Luis nodded. "La Perdida." *The Lost One.*

Ice slid down my back.

"Luis," Bones said, voice flat as a blade, "look at me."

The man obeyed instantly.

"You didn't tell them anything," Bones said. "You didn't speak into that radio."

Luis shook his head. "No—no, I didn't. I didn't have time. You—all of you—moved too fast."

Bones leaned closer. "If you had?"

Luis's voice cracked. "They would've come. They don't care who else dies around the target."

The target.

Me.

He meant me.

Voodoo's jaw clenched, and I saw his fingers flex once like he wanted to break something.

Bones stood slowly. He exhaled through his nose, long and controlled. Then he looked at Legend.

"He's staying quiet," Bones said. "Tie him. He's not going anywhere until we're done."

Luis started to tremble. "Please—I—"

Voodoo stepped in, voice low but not cruel. "Luis, this is your safest possible outcome. Believe me."

Legend peeled duct tape from his pack with a soft rip and secured Luis's wrists behind him—not tight enough to injure, but tight enough to keep him from running straight back to the people who'd kill him for failing.

Bones turned toward me next, expression shifting from stone to something gentler around the edges. "Dollface?"

I straightened even though my heart still felt lodged in my throat.

"You good?" he asked.

It wasn't a casual question. Bones didn't do casual checks. He was asking if I was triggered, if I needed space, if I was slipping.

"I'm okay," I said quietly.

My voice didn't shake. Good.

Voodoo slid closer, his fingers brushing the back of my hand. "You did everything right."

I didn't look at him because if I did I might not look away.

"Guys," AB said suddenly, tension crackling. "Big update."

Bones pivoted instantly. "Talk."

"I found a ghost container."

Voodoo stiffened. "Where?"

"Pier C," Alphabet said. "Exactly where you thought. But that's not the problem."

Legend raised a brow. "Then what is?"

"The problem," AB said, voice dropping, "is that whatever's inside it... someone scrubbed the record eight hours ago. Completely. No ID. No contents. No weight. It's a blank box."

A chill slid down my arms.

"They're hiding something big," AB continued. "And whatever it is? It's tied to Luis's people. It's sealed but not logged as empty. My bet? It's holding something—or someone."

Bones looked at the unconscious men, then at the duct-taped spotter, then out toward the port. My stomach twisted. He looked at each of us, one by one, silent but in that way of communicating.

"Then we're not done," he said finally. "Not even close." *We move smart. We move fast. We do not leave people behind.*

Voodoo reached for my hand again—and this time I let him hold it.

I swallowed hard, pushing past the prickling fear at the edges of my ribs. "What... what do we do if we find people in that container?"

"If we find people in that container?" Legend echoed, voice low and sure.

His grin sharpened and he shot me a wink.

"We improvise."

CHAPTER

SIXTEEN

LUNCHBOX

The second Bones gave the nod, we started moving. Not running—running gets you clocked. Just a steady, unbothered walk through the steel canyons of Pier C, the kind of pace every dock worker here adopted once they realized time was a suggestion and forklift drivers were gods.

I had point, mostly because people tended to step out of my way without realizing they'd done it. For Bones, they crossed the street, but for me, they just shifted aside and accepted my easy smiles without a second thought.

The air tasted like diesel, old salt, and the coppery edge of trouble. Goblin padded at Grace's heel behind me, his little claws clicking a warning to anyone who got within sniffing distance.

Alphabet's voice came through the comms, sharp and focused. "Container is C7–B block. Southwest corner tower. Third row from the bottom."

"Copy," I murmured, dodging a forklift with a wave I didn't mean. "Any cameras we gotta duck?"

"I would have said two. Both old. Both dumb. But they annoyed me, so you're good."

Good. I liked being good.

Voodoo stayed near Grace, not touching her, but hovering with what had become our brand of casual protectiveness that meant he'd murder someone with a smile if the situation called for it. Bones watched everything—angles, shadows, the rhythm of the port like he could hear danger breathing.

I kept eyes ahead. My job wasn't to worry. It was to move.

And crack skulls when necessary.

We slipped between two container stacks, the air cooler in the shade. I traced the faded stenciling on the metal as we passed—serial numbers, destination codes, layers of history that meant nothing and everything.

"Alphabet," I muttered, "we aiming for cargo or cover?"

"The former," he said. "Container's sealed, but someone logged manual overrides on the locking mechanism. Old-school. Not electronic."

Voodoo whistled low. "That's deliberate."

Bones grunted, which for Bones meant he agreed, understood, and probably hated the implications.

Grace's voice came small but steady. "Why hide something in a container but not digitally?"

"Because the thing you're hiding," I said over my shoulder, "isn't supposed to exist at all."

Her silence tightened my grip on the crowbar strapped to my pack.

We rounded the last bend into the southwest corner. Fewer workers here. Fewer forklifts. Just a quiet stretch of metal and stacked shadows.

Then I saw it. C7–B. Third row. First level.

Locked with a brand-new, polished steel mechanism that didn't match the rust-eaten hardware around it.

Bones stopped beside me. Voodoo exhaled sharply behind him.

Grace whispered, "That's it?"

"Yeah," I said. "That's the one pretending real hard to be normal."

Bones gave me a nod—go.

I stepped forward, dropping my pack and pulling the crowbar free. The lock wasn't chained. It was pinned. Heavy hardware, but not cartel-style. More… government surplus? Weird.

"Alphabet," I said, wedging the bar under the latch. "You seeing this?"

"Yep. And I hate it."

"Join the club."

The first pin popped with a metallic snap. The second resisted. I leaned my weight into it—felt the metal bite back—then gave it a sharp jerk.

Snap.

Silence.

Everyone stilled.

Bones nodded at me. "Open it."

I hooked the crowbar under the door lip and heaved.

The metal groaned, heavy and reluctant, like something inside didn't want to be seen. Diesel air rushed out, stale and old.

I lifted the door high enough for Bones to duck under, then for Grace, then Voodoo.

I went last.

And the second my boots hit the steel floor inside, I knew this wasn't cargo storage.

Too clean. Too quiet. Too intentional.

There were crates—two. A cot. A metal water jug. And far in the corner, a small figure curled into themselves like they'd made the shape permanent.

Grace gasped, a sharp inhale she couldn't help.

The figure flinched.

Bones lifted a hand—halt—but I was already stepping forward. Soft. Slow. Not the "Lunchbox kicking doors" slow —this was the "don't scare the wounded animal" slow.

The kid—because that's what they were, no more than maybe twelve—lifted their head an inch. Eyes hollow. Skin gray. Fear baked so deep it looked like bone.

Voodoo whispered, "Jesus Christ."

Grace moved next to me, voice soft enough to melt iron. "Hi. Hey. It's okay. We're here to help."

The kid blinked, disoriented. Their voice cracked out in Spanish, brittle and tiny. "¿Son... de ellos?" *Are you... with them?*

"No," Grace said softly, crouching and lowering herself without even needing to be urged. Her tiny stature already made her far less of a threat. *"Nosotros somos los que paramos a gente así, ¿ves?"*

We're the one who stop people like them.

The kid's chin trembled.

Before I knew what I was doing, I shrugged off my jacket and held it out. "You cold, buddy?"

They stared at it. At me. Then reached with fingers shaking so hard it hurt to watch.

Grace's breath hitched behind me—a tiny, pained sound.

Bones looked at the rest of us. Something hard settled in his posture, carved in iron.

"This ends now," he said.

Not a suggestion. Not a plan. A promise.

The kind we didn't break.

The kid hauled the jacket around their shoulders like it weighed as much as they did. It swallowed them whole, sleeves dangling past their hands, but they clutched the fabric like armor. Like if they let go, someone would take it —and them—away.

Grace eased closer, slow and gentle, Goblin settling against her leg like he'd decided the kid was under his jurisdiction now.

"*¿Cómo te llamas?*" she asked.

The kid swallowed, Adam's apple bobbing too sharply for someone that small. "Nico," he whispered.

Nico. Jesus.

Grace's eyes softened in a way that made something in my chest twist. She crouched lower, letting him see her face properly. She'd taken off her sunglasses without even thinking about it—probably to look less like a threat, even though she was the least threatening thing in this steel tomb.

"*Hola, Nico,*" she said gently. "*¿Estás herido? ¿Te duele algo?*" Are you hurt? Does anything hurt?

He shook his head too fast to be true. Kids lied about pain like adults lied about guilt—instinctively, hopelessly, thinking it protected them.

I knelt beside Grace, keeping my hands visible. "Hey," I said softly, "we're gonna get you out of here, okay? You're safe now."

Nico's eyes darted to the crates, then to the sealed door, then back at Grace. Terror flickered under his ribs like a trapped animal.

Bones stepped closer—slow, controlled—his voice low. "We need to know if he's alone in here."

Right. The million-dollar question.

Grace nodded once and shifted her weight so she could face Nico squarely. Her hand hovered, not touching him, just close enough he could take it if he wanted to.

"*Nico,*" she murmured, "*¿hay más niños aquí? ¿Más personas?*" *Are there more children here? More people?*

Nico's fingers tightened around the jacket so hard the knuckles went white. His breath hitched in a tiny sound that broke like glass.

For a second, I thought he wouldn't answer.

Then he whispered, voice trembling, "*Dos más. En... en otros contenedores.*" *Two more. In... in other containers.*

Grace inhaled sharply then she translated, but she didn't let it show on her face. She kept steady, grounding him. "*¿Sabes dónde?*" *Do you know where?*

He nodded. A fast, frightened motion. He pointed—weakly—toward the far end of the stack outside.

Bones' eyes went flat and lethal. "Voodoo. Mark the direction. Alphabet—start scanning container logs within that grid. We're finding them. Grace—let him know."

"Already on it," Alphabet said. His voice had lost every trace of humor. "And Lunchbox... you're gonna be pissed."

I already was.

"*Nico,*" she said softly, "*vamos a sacar a tus amigos también, ¿sí?*" *We're going to get your friends out too, okay?*

Nico blinked hard, tears threatening but clinging to the edges. Then he whispered, "*Por favor... rápido.*" *Please... fast.*

That did it.

Whatever fragile thread of restraint I had snapped clean.

Grace reached out, finally letting her hand rest lightly on Nico's arm. He flinched—then melted into the contact like he'd been starving for it. Goblin shifted closer, nose bumping Nico's knee gently, and the kid's fingers disappeared into the dog's fur like he needed something alive to hold onto.

"All right," Bones said, his voice steel-wrapped. "Here's the plan."

He pointed at Voodoo. "You stay with Grace and Nico. Keep them hidden. No one comes near that door."

Voodoo nodded once, jaw locked.

"Lunchbox," Bones said, turning to me, "you're with me."

My knuckles cracked on instinct. "Good. I need to hit something."

Bones didn't smile—not really—but the corner of his mouth twitched. "You will."

Grace looked up at us, eyes shining with fury and fear and something else—determination sharpened to a blade.

"Just bring them back," she said quietly. "All of them."

"We will," I promised. No hesitation. No uncertainty.

Because this wasn't a mission anymore. This wasn't recon, or intel gathering, or even payback.

This was extraction.

This was rescue.

Bones moved to the door. I followed, crowbar back in hand, blood humming like a live wire.

Behind me, Grace's voice drifted soft, comforting, protective. *"Nico, cariño... estás a salvo ahora. Nos tienes a nosotros."* You're safe now. You have us.

For the first time since we found him, the kid's breathing eased. Bones jerked his chin toward the container wall, silent command to get moving. Time to tear this port apart. Because there were two more kids out there. God help anyone standing between us and them.

He pushed out of the container first, all shadows and lethal calm. I followed, crowbar in hand, the metal still vibrating like it wanted another fight. The air outside hit colder, sharper. The stacked steel walls made it feel like we'd stepped out of a tomb and straight into another.

Bones didn't speak—he didn't need to. I fell into stride beside him, matching his angle, pacing low and fast through the narrow corridor between container towers.

"Alphabet," he murmured, "give us the nearest likely matches on Nico's direction."

"I'm on it," Alphabet said. "There are sixteen containers in that line with manual overrides like the one you just popped. But only three had recent access pings."

"Mark the closest."

A faint waypoint pinged in my ear. Ten o'clock. Thirty yards.

Perfect distance for trouble.

We reached the mouth of the next lane—a long stretch shadowed between rows of blue containers. Bones raised a hand, one finger tapping downward.

Hold.

I froze.

Because down the lane, half-hidden by the steel shadows, a silhouette leaned against a container corner—too still to be a worker, too aware to be anything except a problem.

Bones jerked his chin left. I angled right.

We approached like closing jaws.

The guy didn't see us at first—he was staring toward the container we'd just come from, shoulders tight, hand twitching toward his waistband every few seconds. Watching. Waiting.

Looking for us.

Looking for Nico.

Rage crawled up my spine.

Bones was five feet from him when the guy finally sensed movement. He spun—

Too slow.

Bones slammed him against the container harder than strictly necessary, one forearm pinning his throat, the other ripping a pistol from the bastard's belt and tossing it aside like a piece of trash.

I grabbed the front of his jacket before he could drop to the ground, hauling him upright. "Bad day to be working for kidnappers, amigo."

He spit at me.

It hit my chest.

I smiled—the kind of smile that used to scare my old CO. "Oh, you're gonna regret that."

"Lunchbox," Bones warned quietly.

Right. We didn't have time for dental rearrangement.

I twisted the guy's arm behind him, hard enough to make him gasp. Bones leaned in close.

"Where are they moving the children?"

His breathing hitched, panic flashing across his face, but he clamped his mouth shut in defiance.

Bones didn't hesitate. His knee jammed into the guy's thigh, dead center on the nerve bundle. Not enough to break anything.

Just enough to convince him Bones had a map to all the places he *could* break.

The hostile choked, sagging in my grip.

"I don't know," he spat, voice cracking. "They—they were supposed to be here. They were here this morning."

Bones's eyes narrowed. "Past tense."

I shoved him backwards into the container, letting the steel ring. "When did they move them?"

"Just—just before you showed up."

Bones leaned forward, voice dropping into a register that could freeze blood. "How?"

"Vans," the man whispered, voice shaking. "Two white vans. No plates."

Bones released him. I did not. "Where were they heading?"

But he shook his head. "I don't know."

Before I could argue with physics and drag answers out of him—

Alphabet's voice cut through sharply. "I've got something."

Bones spun toward the open lane. "Talk."

"I'm pulling traffic cam access along the perimeter. Two white panel vans exited the north checkpoint seven minutes ago." So he'd meant before we found Nico. Prick.

My grip tightened on the hostile's jacket. "Direction?"

"Eastbound. Toward the 110. They're already off port property."

That meant they were moving fast.

And we were behind.

Bones took a slow breath—the kind that meant someone was about to die—and then spoke, calm as a blade in deep water. Checking for hidden compartments or false walls, he walked the container in a swift sweep.

"Lunchbox. Secure him."

My smile widened. "Gladly."

The guy's eyes went wide. Rightly so.

Bones didn't wait—he started moving back toward Grace and Nico with that long, predator stride.

Alphabet spoke again, urgency sharpening. "Guys... if they're on the 110, they're heading toward the city. Sarmiento's people don't move cargo like that unless they're spooked."

"They're spooked," I muttered, shoving the hostile face-first against the steel and cuffing him with zip ties. "We rattled them."

Bones answered, voice dark. "Good. Because we're not done."

I grabbed the hostile by the back of his collar and started dragging him toward the others. We needed answers and I was in the perfect mood to get some.

SEVENTEEN

GRACE

The air was sharp, diesel and salt and something bitter I didn't want to name. Goblin padded at my side, low growl soft and protective, his little body pressed against Nico's leg like he could somehow carry the weight of the world in fur.

Nico clutched the jacket around him like it was armor, eyes wide and hollow. I crouched down, careful not to smother him, and let him see my hands.

I whispered, voice soft. *"Está bien. Te vamos a sacar de aquí. Estás a salvo ahora."* It's okay. We're getting you out. You're safe now.

He didn't speak for a long beat, just stared, blinking rapidly like he was trying to remember how. Goblin nudged him gently with his snout, tail wagging just enough to say *I've got you too.* I ruffled Nico's hair, soft, careful, and felt the tiniest flinch relax.

"Voodoo?" Bones' voice came sharp in my ear. "Lunchbox and I cleared the yard. One of the hostile guys down. Signs they moved more kids recently. Might've been prepping for transport. We're here for Grace and the boy, go and get the SUV ready."

"Copy that," Voodoo said. He cupped my face once, a stroke of his thumb to my cheek then he was gone. Nico dug his fingers into mine, but he didn't make a sound. I hated that he'd already learned to contain his fear.

Hated it.

I swallowed, my throat tight. "Any leads?" Right now, I was just hoping that Nico didn't understand enough English for it to scare him.

AB cut in, crisp and fast. "Yeah. On the road. Moving north. Could be anywhere along Highway 12 in the next twenty minutes if they don't slow down."

I pressed my forehead against Nico's, whispered, *"Vamos a mantenerte a salvo. ¿Me escuchas?" We're going to keep you safe. You hear me?*

His small nod pressed against me was enough for now. Enough to keep moving because Legend and Bones were there. They carried in another guy and dumped him on Nico's abandoned cot and left him secured. Then they ushered us out before they sealed the container up again.

"Time to go," Bones said. "Stay close. Don't worry about what it looks like this time."

I nodded and slid my sunglasses back on, I also dropped my hat onto Nico's head. I rose slowly, tugging Nico to his feet. He wobbled a little, but he hung onto my hoodie. Goblin's hackles dropped as he stepped closer, letting Nico wrap a tiny hand over his fur.

"Bien," I said quietly. *"SUV. Rápido, cuidadoso, y sin sorpresas." Okay. SUV. Fast, careful, and no surprises.*

We threaded through the steel canyons again, shadows long, containers looming. Every step measured. Every forklift and dock worker accounted for. Legend swept ahead, casual and lethal. Bones flanked the other side, scanning angles I couldn't even name.

Nico whispered my name once, a shaky little thing, and I squeezed his hand. *"Estoy aquí." I'm right here.*

Goblin nudged him again. Protection, insistence, promise.

When we hit the edge of the yard, the SUV waited—idling, hidden enough not to draw attention, ready enough to disappear in seconds. I guided Nico to the middle seat, letting him curl in with the jacket wrapped tight, Goblin hopping in beside him.

Bones climbed into the passenger seat as Lunchbox followed behind me to get into the third row seat. After securing Nico with a seatbelt, I leaned back, eyes on Nico's small face. He didn't say anything. He didn't need to. He just held onto the jacket, held onto Goblin, and we moved out.

"I've mapped a route to let you intercept," AB's voice in the comms cut through, adding a sharp report on traffic and potential checkpoints. "Highway 12, clear. Speed up. ETA to catch them, fifteen minutes if no interference."

I exhaled slowly, letting myself relax just enough to wrap an arm around Nico. He tucked his head between me and Goblin, small, fragile and still wrapped in the jacket.

"Estás a salvo," I murmured again. *"Por ahora." You're safe. For now.*

The road stretched out ahead, the diesel scent fading, but the danger—not gone, not yet. Just postponed. Nico's small fingers twitched as he clasped my hand. It was weird how fast it seemed to go, and at the same time, how interminably long. I kept looking for white vans and not seeing them.

The SUV hummed along Highway 12, the engine low

and steady, a coiled promise of power under our feet. Goblin rested his chin on Nico's shoulder like a shield, tail flicking in sync with the car's rhythm. I kept one arm around Nico, holding him close, trying to transfer calm through nothing but touch and quiet words.

After what felt like too long—I trusted the guys and their skills but this was asking a lot of them—there they were.

"¿Ves los camiones blancos?" I whispered, nodding toward the windshield. *Do you see the white vans?*

Nico's tiny head lifted slightly. His eyes, wide and terrified, tracked the distant shapes, two white vans weaving through the afternoon traffic, hopefully still oblivious to the hunters on their tail.

"Vamos a atraparlos." We're going to catch them. Maybe I shouldn't tell him everything but I would want to know. I'd wanted to know when I'd been terrified out of my mind and I couldn't offer Nico much but the illusion of control right now. So that was what I would offer him.

AB's voice cut through the comms, calm but tense. "Both vans heading north, same speed as you. One's hugging the shoulder, the other's riding center lane. Looks like they're coordinating. ETA to intersection 17 is six minutes."

My stomach tensed. "What if they split up?"

Bones' glanced at me from the front seat, his gaze firm and reassuring yet resolute. "Don't borrow trouble, Dollface. We handle what comes."

I exhaled slowly, trying to shove the worry down, as Voodoo kept us in their blind spot.

AB's voice sharpened, a little edge now. "Traffic slowing ahead. I've got some help from local patterns—adjusted lights on your path. You'll gain on them fast, but be ready for aggressive drivers."

Legend chuckled, leaning slightly in his seat. "Really glad Alphabet's on our side for this one. Otherwise, we'd be playing bumper cars with city traffic."

The vans were close enough now that I could make out the outline of the roof racks. Bones leaned forward, scanning the highway with lethal precision. "Keep steady. Don't spook them. Lunchbox, be ready to block if they try anything."

I felt Nico tense against me. His small hands clutched my jacket, digging into the fabric as though it could somehow anchor him to safety. *"Estamos casi allí,"* I whispered softly. *We're almost there.*

A flash of brake lights ahead made my pulse skip and I sucked in a breath. One van swerved slightly, testing the lanes. Voodoo matched the maneuver effortlessly, a smirk tugging at his lips. "Relax, Firecracker. Alphabet's got this. We'll catch up before they even know what hit them."

I exhaled again, holding Nico a little tighter. *"Está bien. Lo tenemos."* *It's okay. We've got this.*

Highway 12 stretched out, emptying into long strips of asphalt and industrial backroads. The vans were just ahead, speeding toward the intersection AB had marked. Every second brought them closer, every turn a chance to slip, a chance to catch them—or lose them.

The vans grew larger in the windshield—white, nondescript, and so heavily identified as serial killer vans it almost made me laugh. White, the most common vehicle color in the world, was the kind of vehicle you wouldn't look at twice unless you already knew monsters were driving them.

Traffic thickened as we neared intersection 17, the sun

was already beginning to dip in the west and cast a burnt orange warning flare. Drivers were hitting brakes. Lanes bunching. The kind of congestion that could either hide the vans... or bury us.

"Alphabet," Voodoo muttered, knuckles tightening on the wheel, "they're gonna slip the net if we hit a full stop."

"Relax," AB answered, voice low but smug enough that I could picture him grinning at his screens. "I'm about to make this the world's most cooperative traffic jam."

Bones raised an eyebrow. "Cooperative?"

"Working on it... annnnnd—lights switching now."

Ahead of us, every traffic signal along the perpendicular cross-street flicked from green to red in synchronized precision. Cars hit brakes. Horns blared. The vans were forced to slow, boxed into the middle of the pack.

Legend let out a low whistle. "Yeah... I'm really damn glad Alphabet's on our side."

I didn't argue. I breathed. But the relief was short-lived. One of the vans jerked sharply into the right lane, the other drifted left, inching apart, creeping toward the possibility of splitting.

A spike of fear shot through my chest. "They're—they're splitting up."

Nico tensed, head snapping up, eyes wide. He didn't understand everything, but he understood enough. Goblin whined, leaning into him.

Bones turned in his seat, voice quiet but firm. "We don't chase two. We force them back together."

"How?" I breathed.

"Like this," Voodoo said under his breath. "Alphabet—need a window. Right lane."

"I see it. Opening in three... two... aaand go."

The lane to the right cleared like someone parted the

ocean. Voodoo slipped the SUV into the space, accelerating just enough to match the vans' speed. Bones watched every mirror, every angle, hands braced on the dash like it was an extension of his body.

"Lunchbox," he murmured. "Get ready."

"Always am," came the amused rumble from the back.

Goblin gave a sharp bark—soft but insistent, like he sensed the shift in energy. Nico clutched the little dog's vest and my arm at the same time, trembling.

"Está bien," I whispered, brushing his hair back. "Solo un poco más." *It's okay. Just a little more.*

Ahead, the vans grew close again as Voodoo angled us neatly between them—one on each side now, the perfect trap position. If either tried to bolt, we'd see it first.

"Vans approaching the red at intersection 17," AB narrated, tension threading through each word. "If they run the light, they'll get boxed in by oncoming traffic. If they don't…"

"Then we make our move," Bones finished.

Voodoo flexed his fingers on the wheel. "Grace. When we hit, keep Nico down and hold tight."

My heart pounded, but my voice stayed steady. "Lo tengo, mi amor," I whispered down to Nico. *I've got you, sweetheart.*

The vans approached the intersection—one slowing, one hesitating, both caught in the web AB had spun for them.

This was it.

Bones' voice dropped to a low, lethal calm.

"On my mark."

The moment froze sharp and thin.

Two white vans boxed us at the intersection. Engines

humming. Brakes squealing. Traffic held in place by AB's digital chokehold.

Bones leaned forward, voice low and lethal. "Mark."

Voodoo hit the gas.

We cut off the lead van with a clean, angled block that pinned it behind a delivery truck. The second swerved left —straight into the trap—only to find the lane sealed by the SUV's back quarter panel.

Perfect.

"Grace—heads down," Bones ordered.

I folded over Nico, wrapping my arms around him as Goblin wedged himself between us and the window. His low growl pulsed against my ribs—protective, fierce.

Legend braced behind me. Both vans screeched to a full stop.

AB crackled over comms, breathless. "All right. They're boxed. No exit lanes. No reverse path. You're green."

Bones was already unbuckling.

"Lunchbox—left van. I've got right. Voodoo, Grace, hold position until we clear."

"You got it," Voodoo muttered. "Bring back souvenirs."

The doors burst open.

Bones hit the pavement first, silent and deadly. Legend followed, rounding the left van with a predator's precision. I kept Nico tucked close, Goblin's paws planted on my lap as he scanned the windows with tiny, furious intent.

The right van's driver cracked the door an inch—panic in the motion. Bones yanked it open, slammed the guy's wrist against the frame, disarmed him before he even understood what was happening, and dragged him onto the asphalt.

Legend ripped the left passenger door wide. Someone lunged at him—wild, cornered. Legend stepped aside, grabbed a fistful of shirt, and introduced the man's head to the doorframe with a brutal thunk.

Inside the vans, movement. Not adult movement. Smaller. Softer. Huddled.

Oh God.

Bones growled. "Grace—stand by."

He and Legend opened the sliding doors in unison.

And the world shifted.

Shapes in the dim interior. Thin limbs. Wide eyes.

Blankets wrapped around trembling shoulders.

Four kids total. Two in each van.

All of them too quiet.

Nico whimpered—a tiny, broken sound. Goblin whined low, vibrating with distress.

Bones didn't flinch, but something in his jaw cracked.

Legend blew out a breath, voice hard with fury. "Grace. Bring Nico. Slowly."

Voodoo was out of the driver's seat and opened my door before I unbuckled. Then I was sliding out with Nico clinging to me like I was the only solid thing left in the world. Goblin hopped down, planting himself at Nico's side.

"Está bien, mi cielo," I whispered into his hair. "No estás solo." *It's okay, sweetheart. You're not alone.*

When we reached the first van, the children shrank back, flinching at movement, at sound, at everything.

So I dropped to my knees.

Nico didn't hesitate—he let go of me just enough to kneel too. Goblin pressed between us and the open van door, tail low but not threatening, just present, grounding.

Softly, I spoke to the nearest little girl. "Hola, mi amor… estamos aquí para ayudarte, ¿sí?" *Hi sweetheart… we're here to help you, okay?*

Her lip trembled. She nodded once.

Legend muttered quietly behind me, "Hell."

Bones' voice was quieter still, meant only for our team. "Get them out. Gentle. Quick."

The kids came out like shadows—tiny hands reaching, legs unsteady. Some clutched blankets. One boy carried a stuffed toy missing an eye. Another little girl looked at Goblin and burst into tears—silent tears, her chest shaking.

Goblin stepped forward and licked her wrist. She folded over him like he was the first safe thing she'd felt in days.

Bones swallowed hard. His voice stayed level. "Load them in our SUV. Grace takes point."

Legend moved fast but gentle, lifting the youngest with care. Voodoo picked up another who couldn't quite stand. Bones handled the last two, guiding them with slow, deliberate movements, like they were made of glass.

I kept Nico's hand tight in mine, guiding him and Goblin back to the SUV.

"Todo está bien," I whispered to the group, switching between English and Spanish. *"Están a salvo. Los tenemos."*

Everything's okay. You're safe now. We've got you.

We loaded them in—middle row, third row, stuffed animal reunited with trembling hands. Goblin crawled right into the center of them, letting them hold onto him, six small hands gripping his fur.

Nico stayed pressed to my side—but he was watching them now, eyes big and worried instead of terrified.

Then AB came back on comms—this time not frantic, but furious.

"Guys," he said. "You need to move. Now."

Bones climbed into the passenger seat as Voodoo slid behind the wheel.

"What's coming?" Bones asked.

"Backup," AB said. "Heavy. Fifteen minutes out. But—"
He paused.

"But what, Alphabet?" Legend snapped.

"We need to relocate the kids and we're going to need backup of our own," he said, voice low.

"What's up?" Bones asked even as Voodoo got us moving. The vans created another traffic jam, but we were able to slide between. "There's a bigger transport. Heading toward the port. Full blackout. Doesn't want to be seen."

My blood chilled.

"ETA?" Bones asked even as he turned toward us, his gaze flicking over the five children huddled together and Goblin on the floor.

"We have maybe an hour." Though AB's tone implied we would be lucky as hell to get that much.

"Get us a secure location for Grace and the kids," Bones said.

"On it," AB replied.

Then Bones transferred his gaze to me. The question was in his eyes. We couldn't take five kids into any kind of combat. They'd also made me a promise, and we were still looking for Amorette. At the same time, this operation needed to be shut down whether we found Amorette or not.

I glanced at the kids then at him as I nodded. "Just leave a weapon."

"We will." Bones nodded once. "Alphabet?"

"Secure location acquired, sending you the address."

My heart slammed against my ribs. The only sound in the SUV was the faint snuffling of the kids, and the harsh sounds of my own breathing.

"Give us the SITREP," Bones ordered after a beat. "We

need to be ready to roll once we've gotten the kids locked down."

I listened as AB briefed them, the whole time, Nico held fast to my hand. One of the little girls had gripped my wrist. We had to burn all of these operations down.

Every.

Single.

One.

EIGHTEEN

BONES

The SUV was too full of breathing.

Too many small, uneven inhales. Too many soft, strangled sniffles. Too much fear packed into one metal box rattling down a port access road.

And every sound carved itself somewhere under my ribs.

Still, my head stayed clear. It had to.

Voodoo drove like the vehicle was an extension of him. Lunchbox kept watch out the back window, every muscle coiled. Grace sat in the middle row, kids anchored around her and Goblin like gravity.

I watched all of it. I always did.

Alphabet's voice crackled again in my ear, cool and clipped. "Sending the final pin drop. Maintenance outbuilding behind an old inspection lot. Cameras are down. No foot traffic. You've got fifteen minutes before someone with guns and bad intentions realizes those vans aren't on schedule."

"Copy," I said.

Grace didn't look at me, but she was listening. She always was.

The smallest kid—little girl with the stuffed toy missing an eye—had her face buried in Goblin's fur. The dog didn't move except to give a low, steady thrum of protective noise from his chest. Nico sat plastered to Grace's left, staring out the window like the world was made of monsters.

He wasn't wrong.

Lunchbox leaned forward between the seats. "If they're running blackout on that bigger transport, we're not dealing with an average delivery."

"Never said we were," I muttered.

"We need more than the four of us," Voodoo said. "And maybe a tank."

Lunchbox snorted. "I can be a tank."

"You're shaped like one," Voodoo added with a laugh.

"Thank you." Lunchbox grinned. "I'll take point."

The kids startled at the laughter, but little Nico proved to be a trooper and he smiled.

The safe building Alphabet found came into view—a squat concrete block at the edge of the old port inspection lot, fenced off and abandoned. Perfect for hiding. Perfect for protecting.

"Voodoo," I said, "circle once."

He did, slow. My eyes tracked everything—the sightlines, the blind corners, the possible exits, the two routes that could be used to funnel an ambush. Nothing moved except a gull picking at a paper bag.

"Clear," I said.

We rolled up to the rear of the building. Lunchbox hopped out first, crowbar in hand, to sweep the perimeter. I took a second sweep of the interior—doorframe sturdy, floor dusty, windows boarded.

Secure enough.

"Grace," I called softly. "Bring them in."

She unbuckled, then led the kids out to follow her. Nico's hand was in hers, the other children linked hands together, a chain of ducklings sticking so close they looked tied together. Goblin herded them with soft nudges, tail down but wagging just enough to say safe safe safe.

I stood in the doorway, a Glock in hand, a pair of clips and a taser. Once they were inside, I passed Grace what she needed. "One is already in the chamber. If anyone comes through that door that isn't us, you shoot first and ask questions later."

Grace's eyes shone even though she was shaking. "We'll be fine."

"Yes, you will." I touched two fingers to her chin, then tapped her comm unit. "You'll be able to hear us, but I want you to mute your end unless we need something or you do."

She nodded again. "Goblin and I can do this."

I pressed a firm kiss to her lips, not stretching this out any longer than we needed to. Voodoo had rolled out a length of chain to wrap around the outer doorhandles, we'd "secure" it so it looked locked from the outside once we were there.

Then Grace's voice—quiet—found me in the dim.

"Bones?"

I turned.

She swallowed. For a second, she looked small. Not weak—never that—but weighed down by what she'd just carried out of those vans.

"What do I tell them?" she whispered.

The kids watched her with hollow eyes. Nico clung to her sleeve. Goblin sat pressed to her ankle.

I didn't sugarcoat it. Couldn't.

"You tell them they're safe," I said. "Because right now, they are."

Her throat worked. She nodded.

"You come back," she said—soft, not pleading, just truth.

I didn't promise, but I had no intentions of disobeying the order.

"We burn it down," I said instead. "Then we come back."

Alphabet chimed in. "Bones. Clock's ticking."

I touched Grace's shoulder once—deliberate, solid— then stepped back through the door.

She watched me until it shut.

I heard the click as she slid the interior bolt.

Good.

Voodoo did the final touch, then we were back in the SUV. The day had grown longer and longer. Somewhere in here, late afternoon had become evening.

"Movement confirmed." Alphabet said. "The blackout transport just changed course. Heading straight for the port."

Voodoo shifted into drive, face going hard.

"Think they are sending a hit squad for the kids or for their men who fucked up?" Lunchbox asked.

"Both," I said, doublechecking my gun. "Body armor for this." We didn't have everything I'd like, but we still had enough. Lunchbox was opening a case in the back.

Voodoo floored it.

"Give us an overview of the pier and the port," I said as I pulled the vest on that Lunchbox passed up.

Alphabet didn't waste a second.

"Copy. Overview coming up. Pulling satellite and traffic feeds... hold—" A pause, then the shift in his voice that always meant *he saw something he really didn't like*. "Okay. Listen close. Pier C is locked down tighter than usual. Almost no forklift traffic. Yard workers moved off main lanes. Either someone knows they've got company coming... or someone cleared the board to make room for this transport."

"That's deliberate," Voodoo muttered.

"Every bit of it," Alphabet confirmed. "Truck's about a mile out. Long-bed hauler. Heavy suspension. No plates. Running cold—no transponder, no scanner ping, nothing to give me a digital fingerprint. That alone pisses me off."

"Tell us about their route," I said.

"You're going to intercept near the west access lane," he answered. "Transport's coming up the outer road, hugging the fence line. If they keep pace, they'll hit Dock 22 in four minutes."

Legend scoffed. "That's one of the loading docks for personal imports?"

"Yes, and from what I can see, it's been used a lot recently." Alphabet said, voice grim. "Means they are comfortable here."

Voodoo pushed us into the outer lane, weaving between warehouse trucks with surgical precision. We merged onto the service road, keeping speed without drawing eyes. The port lights threw long golden streaks across the asphalt— barren, eerie, wrong.

The kind of wrong that made the hair at my nape rise.

Lunchbox leaned forward. "You want us tight on the tail or hanging back?"

"Hanging back," I said. "Two hundred feet. I want a

buffer if they've got shooters in the cab or someone in the rear compartment."

Legend rolled down his window an inch, eyes narrowed. "Think they're expecting company?"

"They're expecting someone," I said. "Maybe not us."

Voodoo's jaw flexed. "But they'll get us anyway."

The road curved, revealing the silhouette of the truck—a hulking shadow moving slow and steady, too heavy to be legal, too intentional to be innocent.

There it was.

The blackout transport.

Not a standard freight hauler. Taller. Reinforced. The kind of truck used to move something that wasn't supposed to exist.

"Alphabet," I murmured, "scan for escort vehicles."

"Two cars behind it—unmarked." He was already ahead of me. "One pickup ahead of you. None of them have plates. All three are maintaining a perfect triangle around the truck."

"So a convoy," Lunchbox said. "Love that."

"No," I corrected. "We've got a cage."

Legend cursed under his breath. "They're guarding it. Hard."

"And we're behind their cage of three vehicles," Voodoo said. "Means if we get closer, they'll box us out."

"And if we stay back too far?" Lunchbox asked.

"They'll know we're tailing," I said.

So we kept that perfect two-hundred-foot distance. Close enough to see everything, far enough not to spook the whole parade.

The truck's brake lights flashed once—too sharp, too quick.

"That was a signal." Voodoo blew out a breath.

"Yeah," I said, narrowing my eyes. "Calling a check."

The vehicles in the cage tightened half a lane inward.

Alphabet hissed. "Shit. They're checking for tails. Don't do anything stupid."

"Define stupid," Voodoo muttered, but he kept us steady and we didn't try to close the distance or shift lanes.

The transport rumbled past a row of idle cranes, then made a wide, sweeping turn deeper into the heart of the port—toward the restricted loading zones.

Alphabet's voice returned. "You're heading toward the decommissioned section of Pier C. You'll lose public coverage soon. All cameras past this point feed to internal servers."

"Already handled that?" Voodoo asked.

Alphabet snorted. "Please. They won't be watching anything but black screens for the next hour."

Good.

The convoy approached a steel checkpoint gate—one that should've been guarded.

It wasn't.

Instead, one man in a reflective vest stepped out, waved the truck through with zero ID check, and never once looked at the trailing vehicles.

Inside job. Completely.

The transport rolled into the restricted pier.

Voodoo slowed at the gate, just enough to look like we weren't following them. The gate guard glanced at us, hand drifting toward his radio.

Lunchbox reached across the seat and brandished his dock badge—one of the good fakes, the kind we tried to avoid using but came in handy in situations like this.

The guard flicked his eyes over it before waving us

through. Yeah, he wasn't all that interested in this, so move us along.

Lazy.

Complicit.

Dead in a few minutes if he kept working with the wrong people.

We moved deeper, the warehouse shadows growing long and the sea breeze turning metallic. Voodoo killed our headlights. We glided down another lane of containers, tracking the convoy on the other side.

The convoy turned again—this time toward a row of sealed containers staged at the waterline. The same place we'd found the kids.

My pulse ticked once.

We pulled between the containers. The floodlights were totally out. The convoy idled, their engines loud enough to catch over the waves, the wind, and the hum of equipment in the distance.

Alphabet's voice sharpened. "That's Dock 22. That's where they loaded the others two nights ago."

The truck slowed.

Stopped.

And then—

The rear door of the blackout transport cracked open two inches. Just two. Enough to let someone inside peek out. Not enough for us to see who—or *what*—was in there.

Lunchbox muttered, "Anyone else getting the feeling this is about to go sideways?"

Voodoo fingers drummed against his thigh. "Sideways, upside down, on fire—pick one."

I stared at the transport. At the shadow behind that cracked-open door. At the guard pacing with a hand on his belt. At the escort cars boxing the area. At the containers painted with serial numbers Alphabet flagged earlier.

Then I breathed once, deep. "Grace?" I gave her a moment, a soft beep told me she had unmuted

"We're good," she murmured. I nodded even if she couldn't see it. "Going quiet again." Another beep as she muted on her end.

"We get closer," I said.

Legend blinked. "Closer? As in—"

"As in we get eyes inside that truck," I said. "Before they unload whatever they're hiding."

Lunchbox's grin spread slow and feral.

"Been waiting for you to say that."

I cracked the door.

The night air hit my face—cold, sharp, electric.

"Alphabet," I murmured, stepping out. "Keep us off the grid."

"You bet your ass I will," he said.

The convoy moved. People shifted. Weapons glinted.

And as I stepped forward into the belly of the pier, one thing settled like steel inside me—this was always going to end in blood.

The wind shifted—salt, diesel, metal—and carried just enough sound from the convoy for me to count bodies.

Three by the escort sedans. One pacing at the rear of the transport. Two at the pickup. One at the checkpoint shack.

Six. Not many. But enough to ruin this pier if we made a mistake.

Voodoo slid up beside me, eyes scanning angles. Lunchbox moved ahead like a shadow with teeth. I stayed low, Glock ready, senses tuned. Alphabet's voice crackled in my ear.

"Eyes on everything. Seven targets, low alert, keep it clean," he said.

"We go quiet," I muttered. "No gunfire unless absolutely necessary."

Lunchbox smirked. "Been waiting to do this."

Voodoo nodded once.

We moved.

TWO AT THE sedans were leaning against their cars, smoking, careless. Dead men walking. The third stood a few feet away, radio or cell phone in hand like he was waiting for a call.

Lunchbox took the left, I went right, Voodoo covered the center. Shadows sliding across concrete.

Lunchbox reached his guy first—hand clamped over the mouth, a quick twist to the wrist, and the man went down silent. I moved my target next, elbow driving into the back of his skull just enough to make him fold. Voodoo eased the second down with a chokehold before he could react.

All three unconscious before anyone could even think to reach for a gun.

I was on the man pacing behind the transport. Arm across the throat, wrist twisting, and the man crumpled. No noise, no chance to scream.

With hand signals, I sent Lunchbox and Voodoo after the two by the pickup. They moved like a pair of ghosts, siding behind them and taking them down in controlled chokes.

The last one was the man in the reflective vest—eyes sharp enough to ruin everything if he saw us.

Voodoo and Lunchbox actually did rock, paper scissors

for the asshole and I rolled my eyes. But Voodoo's scissors sliced through Lunchbox's paper. Just as swiftly, Voodoo took out his target.

I tapped a message to Alphabet via the comms. *SITREP*

Alphabet confirmed. "No alerts. You're ghosts. Clean sweep so far."

Seven bodies down. All unconscious.

We regrouped behind the transport, movements smooth, breaths calm. Alphabet's voice floated in the comms.

"All feeds still black. You're clear."

Voodoo stepped up beside me, eyes on the cracked-open rear door. Lunchbox exhaled. "Warm-up's done."

I nodded. "Time for the main event."

Hand on the door, I felt the dark inside exhale at us.

"Eyes up," I said, voice low steel. "No mistakes."

We ghosted forward.

Three shadows slipping through darker shadows, silent as we could get on concrete that wanted to echo every damn step. With the escort team down, we just needed to deal with the guards on the transport itself.

Lunchbox tapped my arm once—two guards nearest the truck, one on patrol near the containers, and another lingering by the cab.

Four total.

Doable.

I gestured left. Lunchbox peeled off, melting into the container shadows with the kind of fluidity a man his size shouldn't have. Voodoo circled right, keeping low. I headed dead center toward the pacing guard.

The man hummed under his breath—nervous energy. Didn't matter.

His head turned at the wrong moment.

My forearm clamped around his throat, cutting off air and voice. He kicked once, twice—weak. Training, panic, both in the wrong order. I guided him down in total silence, lowering his body until it touched concrete with all the weight of a falling leaf.

One down.

Lunchbox grabbed his target from behind a stack of crates, slammed him into the steel wall just once, and caught him before he hit the floor. Voodoo's target crumpled without a sound.

Three down.

We waited for the last—the one near the cab—to turn his back.

He did.

Lunchbox was on him before the man realized the world had shifted. A quick chokehold, a soft thump, body tucked under the truck frame.

Four down.

Good.

We moved to the transport.

Up close, the blackout hauler was worse. Taller. Reinforced. The kind of metal that didn't flex in temperature changes. Something purpose-built for hiding human cargo.

I exchanged a look with Voodoo, then signaled Lunchbox up.

We went to the rear.

Lunchbox eased the latch. It was heavy, secure, recently locked. But nothing we couldn't handle. The door shifted an inch.

Inside, I heard something—

A stifled sob.

Voodoo's jaw locked. "People."

"More kids?" Lunchbox whispered.

"No." My gut knew before the door swung enough to show us.

I opened it wider.

Rows. Layers. Bodies huddled together.

Women.

Dozens of them.

Young—too young—pale faces washed in the dim red emergency light the transport used to hide its movement. Eastern European features. Some with bruises. Some shaking. All terrified.

Some held each other, whispering. Some stared with hollow, resigned eyes. Some recoiled instinctively at the movement.

One finally spoke in a trembling voice.

"Prosím... neubližujte nám."

Slovak. Czech. Something close.

"Please... don't hurt us." Grace translated without me needing to ask.

Voodoo exhaled slowly. "Jesus Christ."

Lunchbox shoved a hand through his hair, fury shaking in his shoulders. "They were going to unload them. Tonight."

If we hadn't found them?

Sold.

Vanished.

Forgotten.

One woman—older, maybe late twenties—pulled a girl behind her, shielding her with her body. She stared at me like I was another monster.

I kept my hands visible, palms up. "We're here to help," I said softly, knowing they wouldn't understand the words but maybe the tone.

The older woman's breath hitched.

Lunchbox whispered, voice a raw scrape, "Bones… we can't move this many by ourselves."

"I know."

"We need Grace," Voodoo muttered.

"We can't bring her into this," I said. "Not until it's secure."

We were about to figure out how the hell to extract thirty terrified women when a crackle sounded from one of the downed guards' radios.

All three of us froze.

Voices spilled out—flat, efficient, emotionless.

"Timoson, report. The vans never arrived."

"Status on cargo prep?"

Static.

"Timoson, respond. The sweep team is inbound to clean your mess. ETA nine minutes."

Lunchbox's grip tightened on his gun. "Cleanup crew. Not the 'brooms and mop' kind, either."

"No." My voice came out hard, cold.

This was the kind of squad sent when problems needed to disappear. All of them. Bodies. Evidence. Survivors.

Cargo.

"They're coming to wipe this whole pier," Voodoo said.

"And everyone in it," I finished. "Including them."

I looked back at the women—dozens of eyes staring at us, trembling, waiting for the next horror.

"Okay," I exhaled. "We improvise."

That was how we put Voodoo in the cab to drive the transport with Lunchbox riding shotgun and I set up for the cleanup team.

It was going to be messy, but what the hell.

"I've got eyes, Cap," Alphabet said. "We can do this."

Yes. Yes we could.

NINETEEN

GRACE

The kids were quiet for now. Too quiet. That's usually when the fear starts creeping in, like a shadow stretching across the floor. At least, it was like that when I was a kid. God, I couldn't have imagined going through everything I already had at my age *now*. If I'd been a kid?

A shudder went through me. I knelt next to Nico, his little hand still clinging to mine. "Hey," I said softly. "We're okay. Remember? We're okay."

He didn't answer. His eyes tracked the walls, every creak or groan of sound seemed to make him flinch. Goblin lay at my feet, low thrum vibrating in his chest like a motor —steady, unshakable. That alone helped.

A crackle, then Bones' voice, rough but controlled came over the comm. "Clear at the truck."

I'd been listening to them every step of the way.

"Voodoo and Lunchbox are taking the rig. Alphabet— get them an exit strategy and make sure it's clear."

"Go with them, Cap," AB said.

"No," Bones replied and I swore my heart spasmed.

215

My stomach clenched. It felt like we'd just gotten him back, I didn't want to risk losing him again. My hands tightened around Nico's. "Bones..."

"Shh," he said, and though his tone was softer the order underlying the syllable was no less fierce. "They're coming for me."

I swallowed. My throat was tight. I tapped the comm to silence my end. I wasn't alone. There were two other soft beeps that followed mine. Legend and Voodoo, AB would stay on with Bones. We'd moved as a unit, but bit by bit, we'd broken off into smaller teams.

Now Bones was alone. My heart did a violent little wrench.

I glanced at the others. The little girl with the stuffed toy missing an eye was hugging it like it was the only thing in the world keeping her alive. I smiled, even though it didn't reach my eyes.

"It's okay, sweetie. Goblin's right here. You're safe. I promise."

I translated it too, because it forced me to calm down. Panic tended to make me think in English, so it seemed reasonable they would default to their own languages.

One by one, I checked on the others. Words didn't have to make sense. The tone mattered. Calm, slow, solid. That's what they needed. That's what I gave.

Bones' voice came again. More frantic now. "Rig's out, I've got a hit team—four of them—coming through the west containers. I'm holding."

My stomach dropped.

"Dollface," he continued barely pausing for a breath. "I've got this, but you can turn the comm off so you don't have to listen."

Fuck. That.

I gritted my teeth and held my tongue. I couldn't fix this from here. Not yet. My job was the kids. My job was keeping them alive. And I could do that.

The youngest, the little boy clinging to Goblin's tail, whimpered. I scooped him onto my lap, rubbing his back. "It's okay," I said softly. "They can't get to us. Bones and the others are making sure of that. You're safe. I promise."

My comm pinged again. "We're out." Legend's voice rolled over me in slow, smooth, and deliberate fashion as he confirmed Bones' earlier report. "Clear in two. Don't do anything stupid back there, Bones."

"I don't plan to," came Bones' sharp reply.

My comm beeped again, I didn't recognize this one. "Grace," AB's calm, clipped voice cut in. "I swapped our channel for a moment. I've got backup coming in and Feds on standby. They'll hit the perimeter and sweep in once we have visual clearance on the evac. One of us will bring them to you when it's time. You're not alone."

I let out a breath I didn't know I was holding. "Copy," I said. "Put me back on with Bones?" A whisper of noise that sounded like a kiss before the comm beeped and the sound of vehicles and shouting in the distance came over the comms.

"Help is coming," I whispered, forcing my tone to be upbeat. "We're safe. Goblin agrees." Thankfully, the Staffy gave me a long, comforting look and thumped his tail.

A rumble of engines sounded outside. They weren't close, but the vibrations carried. One of the girls clutched the stuffed toy to her chest and buried her face. I leaned close, voice low and steady. "Nothing's going to touch us. Not here. Not tonight. You're okay."

She crawled over to curl up in what little of my lap was left. The kids were forming a bundle with me and Goblin on either side of them. It didn't surprise me when Nico wrapped a thin arm around the youngest girl even as the littlest boy rubbed his dirty, tear-stained face against my sweatshirt.

Bones' voice came again, more urgent now. "They're pushing through the containers. I've got one down... two more—"

The tension in his voice threatened to gut me. "Do you want me to tell you a story?" It was reaching and now that I'd offered, my mind went a little blank.

There was a metallic crash, the echo of combat. My stomach twisted.

Nico looked at me with a sheen of tears in his dark brown eyes. Tears he refused to shed, but blinked furiously to keep back. It was hard to fight the urge to cry. But I was proud of him for doing it.

"Story?" His request came out a little stronger than my offer.

"Sí, story," I said softly, smoothing Nico's hair back. "Let's tell a story. One that's... brave."

The littlest girl peeked at me from under her toy with its stitched eyes glimmered in the dim light. I swallowed, trying to hold the knot in my chest at bay.

I took a slow breath, the kids pressed close, and began in a whisper, *"Había una vez una tortuga que quería tocar el cielo."*

The little turtle who wanted to touch the sky.

Nico's hand tightened around mine. He didn't speak, but he listened. The youngest girl clutched her toy, head tilted to look up at me. Goblin lay like a shield at our side. I kept my tone calm, steady, soothing.

Over the comm, Bones' voice crackled again. "Two down. West side—moving faster."

I swallowed, forcing my words to remain soft. *"Esta tortuga no era la más rápida ni la más fuerte, pero tenía un corazón muy valiente."*

Not the fastest. Not the strongest. But very brave.

I glanced at Nico. His eyes were wide, tracking sounds beyond our little building. He didn't need translation for the fear, but he needed me to be brave for him.

"Un día decidió que nada—ni el viento, ni la lluvia, ni los animales más grandes del bosque—podía detenerla."

Nothing could stop it.

The metallic clang of Bones' gunfire echoed faintly through the comm, far off but sharp enough to make me flinch.

"We've got another moving in on the north dock," he said, voice tense but controlled. "I can handle it."

I nodded to myself. My job was here. The kids. The story. My hands rubbed the youngest boy's back. *"Pero la tortuga sabía que a veces se necesitan amigos. Amigos que te ayudan a subir y te protegen cuando el camino es peligroso."*

Sometimes you need friends.

Goblin thumped his tail, and one by one, the kids leaned closer, forming a bundle around me. I could almost feel their tension seeping into my lap. I whispered, *"Y la tortuga encontró un amigo muy grande, un perro fuerte que estaba a su lado."*

A big friend. A strong dog.

Through the comm, I heard a shout, not Bones' voice— closer, faster. "We are clear," Voodoo said.

I kept going, soft, slow. *"Y cuando el viento soplaba demasiado fuerte, el perro decía: 'No te preocupes, estoy aquí.'"*

"Don't worry, I'm here."

A crash from the pier made the kids flinch. I held them tighter. *"Juntos, la tortuga y el perro caminaron hasta la cima de la montaña. El sol brillaba sobre ellos, y sabían que aunque haya peligro, nunca estaban solos."*

Even when there's danger, they weren't alone.

Bones' voice roared back over the comm, closer, ragged: "North dock cleared. Hit squad—three more. I'm holding."

Minutes stretched like hours.

I swallowed. The story didn't falter, even though my heart felt weighed down in titanium chains. *"A veces, los más pequeños son los más valientes. Y con amigos, siempre llegamos a casa."*

The smallest can be the bravest. With friends, we always make it home.

The youngest boy sniffled into my sweatshirt. I whispered directly to him, softly translating the words. *"La tortuga aprendió que ser valiente no es no tener miedo... es seguir adelante incluso cuando tienes miedo. Y nosotros... podemos hacer lo mismo."*

Bravery isn't not being afraid. It's moving forward anyway. And we... we can do the same.

A long silence fell over the room, the kind that feels like the eye of a storm. And then, faint but distinct, the low rumble of engines. AB's voice cut in sharp, clipped, a lifeline over the static: "Backup's on site. Feds moving in. You're not alone."

I let out a breath I hadn't realized I'd been holding. I repeated softly to the kids, as much to remind myself: *"Estamos bien. Estamos seguros. Goblin está aquí. Todos estamos juntos."*

We're okay. We're safe. Goblin's here. We're all together.

And even as the distant chaos continued, even as Bones fought his way through the pier alone, I told the story again —slow, soft, brave—because in this moment, our courage, like the turtle's, was the only thing keeping us moving forward.

I tightened my grip on the youngest boy as the engines grew louder. In the distance, I swore I could hear the clatter of footsteps and shouted orders carrying faintly over the comms. Bones was still on his own, holding the north dock against the rest of the hit team.

I whispered, *"Y la tortuga miró hacia atrás y vio que sus amigos estaban allí. Siempre a su lado, incluso cuando el camino era peligroso."*

The turtle looked back and saw his friends. Always by his side, even when the road was dangerous.

Another metallic clang. Bones' voice cut sharply over the comm. "Two more down. One left—northwest corner. I've got eyes on him. He doesn't know I'm here."

I held my breath. My hands trembled just slightly. Nico leaned into me, his face pressed against my shoulder. *"Estamos bien, pequeño,"* I said softly. *"La tortuga tiene amigos, y nosotros también."*

We're okay, little one. The turtle has friends, and so do we.

The youngest girl clutched her stuffed toy closer, muttering something under her breath.

I answered her little prayer whether she meant it for me or not. *"Sí, querida. Nadie puede hacernos daño mientras estemos juntos."*

Yes, darling. No one can hurt us while we're together.

Bones' voice returned, ragged but controlled. "Got him. Clear. West side's moving out. Repeat, everyone is down and accounted for."

AB's voice came in, clipped and calm: "Perimeter's secured. Federal teams moving in now. You've got visual clearance soon."

The kids were tense, waiting for my reassurance. I wrapped my arms around the two youngest, pulling them close. *"La tortuga y el perro cruzaron la cima de la montaña, y vieron que el sol brillaba para todos ellos. No importa lo que pase... siempre hay luz."*

The turtle and the dog reached the top of the mountain, and the sun shone on them. No matter what happens... there's always light.

I glanced at Nico. His dark eyes tracked every shadow, every movement outside the window, but there was a faint spark of calm in them now. *"Bones está bien,"* I whispered. *"Voodoo y Legend también. Todo está bajo control."*

Bones is okay. Voodoo and Legend too. Everything's under control.

A sudden horn from the pier made the youngest girl squeak. I held her tighter, whispering fast but gentle. *"Recuerda la historia. La tortuga no corría, no saltaba, pero avanzaba, siempre con sus amigos."*

Remember the story. The turtle didn't run, didn't jump, but kept moving forward, always with friends.

Another comm ping. Bones' voice, low and relieved, came through. "Dollface?"

I brushed my comms unit. "I'm here," I murmured even as I let out the breath I hadn't realized I'd been holding. My knees ached from staying kneeling, holding the kids, keeping them calm. "Just telling the kids a story." I brushed the comms again before I continued. *"Veamos la luz,"* I whispered to them, translating it softly. *"Así como la tortuga y el perro... la luz siempre vuelve."*

Let's see the light. Just like the turtle and the dog... the light always comes back.

"That's our girl," Bones murmured and my heart did a fistbump to my ribs. They were okay.

I kept repeating that inside.

They were okay.

Outside, the distant rumble of tires on asphalt and shouted orders carried through the steel walls. The kids shifted, sensing the tension lifting, if only slightly. Goblin thumped his tail and nuzzled the littlest boy. I pressed a soft kiss to Nico's temple. *"Ya casi estamos,"* I murmured. *"Casi seguros."*

We're almost there. Almost safe.

And even as the night pressed against the warehouse walls, even as the echo of combat faded into the distance, I kept telling the story, slow and soft, letting it thread courage through the room. Bones, Voodoo, Legend—they'd cleared the worst, and we were going to make it out. Because like the turtle, sometimes courage is just moving forward with friends beside you.

It took another hour. An hour of whispered stories, careful translations, and listening through the comm as Bones and the others made sure the last pockets of threat were neutralized. My legs ached from kneeling, my arms from holding the children close, but I didn't dare move until I had confirmation.

Then, finally, the voices I'd been waiting for—lively, reassuring, Spanish-accented—cut through the static.

"Grace," Bones said, low and steady, "we're here."

I froze for a heartbeat, heart hammering. Then, careful not to disturb the kids more than necessary, I rose, then moved over to the door and slid the lock back. It clicked open—a small sound, but to me it felt like the first breath of freedom. I pressed my ear to the crack for a moment, listening, before letting the door swing wide.

There was Bones, flanked by two others I didn't recognize. One of them was a medic, the other a man Bones introduced simply as a "friend." Both spoke in Spanish, addressing the kids with a calm authority that immediately made them relax.

"You can trust them," Bones said softly, meeting my eyes. Red marks that I knew would turn into bruises shadowed his face, and his lower lip was cut. If he'd been bleeding, he'd cleaned it up.

AB's voice followed over the comm, echoing the same reassurance. "They'll take care of the kids. You've done your job. Now let them do theirs."

I hesitated. My hands lingered on Nico's shoulders, stroking the youngest boy's hair. I didn't want to let go, but I knew they were safe. I gave the smallest nod I could manage and began transferring the children, one by one, into the arms of those who could keep them calm, fed, and protected. The relief in their eyes mirrored my own, even as my chest ached at the thought of letting them go.

Once the last of the kids were safely settled into the arms of Bones' medic and his friend, I finally let myself breathe all the way through.

Bones' arms wrapped around me again, tighter this time, grounding me as though he could absorb the weight that was crushing down on me. My cheek rested against his chest, listening to the steady beat of his heart, I let my shoulders relax.

"We did it," I whispered, voice trembling, though the words weren't for anyone but me.

"You did it," Bones corrected gently, pressing a kiss to my temple. "You kept them alive. You were brave."

It was still a we, but I was far too tired to argue with him right now. So, I just let the exhaustion wash over me, mingling with relief and grief, with hope. We hadn't found Amorette yet, but in this small victory, I felt her presence more vividly than ever. Saving these people, protecting the children... this was the work she would have done.

For the first time in hours, I closed my eyes, letting myself sink completely into the safety Bones offered. The warehouse, the night, the distant sounds of evacuation—all of it could wait. Right now, we were alive, we were together, and for the first time in a long while, that was enough.

I breathed him in then whispered, "Thank you." He came back. Just like I'd asked. He tightened his hold, and for a long, perfect moment, the world shrank to just us.

"So..." AB said into the quiet over the comms. "What are we doing for food? Cause I don't know about you guys, but I'm starving."

TWENTY

GRACE

We were in New Jersey. Quiet. Brick townhouse, narrow street, the kind of place that could almost pass for normal if you squinted hard enough.

Almost.

I was curled up in an armchair, wrapped in a blanket and cradling a cup of hot cocoa. Goblin at my feet, thumping his tail against the floor like some low, steady heartbeat even though his eyes were closed. Bones, Voodoo, and Legend were sprawled across the living room in various degrees of exhaustion. AB was in the corner, laptop open, monitoring communications that might not even exist yet.

The window blinds were all closed and heavy curtains blocked out any light that might try to sneak in. I wasn't even certain whether it was four in the afternoon or four in the morning. Time had lost all meaning while we took care of the fallout from the pier.

The kids and women we'd rescued were already being shepherded to safe houses by teams that moved faster and quieter than I could have imagined. The guys insisted they were in good hands, people who would take care of them and see them either into new safer locations or get them home. It was a lot like what the guys had done with the people I'd been rescued with by the Vandals.

Well, what they'd *tried* to do with me before everything went sideways. It seemed a million years before and just yesterday in the same breath. I really couldn't imagine my life without all of them in it. Yet, if AB and Legend hadn't waited once they dropped me at my place, I might have ended right back where I'd been, and I'd have never seen them again.

The latter disturbed me far more than the former. I'd survived the former, I didn't want to learn how I would handle the latter.

Ever.

Once we got to the safe house, we'd all taken turns to strip, shower, and put on clean clothes. I'd half-expected one of the guys to join me, but rather than climb in the shower, Bones and Legend waited as I showered while Voodoo was in the second bathroom, then AB followed him. Legend actually brought me my first round of hot cocoa so I could sip it once I was clean.

Awareness of them watching me actually provided a lot of comfort. I stuck around for Bones' shower too and offered when it was Legend's turn. He'd winked and sent me out to get dressed. I was wearing one of Bones' sweatshirts and a pair of Alphabet's boxers. Voodoo was going to get me more clothes the next day.

Right now, I really didn't care. At least this place boasted three king-sized beds and one room with a queen. It was a lot more comfortable than the standard safe houses we'd used, but I was only guessing. It wasn't like the other places were just bare bones.

Still, Legend had taken the time waiting for his shower, getting food going. That included two entire pans of enchiladas and beans. Hot, filling, and tasty, I'd devoured mine without an ounce of complaint for the carbs.

"Feds got Sarmiento and two of his lieutenants," AB said, voice calm as he scanned his screen. His hair was still damp and drying in little waves. "Bad timing on their part showing up right in the midst of the pier raid. Clean sweep."

Bones let out a long breath, finally allowing some of the tension in his shoulders to go. "Good," he said. The bruises on his face were growing more distinct. The reddened mark on his jaw would be a dark shadow. "One less headache."

I took another long sip of the hot cocoa. It was dark chocolate, sweet, and thick. It was perfect. I didn't know if he made it like I had or just his own way and honestly, I didn't care. It was like a chocolate hug and kiss rolled into one. The edges of exhaustion were gradually expanding to fill my whole being. My muscles ached in ways I hadn't noticed while on high alert, and my heart still thumped like a drum in my chest.

Voodoo cracked one eye open, murmuring, "Quiet for once. I almost don't know what to do with it."

Legend, leaning back in a chair, muttered, "Enjoy it while it lasts. We all know it won't."

Bones' gaze found mine, and it wasn't anything I could call soft, exactly, but it was steady. "We need a plan," he said.

"We do," I agreed. "But..."

At the caveat, I had all of their attention from Voodoo's seemingly sleepy-eyed gaze to Bones' sharp and assessing one. Legend shifted, stretching his legs out and interlacing his fingers together as he fixed a studious look on me.

"But?" AB prompted, setting his laptop aside to rise and stretch. There was a distinct hitch in his stride and I wasn't the only one who noticed. Goblin lifted his head, ears swiveling to focus on AB as he began a slow, easy walk around the room. He'd spent a lot of long hours hunched over his computer. I didn't doubt he was stiff.

"All of you need to sleep, we need to recuperate and recover before we dig in again." We hadn't truly stopped moving in over a week. We'd had more than one fight and we hadn't even taken a break after dealing with McClean.

I didn't think about either man. They were dead and gone. We would still look for Mrs. Sinclair and we'd left Hannah Torres with our information. AB promised he'd get me updates on the women we freed and the kids. Little Nico hadn't wanted to go, but as much as I was sorry to see him off—I wasn't mom material.

Our life right now was not conducive to having kids around. It just wouldn't be safe for them. That kept trying to trigger off another series of thoughts, but I was too damn tired to think about it either. I'd never pictured myself as a mother, and I didn't expect that to change anytime soon.

"What will you be doing while we're sleeping, Firecracker?" The soft, almost wry amusement in Voodoo's voice nearly made me laugh.

"Well, I won't be darning socks." Did people even *darn* socks anymore? The idea seemed ludicrous and the dry comment made all of them smile.

Voodoo's smile sharpened. "Good. Because my socks are perfect, thank you very much."

"You buy yours in bulk at Costco," Legend said without looking up from his plate. "There is no 'perfect.' There's just 'cheap and identical.'"

"Identical is efficient," Voodoo shot back.

"Identical is boring," Legend countered.

"Identical is reliable," AB chimed in, deadpan.

Bones snorted, shaking his head. "We're debating socks now? Really?"

I grinned into my cocoa. "You're all punch-drunk."

"Absolutely," Voodoo agreed without shame.

Legend pressed a hand to his chest, putting on gravitas he absolutely didn't have. "We are branching into domestic topics as a method of decompression. It's healthy."

"Or sleep deprivation," AB added.

"Or both," I said.

They all looked at me again—the kind of collective attention that would have intimidated the hell out of me a year ago... now it mostly made me want to roll my eyes and smile.

Bones lifted his chin at me. "So. You told us to sleep."

"Yes," I said.

"And you?" Legend asked, narrowing his gaze.

"I'll sleep too," I promised.

"No," Voodoo corrected, raising a finger. "The question isn't whether you'll sleep. The question is where."

"Oh lord," I muttered. "Here we go."

Legend perked up like he'd been waiting for this. "We've got three kings and a queen. Goblin already claimed the couch, so that's off the table. We can't let you sleep alone after the day we've had—"

"—or the week," AB added.

"—or the month," Voodoo finished helpfully.

Bones' jaw flexed. "She's sleeping with me."

The immediate chorus of "Nope," "Hold up," and "We're doing this properly" nearly made me snort cocoa out my nose.

Voodoo raised his hand. "For the record, I am comfortable being the sacrificial pillow. I don't snore, I don't steal blankets, and I am excellent at regulating body temperature."

"That's because you're part reptile," Legend said.

"Exactly," Voodoo replied smugly.

Legend pointed at himself. "I, on the other hand, am the superior option because I actually know how to share a bed. I don't flail, I don't roll, and I don't hog the mattress like a certain Captain we all know—"

"I do not hog the bed," Bones growled.

"Cap, with love?" Legend said sweetly. "You absolutely do."

AB, who had been silent through all of this, sipped from a water bottle. "I'll room with her."

All three men turned a gimlet eye on him.

He shrugged. "I don't snore either. I'm also the least injured at the moment. I can wake easily if something happens."

"That's true," Voodoo conceded.

Legend squinted. "But you run hot as hell. You'll bake her alive."

"I'll survive," I muttered. "I have plenty of times before." I also didn't mind being wrapped up in an AB blanket.

Bones growled again. "She's with me." He looked ready to bite someone's head off if necessary.

AB crossed his arms. "We're making a decision, not submitting to your territorial whims."

"Territorial?" Bones scoffed. "I'm practical."

"You're possessive," Voodoo corrected.

Legend grinned. "And bad at hiding it."

Bones glared at them. "She is *safest* with me."

The room fell quiet.

A warm, aching softness slid under my ribs.

Because yes—there it was. Not posturing. Not ego.

Just the truth.

They all felt responsible for me, each in their own way. They all cared. A lot. And beneath all the banter they were just trying to figure out how to keep me safest, keep themselves safest, keep the team intact.

Honestly?

I loved them for it.

Finally, I set my empty mug aide aside and held up a hand.

"Okay. Enough. You all need sleep more than you need to fight over who gets to take up half a mattress." I loved sleeping with all of them, so it wasn't even a debate on preferring one to the other.

"Quarter," Legend corrected. "Bones doesn't just hog the bed, he—"

"Lunchbox," Bones said warningly. The air crackled between them as they let off steam in a playful fashion. These men loved each other, and they loved to give each other shit.

I laughed softly. "Here's what's happening. We are all exhausted. We can barely keep our eyes open. I'm not sleeping alone and I'm not sleeping on the floor. So the simplest solution?"

Four men blinked at me like I'd just delivered an unexpected plot twist. I shrugged, because rarely did I manage to get one over on *one* of them, much less all of them.

"We share a bed."

There was a beat of silence as they all stared at me.

"We might be a bit snug, but we'll fit."

Then:

Voodoo: "Dibs on not being in the middle, I get too warm."

Legend: "I vote Grace in the middle."

AB: "That is the only strategically sound configuration."

Bones: "Fine. But I'm on her left."

"Why left?" Legend asked.

"Because that's where I sleep," Bones said.

"That's not—" Legend started.

I cut him off with a yawn so big my jaw clicked. "Guys? Pick your sides. I'm going to bed before I fall asleep standing up."

Bones was up first—like his body had been waiting for me to say the words.

Legend pushed to his feet next with a muttered, "Called it," while Voodoo grinned and AB simply nodded like this was the inevitable outcome he'd calculated hours ago.

Goblin glanced at us, then climbed up onto the couch. He turned in a couple of circles, then sighed as he settled in and his eyes were closed immediately.

After giving him a loving scritch, I leaned over to press a kiss to the top of his head. "Sleep well." His tail thumped once as I headed up the stairs. Bones was already waiting for me and he motioned me ahead, then fell in behind me.

Behind me, Voodoo murmured to Legend, "I'm telling you, I'm not cuddling you if you drift into my space."

"Please," Legend scoffed. "You couldn't handle cuddling me."

"Boys," Bones growled.

And even half-asleep, bruised, and dragging their feet...

They made me happier than I ever imagined I could be.

Bones led the way toward the bedrooms, slow but purposeful, like his body was running on fumes and stubbornness alone. The upstairs hallway was narrow, dim, quiet except for the soft steps behind me. Bones opened the door to the largest room and paused. "We're combining beds."

I blinked. "What?"

Legend brushed past us with an evaluating look at the layout. "Oh yeah. Lose the nightstands, then put Queen goes against one wall, king wedged against the other, create one giant sleeping surface."

Voodoo was already in the doorway of the next room, inspecting the queen bed like he was planning a heist. "Alphabet, grab the other side."

AB didn't even argue. He just said, "On three," and the two of them lifted the frame like it weighed nothing. It definitely did not weigh nothing—I'd tried moving one of those once and nearly dislocated my whole soul.

Bones muttered, "Idiots," but he got the nightstands moved and helped Legend shove the king over before he paused to watch. He always watched. Making sure everyone was okay even in the most ridiculous of moments.

Legend stripped the blankets off the king-sized bed and rolled them to the side. "We're gonna need all the pillows."

"All of them," Voodoo echoes solemnly, as though this were a tactical operation.

AB and Voodoo backed through the doorway, carefully maneuvering the queen mattress and frame. The two of them lined it up with the side of the king bed while Legend guided angles like an air traffic controller.

Bones helped too—he just did it with a growl and a wince every time his ribs objected.

Ten minutes later, they'd created a monstrosity: a bed so large it could probably host a small conference.

Legend surveyed their work, hands on hips. "Behold. The Sleep Platform."

Voodoo added, "The cuddle battlefield."

AB: "The tactical rest array."

Bones: "The bed."

I covered my laugh with a hand. God, the tension hadn't fully left any of them, but this? This helped. The normalcy. The ridiculousness. The way they were all a little punchy and overtired.

Bones looked at me again—steady, grounding. "You good?"

"I'm great," I said. Thankfully, it wasn't a lie.

I walked to the bed, reached for the hem of Bones' sweatshirt...and peeled it off. The boxers went next and I left them in a neat pile at the foot, where I could claim them in the morning.

Every man in the room froze.

"Guys, you're all basically space heaters. If I wear anything, I'm absolutely going to wake up cooked alive." If anyone decided to play, well, there was something to be said about not getting tied up in my clothes.

Voodoo nodded immediately. "Accurate."

Legend cleared his throat. "Uh—yes. That is...practically sound."

AB offered a courteous, "We'll keep the blankets light then," as though we were discussing spreadsheets.

Bones didn't move. Didn't blink. Just watched me with this quiet, protective intensity that made my chest warm. "You cold?"

"Nope." I climbed onto the middle of the giant bed and sank into the mattress. "But I will be if you all don't stop staring and get in here."

That snapped them out of it.

Voodoo claimed the far right of the queen, grumbling about "optimal airflow." Legend took the far left on the queen side. AB positioned himself between Legend and where I was sitting, efficiently adjusting pillows like he was arranging data sets. Then he unstrapped his prosthetic.

Once he had it off, I held out a hand and he eyed me for a moment, then handed it to me. I crawled to the foot of the bed and set it on top of my clothes. Aware of their gazes without turning around, I gave my ass a little wiggle. "Get a good look gentlemen, but tonight—or whatever the hell the time is, that's all it's going to be."

A soft chuckle rumbled out of them as I crawled back up to my spot.

Bones slid in on my left, careful of my space, even though I knew he wanted to fold around me immediately. He'd wait—even exhausted—until I made the first move.

I didn't make him wait long.

I nudged into his side, careful of his ribs, then rested my head on his shoulder. He exhaled, the tension in his chest easing like someone had unlocked it. His hand found my hip. Gentle. Grounding.

Legend stretched out, arms over his head. "If anyone snores, I'm suffocating you with a pillow."

"Try it," Voodoo said, already half-buried in blankets.

AB lay back, hands folded across his stomach. "Statistically speaking, Voodoo is most likely to snore."

Voodoo didn't even open his eyes. "Statistically speaking, I could take you in a fight."

AB: "Incorrect."

Legend: "Boys."

Bones: "All of you shut up."

I smiled into his shoulder. "I love you guys."

Four quiet voices answered in their own ways:

Voodoo: "Love you too, Firecracker."

Legend: "Obviously."

AB: "Likewise."

Bones, softest of all despite the gravel in his voice, "Sleep, Grace."

My heart jerked at Voodoo's soft declaration as if it was the most natural thing in the world. A smile curved my lips and I let out a sigh. Tomorrow, I planned to kiss the hell out of him for that.

The whole bed shifted as they settled around me, their presence familiar weight bracketing me on all sides. The room smelled like soap and exhaustion and *them*.

For the first time in what felt like forever, my muscles unclenched completely. It didn't take me long until I was drifting. Content to float on the tide of their breathing rising and falling around me, I didn't fight the sleep that pulled me down even as AB interlaced his fingers with mine.

We were here, we were together—and in that moment, bruised and bone-deep tired and finally still...these beautiful men were safe, they were warm, and they were *mine*.

TWENTY-ONE

GRACE

I was floating in a warm, heavy darkness, the kind of sleep that feels like sinking to the bottom of the sea. There was no sound, no light, just the profound quiet of exhaustion finally claiming its due. The world had narrowed to the steady rhythm of breathing around me, the solid weight of AB's fingers still laced with mine, the firm line of Bones' body against my side. It was perfect. It was peaceful.

A hand on my hip, warm and calloused, pulled me gently from the depths. Not a jolt, but a slow, deliberate drag toward consciousness. I blinked my eyes open, but the room was pitch black. The only light was the faint, hazy glow from the street outside, muted by the heavy curtains. For a moment, I was disoriented, my mind still fuzzy with sleep. Then I felt the shift of the mattress beside me and heard a soft murmur right against my ear.

"Grace."

Bones. His voice was a low, rough rumble, a vibration that traveled straight through my bones. It wasn't a question. It was a summons.

I shifted, my body still heavy and pliant with sleep. "Mmm?" was all I could manage. The sound was barely a breath.

His hand tightened on my hip, his thumb stroking a slow, deliberate circle over my skin. "Shhh," he murmured, his lips brushing against the shell of my ear. "Stay quiet. Just feel."

My heart gave a slow, heavy thud, waking up faster than the rest of me. His other hand slid from my shoulder down my arm, tracing the line of my body until it reached my waist. He was being so careful, so deliberate, as if he were trying not to wake the dead. Or maybe just not wake Legend, Voodoo, and AB. The thought was so absurd it almost made me giggle, but the sound caught in my throat as his fingers splayed across my stomach, his palm a brand of heat against my cool skin.

He nudged me with his body, a gentle pressure that was impossible to misinterpret. I rolled onto my back, the sheets whispering around me. The bed was a landscape of warm bodies. AB remained a solid, unmoving presence on my other side, his breathing deep and even as I slid my hand from his. Further off, I could hear the soft snores Voodoo had denied, and Legend's quiet, rhythmic breathing. We were a tangle of limbs and blankets, a fortress of exhausted bodies.

Bones moved over me, not covering me completely, but bracing himself on one elbow beside my head, his legs tangling with mine. He was a shadow in the dark, a solid, comforting weight that smelled of soap and bone-deep weariness and something else. Something that was purely *Bones.*

"Bones," I whispered again, my voice a little clearer this time. "What are you—?"

He cut me off with his mouth. It wasn't a demanding kiss, not a hungry one. It was slow, deep, and exploratory. A kiss that said *I'm here* and *You're mine* and *We're alive.* His tongue swept against mine, a slow, languid dance that made my toes curl and my blood heat. His hand slid up from my stomach to cup my breast, his thumb brushing over my nipple, which pebbled instantly at his touch.

A soft gasp escaped me, and he immediately stilled, pulling back just enough to murmur against my lips. "Shhh. Quiet, Dollface. Just feel."

I nodded, my movements jerky in the dark. I understood. This wasn't about loud passion or frantic need. This was something else. This was a silent, secret conversation in the middle of the night. A reaffirmation of life after we'd danced too close to death. A way to burn off the lingering adrenaline that sleep hadn't been able to chase away.

His hand began to move again, a slow, maddening exploration. He traced the curve of my waist, the dip of my hip, the sensitive skin of my inner thigh. Every touch was a spark, every caress a slow burn. He was driving me absolutely mad with his deliberate, controlled movements. My body, which had been moments ago slack with sleep, was now humming with a quiet, desperate energy. I wanted to arch into his touch, to cry out, to demand more, but his soft, repeated "shhh" was a constant reminder of where we were. Of the three other men sleeping just feet away.

It made everything more intense. The need to be silent, to keep our pleasure contained within this small, dark space between us, was a heady kind of torture. His fingers found my core, sliding through the slick heat that had gathered there. I bit down hard on my lower lip to keep from moaning as he circled my clit, the pressure light, teasing, perfect.

"Bones," I breathed, his name a desperate plea against his mouth.

"I know," he murmured, his voice strained. "I know, Grace. Just... let me."

And I did. I let him. I let him drive me to the edge with nothing but his hands and his mouth and his whispered commands to be quiet. He slid one finger inside me, then another, his thumb still working that maddening circle. My hips began to move of their own accord, a slow, rolling rhythm that met his strokes. I could feel the tension coiling in my belly, tight and hot and ready to snap. My hands fisted in the sheets, my breath coming in short, sharp pants that I tried to muffle against his shoulder.

He shifted, settling more firmly between my legs, and I felt the hard, heavy length of him press against me. He was just as affected as I was, his control a fragile thing I could feel straining at its edges. He kissed me again, deeper this time, a silent promise of what was to come.

"Please," I whimpered, the word barely audible.

He didn't make me wait any longer. He positioned himself, then pushed inside me in one slow, smooth stroke. I choked on a gasp, my body arching off the bed as he filled me completely. He stilled, giving me a moment to adjust, his forehead resting against mine. We were both breathing hard, the sound loud in the quiet room.

"Okay?" he whispered.

I nodded, unable to speak.

He began to move, a slow, deep rhythm that was both torturous and exquisite. Every thrust was a silent declaration, every retreat a promise to return. He was watching me, I could feel it, his gaze intense even in the darkness. He was committing this to memory, just as I was. The feel of him, the sound of our breathing, the scent of our skin.

He shifted his angle slightly, and the head of his cock brushed against that spot deep inside me. My eyes flew open, and a strangled sound escaped my throat. He immediately clamped a hand over my mouth, his touch gentle but firm.

"Shhh," he reminded me, his voice a low, urgent whisper against my ear. "I know. Just let it happen."

The pressure, the pleasure, the need for silence—it all combined into a perfect, stormy crescendo. I came with a silent scream, my body clamping around his as wave after wave of pleasure washed over me. It was intense, overwhelming, a release so profound it left me shaking.

He followed me over the edge with a low, guttural groan that he muffled against my neck, his body shuddering against mine as he found his own release.

For a long moment, we just lay there, tangled together, our hearts pounding a frantic rhythm against our ribs. The air was thick with the scent of sex and sweat and satisfaction. He was still inside me, a heavy, comforting weight that I didn't want to let go of.

Finally, he lifted his head, his lips finding mine for a soft, gentle kiss. A kiss that was full of everything we couldn't say out loud.

"Go back to sleep, Grace," he murmured, his voice soft and full of a tenderness he rarely showed the others. "I've got you."

As he shifted to pull out, I tightened my arms around him, holding him close. I wasn't ready to let him go yet. I wasn't sure I'd ever be ready to let any of them go again. He seemed to understand, settling back against me with a soft sigh, his body relaxing into mine.

Sleep, when it came again, was a deep and dreamless thing. I was anchored to Bones, his body a solid, warm wall behind me, his arm a heavy weight across my waist, holding me close. The world had shrunk to the space between us, a pocket of safety in the dark. I drifted, secure and sated, the lingering ache between my thighs a pleasant reminder of our secret, silent encounter.

The next time I surfaced, it was different. A gentle but persistent pressure was pulling me away from my warmth. I was being untangled from Bones' embrace, his arm carefully lifted from my hip. A soft groan of protest rumbled in my chest, but a hand was there, stroking my hair back from my face.

"Shhh," a familiar voice whispered, a low, amused tenor that was distinctly not Bones. "Come here, Gracie. My turn."

Legend.

My eyes fluttered open, and I could just make out his silhouette in the gloom. He was kneeling on the floor at the foot of the bed, his expression unreadable in the low light. He eased me from the mattress, his hands strong and sure on my waist, guiding me down until my knees met the plush carpet. Bones didn't even stir, a testament to his utter exhaustion. On my other side, AB was a still, silent mountain, and Voodoo's soft snores continued unabated from the far side of the bed.

I blinked up at Legend, my mind still fuzzy with sleep. "Legend?"

He didn't answer with words. He answered with his body. He was already kneeling, his legs spread slightly, and in the dim light, I could see him. His cock was thick, straining, the head flushed and dark and so ready it made my breath catch. He reached for me, his hands gripping my hips, and pulled me forward, onto his lap.

"Ride me," he commanded, his voice a raw, urgent whisper.

I didn't hesitate. I rose up on my knees, positioned myself over him, and sank down. The thickness of him spearing me stole the air from my lungs. It was a sudden, intense stretch, a deep, full pressure that would have been almost too much, too fast. But it wasn't. I was slick and open from Bones, from his cum still coating my insides, and Legend slid into me with an ease that was as shocking as it was intoxicating.

A sharp, breathy gasp escaped me, and his mouth was on my chest instantly, sucking and nipping at my breasts, his tongue swirling around my sensitive nipples. The dual sensations of him filling me so completely and his mouth on my skin sent a jolt of pure electricity straight to my core. My hands found his shoulders, my fingers digging into the hard muscle as I tried to ground myself.

He lifted his head, his eyes locking with mine in the near-darkness. Then he kissed me, a deep, possessive kiss that tasted of hunger and a dark, playful promise. He broke away, his lips hovering just over mine.

"Ride me," he repeated, his voice a low growl. "Ride me until you come."

A breathless, incredulous laugh escaped me. The sheer audacity of it, of him orchestrating this in the middle of the room while the others slept, was heady. I leaned in, my lips brushing against his ear. "Do we have to be quiet?" I whispered, the words a challenge, a tease.

He grinned, a flash of white teeth in the gloom, and his hands tightened on my hips, urging me to move. "Sure," he murmured, his voice laced with wicked amusement. "But if they want to wake up and watch... I'm fine with that too."

The playful words sent a fresh wave of heat through me,

a thrill so potent it made my head spin. The idea of being watched, of them waking up to see me like this, with Legend buried deep inside me, was an intoxicating secret. I began to move, a slow, rolling rhythm that had me lifting up and sliding back down his thick length. Each downward stroke was a delicious, deep friction that made my toes curl.

He let me set the pace, his hands guiding me, his thumbs stroking the skin just above my hips. He watched me, his gaze hot and heavy, drinking in every shift of my expression, every soft sigh that I couldn't quite suppress. The room was silent except for the soft slap of our skin and the quiet sounds of our breathing. I was lost in it, lost in the feel of him, the dark promise in his eyes, the sheer, unadulterated pleasure of it all.

I could feel the tension building again, that familiar coil tightening low in my belly. I moved faster, chasing it, my body taking over, my hips grinding against his. Legend's hands slid up my back, pulling me down until my chest was flush against his, his mouth finding my nipple again, sucking hard.

That was all it took. The sharp, delicious pull of his mouth sent me over the edge. I came with a muffled cry against his shoulder, my body shattering, my inner muscles clamping down around him like a vise. He groaned, a low, guttural sound of pure satisfaction as he followed me, his hips jerking up into me once, twice, before he stilled, his own release flooding me.

We stayed like that for a long moment, locked together, our bodies trembling in the aftermath. I was boneless, utterly spent, my head resting on his shoulder as I tried to catch my breath. He held me, his arms wrapped around me, his face buried in my hair.

Finally, he lifted his head, his lips finding mine for a

soft, lingering kiss. "Good girl," he murmured, his voice thick with satisfaction.

A small, tired smile touched my lips. He eased me off his lap, his touch gentle, and helped me to my feet. My legs felt like jelly, and I swayed slightly. He chuckled softly, steadying me with a hand on my waist.

"Back to bed with you," he whispered.

"I need to clean up," I mumbled and he used two fingers to push the cum sliding out of me back up.

"No, I like you like this. All filthy and filled from us."

I really didn't have it in me to argue as he lifted me easily and settled me into the warm spot between AB and Bones again, but this time, I was facing Legend. He stretched over me a moment longer, just watching me, a look of raw, possessive tenderness on his face. Then he leaned in, pressed a soft kiss to my forehead, and whispered, "Go to sleep, Gracie."

Stealthily, he withdrew and returned to his own spot on the bed and I closed my eyes. A feeling of profound contentment washed over me. Sleep came quickly this time, pulling me under with the promise of more secrets to be shared in the dark.

The third time I woke, it was to the soft, pearlescent light of dawn filtering around the edges of the heavy curtains. The world outside was beginning to stir, but in our little cocoon, all was still. I was lying on my side, facing AB, his arm draped loosely over my waist. The others were breathing deeply around me, lost in their own dream worlds. The air was cool on my skin, but AB was a furnace of warmth beside me.

I blinked my eyes open slowly, and his were already open, watching me. There was no intensity in his gaze this time, no dark hunger. It was soft, open, and impossibly tender. He leaned in and pressed a gentle, lingering kiss to my lips. It was a kiss that said good morning, a kiss that was full of a quiet, steadfast affection that made my chest ache.

His fingers came up to stroke my cheek, his touch feather-light. "Hey," he murmured, his voice the softest I'd ever heard it.

"Hey," I whispered back, a sleepy smile curving my lips. I snuggled a little closer, content to just float in this peaceful moment with him. But as I shifted, I felt him flinch beside me, a sharp, almost silent intake of breath. I pulled back just enough to see his face. His brow was furrowed in a line of discomfort.

"What is it?" I asked, my voice barely audible.

He gave a small, self-deprecating shrug. "Just a cramp. And I'm sore." He gestured vaguely with his free hand toward his thigh. "Too many hours folded over that laptop."

I knew that feeling all too well. The ache of being held in one position for too long, the muscles protesting in stiff, angry knots. I looked at the tense line of his jaw, the faint exhaustion still lingering in his eyes. An idea, warm and wicked, began to form in my mind.

I leaned in, my lips brushing against his ear. "Do you want a distraction?" I whispered.

He let out a soft, breathy chuckle, the sound vibrating against my cheek. "What did you have in mind?" he asked, his voice laced with genuine curiosity and a hint of intrigue.

I pulled back just enough to meet his gaze, and I gave him a slow, deliberate wink. "You have to be quiet," I whispered, my tone a conspiratorial caress. "But I think this could work."

Understanding dawned in his eyes, followed by a flash

of heat that made my own body hum. He didn't say a word, just watched me, his gaze intense and unwavering as I began to move. I kissed a slow, deliberate path down his chest, my lips tracing the hard lines of his muscle, my tongue flicking out to taste the salt of his skin. He was warm, solid, and he tasted like home.

I continued my journey south, my mouth exploring the ridges of his stomach, my hands stroking his hips. I could feel his muscles tense beneath my touch, could hear the way his breathing hitched in his throat. I reached the waistband of his sweatpants and hooked my fingers into the soft cotton. I looked up at him one last time, my eyes asking for permission. He gave a single, sharp nod, his jaw clenched with anticipation.

I tugged the sweats down, just enough to free him. He was already hard, thick and heavy in my hand, the tip flushed and beading with moisture. I leaned in and took him into my mouth, a slow, deliberate glide that had him sucking in a sharp, silent breath.

Loving that I didn't need to rush, I took my time. This wasn't about frantic need or a race to the finish. This was about him. About taking care of him. I moved with slow, deliberate care, my tongue stroking the sensitive underside, my lips creating a tight, slick friction as I bobbed my head. I used my hand to stroke what I couldn't take, my fingers curling around his base, my thumb brushing against his balls.

His thighs began to tremble and his hand came up to tangle in my hair. He fisted his grip but seemed to keep from yanking it. He was trying so hard to be quiet, to keep his pleasure contained, and it was the sexiest thing I'd ever felt. Every suppressed groan, every sharp inhale, every subtle shift of his hips was a testament to the control he was exerting, and it drove me absolutely mad.

I took him deeper, relaxing my throat, swallowing around him. The guttural sound that escaped him was muffled by the pillow he'd pressed to his face, and I felt a surge of feminine power. I was doing this to him. I was the one making him fall apart.

He inched closer, his body tightening like a drawn bow. I increased the pressure slightly, my strokes becoming a little faster, a little firmer, my tongue working him relentlessly. And then he was coming, his hips bucking up into my mouth as he spilled himself down my throat with a long, muffled groan.

Sealing my lips around him, I swallowed every drop until he was completely spent. I savored the ache in my jaw, the slight burn in my throat, the intimate proof of his pleasure. It was a mark of possession, a silent claim, and I wouldn't have traded it for anything.

I slowly released him, pressing a soft, final kiss to his tip before tucking him back into his sweats. When I looked up, he was watching me, his chest heaving, his eyes dark and heavy with an emotion that went far beyond simple satisfaction.

He reached down, hooked his hands under my arms, and dragged me up his body until our faces were level. He crushed his mouth to mine, a deep, hungry kiss that tasted of him and of me and of everything we'd just shared. It was a kiss of gratitude, of possession, of pure, unadulterated need.

When he finally pulled back, his forehead was resting against mine. "Do you feel better?" I whispered, a smug little smile playing on my lips.

He let out a low, rich chuckle, the sound vibrating

through his chest and into mine. "Immensely," he murmured. "Want me to..."

I pressed a finger to his lips, I'd come a few times already tonight. "This was about you," I whispered, nuzzling another kiss to his lips. "I love making you feel good."

"Then mission accomplished, Gracie." He shifted, rolling onto his side and pulling me with him, pillowing my head against his chest and tucking the blankets around us.

A part of me wondered how Voodoo would wake me up even as sleep pulled me back down with a smile on my face.

TWENTY-TWO

VOODOO

I woke up to the scent of her. It wasn't just the clean, sweet smell of Grace's skin, though that was always there. It was the scent of sex—musky, sharp, and undeniably hers, layered with the deeper, rawer heat the other men had left on her. A claim staked in the dark.

My eyes were already open. I'd been awake. I'd been awake when Lunchbox eased her from Bones' arms, the dip of the mattress pulling me from a light doze. I'd been awake while her soft huffs and his grunts punctuated the slapping of their skin.

I was awake when she came back, the scent of her satisfaction mingling with Lunchbox's sharper, spicier scent. I'd listened to the soft, muffled sounds, the rustle of sheets, the quiet gasps she tried so hard to swallow. When Alphabet twitched with his sudden cramp, I'd been about to offer help—but my firecracker got there first.

Watching her suck him off had been an exercise in torture. Perfect, sensual, hedonistic *torture.* Each time, my dick had gotten a little harder, a little more insistent, until now, in the pale light of dawn, it was a steel bar against my stomach, so hard it actually fucking hurt.

Assholes. The lot of them. They'd kept me up most of the night, taking their turns with our girl while I was left to listen, to imagine, to ache. I could hear them now, the deep, even breathing of the dead asleep. Bones, Alphabet, Lunchbox. All of them sated and dreaming.

But I wasn't.

My gaze fell on her. Grace was curled against Alphabet's chest, her face tucked into his neck, looking soft and well-fucked and utterly beautiful. A slow grin stretched my lips. They'd had their quiet, secret moments in the dark. They'd had their gentle, tender wake-ups. They'd had their fun.

My turn was going to be loud.

I slipped from the bed without a sound, my movements fluid and practiced. I stripped my sweats and t-shirt on the way to her. I paced along the edge of the monstrosity of a bed until I stood at the foot, looking down at her. Alphabet's arm was still draped over her, but it was a loose, sleepy hold. I reached down, my fingers wrapping around her ankle.

Her eyes fluttered open, hazy with sleep and confusion. She looked up at me, and a slow, sleepy smile bloomed on her face. "Voodoo," she whispered.

"Firecracker," I murmured back, my voice a low growl. "Time to get up."

I tugged, and she came willingly, a pliant, warm weight that I easily pulled from Alphabet's grasp and down to the foot of the bed. I knelt on the floor, positioning her on her back and laid out before me, her legs spread. The others were beginning to stir, the scent of her and the movement finally penetrating their sleep-fogged minds. I didn't give a shit. Let them watch.

I didn't start with my cock. I wanted her ready. I wanted her begging. I slid two fingers inside her, and she was slick, wet, and open. A testament to the night. A fucking playground. I curled my fingers, finding that spot instantly, and began to stroke her, hard and fast.

Her back arched off the mattress, a sharp gasp tearing from her throat. "*Voodoo...*"

"Yeah, that's it," I grunted, my thumb finding her clit and rubbing in tight, merciless circles. "Let them hear you, Grace. Let them know what I'm doing to you."

It didn't take long. Her body was already primed, already humming with leftover pleasure. Within a minute, she was coming, her inner muscles clamping down on my fingers as a sharp, keening cry escaped her lips. I felt the bed shift as Bones sat up, his gaze sharp and assessing. Lunchbox was propped up on an elbow, a slow, knowing grin on his face. Alphabet just watched, his expression unreadable.

I didn't give her a chance to come down. I positioned myself between her legs, notching the head of my cock against her entrance. Then I drove into her in one hard, deep stroke. Her scream was cut off as the air was forced from her lungs, her eyes going wide with shock and pleasure. I didn't wait. I didn't let her adjust. I set a brutal, punishing rhythm, my hips snapping against hers, fucking her so hard the entire bed started to rock.

"Voodoo!" she cried out, her hands fisting in the sheets. "Oh fuck, Voodoo!"

I leaned over her, my body covering hers, my mouth next to her ear. "You like that, Firecracker? You like being fucked where everyone can see?" I reached down with one hand, pinching her nipple, rolling the hard peak between my fingers. She sobbed, her hips bucking up to meet my thrusts. My other hand snaked between us, my fingers finding her clit again, rubbing it in time with my strokes.

I was fighting my own release, gritting my teeth, holding it back. I wasn't done with her yet. I wanted more. I wanted to drown in her. I wanted her to scream so loud they'd hear her in the next town.

I pulled out, ignoring her cry of protest. I flipped her over, manhandling her until she was bent over the bed, her hands braced on the mattress and their gazes firm on her. I nudged her legs wider with my knee. Then, gripping her hips, I bent over her, my chest to her back, and slammed back into her.

The angle was deeper, more intense. I fucked her hard, my balls slapping against her with every thrust. I reached around, one hand teasing her nipples, the other sliding down to rub her clit. Then I let my fingers drift lower, tracing the tight, puckered ring of her asshole.

She went rigid, a choked gasp escaping her. I circled it, teasing her, applying just the slightest bit of pressure. That was it. That was what broke her.

"*Fuck!*"

Her scream ripped through the quiet room, raw and uninhibited and absolutely fucking perfect. It was a sound of pure, unadulterated pleasure, and it was all for me. Her pussy convulsed around me as she came, and that was all it took. I let go, my own orgasm ripping through me like a tidal wave. I buried myself deep inside her, my body shuddering as I poured myself into her.

For a moment, the only sound was our harsh, ragged breathing. I slowly pulled out, and she collapsed onto the mattress, a boneless, trembling heap. I looked up. Bones, Lunchbox, and Alphabet were all staring at her, their expressions a mixture of shock, amusement, and a raw, undisguised hunger. They looked like a pack of wolves who'd just watched another predator take down the kill.

Assholes had kept me up all night. Turnabout was fair play.

I lifted Grace into my arms, her body limp and beyond relaxed against mine. She blinked up at me, a dazed, sated smile on her face. I carried her toward the adjoining bathroom.

"Round two," I murmured against her hair.

I pushed the door open with my foot and stepped inside, kicking it shut behind me. Bones spit out a sharp angry curse from the other side of the door. Triumph filtered through the passion. I'd gotten even for the shower stunt he'd pulled on me. I turned on the water, letting it run hot as I held her, the sound of the spray drowning out anything else. Just me, my girl, and the sweet sound of payback.

The steam from the shower clung to the air, thick and warm, smelling of soap and her. I had Grace backed against the tiled wall, her legs wrapped around my waist, my cock still buried deep inside her. She was limp against me, her head resting on my shoulder, her breath coming in soft, satisfied little puffs against my neck.

I'd already made her come once with my mouth, lapping up the combined taste of all of us until she was a trembling, whimpering mess. Then I'd fucked her against the wall, slow and hard, just to feel her clench around me when she came again.

"Alright, Firecracker," I grunted, my voice rough. "Time to actually get clean."

She let out a weak, breathy laugh as I lowered her to her feet. Her legs were shaky, and she had to brace a hand against the wall to steady herself. I took my time, soaping up a washcloth and running it over every inch of her skin. It was less about getting clean and more about claiming every part of her, marking her with my touch, my scent. She just stood there and let me, her eyes half-closed, a contented little smile on her face.

When we were done, I shut off the water and grabbed a fluffy towel from the rack. I lifted her out of the tub, setting her gently on the bathmat before I began to dry her. I was methodical about it, rubbing the soft cotton over her skin, starting with her arms and moving down her body.

She was so relaxed and at ease, I didn't think I'd ever seen her drift like this. The cat that got the cream. A deep, pretty flush colored her cheeks and the tops of her breasts, a flush that had nothing to do with the heat of the shower and everything to do with me.

I knelt in front of her, drying her legs, and she giggled. It was a light, happy sound, full of an exhaustion so profound it had tipped right over into giddiness.

"What's so funny?" I asked, looking up at her and utterly enjoying the view.

She shook her head, her damp hair tumbling around her shoulders. "Nothing," she said, but then another giggle escaped. "Okay, not nothing. I'm just thinking."

"Dangerous," I teased, running the towel up the inside of her thigh. She shivered.

"I'm just thinking," she said, her voice dropping to a conspiratorial whisper, "that I am going to be walking funny for the rest of the day."

I let out a low, triumphant chuckle. "Good," I said, pressing a soft kiss to her hip bone. "A reminder."

"A reminder of what? That you're an animal?" she shot back, but there was no heat in it. Only affection. "That you're all animals?"

"That you're mine," I corrected, my voice going low and serious. I stood up, tossing the towel aside and pulling her into my arms. Her skin was still warm, her body soft against mine. "Ours. And that I take care of what's mine."

She looped her arms around my neck, tilting her head back to look at me. Her eyes were shining, a brilliant, happy blue in the soft light of the bathroom. "You're all ridiculous," she murmured, but she was smiling.

"Maybe," I conceded, leaning down to kiss her. It was a slow, deep kiss, a kiss that tasted of satisfaction and something more. Something that felt a whole lot like forever. "But you love it."

"God help me," she breathed against my lips. "I do." Another soft sigh after our kiss. "Voodoo?"

"Hmm?"

"You said you loved me last night."

A warm feeling settled in my chest. Once upon a time, the idea of saying those words to a woman would have been anathema. What the hell did I have to offer to one? But Grace? Grace had been filling in all the gaps in my soul since we rescued her all battered and bruised. Since the night in a hotel room when she let me help her forget for a little while...

"Yes."

"Did you mean it?" All at once, I wanted to kick myself, she shouldn't have to ask me that.

"Yes," I told her, dipping my head to press a softer kiss to her lips, an oath, a promise, a dare.

Her eyes shone as she stared up at me. "I love you so much."

"You have no idea how much I treasure that, and you." I scooped her up and kissed her longer this time. Taking the time to fully explore her lips, her mouth, to savor and to taste. "You're the best damn thing that ever happened to me, Firecracker."

Then, because they'd let us have this time, I nudged the door open and carried her back into the bedroom. The three of them were still there, propped up against the pillows, watching us. There was no anger in their eyes, no resentment. Just a deep, simmering heat and a measure of their own hunger. They looked like they'd just watched the main event and were waiting for the encore.

I laid Grace down in the middle of the bed, right in the space they'd left for her. She landed with a soft little oof, sprawling out like a starfish. She looked at them, a slow, wicked grin spreading across her face.

"Well?" she said, her voice husky and full of challenge. "What are you all waiting for?"

And just like that, the exhaustion was gone. The tension was gone.

I settled back on the edge of the bed, watching her. Grace was a fucking vision, sprawled out in the middle of our makeshift bed, her skin flushed and glowing, her hair a wild, damp tangle around her face. She looked thoroughly, beautifully, and completely fucked. And she was smiling. A real, genuine, ear-to-ear smile that made my chest feel tight.

Bones was the first to break the silence, his voice a low, cautious rumble. "You sure you're up for this, Dollface?" He was always the one to worry, the one to check the margins, to make sure she wasn't going to break.

Grace's head lolled to the side, her gaze finding his. Her smile didn't falter; it just sharpened, all sassy and full of fire. "I can handle you," she said, her voice a husky purr. She let her eyes drift from Bones to Lunchbox, then to Alphabet, and finally back to me. "I can handle all of you."

The sheer, unadulterated confidence in her voice was a fucking turn-on. We all knew she could. We'd just spent the night proving it. But to hear her say it, to see the challenge in her eyes... that was something else entirely.

Just as she finished her declaration, a loud, insistent growl rumbled through the quiet room. It came from her stomach. The sound was so unexpected, so perfectly normal in the middle of all this, that it broke the tension like a rubber band snapping. Her eyes went wide for a second, and then her grin widened.

"But," she announced, her tone full of theatrical importance, "I do demand breakfast after."

Lunchbox, ever the one to seize an opportunity, snaked a hand out from under his blanket and wrapped it around her wrist. He tugged, and she went willingly, rolling across the mattress until she was flush against him. He pulled her in for a deep, lingering kiss, a kiss that was full of promises and a hunger that was just as on the edge of desperate as it had been a few minutes ago.

When he finally let her up for air, he rested his forehead against hers. "I'll feed you anything you want, Gracie," he murmured, his voice a low, intimate promise.

Grace's eyes sparkled with pure, unadulterated mischief. She slowly, deliberately, began to walk her fingers down his stomach, tracing the lines of his abs until they reached the waistband of his boxers. She paused, her fingers tapping lightly against the fabric right over his cock, which was already showing a renewed interest.

"Anything?" she whispered, the single word a loaded question full of sin and suggestion.

I couldn't help it. I threw my head back and laughed, a loud, booming sound that filled the room. The whole situation was fucking ridiculous. We'd just spent the night taking turns with her, a silent, competitive marathon in the dark, and now here we were, negotiating breakfast like it was a peace treaty. My firecracker, holding court in the middle of the bed, completely naked, sore, and demanding pancakes while teasing Lunchbox about a different kind of meal.

It was perfect.

Glancing at the faint light coming through the curtains, I figured it had to be pushing noon. Breakfast was more like a late brunch. And from the way Grace was shifting, trying to find a comfortable position, my firecracker was definitely going to be walking funny for the rest of the day.

Winning all around.

TWENTY-THREE

GRACE

Late afternoon sunlight slanted through the blinds, painting stripes across the kitchen floor. I leaned against the counter, squeezing a lemon slice into a glass of iced tea. The warmth of the house seeped into my bones. The night—and day—had left us all ragged, but content in ways I hadn't thought possible.

Legend was in his element. Two massive pans of lasagna were bubbling in the oven, garlic bread lined up on a sheet tray, and a salad sat waiting on the counter. The smell of rich, meaty sauce curled through the house, wrapping us in comfort and hunger. He glanced my way, a crooked smile playing on his lips. "Nibble on this while I finish the last of the salad?" he said, waving a forkful of crisp lettuce in my direction.

I grinned. "You know me too well."

Voodoo was on a phone in the corner, low tones flowing, fingers tapping on the counter for rhythm. AB had his laptop open, a labyrinth of tabs and documents spread across the screen, eyes scanning faster than I could follow. Bones sat at the table, quietly carving up notes from our last interrogations, occasionally grunting when he found a connection.

It was domestic, somehow. And yet the undercurrent of danger never left.

"We're not just playing house," I murmured, taking a bite of the salad. Crisp, tangy, and perfect.

"No," AB said, not looking up. "We're putting together profiles. La Madrina, Castillo. Names, patterns, connections. It's not cute, but it's necessary."

Voodoo lowered the phone, rubbing at his eyes. "I got the latest contacts lined up. We'll cross-check with the names we pulled from Ignacio and Sinclair. Start filling in gaps."

Bones looked up from his notes, reading out the fragmented recollections,

"Phillip Rojas—de Roja—red. He added red hat or red fish.Then another was a Felipe or Phillip with a very strong British accent. Spanish last name, British accent."

He snorted. "He said there was a Xander something, German or South African, so that gives me Dutch. Also it would match Zander Visser."

He flipped to another page."Next two were… garbled," Bones admitted. "But a starting point."

"Mykel, Michael, Mikael. Then Jochem, Jorchan, or Jon though he said it might be Russian but definitely Eastern European."

"Those aren't the same thing," I said as I took a sip of the tea. I had no idea when Legend decided to make it up, but everyone was having some. Despite the chill outside, it seemed perfect to go with the lasagna.

With a hint of a smile, Bones glanced at me. "No, they aren't. But this is where we are."

AB's brow furrowed. "The Michael one… that has to be

Maikel Castillo. Castillo Cartel. Skin trade. That's one branch of their operations. Nothing good there." He paused, fingers hovering over the keyboard. "We'll need to cross-match with existing intelligence and see who's clean—or not."

I chewed on my lip. The names, the accents, the half-remembered details... it was like piecing together a map of snakes that coiled and wound in and around each other. Every thread pulled revealed another lurking danger.

"Legend," I said, trying to lighten the moment, "when are you going to let me sneak a piece of that garlic bread before it disappears?"

He glanced up, mock indignation in his eyes. "The salad is your warm-up. You get the real prize when it comes out of the oven. But I'll save you a slice... if you promise not to collapse over it."

Voodoo snorted, leaning back in his chair. "Our girl hasn't collapsed yet. Not emotionally, physically... and morally. A slice of lasagna won't tip her over the edge."

"I'm holding out for a second slice," I said. Goblin brushed against my leg as if he agreed, tail wagging.

The room was alive with small domestic battles and the murmur of serious work. Somehow, in the middle of scheming, research, and lasagna, it felt... like home. Safe.

The safe house felt safe. I shook my head. That was what it was supposed to feel like and yet, I almost wished we were back at Base. That all of this was solved and Am was home and...

Some of my good mood ebbed.

I didn't realize Bones had been watching me until he pushed back from the table. "Don't do that," he said quietly.

"Do what?" I tried for light, but my voice didn't quite make it.

AB didn't even look up from his computer. "She's spiraling. She's thinking about her sister."

Voodoo slid his phone into his back pocket. "And—Base," he added, head canted as he studied me. "Probably imagining every worst-case scenario all in a row. Firecracker, don't make us pry you out of your own head."

Legend's spoon froze mid-toss in the salad bowl. "We're okay," he said softly. "You're okay. We're going to get her back." His tone was light, but the promise underneath was steel.

I swallowed, staring into my tea like the lemon slice could give me the answers. "I know. I just... I want her safe. I want all of this over. I want to stop finding new snakes under every rock."

Bones crossed the room in three deliberate steps. His fingers brushed under my chin, tilting my face up until my eyes met his. "We'll handle the snakes," he said. "You just keep breathing."

My throat tightened. Not painfully. Just... truthfully. "And looking pretty?" I went for light, but the words still came out a little thick.

"You don't have to try to do that," Bones told me. "You just *are*. But if you need to scream, to cry, to throw things—aim at Voodoo, I'm still healing."

Laughter broke through me and I cracked up. I wasn't alone as chuckles erupted from the guys. Voodoo even winked at me when I glanced at him.

Legend clapped the salad bowl down with theatrical flourish. "Speaking of snakes, one of these names Sinclair gave us? The Eastern European one? Alphabet thinks that one might connect to the Kirov arm of Castillo."

AB nodded, finally looking up. "Kirov Syndicate does a lot of business with the Castillos—more than I expected based on what I'm seeing here. Logistics, transport, weapons, laundering. If they've got a representative in La Madrina's upper echelon, that's... concerning."

"Understatement," Voodoo muttered.

"How?" I set my glass down. "I don't know all of these guys, does that mean La Madrina isn't just a cartel or a trafficking outfit.?"

AB turned the laptop toward me. Several profiles, photos, and redacted reports filled the screen. "They're a consortium," he said. "A network. Not one family, not one nationality. They operate like a private equity firm that happens to specialize in every awful thing imaginable."

"A fucking hydra." Bones' jaw flexed. "We cut off one head, others spring up."

Voodoo waved a hand. "Sure, but we're not aiming to take down the whole organism." He paused a beat then shot me a look. "We're not going for the whole thing *yet*." That amendment was definitely for me and each time I didn't think I could love them more, they did things like this. "For the *moment*, we're targeting the nodes most likely connected to Am's disappearance. La Madrina is a threat, yeah, but we can't discount the Castillo Cartel."

"Maikel Castillo," Bones repeated, settling a hand on my lower back and beginning to rub a slow massage to ease the tension making it taut. "I agree with Alphabet's assessment there. Do we have a full profile on him?"

"We will by the time we finish dinner," AB said, glancing at me with raised eyebrows as if verifying I was okay with this. I knew, without a doubt, that he would work right through food if I needed it.

"After dinner is fine," I murmured, leaning into Bones'

caress as he shifted to work both of his thumbs into the knot between my shoulder blades. I wanted to melt.

Legend opened the oven to check the lasagna, and a wave of molten, savory aroma washed over us. Cheese bubbling, sauce simmering, garlic perfuming the whole house. It almost felt indecent compared to what we were discussing.

"Lasagna and organized crime," Voodoo said with a lazy grin when my gaze landed on his. "This is balance, baby."

A smile curved my lips. He loved me. That just set off a stupid set of bubbles detonating through my system. Was it cognitive dissonance to be so happy and so worried and freaked out all at the same time?

Probably. But, here we were.

I exhaled slowly, letting the warmth from the kitchen seep into the fear that kept rattling around inside me. "Okay," I said. "To sum up, Maikel Castillo is one of the names. Zander Visser is another. And Phillip Roja... or Rojas... we still need to chase the spelling."

Legend nodded. "AB's running variations. British accent, Spanish last name—it narrows things."

"Unless it's fake," I pointed out.

"Then we cross-reference accents with travel corridors, visas, or shell corporations," AB replied. "Accent's harder to fake consistently over a course of years."

"So we hunt through a forest of snakes," I said softly.

Bones touched my shoulder. "It's not strictly hunting. We're tracking. We may have to backtrack, but we're still taking it one step, one print at a time."

Legend slid the garlic bread into the oven, humming under his breath. "Besides," he added, "we're doing it together. Makes us damn hard to beat."

"And we have lasagna." Voodoo tipped his head back

and rocked his chair up on two legs as he let out a devilish chuckle. "Evil organizations fear lasagna."

That earned a laugh from all of us, small but real.

Goblin trotted over, nudging my leg until I bent to scratch behind his ears. His tail thumped, steady and grounding.

Home. Or the closest thing to it.

I wasn't foolish enough to believe we were safe in the world—not with the names being laid out on AB's laptop like little flags on a battlefield.

The oven timer dinged, and Legend grinned like he'd just won a championship. "Darling Gracie, and the rest of you reprobates, lasagna is officially served."

Bones gave my waist a squeeze before he dipped his head to press a kiss to my throat. "About time. I was beginning to forget what food looked like outside of a protein bar."

Voodoo leaned against the counter, arms crossed, smirking. "You're not going to melt if you wait five more minutes, Cap."

"I'm not melting, I'm starving," Bones countered, and the argument dissolved into laughter.

Legend swept the pans onto the table, steam curling upward, rich sauce and cheese wafting through the kitchen. Garlic bread followed, golden and crisp, and he set down a large bowl of salad with a flourish. "Now, who wants to eat like civilized humans instead of zombie mercenaries?"

I perched at the end of the table, Goblin circling my feet, tail flicking in anticipation. Legend gave me a playful smirk. "Or... civilized humans with a very special guest in their lap."

Before I knew it, he had scooted his chair out slightly,

and I settled onto his lap. "What are you doing?" I asked, half amused, half expecting a trick.

"Feeding you," he said simply, sliding a forkful of lasagna onto my plate and offering it up. "You look too good to let you shovel it into yourself alone." His warm gaze held mine, mischievous and soft all at once.

I laughed, taking a bite. "You're terrible."

"I'm wonderful," he corrected, feeding me another bite with a grin. "And don't even think about arguing. You're in my lap."

Bones groaned. "I can't even look at this without my teeth rotting from the sugar."

Voodoo leaned back in his chair, arms folded. "Jealousy is unbecoming, Bones."

"I'm not jealous," Bones muttered, but his jaw gave him away.

"You're all ridiculous." AB just smirked, still scanning the laptop while stealing a few forkfuls of salad.

"AB, you should take a break."

He winked. "Five more minutes."

I took another bite, letting the warmth of the food and Legend's easy attentiveness wash over me. For a while, we didn't talk about names, cartels, or La Madrina. We just ate, teased, and laughed, the sounds and smells wrapping us in comfort.

Goblin bumped my knee, but Voodoo rose and got him his dinner. "Sorry buddy," he murmured. "I blame Lunchbox."

"Me too," AB concurred and the guys laughed, not that Legend seemed to mind.

I leaned back slightly, sighing contentedly. "I could get used to this. Domestic chaos with lasagna and you guys making stupid faces."

"Domestic chaos is my specialty," Legend said, holding up the crispy, delightfully savory, garlic bread for me to bite into and I let out a lusty little sigh. It tasted even better than it smelled. "And yes, we adore your stupid expressions, too."

Bones snorted. "She's enjoying it. Stop pretending this isn't what you're here for."

"I am enjoying it," I admitted, smirking through a mouthful. "It's... nice. Real."

Voodoo leaned forward, tapping a fork against his chin. "We need more of this. Otherwise, you get cranky. And trust me, cranky Firecracker is terrifying."

I laughed again, reaching for the piece of garlic bread on the side of my plate. Legend caught it first. "Nope," he said, lifting another forkful of the cheesy lasagna to my lips. "You get everything in moderation. Even happiness."

I leaned forward, biting the lasagna, and caught the gleam in his eye that was half mischief, half affection.

The warmth of our laughter, the smell of the food, and the steady presence of the men I trusted—it all pressed together like a shield around me. For a little while, I allowed myself to believe nothing could touch us here.

Then the quiet beep of AB's laptop cut through the kitchen. One soft, insistent tone. Search complete.

Everyone froze.

AB's fingers hovered over the keyboard. "Uh... that's... interesting." His brow furrowed as he scanned the screen.

Legend straightened in his chair. "Interesting how? Good interesting or bad interesting?"

AB's eyes darkened. "Both, maybe. I've got movement on Maikel Castillo. Him and a couple of others linked to the cartel. Patterns shifting. We might have just found their latest operational node."

Bones' jaw tightened. "Figures."

Voodoo let out a long breath. "Well, that escalated fast."

I slid off Legend's lap, my stomach knotting slightly, the comfort of dinner and teasing slipping away. "Show me," I said quietly.

AB turned the screen toward us, the glow painting our faces. "This isn't small," he said. "And it's not going to be easy. But it's a start. And we have to move carefully."

Legend's hand found mine across the table. "We do this together," he murmured. "Like everything else."

I nodded, swallowing hard. The domestic bubble we'd been in—warm, teasing, safe—had burst. But now, like always, we were together. That made the danger manageable.

For now, at least.

TWENTY-FOUR

ALPHABET

The sun beat down on the tarmac as our little charter touched ground, heat shimmering off the concrete like a mirage. Bones was already scanning the horizon, Voodoo quietly muttering into a phone headset, as he locked down vehicles, backup, and supplies. Lunchbox handled the flight and the landing with his kind of calm competence.

Goblin dozed next to me, head tucked against my left foot with his tail flicking lazily, so patient with all of us. Grace sat next to me, a digital tablet open where she was scanning news from a few different countries. The fact she could read as well as converse in multiple languages let me assign a task for her.

I ran a hand over my face. Time had blurred since New Jersey. Days, nights, late nights, early mornings... and somewhere along the line, Miami had become the next logical step. Yakov Dvorak—our closest lead to one of the names Sinclair had butchered in his interrogations—was here. Somewhere. We were going to have a little chat with him.

I muttered under my breath, mostly to myself, "And Sinclair really was an idiot."

Bones glanced at me, one brow raised. "You think?"

"I know," I said, flat and honest. "I mean, the guy couldn't remember his own name, let alone match accents to last names. British Spanish? German South African? He was barely coherent."

Voodoo snorted without looking up. "You're being charitable."

I grinned, though the tension in my chest didn't ease. I'd call it professional courtesy, but that prick didn't deserve anything resembling it.

Lunchbox shook his head, eyes on the runway as he taxied toward the hangers. "You're enjoying the chaos more than you're letting on."

"Maybe," I admitted. "Maybe I am. Doesn't mean I'm not ready to put a bullet in Yakov's—" I caught myself, though Grace's amused eyes said she'd heard that last unspoken syllable. "—have a *conversation* with him."

She snorted and leaned in to brush a kiss against my cheek. "Conversation first. Bullet later?"

Delight flared under the tension coiled in my gut. I'd never imagined a Gracie in my life—never mind woven into all of ours. But she fit, seamlessly. Her personality, her ferocious spirit, that unshakeable determination—hell, even the sensual way she melted for us when she wanted to. I couldn't have pictured any of this before her. Now I couldn't imagine a world without her.

Miami's heat pressed against the cabin walls, and the air conditioning fought valiantly to keep the sweat at bay. I could already feel the temperature climbing inside as Lunchbox taxied us to our rental slot.

"You think he knows we're coming?" Voodoo asked, tilting his head toward me.

"Maybe," I said finally. "Maybe not. Depends on who's been in his circle recently. But he's careful. Calculated. He won't act before he has to. Or how much information on the FBI 'sting' at the Delaware port has been shared."

"It's not in the news," Grace said. "Not here or overseas. I've been watching for it over the past few days. Nothing."

I leaned back in my seat, fingers drumming lightly against the armrest. "Then hopefully, we're ahead of this curve."

Whether we were or not, we'd get him. Then he'd talk. The only real questions were how long it would take and how much force we'd have to apply. Miami wasn't going to be clean or easy. Nothing ever was. But we were ready.

The chances of our target sitting somewhere, thinking he was untouchable were high. That also meant we had some time to close the trap on him. The fact he was a possible link to the Madrina outfit, the Kirov Syndicate, or both. If both, then he was the elusive one Sinclair couldn't, or wouldn't, remember.

"Don't mind me, I'm hoping Mr. Dvorak is as on point as Sinclair. Easier conversation that way."

Voodoo twisted to look at me. "You're hoping he's incompetent, just so we can get in, talk, and get out?"

"Absolutely," I said with a shrug. "I'm here for efficiency."

Lunchbox leaned back, eyes closing briefly. "Efficiency, style, and chaos. That's our motto, Alphabet. Don't forget it."

"I thought your motto was 'we improvise,'" Grace said, shutting off her tablet.

Bones snorted. "No, that's just our style."

The banter eased the tension in my shoulders and the ghost of a cramp in my thigh. I rubbed at it slowly, to help with stretching it. Too many hours locked in the same position was increasing the discomfort.

"Cars are here. Might need to pick up some other gear, but I've had our safe house cleared and stocked." Voodoo was already unbuckling his seat belt as Lunchbox began shutting down the engines after the wheel chocks were in place.

We split once baggage and gear were loaded. Miami humidity hit like a wet towel the second we stepped outside the air-conditioned cocoon, and by the time Goblin hopped into the backseat of the black SUV Bones was driving with Grace. Neither of which looked any happier about the weather than I was.

I gave myself a couple of minutes to stretch before I climbed into the passenger seat. Bones adjusted the mirrors, flipped the A/C to blast, and muttered, "Miami. Damned frying pan."

"I was already missing Montana," I said, buckling in.

His grin was sharp. "Same."

Static crackled in my earpiece as Lunchbox's voice came online. "Everybody green?"

I tapped my mic. "Yep. We're rolling."

Voodoo chimed in next from their SUV. "On your six. Firecracker, you good?"

"I'm perfect," she said, leaning forward between the seats. "Are we heading to the safe house first or...?"

"My Miami contact confirmed Dvorak was at a warehouse in Little River this morning. Left fifteen minutes before wheels down," Voodoo answered.

We pulled out of the private side of the airport, weaving into traffic. Miami had its own pulse—cars darting, horns blaring, palm trees whipping in the wind. So alive it was almost distracting.

Bones grunted. "Good timing. For once."

"We need to check traffic cams," Lunchbox said, tone shifting into mission mode. "You're up, Alphabet."

I already had my laptop open and attached to the wifi available in the vehicle. Honestly, the ability to be online everywhere made my job so much fucking easier. I flicked through the feeds, fingers flying, hacking into the city's real-time camera loop under multiple spoofed addresses. Dvorak wasn't careful. He was arrogant. He moved like he wasn't afraid of being followed.

"Got him," I said. "Silver BMW, custom plate. Heading east. Looks like he's heading to the Marina District. Or one of the hotels in that area."

"Good to know he's stupid," Voodoo muttered.

Grace leaned in, eyebrows rising. "Is he stupid? Or is he arrogant? How could he even know we would be looking?"

"Arrogant. Someone in his position should assume someone is always looking." Bones shook his head. He wasn't wrong. Anyone in a position of power who handled the kind of things Dvorak did was practically waving a red flag to get attention with his custom plates.

Nose wrinkling, Grace leaned back in her seat. "So we're heading to a marina?"

I marked the route on our shared map. "ETA for us, twenty minutes with traffic."

Grace touched my arm, a soft brush grounding me. "What if he changes his route?"

Blowing out a breath, I headed back to monitor the reports coming in from the bot I'd released. "Tracking his license plate right now, any deviations, including not exiting near the marina and I'll have the updates."

Bones navigated over to the fast lane like a Nascar pro. "How do we want to handle him? Bag and tag? Surveillance? Intimidation?"

Amusement speared me at Bones' list. All were viable.

"Conversation," Grace said sweetly.

I shot her a look. "Conversation first."

Her smile widened and while sunglasses hid her eyes, I'd bet they were glowing. "Bullet later."

Voodoo laughed. "You sweet talker."

The warmth of that settled in my chest—quick and bright, like a spark in dry tinder. I scanned the traffic feed again. "Okay. Dvorak just parked. Marina District. South pier."

"Tourist side or private docks?" Bones asked.

"Private."

Voodoo whistled. "Expensive taste. Means he thinks he's safe."

"He's not." I shifted screens to look for cameras at the marina. I wanted to know where Dvorak was going. Specifically.

The Marina District glittered like money dipped in sunshine. Private yachts, sleek hulls, polished rails. Everything gleamed with the quiet smugness of the wealthy who thought they were invisible.

Bones pulled into a lot two blocks away, tucked the SUV between a pair of oversized pickup trucks. Voodoo and Lunchbox parked opposite us.

Salt wind hit the second our doors opened, humid and warm enough that even Goblin huffed.

I did a quick scan of the marina feeds from my phone, linking them to my laptop.

And there he was.

"Target visual," I murmured, angling the screen so

Grace could see. "White-and-graphite yacht, private slip F-12. Dvorak's on deck."

Bones followed my gaze. "What's he doing?"

"Pretending he's on vacation," I answered as Voodoo and Lunchbox joined us. "Drink in hand. Shirt unbuttoned. Absolute prick energy."

Grace squinted at the feed. "That yacht is—something else."

"Understatement," Lunchbox muttered.

"We need him off the boat. Or isolated on it." Bones was already tracking angles, exits, and choke points.

Grace tilted her head. "I could distract him."

Bones gave her a long, slow look. The kind that said *absolutely not, what the hell are you thinking* without a single word.

She blinked back at him. "What? This is definitely bikini weather. And he's on a boat. Approaching directly would be a challenge, right?"

I didn't argue with her. Because she wasn't wrong. If anyone could convince him it was Gracie, the Bones whisperer.

Gracie strolling down that dock would draw every hetero eye for fifty yards. Probably more, really. Voodoo pressed his lips together like he was trying not to grin. Lunchbox failed at trying not to grin.

Bones closed his eyes briefly like he was negotiating with the universe. Then he exhaled through his nose. "Alphabet, get us access to the private docks."

"Already on it," I said, fingers flying. The marina's security system was a joke. "We'll be able to slide right through the gate for the next fifteen minutes or so."

Bones jerked his chin. "Voodoo. Lunchbox."

Both men straightened.

"Rock, paper, scissors. One of you goes water-side, approaches from the stern."

Voodoo groaned. "Really?"

Bones didn't blink. "Really."

They squared off like five-year-olds.

"Rock, paper, scissors—shoot!"

Lunchbox threw scissors.

Voodoo threw rock.

Lunchbox swore under his breath. "Damn it."

But Voodoo grinned like a wolf. "Enjoy the swim."

Bones cut their bickering with a low growl that snapped them both to attention. "Voodoo, get eyes on the starboard walkway. Lunchbox, water approach. Alphabet covers cameras. I'll monitor movement."

Then he looked at Grace.

"Dollface," he said low, warning already woven into his voice, "you're distraction only. No contact. No approach. No physical closeness."

She flashed him a grin that was one hundred percent trouble and sunshine. "I know. Just distraction."

That didn't reassure any of us. She was already stripping, right there, between the car doors with Voodoo and Bones playing blocks as Lunchbox stripped off his own shirt and down to shorts.

The bikini she put on should be illegal.

"Why is that in her wardrobe?" Bones asked abruptly but Voodoo just grinned.

"Because I knew she'd look fucking fantastic in it."

He wasn't wrong, it was damn near the same blue as her eyes and the silky triangles barely covered her anywhere. It was probably good she did laser treatments or wax or whatever it was she'd told us about, because the one at her groin wouldn't have hidden a single curl.

Now I kind of wondered what the all natural look would be like for her. Maybe I could tempt her into growing it out just to tease me.

Shaking off that distracting thought, I split my attention between Grace sliding on the strappy-heeled sandals and watching as Dvorak put a phone to his ear. Another man had come up on deck, but he was bringing Dvorak another drink and it looked like something to eat.

Maybe a guard. Maybe not. But definitely an employee.

Grace grabbed a beach tote from her bag and shuffled some stuff over. "Okay, good to go and the taser is loaded just in case."

Lunchbox barked a laugh. "That's our girl."

Bones muttered something under his breath that I was almost sure approximated, "*I'm going to lose my mind.*"

Grace leaned up to kiss his cheek, and whispered, "I'll be good."

Bones did not believe her. None of us did. But she would be effective.

I pulled the dock schematics up on the laptop and tossed a waterproof comm to Lunchbox. "Your best angle is the rear swim deck. Cameras loop for the next twelve minutes."

Lunchbox took the comm, rolling his neck like he was prepping for a prize fight. "Copy that."

Bones shot us all a look, his expression blanking as he went into "go" mode. "Let's move."

The team scattered—Bones to the overlook, Lunchbox toward the back pathway, Voodoo toward the seawall, and Grace heading for the dock gates.

I stayed in the car with the wifi and the air conditioning, monitoring feeds and updating the team. Goblin stuck his head through the seats for a pet and I scratched him between his ears.

"I know buddy, we're in wait mode again."

Miami sun glared off the water. Waves lapped the hull of the yacht and Yakov Dvorak lounged like he owned the world. Not for long.

Not when Grace hit the dock like she'd been born to it.

I mean—she kind of had. She walked with confidence, and a kind of sensuous purpose that made people take notice. Her sensuality was so natural, though, none of it feigned. But this? This was a whole different level.

That bikini threatened to end a lot of lives today. I appreciated my various camera angles so I could watch her, watch her back, and on the people around her. She—well, she was always going to be the best damn part of my job.

Her hips rolled with an effortless sway, sun catching on her skin like she'd been brushed in gold, that tiny blue bikini moving like it had signed some kind of legal agreement not to slip even a millimeter.

"Jesus Christ," Voodoo muttered over comms from his dock vantage. "She looks like trouble wrapped in sunshine."

"She *is* trouble wrapped in sunshine," Lunchbox said, smug as hell, somewhere in the water as he moved toward the stern. "Our trouble."

Bones' voice came in low, controlled, already on edge. "Three men approaching from starboard pier. All ogling. If one of them even tries to talk to her—"

"Something-something violence?" I supplied.

"Exactly," he growled.

Grace kept strolling.

Every yacht crew member in a twenty-yard radius forgot how to do their jobs. A deckhand dropped a coil of rope. A captain almost tripped over his own feet. Two dudes in board shorts actually walked into each other head-first.

Grace didn't even glance at them. She knew the world watched her and she took it as her due. The funny thing was, our Gracie was not this ethereal dream strolling in the sunshine. She was warm, funny, more than a little sassy, and loving as hell. Nothing remote about her.

Her tote bag swung lightly off her shoulder, the heels she'd slipped on clicking a rhythmic beat along the planks.

"Taser still in the tote?" Voodoo asked.

"Loaded," she answered, casual as sunshine. "Not planning to use it."

"Good girl," Bones said automatically—then choked when one of the board-short idiots tried to wave her over.

Grace didn't slow. Didn't even flick her sunglasses their way.

Bones muttered something savage that was too low for me to fully catch, but I was pretty sure had to involve where he would shove that guy's body parts.

I grinned. "Target's looking. He sees her."

On my feed, Yakov Dvorak straightened. He'd been lounging with a drink, trying too hard to be suave, but Grace killed whatever composure he had left. He was up, leaning over the rail, trying to get a better look at her like he expected the universe to hand-deliver her to him.

Grace paused right at his peripheral vision.

Just a half-step.

Just enough to make him think he mattered.

"That's a damn nice pause," Voodoo commented.

"Let her work," Bones growled.

Dvorak's voice carried faintly over her comm. Accented, confident, sleazy.

"Hey! Beautiful! Come up, have a drink!"

Grace tilted her head, sunglasses glinting, pretending like she *might* consider it.

That was all the bait he needed.

Dvorak moved to the stern, waving her closer like a man who'd never encountered consequences. "Come, come—don't be shy!"

Grace's smile was sweet enough to rot teeth. "Oh, I'm not shy."

I almost choked on a laugh.

Over comms, Bones muttered, "I'm going to murder him."

Voodoo: "You say that like it's new."

Bones: "He's inviting her up."

Me: "He thinks he's winning."

Bones: "He's not."

Grace drifted closer to the boat, stepping into the perfect sightline Voodoo had plotted. She tucked a stray curl behind her ear, lifted her chin, and looked up at Dvorak in a way that suggested she liked attention—but on her terms.

And the moment he stepped down onto the swim deck to meet her—

Lunchbox struck.

A blur of motion beneath the water.

A flash of arms around Dvorak's legs.

A muffled yelp.

And then—

Splash.

Dvorak vanished beneath the surface like a stone tossed by an angry god.

Grace didn't flinch. She just pivoted smoothly and continued her stride, as serene as a model on a runway, letting the men behind her erupt into shouts and whistles like they had nothing to do with her.

I lost it. Straight-up barked a laugh in the SUV.

Bones let out a gust of air that might've been relief or amusement or some dangerous mix of both.

Voodoo snorted. "Just like taking candy from a baby."

"I got him," Lunchbox said a second later, voice triumphant as he hauled Dvorak under the dockline. "Package secured."

Grace kept walking—hips swaying, sunglasses on, tote bouncing—never once looking back.

I shook my head, still smiling like a fool.

"Good work, Gracie," I muttered, heart doing something stupid. "Weapons-grade badass. Pretty sure I just fell in love with you twice while watching."

Bones exhaled. "Get her back to the SUV."

"On it," Voodoo said, already moving.

I leaned back in my seat, pulse steady and satisfied.

Target snatched. Grace flawless. Mission unfolding exactly the way we'd wanted.

Her voice came back warm and smug. "Told you I'd be good." She was so much better than good it was ridiculous.

"So good," I said, "you are definitely getting at least two cookies."

That earned me a throaty laugh and I grinned.

TWENTY-FIVE

GRACE

The Miami safe house was cool, dim, and smelled faintly of industrial cleaner and old hardwood. It was not as nice as the last place in New Jersey, but definitely nicer than a couple of the other bolt holes we'd used. They really had mastered the art of functional, quiet, and safe because my dangerous men had decided to make it so.

Dvorak was downstairs in the reinforced laundry room, zip-tied, gagged, and very, very angry. He'd been sputtering in Russian, German, and I was pretty sure Czech or maybe all three before they shut the door. Now it was blessedly muffled.

We weren't touching him.

Not yet.

Apparently, you didn't interrogate when you were tired and hungry. Bones said he already wanted to hurt him, but we needed it to employ *productive* techniques not just pain. I was still learning how this world worked.

Upstairs, in the open kitchen, the guys had torn into takeout cartons. We had a little bit of everything from everywhere. I was actually a fan of the tenders and fries so I stuck with them. Fried food or not, it was damn tasty. Goblin sprawled under the table, tongue lolling, waiting for someone to drop chicken.

Legend finally stopped pacing and leaned against the counter and gesturing with one of his french fries. "He's going to be a problem."

Bones grunted. "He's already a problem."

"Most problems can be solved with a wrench," Voodoo said cheerfully. "Or the threat of one."

I lifted my brows. "You think he'll respond to tools?"

AB snorted around a mouthful of noodles. "In my experience *everyone* responds to tools."

"People are simple creatures," Voodoo said. "Fear is universal."

Bones passed him a water bottle. "Fear only works when they believe we're willing to use it."

"We are." Legend looked up then, eyes sliding to me for a second.

I couldn't argue with that. I'd seen what they were capable of—merciless precision when necessary. It should have scared me. I think it had once... but honestly, now? No, it didn't frighten me and it never would. Because they were never merciless with me. They let me step out when I needed it and be a part of it when I needed that too.

I leaned forward, elbows on the kitchen island. "What does he want? What does someone like Dvorak care about?"

"Money," AB said. "Power."

"Not dying," Voodoo added.

Bones shook his head. "He's loyal to someone bigger. He'll stall. He thinks he can outlast us."

"That's adorable," Legend said with a thin smile. "He doesn't know us yet."

Goblin made a huffing noise like he agreed.

I swallowed a piece of spicy rice and watched them—my men—fall into the same easy rhythm they always did. Even in the middle of chaos, they fit together like puzzle pieces. AB was thinking three steps ahead, Voodoo three steps sideways, Legend ready to blow it all to hell, and Bones grounding everyone.

Me? I was... learning where I fit. Lucky for me, it seemed to be everywhere and nowhere at once.

"What if he doesn't break?" I asked.

Bones met my eyes. His were that dark, stormy gray, steady, warm at the bottom in a way that always made my chest go soft. "Everyone breaks."

"Well, that's grim," I said, going for the levity that made the corners of his lips curve upwards.

"Accurate though," AB added.

Legend set his food down with a sigh. "We just need what he knows about the Madrina connection. Then whether this ties to the Kirov Syndicate or some rogue faction. He's a step to the next part."

"He knows a name we don't," Voodoo said, wiping his hands. "I can feel it."

"Well, we can't exactly wait for him to feel chatty," I said, leaning back. "How long do you think we have before someone knows he's missing?"

"Not that long." AB wrapped more noodles around his fork. "I can scrub some digital traces, but not all. If he has an alert protocol with his organization, a timer's already running."

Bones braced both hands on the counter, head down for a moment.

Legend's gaze flicked to him. "What does your gut say?"

"Still debating that." But Bones focused on me, not Legend. "What is your impression of him?"

That question startled me. "Really?"

He nodded once, straightening and folding his arms as he regarded me. "You have a fresh point of view. That can be useful."

I thought for a minute, chewing slowly. "He's arrogant. You saw it—he walked onto that deck because I smiled at him."

Bones grunted. "That's not unique."

"No," I agreed. "But the way he carries himself? He isn't used to being powerless. Or ignored. Or dismissed." I replayed the way he strode across that deck and then down to the platform to get me to come aboard. He had no doubt at all that I would *obey*.

"Starve him of attention," AB said slowly.

"Reverse interrogation?" Voodoo glanced from me to AB. "Think that would work?"

"If he's as arrogant a prick as he was acting, Gracie is right. We starve him of attention. We don't threaten him, talk to him, or even look at him. Just leave him in that room in the dark."

"Until he's desperate for the interaction, for something..." Legend rubbed a hand along his jaw. "Could take us too long to action anything, especially if he digs in."

"Maybe," Bones said. "But we can afford a few hours to test the theory."

"I don't think it will take that long," I admitted and when Bones raised his brows, I shrugged. "He's not a guy you say no to. I've dealt with lots of those over the years. They don't hear no, they don't see it, they don't want it. You have to praise and pamper their egos to get them to think they said no. Ignoring him is going to make him angry."

The slow, dangerous smile that curved Bones' lips sent a flutter through my system. He was so damn handsome when he looked like that.

"I like it. Cold isolation. No sensory input. No timeline. No context. Let him sit in that room and realize we don't actually need anything from him."

"But we do," Voodoo said.

"We do," I agreed. "But he won't know that if we aren't asking him."

Legend let out a low whistle. "Look at you. Scary brilliant."

Warmth hit my cheeks. Embarrassing.

"Told you, weapons grade badass," AB said and his blue eyes practically sparkled. "Wanna take Goblin for a walk with me? It'll hopefully be a little cooler now."

"I do," I said, closing the box on my food. "Let me grab shorts and a tank top." I was still in the bikini. As nice as the a/c was in here, I was only just now starting to get pebbling on my skin.

"Damn," Voodoo said with a grin. "I am really enjoying that bikini."

"Remind me to burn it later," Bones said, but there was absolutely no heat in his growl. He caught my arm and tugged me back for a kiss. "Take a weapon with you."

"I will," I promised, though he swallowed the words when he deepened that quick kiss to something a lot deeper, wetter, and groan worthy.

"Hands off, Cap, she said she was going to take a walk with me," AB said, though there was laughter in his voice.

"Fine," Bones said, right before he actually nipped my lower lip. There was no mistaking the stiffness in his jeans or the fact his eyes were scorching.

He finally let me go with one last murmured, "Weapon.

Pocket." Then he smacked my ass—slow, claiming, absolutely unhelpful—and turned back to the table.

AB snickered. "Subtle."

Bones didn't even glance over. "Wasn't trying to be."

I rolled my eyes, grabbed my shorts, tank top, and a cross-body bag that would still hide my taser, and got changed. The tank was soft and loose, the shorts comfortable, and the night air would feel good after the day's humidity.

Goblin perked up the second we walked toward the door, tail thumping as he trotted ahead in his harness.

The moment we stepped outside, Miami felt like a different city. The heat hadn't vanished, but the sticky heaviness from earlier had faded. A breeze swept in from the ocean, cool enough to raise goosebumps along my arms. The sky was going dusky—peach melting into lavender—and streetlights flickered to life one by one.

AB walked beside me, one hand in his pocket, the other holding Goblin's leash loosely as he inspected the land around us.

"God," I said on an exhale, "this is so much nicer than earlier."

"No arguments here." He stretched a little, rolling his shoulders. "My brain was melting. Bones looked five minutes from homicide. Lunchbox looked two."

"And Voodoo?"

"Voodoo was considering sacrificing one of us to whatever heat god controls Miami."

I laughed, the sound tumbling out easier than I expected. The breeze tugged at my hair, and AB reached over and smoothed a strand from my cheek without even thinking about it. His fingers lingered.

My chest did something warm and stupid.

We walked half a block before I spoke again. "Hey… I want to ask you something."

AB glanced at me, eyebrows rising, face open and ready in that way he had—like he tuned into me before I even knew what I wanted to say.

"Shoot."

I swallowed. "When you said earlier that you fell in love with me twice… did you mean it?"

A slow, unmistakably genuine grin spread across his face—boyish and wicked and soft all at once. The kind of smile that could ruin a girl forever.

"Gracie." He shook his head, amused. "No."

My stomach dropped.

Then he added, "I think I've fallen in love with you every day since we met."

Heat bloomed under my skin—hotter, deeper than any Miami sun.

He kept talking, voice lower, as sincere as the day he'd made the deal to always tell me the truth if I did the same. "Though really? If we're picking moments? It was the day you nailed Bones in the back of the head with the remote."

A choked laugh ripped out of me. "He deserved it."

"Uh-huh." He grinned wider. "He did, but even when he threw you over his shoulder and carted you up the stairs, you didn't give even an inch."

Pride fisted inside of me. "I almost escaped."

"You did." He shook his head. "Gave me a heart attack when I realized you'd gotten out that window." His lips still curved into that smile that he seemed to reserve only for me. "Took my breath away. Kept fucking stealing it too."

Heat suffused my face and when he caught my hand in his, I interlaced our fingers.

"See, that was it. Right there. You didn't let Bones

intimidate you. You didn't let *any* of us intimidate you. And every time we pushed, you pushed back. You kept us honest."

He paused, eyes softening in the fading light.

"You made us... better."

For a second, the world went quiet—just the slap of palm fronds in the wind and Goblin's happy little huff.

I didn't know what to do with the tenderness in his eyes. I'd learned to read all their moods—Bones' smoldering heat, Legend's stormy intensity, Voodoo's sharp amusement—but AB's softness always hit different. It wasn't loud. It wasn't showy.

It was steady. Quiet. Like he'd opened a door that was for me alone.

Goblin tugged forward, spotting a lizard on the sidewalk, and AB chuckled. "Someone's hunting."

"Let him. He's earned a hobby."

We walked the next few blocks like that, before we began to circle around—hand in hand, breeze cooling the sweat at the back of my neck, Miami humming around us. We weren't in any hurry, just a pair of lovers out for a stroll. It was kind of magical.

Finally, I said softly, "I think I fall a little more in love with you every day too."

AB didn't say anything for a moment. He just stopped walking, turned toward me, and kissed me—slow, careful, reverent. A kiss that said *I hear you. I feel it too. I'm here.*

Goblin tried to wedge himself between our legs halfway through and AB broke away laughing.

"Cockblock," he told the dog fondly.

Goblin wagged his tail, unrepentant.

I leaned into AB's side, heart full, mind clearer than it had been all day.

When we finally headed back toward the safe house, AB murmured, "Let's get inside. The others will want to get started soon."

"They're going to interrogate him now?"

"Nope," he said, still grinning and I blinked up at him.

"Then what do they want to start?" But as soon as I asked, I knew the answer and the playful way he waggled his eyebrows told me I was right. "Are you guys going to rock, paper, scissors it?"

He laughed, that deep, warm timbre that sent butterflies bursting through me. "Maybe. Maybe we'll go for poker again…"

Then he shot me a sly look.

"Or maybe we'll just go in and find a bedroom and not mention it and let them come find us?"

"God, woman, I really do love how you think." He dropped another fierce kiss on my lips. "Don't ever leave me, Gracie. Cause you really do get me."

"I promise." Because they got me too. All four of them. "AB?"

"Hmm?"

"Do I ever get to learn your birth name?" I wasn't gonna say real, not anymore. They were their real selves with me.

He shot me a sidelong look. "I'll think about it."

"Well," I said with a little skip. "That's not a no." Maybe orgasm denial would net it for me.

Oh, now there was a thought.

He eyed me again. "Not sure I like that look on your face."

"What look?" I turned wholly innocent eyes up at him.

"Don't like that one either."

I was still giggling when we made it back to the safe house.

TWENTY-SIX

GRACE

It took nine hours for Dvorak to finally crack.

Nine. Hours.

Eleven if you counted the two hours after dinner they'd left Dvorak to stew in the dark silence of the reinforced laundry room. Then, hours involving him sweating through the zip cuffs, hours of Bones and Voodoo tag-teaming him like it was a sport, nine hours of me sitting in the corner looking deliberately bored out of my mind. That last part was actually the hardest—holding still, holding quiet, pretending the whole thing wasn't picking at me like sandpaper under the skin.

The best part of it all was studying how they worked the man's arrogance against him. Bones paced in front of him, arms crossed, muttering insults in that deadpan way that made them sound like clinical diagnoses. Voodoo followed it with his brand of slow-burning menace, talking almost softly while he poked holes straight through Dvorak's defenses. They didn't rush. They didn't need to. They'd both smelled blood in the water from hour one.

Legend and AB were in reserve. AB would research any

data we received and Legend just made silent appearances with food or drinks for us. He played the role of manservant in his own way. Each time he came and went without so much as acknowledging Dvorak whether he was speaking or not, seemed to agitate the man even further.

It was *almost* funny.

Through it all, I watched. That was my job today—sit, stare, and be forgettable.

Except Dvorak kept glancing at me.

Not often. Not obvious. Just enough for the back of my neck to prickle every time he did it.

"Let's start again," Bones drawled around hour eight, leaning his hip against the table. "You keep telling us you're important, but so far all I've heard is hot air and a tragic understanding of modern deodorant."

That earned a twitch. The vein in Dvorak's forehead throbbed more frequently now. A traitor that confessed how on edge no matter how he tried to play it.

Voodoo grinned like he'd been waiting for it. "Don't fade on us now, *blbec*. You insist that La Madrina's been pulling everyone's strings. Which strings, exactly?" He paused then, switching his attention to Bones, a faintly disgruntled look on his face. "But how much could an errand boy really know?"

Simple pleasure burned in me at Voodoo's spot-on pronunciation. He'd asked me for a couple of words for dumbass or jackass, in Czech. Insulting a man in his own language was another way to knock his pride down. I'd boiled it down to one word, it was a rough translation and not as vulgar as some of the others, but Voodoo *nailed* it.

Bones merely shrugged. "Depends on what errands they sent him out on, I suppose. But considering how easily we snared him and how lax his security..." He didn't even bother to finish the comment, because his tone held nothing but contempt.

Dvorak puffed up, his arrogance blooming like mold. "You Americans think you understand anything," he sneered. "La Madrina's network reaches farther than you can imagine. Korkov aligned with us because he saw power—real power. And the syndicates—" He caught himself, too late.

Bones lifted his brows. "Syndicates plural. Good to know."

"Huh," Voodoo said, affecting real surprise. "Maybe we're getting somewhere."

Awareness of his slip hit Dvorak's expression like cold water. He leaned back, chin high, masking it with derision. "It doesn't matter. None of this concerns you."

"No?" Bones jerked a thumb at me without looking. "What about her?"

I stayed slumped in the chair, arms folded, face neutral. My eyelids felt heavy from the act—boredom as a weapon.

Despite his attempt to ignore me, Dvorak failed—at least briefly—when his gaze flicked toward me once more. "Castillo business is irrelevant," he said dismissively. "You are irrelevant. Whatever storm you people bring among yourselves, it has nothing to do with La Madrina."

Nothing to do with La Madrina. Nothing to do with me.

That should've been reassuring.

It wasn't.

Because when he looked at me—really looked—there was something sharp underneath. Not recognition, not exactly. More like he was trying to place a smell or a taste he almost knew. It was uncomfortable, being relegated to a thing instead of a person.

I tapped my fingers against my thigh to keep the unease

contained. So, he indicated he didn't know me and logically, fine, that made sense. His comments on the Castillos were vague, surface-level. Nothing personal. Nothing specific. Also, fine. Madrina and Castillo were named separately by Sinclair based on what the guys said.

Maybe they were all competitors and one really did not have anything to do with the other. The whole thing gave me a headache. I increased the pace of my tapping, trying to keep myself in check. Particularly because each time he glanced at me, it was like fingers brushing the back of my neck.

Voodoo must have noticed, because he tilted his head, flicking a glance at my hand as he shifted position and placed himself between me and Dvorak. It was so smooth, I almost missed it.

Relief spread through me at the interruption of Dvorak's gaze. I blew out a breath and let my expression relax minutely. The contradicting sensation of pretending to be bored when I just wanted to scream at the man to get answers was stretching me taut.

"You're doing great," Voodoo said, cheerfulness bordering on suspicion. His emotional whiplash routine was getting absurd—skeptical, theatrical, grim, dismissive, repeat. "No, really. Keep monologuing. We'll have a full organizational chart by dinner."

Dvorak snarled.

"Clock's ticking." Bones deadpanned. "And we've got nowhere else to be."

Nine hours. Nine grinding, strategized hours.

And finally—finally—after all of that, Dvorak *broke*. It didn't happen slowly, even if we'd been wearing him down. After those initial slips, he'd grown almost stone-faced, refusing to say a word

He talked about La Madrina's expansion, about Korkov's role, about the syndicates she was stitching together like a patchwork empire. It wasn't a full picture—just enough to confirm they weren't working alone, that the consortium was growing because they were taking over areas where other syndicates and cartels were waning.

It was kind of sickening, really, how proud he was of all his "successes," like undercutting his competition before muscling them out. How he negotiated deals on fucking *price control* and *market share.* How they were utilizing new forms of *advertising* to get the message out.

The worst part was he could have been talking about cars or appliances for all the weight he put on the people who were their *product.* Beneath all of the nauseating details was the way he kept glancing at me. Particularly when Voodoo or Bones let him see me amidst their circling.

Their path confused and needled him because they didn't allow him to control the narrative or hold their gazes. Literally, they took all of his agency. On some level, I'm sure that ate away at him without him even understanding that they were reducing him to "product" the same way he did others.

I kept my face blank. My pulse wasn't.

When he finally sagged back in his chair, silent and shivering with exhaustion and fury, I rose. My legs were stiff from being still too long, but I kept it casual, stretching like this had all been tedious.

Bones shot me a question with his eyes.

I answered with a tiny shrug.

Because I didn't know either.

But as I drifted out like I didn't have a care in the world, something cold settled in my chest. Dvorak didn't *know* me, but somehow he recognized me on some level? At this point, I didn't know what was worse. Because if he didn't know *me*, then he didn't know *Am*.

That hurt a lot more than I expected it to. Because after that conversation, I should be much happier about the idea he didn't know her.

The second the door sealed behind us, the silence hit different. Thicker. Cleaner. As if the air out here hadn't been scraped thin by Dvorak's voice and his arrogance and the nine-hour tug-of-war over his ego.

The soundproofing swallowed the last of him, and I hadn't realized how tight my shoulders were until they dropped all at once.

The hallway outside the laundry room was washed in early sunrise—those pale, washed-out colors right before the sky decided what mood it wanted to have. Pink, blue, soft gold bleeding slowly through the reinforced windows like someone had dialed the saturation up too fast.

It was almost too bright.

I blinked against it, lifting a hand to shade my eyes. After hours in that dark, the light felt invasive.

Legend stood waiting for us, leaning against the wall with a tray balanced on one forearm. Breakfast sandwiches, bottled water, steaming coffee. Before anyone else could move, he crossed to me and put the coffee in my hands. *Hot.* Painfully so. Perfect.

He took the empty space in front of me without asking and wrapped me in a hug that was long and warm and grounding. I let my forehead rest briefly on his shoulder, inhaling the scent of soap and something faintly herbal.

"I *got* you," he murmured. Not loud. Not for anyone else.

Then he stepped back, eyes scanning me once before he nodded like I'd passed some invisible assessment.

Bones and Voodoo grabbed their food automatically, both more tired than they'd admit. Bones' jaw twitched. Voodoo scrubbed a hand over his face. Nine hours had to weigh on them too.

AB emerged as we reached the kitchen from the room he'd turned into a makeshift office, tablet in hand, bags under his eyes that were the perfect complement to our own.

"Okay," he said without preamble, "so I went through everything we pulled off Dvorak's devices. And cross-checked with the verbal intel you three wrung out of him like sociopaths." He gestured vaguely toward Bones and Voodoo, who gave him matching middle finger shrugs.

AB didn't smile.

"It's not the lead we hoped for," he continued bluntly. "Not... really a lead at all. Not directly."

A tightness pulled between my ribs. Not surprise. Just another echo of disappointment I wasn't ready to name.

Bones swallowed a mouthful of sandwich and washed it down with coffee. "Give it to us straight."

I slid into a chair at the dining table, both hands wrapped around the coffee. Even my eyelashes felt tired at the moment. Legend slid a breakfast sandwich in front of me along with hash browns, actual real, crispy cooked and fresh hash browns.

AB blew out a breath and tapped the tablet. "Best theory? Dvorak's people—Madrina—were running a separate operation alongside Ignacio. Parallel tracks. And based on financial discrepancies and shipment logs..." His voice softened. "...Ignacio was definitely skimming."

My jaw clenched. Hard.

"So," AB said gently, "when their people raided one of Ignacio's off-books transport hubs, it's very possible you were caught in that sweep. Wrong place. Wrong time. Wrong man lining his pockets."

My stomach twisted. Familiar discomfort. The kind that never quite left.

"But," AB added, more cautiously now, "there's nothing definitively tying you to Madrina's group before that point. No prior notation. No identifiers. No auction codes. Nothing personal. Which means..." He hesitated.

Voodoo lifted his chin softly. "Means we still don't know."

AB nodded.

"And," AB continued. "While we still have some threads to pull, we are running out of avenues to look."

My heart was a rock in my chest. "Wasn't there another name? The Maikel one?"

"He's dead," AB said. "Not a lot of data on that at the moment. Just—regime change. Looks like an internal war, not a lot of clear data at the moment, just..." His sigh said everything.

A thick quiet settled over the table. The heavy drape of it threatened to muffle the rest of the world. After all of it, we'd found so much and were no closer.

Legend crossed his arms, face unreadable. Bones dropped into the chair next to mine as Voodoo's gaze flicked to me, sharp and careful. But I was looking right at AB when he glanced up from his tablet, guilt etched into the lines on his face.

Unsurprisingly, it was Bones who broke the quiet. His somber, authoritative presence steadied me as he wrapped a hand around my nape.

"Grace." His tone was even gentler than I expected. "Do you want to keep looking?"

Just like that, every breath in my lungs froze. The room

felt too bright again. The sunrise too sharp. The coffee scalded my fingers but I held onto it like it anchored me.

I looked at each of them—these men who had dragged me back from hell, who followed me into shadows they never owed me. Men who were asking—not assuming, not pushing—what I wanted.

What *I* wanted.

Did I keep searching for answers that might not exist? Did I chase ghosts and fragments, push deeper into wounds that might never close? Did I want the truth badly enough to risk what it might do to me?

Or had I already seen enough to know that certainty was a luxury I'd probably never get?

"I..." My voice caught. I swallowed and tried again. "I don't know."

And the awful, honest part of it was—

I wasn't sure I ever would.

The words felt thin the moment they left my mouth—fragile, like they might splinter in the air if anyone breathed too hard.

No one did.

Bones didn't flinch. Voodoo didn't crack a joke to fill the silence. Legend didn't step closer. AB didn't try to offer some soft consolation or workaround. They all just... stayed. Present. Watching me without staring me down.

It was almost worse.

I dragged a hand through my hair, breathing out slowly. "It's like—I finally think I'm getting somewhere, and then it curves back into a dead end. And every time we hit another wall, it feels less like we're getting closer and more like we're just confirming that everyone involved—Ignacio, La Madrina, whoever—treated people like inventory. Which means I could've been anyone. A body in a room."

Meant she could have been anyone. If I didn't end up somewhere, maybe Am didn't...

My voice went quiet. "I don't know if there's an answer. Not anymore."

Legend's eyes softened, but he didn't intrude on the space I was fighting to hold. "Not every story's clean," he said, voice low.

Voodoo nudged the wall with his shoulder. "Sometimes the closest thing you get to peace is knowing which doors *aren't* the right ones."

"That's still progress." Bones massaged the tense muscles at my nape, his fingers working slowly as if he could help drain it all away.

Maybe. Maybe not.

I stared down at the coffee between my hands. Steam curled up toward my face, warm, comforting, grounding— something simple in the middle of everything that wasn't.

"I'm tired," I admitted. "Of chasing shadows that might not even be hers."

AB cleared his throat. "Then you don't have to keep chasing it." His tone was steady but not forceful. "We can stop. We can shift. We can reroute. You're in control of the pace."

I let that sit. My heart thudded hard against my ribs— slow, heavy, unsure.

"I don't want to... quit," I said finally. "But I don't know how much further I can push without losing myself in the process."

"Then say that." Bones' voice softened—not gentle, but solid. The kind of voice that made you feel like if the floor gave out, he wouldn't. "Tell us where you want the line."

My throat tightened. "I don't know where the line is yet."

"Okay," Voodoo said simply. "Then we'll help you find it."

No pity. No pressure. No one jumping in to fix things for me.

Just... support. Plain and uncomplicated and terrifyingly steady.

Legend stepped closer—not crowding, just easing into my orbit like he'd been keeping pace with my heartbeat. "Grace," he murmured, "you don't have to decide today. Or tomorrow. Or anytime soon."

My eyes burned, but I blinked it back hard. Until I decided, we were out here burning through their resources, their networks, their time—time they didn't owe me. They'd already done so much more than anyone ever had.

Legend held my gaze. "But whatever you decide—we're not letting you face it alone."

Something in me loosened. Not fully. But enough that I could breathe again without feeling like my ribs were made of wire.

"I don't know what I want," I repeated, quieter now. The truth sat heavy on my tongue until another truth pushed past it. "Except you. All of you. I want all of you in this with me. I want to..."

The words jammed in my throat. Tears caught behind them like gravel. I couldn't let go of Am. Couldn't let myself imagine the world where she was... gone. But I didn't know where to look next.

"Do we have any other leads?" I asked, though my heart already braced for the answer.

As my gaze moved from one face to the next—Voodoo, Bones, Legend, AB—I read it clearly. The answer was *not really*. Not cleanly. Not anymore.

"We're not done here," AB said firmly. "There are still some stones we can kick over."

But his eyes told the quieter truth, those stones might not hide anything.

I closed my own eyes and leaned back into the warmth of Bones' hand at my nape.

"Firecracker." Voodoo's voice was soft enough I almost missed it. When I opened my eyes, he'd moved—kneeling beside my chair, level with me. "We can finish up with Dvorak. Turn everything over to the Feds. Let them take the hammer to Madrina's side of the wall. Then we regroup. That's not the same as giving up."

"No?" I whispered. Wanting so badly to believe it.

"No," Bones answered, as unshakeable as bedrock. "It means we're giving ourselves breathing room. We rest. Recover. Restock. Get our feet under us. Meanwhile, Alphabet keeps digging, we keep our contacts in the loop, we tug threads and watch what shakes loose. And when we have intel..."

We move.

That promise lived bright and certain in their eyes.

"Until then... we go back to Base?" I asked.

Montana. The mountain. Their quiet place. Our safe place.

"Yes," Legend said, sliding his hand over mine on the table. "We take you home, Gracie."

Voodoo set his hand over Legend's. "We let you heal."

"We help you heal," AB corrected softly, adding his hand to theirs.

Bones covered them all with his own, squeezing the back of my neck gently. "And we don't give up. Ever. We're with you, Dollface. All the way."

Then Goblin shoved his head right up between all our

arms and nudged my knee with his nose like he was impatient to be included.

A watery laugh broke out of me. "What do you say?" I asked him. "Ready to go back to Base?"

His sharp bark echoed in the hallway—and the guys laughed, real and warm, something bright cracking through the exhaustion around us.

We weren't giving up.

I wasn't giving up on her. I never would. But I wasn't alone, and pretending I was didn't help any of us. We were stronger together—broken pieces braced against each other.

"Then let's go home," I said, more certain this time.

TWENTY-SEVEN

BONES

Two weeks after returning to Base, Montana welcomed us back with a snowstorm. Big, heavy flakes drifted past the windows like someone was shaking out a feather pillow over the mountains. The world outside was quiet, soft, and white—too peaceful compared to where we'd been, but that was the point of coming home.

Inside, the fire snapped and cracked in the stone hearth, throwing gold light across the living room. I sprawled in the large armchair, watching the flames chew through a fresh log. The whole place smelled like pine, cedar, and the faint sweetness of whatever Lunchbox had simmering in the kitchen. Something with apples, probably. He'd gotten even more weirdly domestic than ever.

The others were scattered around the open space. Voodoo pretended to read on the couch but was mostly watching Grace with the same quiet intensity I felt. Alphabet sat by the big window with his laptop open, fingers flying while Goblin snored at his feet, tail twitching every now and then.

And Grace…

Grace stood near the fire, arms folded, wearing one of my hoodies that swallowed her frame. She was staring into the flames like they were telling stories she wanted to hear.

We were settling back in. Slowly. Awkwardly. Carefully. Base had always been a retreat for the four of us—a place to breathe, to reset, to be something close to human again. But now it was hers too. Had been hers for a while, even if she never said the words out loud.

The trick was making sure she felt it.

Voodoo looked up at me from the couch, eyebrows raised as he asked without words whether I was going to say something to her or just keep hovering.

Hovering. The thought resonated with my internal disgust and I resisted the urge to grunt. I didn't *hover*, despite the number of times he or Lunchbox brought it up.

Alphabet snorted faintly and I spared him a withering look that didn't make him do anything more than grin. He was already focused on his laptop again and missed it. Or maybe he just ignored it.

We were all making time to be out here. In the past, we returned to Base, debriefed, treated any injuries, then retreated to our various corners and—

And nothing.

Alphabet did his work. Voodoo would read or research. Sometimes, he went out hiking as did Lunchbox. I— trained. It was what I had and what I did. I made sure they had what they needed and I trained.

The night before, we'd all gathered in here with popcorn, drinks, and slices of cake, which made Grace laugh, to watch a movie. Lunchbox had whipped up the cake because our beautiful girl had complained about the lack of chocolate to go with the popcorn.

We had chocolate bars, but she wanted those for the hot cocoa she made. A treat she'd introduced me to a couple of days before. I'd never been a fan of the stuff, but for Grace? Well, I'd drink it every day if she made it.

No, this time, coming back to Base had revealed differences in all of us. We spent more time *together* without working. Movies. Games—though it amused me to discover that Grace was quite good at first person shooter games. Something that Alphabet absolutely delighted in.

Lunchbox was teaching her to cook and she'd only set fire to the stove top once. Voodoo took her down to the gym and dancing two days after we'd gotten back. I'd never envied my team before. Yet, here I was, envying them their ease with her.

They didn't call what they were doing hovering. I resisted another snort. I didn't want to draw her attention to our focus. Not while the firelight played over the soft curves of her face and highlighted her in this soft golden light. We were all watching her, but they found ways to play with her, and I hadn't.

Maybe she wasn't as aware of it as we were, but there was a lost air about her that made her seem so infinitely fragile. After everything—the interrogations, the rescues, Dvorak's twisted game play, the dead-end leads—Grace needed space. Except she didn't always know how to ask for what she needed, and we didn't always know when to give it. So we watched. And waited. And stayed close.

The renovations upstairs were finally done. That had been a whole project of its own—Lunchbox and I had sketched it out over the course of our first thirty-six hours home. We had most of what we needed in storage, but we'd made two trips to town to fully stock the house and to pick up everything else.

It took us a week, but we'd devoted our time to the renovation. Knocking out the wall between my bedroom and hers doubled the size of the space. We'd painted it, letting her choose the palette after we'd sanded it smooth. Her choices included Indigo Ink for the "accent" wall, golden umber for the carpet and earthier accents on the curtains—seriously choosing those had been amusing—and walnut for the wood.

"The darker grain stands up beautifully against Indigo, and creates a high-contrast look with the umber. It's luxe, but also grounded," she'd said, when she held up the samples together. "Do you like it?"

Of course we liked it. Grace had come to life while she sorted through all the options and she'd made all of us choose from her favorites.

"It has to reflect all of you too."

In the end, the room came together beautifully. It still boasted the largest bathroom in the house and there was room to add an electronic fireplace that boasted multiple colors.

Voodoo had made a good call with that one. We'd added a pair of sofas up there to the space, once we'd finished the custom-built bed that took up one whole wall of the room. It would fit all five of us quite comfortably.

Lunchbox supervised the carpentry once Voodoo sourced the custom mattresses—a *pair* of Alaskan kings. They were the biggest I'd ever seen. But Alphabet had hunted down bedding in the same shades of umber and matching indigo for the pillows to match the room.

I'd never spent that much time thinking about how something *looked*. Functionality? Yes. Comfort? Yes. But looks? At the same time, I would have spent twice as much time on all of that because Grace had come back to life while we worked on it.

She didn't know the first things about sanding, hammering, painting, *or* building, but didn't shy away from a single activity. Not once. Though after the first time she threatened to throw a hammer, we established rules.

The last had been the art and the photos—she'd wanted pictures of us on the wall. All of us, so...we'd gotten to work. It was still in progress, but I had my own favorite up there. One that someone had snapped of her sound asleep and curled up against my chest. I had no idea which of them had taken it or when, but it went with the one of her curled up with me in the back of the van in France.

The day we finished, that was where all of us slept—including Goblin. What surprised me most wasn't the bed itself—it was how natural it felt now. Crawling in beside her. Feeling her pressed between us, safe and sound, her breathing softening as she drifted off—it was everything. The first few nights had been awkward as hell. Too many limbs. Too much shared warmth. Too much awareness.

Occasionally needing to smack the boys upside the head and once threatening to send them to their own rooms. Though, admittedly, Grace's laughter over that had been worth the irritation.

Now?

It wasn't weird at all. It was... home.

Grace shifted by the fire, shoulders drawing tight as she folded her arms. Even in silhouette she seemed to vibrate with upset. If I had to guess, she was spiraling into her thoughts again—too deep, too fast.

My cue.

I pushed up from the chair and crossed the room, stopping a step behind her so she didn't feel cornered. "Fire's not going anywhere," I said. "You can blink, you know."

She huffed a quiet breath. "Wasn't staring."

"You were absolutely staring," Voodoo said from the couch.

Grace flipped him off without turning around.

I smiled. Middle fingers had also become a familiar salute from her. Construction had freed her up her cuss like a sailor. Though I was determined to teach her to cuss like an Army grunt. We were just better. "How's the shoulder?"

She rolled it experimentally. "Better. Bruise is fading." A momentary distraction in our hand-to-hand three days before and she'd twisted her grip wrong, nearly dislocating her shoulder. I still winced when I thought about it.

"Good. Tomorrow, we pick back up with lessons."

She groaned like I'd announced her execution. "Bones…"

"You asked me to teach you," I reminded her, nudging her lightly. "And you're doing damn well. But you're not getting out of footwork drills."

"That's cruel."

"That's survival."

She looked up at me then, eyes reflecting the firelight—tired, but steadier than before. "Okay," she said softly. "Tomorrow."

We stood there for a moment, just listening to the crackling fire and the wind brushing against the windows.

I didn't touch her. Not yet. But she leaned just a fraction closer, enough that her shoulder brushed my arm. On purpose.

It felt like something real. Something earned. Something we were building together—slowly, carefully—brick by brick.

Behind us, Legend called out, "Dinner in ten!"

Grace sighed. "Are you sure I can't help?"

"You're helping me just fine *way* over there," he said with just enough laughter and humor in his voice to make her smile.

I looked down at her. "You hungry?"

"A little."

"Good. Eat. Then sleep. You need rest."

Her lips curved upward. Barely, but it counted. "What about you?"

"I'll sleep." I shrugged. "We all will."

"In our gigantic, ridiculous bed?" A note of real teasing crept into her voice as the firelight chased the shadows out of her eyes.

I snorted. "Dollface, that thing isn't a bed. It's a landmass. I'm pretty sure we need a map, a compass, and emergency rations just to locate each other in it."

She twisted toward me, grinning up with a spark I hadn't seen all day. "So what I hear you saying is that we should run some survival drills up there?"

The sultry glide of her voice hit me low and hot, damn near buckling my knees.

"If it involves full-body contact?" I arched a brow at her. "You won't hear a single complaint. From any of us."

"Hoowah!" Voodoo crowed from the couch, shameless and triumphant.

Grace broke into bright, helpless laughter—warm and alive—the shadows in her eyes scattering like they'd never existed.

Much better.

LEGEND

Two weeks back at Base, and Montana had done what Montana did best—buried the world in white and dared us to be anything but still.

Snow drifted past the big windows in lazy sheets, thick and soft as down. The fire crackled in the hearth, steady and warm. Goblin snored under Alphabet's desk. Voodoo pretended to read. Bones pretended he wasn't hovering. As for me? I was in the kitchen pretending not to stress-bake a third cobbler.

And Grace...

Grace stood near the fire wearing Bones' hoodie and a look that said she was two thoughts away from falling down some dark tunnel. She tilted toward the heat like a flower leaning toward the sun. She didn't even realize she did that—seeking warmth without asking for it. Seeking us without admitting it.

We were all adjusting to being home again. But she was the one relearning how to breathe.

Bones had gone to her first, because, of course he had. He always moved to protect without thinking, and she always softened just a little when he did. I watched them from the kitchen counter as I chopped more apples for the cinnamon apples for Gracie's morning pancakes. She had a weakness for them. Hence the apple cobbler for tonight's dinner.

That and Voodoo sourced way too many damn apples, so I had to use them before they went bad.

Bones made her smile, and the tiny flicker of it loosened something tight in my chest.

Good. She needed that. Hell—*we* needed that.

Because the truth was, since coming back, everything

had shifted. We'd always been a team. A family of sorts. But Grace had become the center gravity of this house. Of us. Not because she asked to be. Not because we wanted her to carry anything—fuck she didn't have to do a damn thing but keep breathing. No, she was the center because that was where she fit.

Where she belonged.

Still... belonging and understanding were two different things. The deeper we settled into this... whatever *this* was... the more all the edges of everything left unsaid pulled tighter and tighter.

We'd agreed to so much without ever actually agreeing to it.

The shared bed.

The constant physical closeness.

The way all of us touched her and she touched us.

The quiet assumption that she was ours and we were hers.

The way she fell asleep pressed between us as naturally as breathing.

No one had said it aloud, but every one of us was living it.

Well, that wasn't totally true. Grace had said it. She'd said she loved us. She'd told us that all the way back in France. She loved us and she wanted us. Then in Miami, she said she didn't know what she wanted—except that it involved all of us. *She* wanted *us*.

So, our Gracie,—sweet, brave, traumatized, stubborn Grace—needed more from all of us like oxygen. Needed clarity. Needed truth she could hold in her hands. She needed to hear what we all felt but hadn't given words to.

She needed to know she wasn't temporary.

Bones got her laughing—real and bright—and the

sound filled every room in the house like it always did. As she headed toward the kitchen for dinner, I wiped my hands on a towel and intercepted her gently.

"Hey," I said, brushing my knuckles lightly along her arm. "Can I talk to you for a minute?"

She blinked up at me. "Everything okay?"

"Yeah." I gave her a small smile. "But there's something I think we should say out loud. Something all of us have been... avoiding."

The whole house shifted. They'd heard me. I wasn't so self-absorbed to think they weren't feeling it. Understanding.

Grace took a small breath. A wary one. "Is something wrong?"

"No," I said, stepping closer, letting my voice stay soft but firm. "But you—and us—we're building something. We're living something. And it's long-term. Whether or not any of us have said that out loud."

Her eyes went wide—uncertain, hopeful, scared.

"Legend..." she whispered.

"We're here," I told her. "Not just because you need us. Not because of your sister. Not just because you're hurting —though I'd really like to fix that part. We're here because where you are is home. This has always been Base, but now it's home too because you are here. I think it's time we stopped pretending we didn't all choose this already."

Bones crossed his arms behind her like a wall of warm muscle. "He's right."

Voodoo set his book aside and stood. "We're already in, Firecracker."

Alphabet shut his laptop, voice low but steady. "We should talk. All of us."

Grace looked at each of us one by one—eyes shining,

breath caught, shoulders trembling like she didn't know whether to collapse or reach for us.

So I held her gaze and offered the truth she needed.

"No more guessing," I said. "No more reading between lines. You deserve to know exactly where we stand."

I reached out, offering my hand—not grabbing, not pulling, just offering.

"Let's have the conversation we've all been avoiding," I said softly. "Together."

Her fingers slid into mine.I guided her gently toward the huge dining table. Roasted butternut squash soup steamed in the tureen at the center, braised short ribs sat atop a bed of garlic mashed potatoes, maple-glazed carrots glistened beside them, and fresh homemade bread waited, still warm from the oven. The apple cobbler was cooling on the counter, the scent of cinnamon and sugar already filling the room. A wine glass awaited her while I'd put out beer mugs for the rest of us.

We weren't always so formal at dinner, but I found myself glad as hell I'd decided to go for it tonight. I pulled out her chair and helped her settle in.

"You're not getting out of this," I said lightly, trying to ease the tension she carried like a shield.

Grace smiled faintly, sliding in, her hands brushing mine on the table. "I know," she murmured.

Bones slid in next to her on her left, Voodoo across from him, Alphabet at the far end, Goblin tucked near near his feet, as I settled in opposite Gracie. The table felt impossibly cozy, perfectly sized for us, the fire crackling just right, the snow drifting lazily outside as if the world itself had agreed to give us this space.

I poured her wine, careful not to spill a drop, then handed her the glass.

"I want to start," I said softly, letting my fingers brush hers again. "Because I haven't said it. Not properly."

Her eyes flicked up to mine, curious, expectant.

"I love you, Gracie," I said, simple and unadorned. "I've loved you for a long time. But I didn't say it out loud, because... I wanted you to feel safe, not pressured, not like there was any expectation. I wanted you to choose us the same way we've chosen you."

Her lips parted, and I caught the catch of breath I knew she'd been holding.

Voodoo grinned slowly. "And I've said it too, Firecracker. You've got all of us, every day, every way you want. And I mean that."

Alphabet's calm voice cut through next. "I love you. I've told you before, but it bears repeating. You've got my heart, my trust, and my chaos. You're in it with me, and I'm in it with you."

That was all of us, save for Bones, who canted his head and waited for her to look at him. "You don't have to question whether you belong to us—or we to you. We do. Your place is with us. Ours is with you. I told you once, not a single damn one of us is worthy of you."

"You just had to go and say I love you in the weirdest way?" As dry as I kept my tone, it made the others grin, even Bones. But it was Gracie's fierce smile that brightened the whole room.

"Shh," she ordered. "He's talking."

"As I was saying," Bones continued, giving me a wry look before he focused on her again. "None of us are good enough, least of all me. But you love us anyway and you're letting us love you. So yes, Dollface, if you need to hear those words then hear them loud and clear, I love every damn stubborn inch of you."

Grace's eyes shimmered with unshed tears. She swallowed hard, then glanced at me, then at Bones, then the others. "I... I love all of you too. I've said it. But... I didn't know how much I wanted to hear it out loud. From all of you."

"Sound off, gentlemen," I said as I rose to serve the soup. "The lady needs to hear it."

"I love you," Voodoo said without preamble or hesitation.

"So do I," Alphabet agreed. "I can't get over how much I love you. Still can't believe you think we're lovable, but never letting you go."

"Absolutely never," I concurred and when those stunning blue eyes locked onto mine, I added, "I love you, Gracie."

"Love you, Dollface. And if you ever doubt it," Bones said quietly, brushing her hair back behind an ear. "We'll remind you."

"Every day," Voodoo piled on as he raised his beer mug.

"We're here," Alphabet told her. "We're not going anywhere without you and we're never leaving you."

I set her soup bowl in front of her. "You're pretty much stuck with us, Gracie. Just—remember that whenever we piss you off, okay?"

She looked at each of us in turn, a single tear sliding down her face. "I will if you remember that you're stuck with me too—even if I really piss you off." The last she said to Bones and he cupped her face and kissed her.

"Deal."

Just like that, the stretched bands of tension winding around all of us snapped free, leaving only warmth behind.

"We should eat before it gets cold," I said, motioning to the food. "Because the ribs won't survive without someone appreciating the sweat and tears that went into them."

Voodoo patted me on the shoulder. "Suckup."

"Hey," I argued. "I'm pretty damn impressive."

"Yes," Gracie said with a soft laugh that stroked over my soul. "You are."

"Great," Bones said in the driest tone possible. "I see a contest for impressing her is now going to be the focus of the next few months."

"Going to be? Alphabet said, raising his own beer mug. "It's been on the agenda, Bones. You're just starting in last position... apparently."

That earned another round of laughter.

"I don't know why I put up with you idiots," Bones muttered, but the smirk tugging at the corner of his mouth robbed the words of any bite.

"Because we're lovable idiots," Voodoo said cheerfully.

"Speak for yourself." Alphabet took a sip of his beer. "I am a menace, not an idiot."

Grace laughed again—softer this time, but no less bright. The sound loosened the last knots in my spine. She dipped her spoon into the soup, brows lifting in delight at the first taste, and I felt a surge of smug pride.

"This is amazing," she murmured.

"Thank you," I said. "I aim to please."

We settled into the meal—easy, warm, the kind of comfortable where you could hear the snow falling outside if you listened closely. Grace relaxed visibly with every bite, every joke, every casual nudge or brush of fingers.

The conversation flowed, as it always did when the edges weren't sharp anymore.

"So," Grace said once she'd polished off her soup and

the ribs had made their rounds. "Since this is apparently a night of honesty… can I ask something?"

"Always," I answered.

She toyed with her wine glass for a second. "The renovations. The new room. The bed big enough to land a helicopter on. That was for… all of us, right?"

Bones answered before the rest of us could. "You think we built an aircraft-carrier-sized bed for fun?"

"Yes," Voodoo said. "Absolutely for fun. Also because Bones kicks. Hard."

"I do not—"

"He kicked me off the bed once," Alphabet said mildly. "Just saying."

Grace's hand flew to her mouth, laughing.

Bones glared at all of us. "I don't kick."

"You do," I said soothingly. "But it's adorable."

"It is not adorable—"

"I think you're very adorable," Grace insisted. "Don't listen to them."

His whole expression softened for her. Fuck, Alphabet was right, she really was the Bones whisperer.

"Anyway," Alphabet continued, wiping his mouth with a napkin, "the room was built for the five of us, yeah. Forever-term, not temporary. We want you there. Because you belong there."

Grace's eyes shone again—this time without fear behind it.

"Good," she said softly. "Because I was thinking… maybe once spring comes… we could add a deck?"

I blinked. "A deck?"

She nodded, setting her wine glass down. "Off the new suite. Maybe French doors? So we can walk right out to the view. A place to sit. Maybe some planters. A little garden."

The entire table stilled.

Then Bones shook his head once, expression implacable. "No."

"No?" Grace's jaw dropped.

Voodoo chimed in immediately. "Hard no."

"Security nightmare." Alphabet raised a finger.

Grace looked from man to man, scandalized. "I didn't say retractable glass floors or a giant slide! Just a deck!"

"It would be beautiful," I said diplomatically. Then sighed. "But they're not wrong. French doors are a vulnerability."

"We can reinforce them," she argued. "Didn't you say the glass in all of the windows is bulletproof? Why not those?"

Voodoo leaned in as though letting her in on a secret. "Because bulletproof French doors cost as much as a kidney on the black market."

"Really?"

"Yes," Voodoo said solemnly, holding her gaze. "Really."

Wthout missing a beat, she took a sip of her wine then said, "Good thing none of you are using both."

Alphabet choked on his beer. I burst out laughing. Bones dropped his head into his hand, shoulders shaking.

"Firecracker," Voodoo said proudly, "that was beautiful."

"I'm serious," she said, tapping her fingers on the table. "A deck would be nice. And safe. If you make it safe."

Bones exhaled through his nose like she'd just challenged him to a duel. "If we do this—and that's a *big* if — then we design it. Not prebuilt. Not flimsy. Reinforced everything. The garden planters have to be placed so they don't obstruct line of sight."

"Whatever you say, Captain." Grace smiled slowly.

He narrowed his eyes. "That tone is mocking me."

"Mocking?" She widened her blue eyes innocently. "Never."

Voodoo snickered. Alphabet shook his head.

I covered her hand again. "What he means is—we'll build it. For you. With you. Just like the room."

Grace's smile softened. "I'd like that."

After slamming back his beer, Bones sighed like he'd just aged ten years and resigned himself to fate. "Fine. We'll build a damn deck."

She lit up—actually glowed—with joy so bright it punched straight through my ribs.

Just like that, the teasing died into warmth again, the kind that was patient and slow and full of promise.

Future plans.

Shared space.

Shared life.

She wasn't temporary. None of it was.

TWENTY-EIGHT

VOODOO

Three months back at Base, and spring had finally bullied winter into stepping aside. Montana didn't warm up so much as *thaw*, slow and suspicious, like it expected snow to ambush it at any minute. Which—honestly—was fair.

But today? Today was damn near perfect. Blue skies. Crisp air. Smell of pine waking up again. And the soft thud-thud-thud of construction floating from behind the house, where Bones, Lunchbox, and Alphabet were arguing over load-bearing supports for the deck we were apparently building with the paranoid precision of a military bunker.

Firecracker blamed me for the design plans getting more elaborate every week. I blamed her sparkling blue eyes and the way she said *please* like she didn't know it was a nuclear-grade weapon.

Speaking of...

"Voodoo!" she called from the stairs, tugging her hair into a loose ponytail as she hopped down the last step. "I'm ready."

I was supposed to be heading into town alone to pick

up the custom French doors—doors that had taken four damn shipping hops and a forged delivery route to make sure no one ever traced anything back to Base. Old habits. Necessary habits. And with Grace here? Non-negotiable.

But when she'd said she wanted to come with me—sunshine in her voice, promise in her smile—yeah, I wasn't about to say no.

"Looking good, Firecracker," I said as I grabbed the keys off the hook.

She rolled her eyes. "I'm in jeans and a sweatshirt."

"Exactly. Looking good."

She bumped me with her hip as she passed. "You're biased."

"Obviously," I said, opening the door for her. "And correct." In more ways than one. The pale, haunted look had retreated. She had a healthier glow to her skin, a playfulness that came easier and easier to the smile she often wore.

The nightmares still came, but less and less. Two days earlier, she'd told a story about her sister and her eyes hadn't instantly sheened with tears. Though she'd immediately flicked a look to Alphabet who gave her a quick shake of his head with a measure of regret in his expression.

She'd steeled herself, then lifted her chin and asked us for stories. Stories about when we were younger, home lives, families... None of us could resist her. It didn't take long before we unearthed some hilarious memories that had her in stitches.

Progress.

The breeze hit us the second we stepped outside. Somewhere in the trees, birds were making an unholy racket. Springsong. Life happening again. Looked a lot like Grace these days.

I'd gotten the big truck out of the garage, we needed the extended bed for this trip. When I opened the passenger door for her, she winked then *climbed* into the passenger seat. Once she was in place, she grinned at me with that soft, relaxed look she only got out here—away from shadows, away from memories with teeth.

Satisfied, I closed the door and circled round to the driver's side. As I slid behind the wheel, I tapped two buttons on my phone. It turned on the GPS. We had our own trackers, but habits were habits for a reason. Mirroring me, she pulled out her phone and swiped across the screen to show me she already had hers on.

God, I loved her.

"You excited to get the doors?" she asked, pocketing the phone once more.

"Sure am. Means we can finish the frame next week." I flicked her a look. "You're really getting that deck, huh?"

Grace grinned. "Told you I would win the deck battle."

"You didn't win. You *wore us down.*"

Her snort of laughter was everything. "You agreed before dinner was over. That's not winning?"

"Bones agreed," I corrected. Some reservations had been assuaged when I sourced the doors. More as we worked out how to do it. "Some of us took more convincing."

She laughed, bright and warm, and I'd drive sixteen hours just to hear that sound again.

We rolled down the gravel until it met the mountain road, the forest curling in around us like a living tunnel. She rested her cheek against the window, taking it all in with the same wonder she always did lately—like the world was something she could touch now instead of just survive.

"We should take you deeper into the mountains soon," I said. "Past Harlow Ridge. Maybe hit the falls."

She perked right up. "Yes. A thousand times yes. And maybe camping?"

"I'll allow it," I teased. "As long as you remember that the wildlife out there doesn't give a single damn how cute you are."

"Yet," she corrected. "You haven't seen me try to befriend a bear."

I groaned. "Why would you say something so horrible?"

She snorted. "Legend said the same thing last night."

"Because Lunchbox is a smart man." I flicked her a grin. "Also because none of us want to fight a bear on your behalf."

"You wouldn't?"

"Oh, I would. All of us would. We'd win too. But the paperwork would be hell." Not to mention none of us were fans of being mauled. "Remember what happens to tourists who want to pet the murder cows."

Grace burst out laughing again and then grew quieter, softer, as we dipped around a bend and the mountains opened up in front of us—

"Last night was beautiful," she murmured. "The stars."

Her voice carried that quiet awe she only used with things that made her feel safe. Or alive. Or both.

"Yeah," I agreed. "You know, most folks never get to see the Milky Way like that. Too much light pollution."

"You turned off every single light in the house," she said, amused.

"Operation Stargaze," I corrected. "Very important mission."

She flashed me another dazzling smile. "Thank you for showing me the constellations."

"Anytime," I said. "You picked them up fast."

"I liked how you explained them. How they connect. How old they are. How people used to navigate by them." She paused. "It felt... whimsical and real all at once."

"Good." I reached over and brushed my knuckles against her thigh, brief but intentional. "You deserve things that make the world feel big in the right ways."

She swallowed, staring out at the horizon. Something in her shifted—subtle but real. A tightening. A breath she held a beat too long.

"Voodoo?" she said quietly.

"Yes, Firecracker?"

She hesitated, and that right there was unusual. Grace did a lot of things—ran headfirst into danger, loved recklessly, laughed like she meant it—but hesitation? That wasn't her unless something mattered.

She twisted her hands once, then exhaled.

"I've been thinking," she said finally. "About going back to work."

I didn't react. Didn't flinch. Didn't give her the wide-eyed panic she might've been bracing for.

Instead, I let the truck roll steady down the mountain road and asked, calm as anything—

"Okay. Talk to me."

She looked at me then—really looked—and I saw every piece of what she wasn't saying yet.

Her independence.

Her identity.

Her fear of being fragile.

Her need to stand on her own feet again.

Her worry that we'd try to bubble-wrap her.

Beneath all that—hope.

Because she trusted us enough to tell us.

"I miss it," she admitted. "I miss... feeling capable. Useful. I miss doing something that's mine."

I nodded slowly. "You're allowed to want that."

"You don't think it's too soon?"

"You're the only one who gets to say whether it's too soon," I told her. "Not me. Not Bones. Not Lunchbox. Not Alphabet."

Grace's breath wavered. I reached over and hooked my pinky around hers, gentle and sure.

"And if you want to go back," I said, "then we'll figure it out. Together."

Her shoulders relaxed. A little at first, then a lot.

"You're not mad?" she whispered.

I barked out a laugh. "Mad? Firecracker, I'm proud of you."

She blinked, startled. "Proud?"

"Hell, yes. Wanting your life back? That's strength."

She smiled then—small, aching, honest. The kind of smile that carved itself into a man's ribs.

"Thank you," she said quietly.

"Anytime," I murmured, tugging her hand to me and kissing it before I released her pinky. . "As long as you don't try to befriend any bears at your job."

"I make no promises." The lightness in her tone held elements of teasing. "The business can be pretty brutal."

I groaned again, but my chest felt warm—full.

"I guess I thought that there would be more security concerns..." She chewed on her lower lip. "You think it's safe enough for me to go back? Eleanor is gone, so I'd need a new agent." Sadness trickled into her voice again.

Grace wanting her life back didn't scare me. Grace *not* wanting it back—that was the thing that would've terrified me. I reached over and let my hand rest against her knee—warm, steady, grounding.

"There *will* be security concerns," I said. "Plenty. I've already got a list running in my head."

Her eyes widened a little, but she didn't retreat. She never did anymore. If anything, she took on a measured expression that reminded me of Bones. I doubted either would appreciate the comparison, but I enjoyed it. Particularly because she was a lot prettier.

"Like what?" she asked.

"For starters?" I ticked one finger off the wheel. "We've kept you off the grid for over a year, Firecracker. As far as the public knows, you dropped off the face of the earth. If you walk back into the modeling world tomorrow, every blog, tabloid, and social media account is going to light up like a Christmas tree on crack. People are going to ask where you've been. Why you disappeared. Why you came back."

She inhaled, slow and sharp.

"Second," I continued, "modeling means travel. Shows. Hotels. Public venues. Crowds. Paparazzi. Photographers. People wanting access to you. You can bet your ass that if La Madrina's people—or anyone tied to the shit we've been digging through—are still sniffing around, they'll see you pop up again."

She looked down at her hands. "So… not safe."

"I didn't say that." I softened my tone. "I said there are concerns." It would absolutely paint a target on her. Threat assessments were probably going to be nightmarish. We would need to take real time on them.

Her gaze flicked up, hopeful and uncertain all at once.

"And third," I said, "you'd need to build a whole new team around you. New agent. New contracts. New circles.

That means new people in your life. New connections to vet. Which we can do, but it's work."

There it was again, that tiny flinch when she thought she was going to be a burden.

"Hey," I said, nudging her pinky again. "I didn't say *no*. I'm just giving you the reality. If you go back, we build the safety net before you take the first step."

She nodded slowly. "Okay. That... makes sense."

I could tell she wasn't done, though. The words were bunched up behind her teeth, fighting their way out. So I waited. Let her get there herself.

Finally, she whispered, "I do miss modeling. I miss the creativity. The artistry. I miss... feeling beautiful. Strong. Like I owned the space I walked into."

God. Yeah. I felt that one like a punch.

She wasn't being vain. She was remembering a version of herself she'd been forced to abandon.

"You were good at it," I said. "Hell, Firecracker—you lit up runways. When Alphabet found some of your old campaign videos? I thought Lunchbox was gonna have a stroke."

That pulled a shaky laugh from her. "Legend said he almost tripped over a chair."

"Lunchbox absolutely tripped over a chair," I corrected. "Don't let him lie to you. Man damn near face-planted watching you pose with a scarf."

Of course, it had *only* been a scarf draped creatively. Rather than pornographic, it had been utterly sensual and captivating. Which posed another problem, her body, her call. But anyone being near her while she was that naked would need an even closer look and one if not two of us on set.

Her cheeks pinked in that way that always made me want to pull over and kiss the breath out of her.

"But…" she said slowly, "I also miss the people. The relationships I built." Her throat bobbed. "After Eleanor died, I didn't just lose my sister. I lost my world. All of it. And I don't… I don't want to hide forever."

I reached over and tucked a strand of hair behind her ear—gentle, deliberate.

"You don't have to hide," I told her. "Not anymore."

Her breath hitched.

"If the thing you want," I added, "is to go back to modeling—not because you feel like you should, but because you miss it? Then say that. Say you want it."

She swallowed hard. "I think I do."

"Then we figure it out."

She blinked. "Really?"

"Really," I said. "Grace, if modeling is where you feel most *you*? Most alive? Most in your element? Then we're not gonna lock you up in the mountains and tell you no."

Her shoulders eased. A small smile tugged at her mouth.

"I guess I thought you'd try to talk me out of it."

"Oh, I will," I shot back, "if you tell me you want to go do runway shows in South America with zero support crew and shit security. Or if you say you want to go back tomorrow without a plan."

"I wasn't planning that," she promised.

"Good. Because I like my heart beating inside my chest, not ripped out by Bones." Who would take far more convincing and I didn't have a single argument that would work—yet. I turned that over in my head. Putting her out there would put us out there and any anonymity we relied on now would be eroded.

"So you're not worried?" she pressed.

"I'm always worried where you're concerned," I said simply. "But not because you can't handle yourself—because the world doesn't deserve you."

She froze. Absolutely froze.

Then her voice came out tiny and stunned. "That's... that's a lot, Voodoo."

"Firecracker," I said, "everything about you is a lot. That's the point."

She pressed a hand over her eyes, breath shaking, halfway between a laugh and a cry. When she lowered her hand again, she looked lighter. Brighter. Braver.

"So," I said, "modeling, huh?"

She nodded. "Yeah. I think so."

"Then we'll prep for it. We'll talk to the guys. Start the background safety net. Maybe keep your first gigs low-profile. Controlled. Choose photographers and designers who won't sell their own mothers for a headline."

Her smile grew, hopeful and full. "You really think I can do it?"

"Grace," I said, letting her name land softly but firmly, "I think you can do anything you decide you want."

She stared at me like she couldn't quite believe I meant it.

But I did.

I meant every damn word.

"Voodoo?"

"Yeah?"

She settled her hand over mine on her thigh.

"Thank you."

"For what?" I asked, even though I already knew.

"For not making me feel... fragile."

I lifted her hand to my lips and kissed her knuckles. "Never fragile," I murmured. "Just precious."

She turned her gaze back to the mountains, sunlight catching in her hair, and I knew, clear as the constellations she'd memorized last night, she wasn't breakable. Not anymore. She was rebuilding.

A woman we'd follow her anywhere she wanted to go. Even into town for French doors that cost more than my first car. A future she was brave enough to want? That wasn't even a question.

TWENTY-NINE

ALPHABET

By the time Voodoo's truck rumbled back up the long gravel drive, I'd already run four different search sweeps, two encrypted message threads with overseas contacts, and one deep-dive scrape on every Syndicate affiliate who'd so much as sneezed in the last twenty-four hours.

Nothing. Again.

Goblin nudged my boot with his nose and I reached down to ruffle his ears. He leaned into my hand, warm and solid, reminding me I was *here*, not buried in the digital dark again.

But Amorette *wasn't* here. That part hit me every damn day.

Three months back at Base, and the trail felt colder by the hour. Even so, I kept digging, because I wanted to look Gracie in the eye and mean it when I said, *I did everything I could to find her sister.*

And because we didn't leave people behind. Not ever.

The new deck was starting to look like an actual structure instead of a fever dream. Bones and Lunchbox were knee-deep in lumber, tools, and a debate about torque angles that had devolved into insults about each other's math skills.

Bones hammered something with way too much force. "Lunchbox, I swear to God, if you tell me one more time that I should 'eyeball the measurement,' I'm gonna eyeball you off this deck."

"You *can't* eyeball structural integrity, Bones." Lunchbox held up a level with saintly calm. "We've discussed this."

"You've discussed this," Bones growled.

I smothered a laugh. Then the crunch of tires on gravel had all three of us glancing up. We set aside the tools to circle around to meet them. Voodoo hopped out of the truck first, sunglasses on, smirk firmly in place.

Grace slid out of the passenger seat—jeans, sweatshirt, hair up, cheeks pink from the sun and wind. She looked... good. Better. Lighter.

"Got the doors," Voodoo called, tapping the side of the truck. "And snacks. Firecracker stole half my trail mix but I let it slide."

"It was mostly raisins." Grace held up the bag.

"Blasphemy," Lunchbox muttered. Then louder, "Grab an end?"

Grace headed over to climb up in the truck bed, but Voodoo lifted her off and Bones set her to the side where she burst out laughing at them. Not for the first time I marveled at how seamlessly she fit into our world—even the rough, sawdust-filled parts.

Between the four of us, we unloaded the doors. They were beautiful, heavy as hell, framed in rich walnut to match the suite upstairs. Grace brushed her fingers along the glass like she was imagining the view already.

She would have that view. She'd dreamed of it. Maybe she deserved more than that view. One by one, we carried them around to store in the temp shed, we'd set up under the deck. Now that they were here, we could cut through the wall, but we would need to do some more work to set up for that.

Once they were secured, she stepped back, rubbing her palms on her jeans, her eyes flicked from me to Bones to Lunchbox, and then over to Voodoo.

"So," she said, casual—too casual. "I told Voodoo something today."

Bones straightened, expression shifting into that heavy unreadable wall he used when preparing for something unpleasant.

Voodoo leaned a hip against one of the posts, arms crossed, waiting.

"Shoot," Lunchbox said gently.

"I'm... thinking about going back to work."

Grip going white-knuckled on the hammer he'd just picked back up, Bones went absolutely still. His jaw locked so hard I heard the grind from ten feet away.

"No," he said flatly. "Absolutely not."

Grace blinked. "Bones—"

"No." He stabbed the hammer toward the ground like he was punctuating it. "You've been off the radar for a year. The second your face hits a billboard, we'll have people up our asses."

Lunchbox winced. "He's not wrong. It would put you in the spotlight again. Cameras. Reporters. Schedules. Travel. Less control."

Grace's shoulders nipped inward, barely, the way they

sometimes did when she was absorbing impact. But she didn't back down.

"I miss it," she said quietly. "I miss *me*. Or that part of me."

Scrubbing a hand through his hair, Lunchbox shot me a look. The "are you going to say something?" look.

I didn't. Not yet. Because every scenario was already firing behind my eyes—

Grace doing shoots in controlled environments?

Possible. High monitoring.

Grace traveling out of state?

Complicated. Risk spike.

Grace stepping out in public, photographed, tagged, tracked, discussed online?

At least twenty countermeasures needed upfront.

Bones pacing beside her, protective instincts spiking so hard he'd probably punch the nearest camera?

Guaranteed.

Grace seeing old colleagues, old friends, people who'd known her before?

Unpredictable. Could be healing. Could be a landmine.

Grace wanting her life back?

Necessary.

Grace being hunted again?

Unacceptable.

"Bones," Grace said softly, stepping closer. "I'm not asking to sign a thousand endorsements tomorrow. I'm just... thinking. Maybe rebuilding. Maybe slowly."

"Dollface..." Bones exhaled like she'd punched him in the lungs.

"I'm not fragile," she whispered.

He closed his eyes.

Fuck if I didn't feel that like a knife slipped right between my ribs.

"She's not asking for permission," Voodoo said gently. "She's asking what it looks like."

"We can build safeguards." Lunchbox nodded, thoughtful. "Start small. Interviews with vetted people. Shoots on our terms. Maybe bring an agent on board who understands discretion."

Grace's eyes brightened a little. "Yes. Like that."

Bones shot the three of us the dirtiest look imaginable. "I see how it is. Mutiny."

"Collective problem-solving," Voodoo corrected cheerfully.

"Same thing," Bones muttered.

Grace stepped closer to him and slid her hand along his arm. "I just need parts of my life back."

He sagged. Just a little. Then he covered her hand with his own.

"You're asking me to let you walk into the open," he said. "After everything."

"I'm asking you," she whispered, "to walk with me into it."

Something kicked under my ribs. I finally spoke. "We can do it."

All eyes snapped to me—including Grace's soft, hopeful blue ones.

"We prep," I continued. "We plan. We build a firewall around your name. We manage every appearance, every shoot, every digital trail. We vet your agent, your circles, the locations. We put buffers in place. We decide what level of anonymity you want and where."

Her throat moved in a tight swallow. "You really think it could work?"

"I think," I said, "that the only thing worse than risking letting you live your life... is asking you to keep hiding from it."

She took a tiny step toward me. Goblin rose too, tail thumping once, like he was taking her side simply because she was Grace.

I let a little smile curve my mouth. "We'll make it safe, Gracie. I'll run the logistics. I'll run the checks. I'll run *everything*. But if something doesn't look right? We pull you out."

Her voice shook. "AB..."

"This is non-negotiable," I said quietly. "I want you to be happy. I want you to have the life you want. But I want you alive more than any of that. If something doesn't check out, then we extract—no arguments, no debates."

Her breath caught. Her perfect white teeth scraped over her lower lip. She'd been worrying at it again, turning it redder and making it more plump.

The guys were not thrilled with the response, Bones least of all. I could practically read him running all the possible scenarios to keep her safe. We all were. This was not one time where he would just cave because she wanted it.

The threat was too *real*.

Grace wiped at her eyes and whispered, "So... that's not a no?"

I shook my head slowly. "It's a *not yet*. Until we're ready. Not to mention we need to work out the story to cover your absence. I took care of a lot of your accounts, and handled everything I could remotely..."

Surprise flickered over her face.

"People do *know* you're missing but they don't have any information on it." They'd filed a missing persons case, but the investigators hadn't spent more than a week on it. The case had already been cold when her absence had been reported. No leads, no hints, and no evidence to follow.

Sinclair's people had done too good a job scrubbing Amorette's absence, so it was never tied to Grace's. Since they didn't have any family to report it, she was just... gone. In some ways, it was the safest outcome for Grace. No one knew where she was or who she was with. We could and would keep her safe.

Going back into the world would strip away one real layer of security. She exhaled in relief, trembling at the edges.

Bones sighed long and heavy. "Dollface, *if* you're doing this, I'm escorting you everywhere until you're eighty."

"Deal." Grace grinned, then hugged him. Over her head, Bones' gaze fixed on mine. Taking her back out there would mean changes for all of us. The work we did required us to be ghosts. Ghosts couldn't be in the sun with Gracie.

I nodded once. Guilt raked through me, because I really didn't want her going back to that life. To being treated like a piece of meat put there for others to ogle and desire. The first time someone came on to her or propositioned her, they would disappear.

Lunchbox clapped his hands once. "Steaks are going on the grill in fifteen. Anyone planning to eat should wash off the sawdust."

Bones grumbled, but he kissed her with such ferocity it silenced everyone. Then he headed inside with Voodoo to wash up and Goblin trotted after Lunchbox who followed.

Grace stepped toward me, slipping her arms around my torso. I hugged her back without hesitation. "Thank you," she whispered into my chest.

"For what?"

"For trying. For everything."

I rested my chin lightly on her hair. "I'm not done trying. Not even close." *I'll find your sister. Somehow. Some way. I'll find her...*

~

A WEEK LATER, my office was a cave of cold light and humming processors—every monitor running a different search, every encrypted channel blinking results that told me absolutely nothing new.

Nothing about Amorette.

Nothing that led toward Korkov.

Nothing that connected La Madrina to any recent movement.

Nothing on the Castillos or a half-dozen other South American operations I tracked. There had been a lot of takeovers, assassinations, infiltrations, and surprisingly enough—arrests—over the past few months. All of which promised a shifting power structure and landscape.

But there was nothing but silence on the other fronts. It was the wrong kind of silence. The kind that meant someone else was covering tracks better than I could uncover them.

We'd taken a huge chunk out of the trafficking side of their operations. We hadn't eliminated it. That would be pure arrogance to think we had, but we'd definitely *hurt* them.

Goblin lay stretched out at my feet, chin on his paws, tail thumping once every so often like he knew I needed reminding I wasn't alone. He did that. Chose his moments.

I leaned back in the chair, left ankle propped over the right prosthetic on the desk. An open notebook sat on my lap where I'd been writing out the contingencies for Grace's potential return to modeling.

Potential.

I hated that word more today than I had last week.

"I told Voodoo something today."

"I'm thinking about going back to work."

I replayed it more often than I wanted to admit. Not because I was angry. I wasn't. Worried? Absolutely.

No, it was on a constant loop in my head because the quiet, certainty in her voice had been *hers* again. The Grace from before everything fell apart. Before monsters peeled back the world and showed her its teeth.

That part mattered more to me than all the risks I could list.

But holy shit, I could list a lot. I dragged a hand down my face and forced myself to keep looking at the screens.

On the left: The remains of Eleanor's agency—Drake Talent & Management. I'd traced the transition of power after her death, which was listed as a "freak accident," something vague and insulting. Two junior partners picked up the reins. Neither had her instincts. Neither had her spine. Both had taken on new investors.

Investors whose names were... interesting.

On the right: A scroll of every photographer, designer, stylist, and brand Grace had worked with over the last five years. Fifty-seven names total. Thirty-four still active. Twenty reachable. Ten with questionable ties. Three with direct connections to Rachel Manning—the photographer who'd lent us her Paris apartment.

I flagged every connection, every oddity, every overlap.

Rachel herself? Clean. Too clean. We owed her, but she wasn't stupid. She'd noticed the inconsistencies in the story Grace had told her, and she'd asked questions. Not many questions and even though she accepted it when Grace said she couldn't answer her, I didn't like it.

I didn't like it enough to put her back on the board as someone to just keep an eye on. If I was suspicious of everyone then there was a strong chance no one would surprise me.

Hopefully.

On the screen: A projected security plan. Preliminary. Brutal. Necessary.

Because no matter how I organized it, no matter how much I prepared—every scenario where Gracie stepped back into the public eye put her at risk.

And the worst part? I couldn't escape the idea that this was the absolute *wrong* call.

Not because she couldn't handle it—she could.

Not because she wasn't strong enough—she was stronger than even she knew.

But because the second Grace Black walked back into the world and her face resurfaced, someone—Korkov's people, La Madrina's people, one of the syndicates, hell, even someone we didn't know about yet—would see it.

And then they'd start looking for her again.

A ping hit one of the screens. Goblin's ears perked.

I rolled closer, scanning the notification:

A contact in Barcelona. One I rarely tapped. A quiet favor. Just a breadcrumb.

They'd traced a rumor—just a rumor—of a woman matching Amorette's description in Rio de Janeiro three months earlier. A photograph accompanied it, pixelated to hell and back. Dark hair, right build but so fucking blurry it could have been a mannequin for all the detail visible.

Old. Unverified. Maybe bullshit.

Maybe hope.

I flagged it, coded it, shoved it into the "pursue immedi-ately" file.

Goblin nudged my thigh, sensing the shift. "Yeah, buddy," I murmured. "I know. It's something."

My phone buzzed on the desk.

LUNCHBOX

Fish ready in 20. Grace wants you to taste-
test the garlic butter because she says
yours is better than mine. Lying, obviously,
but come eat anyway.

Despite everything, I snorted. I didn't cook, something Gracie knew well, and the closest I came to making garlic butter was just stirring up Lunchbox's.

Then another message came in.

GRACE

AB? Come out when you can? No rush.
Just... want to see you.

My heart hit the brakes. That was the thing with her—she didn't ask repeatedly. Didn't demand. Didn't push.

But she was getting so much better about asking for what she needed and wanted, when she needed or wanted it. She'd also held to our promise to each other to always say the truth.

And all I could think about was how the hell I was supposed to tell her—

That her going back to work was dangerous. That it risked everything we'd built. That even with all our prepa-ration, all our training, all my surveillance and contingency plans—it still felt like walking her straight into a sniper scope.

I leaned back in my chair, staring at the screens—at every lead I'd chased for her sister, every dead end, every open thread.

At all the ways the world could hurt her again.

Goblin nudged me once more, harder. Like he was telling me to get my ass moving.

"Yeah," I muttered. "Alright."

I shut down nothing—left every search running—locked the screens with a command, and reached down to scratch behind Goblin's ears before pushing to my feet.

THIRTY

Two more months passed, and somehow life had settled into something that felt dangerously close to *normal.*

Not the kind of normal I used to have—bright lights, cameras, runway chaos, schedules planned down to the minute.

This was a different kind.

A better kind.

The deck was finished—broad and warm under bare feet, with a view that stole my breath every sunrise. The garden boxes were planted—herbs, tomatoes, peppers, strawberries—all things the guys pretended they didn't care about but absolutely fussed over when they thought I wasn't watching.

As for our French doors... God, they were beautiful.

Walnut frames, glass panels so clear it looked like the mountains were stepping straight inside. When the morning light hit just right, the whole suite glowed like some kind of daydream.

This place didn't just feel like home. It *was* home.

Life was good. Really, really good.

The guys had taken two missions in the last couple of months—short ones, clean ones. The first was a forty-eight-hour in-and-out that only needed Bones, Legend, and Voodoo. The second required all of them—and me.

I still didn't know how to fully articulate what it meant to be included. Not just tolerated. Not protected into uselessness.

Included.

It reminded me that I wasn't broken. That I could still be capable. That I could want my life back, and while I did, I also valued the life I had *now*.

I'd slowly, carefully reached out to a handful of contacts—people I trusted, or trusted enough with boundaries and encrypted channels. Rachel Manning was one of them.

She was loud, brilliant, sarcastic, and had an uncanny ability to read between every line of every silence.

Which made it all the more alarming when my phone buzzed one late evening with her name lighting up an encrypted app we used because it made the guys happier and me safer while also protecting Rachel too.

We were out on the deck, roasting s'mores over the fire pit. The night air smelled like pine and toasted sugar. I was tucked between Voodoo's legs in one of the oversized deck chairs, Bones and Legend were arguing about the structural integrity of marshmallows, and AB was sprawled on a blanket with Goblin curled at his side.

My phone buzzed again.

I glanced down.

RACHEL (SECURE LINE)

You awake? Need to talk?

My heart slipped a beat.

Rachel didn't do careful punctuation or even more careful questions. Or at least she hadn't since we'd reconnected after AB cleared her as "safe."

I sat up straighter.

"Gracie?" Legend asked immediately.

"I'm fine," I said automatically—too fast for it to sound believable.

The guys went still. Not grabbing, not crowding—just... ready. Every one of them.

I swiped to accept the call and brought the phone to my ear.

"Rach? What's going on?"

A breath, then a familiar voice, husky, low, and tight. "Okay, so, full disclosure? I debated *not* passing this on."

My stomach dropped. "Why?"

"Because it's weird," she said. "It felt... I don't know. Loaded? I've been sitting on it for a couple days, trying to decide if I should even tell you." A pause. "But then I asked myself what I'd want done if the situation were reversed."

Behind me, Voodoo's hands tightened on my hips. Bones stood up like a shadow congealing into a man. AB was suddenly sitting upright, eyes already on my phone. Legend froze mid-reach for a graham cracker.

Swapping us to speaker, I swallowed. "Rachel... what message?"

She exhaled like she'd been holding it the whole time.

"A man showed up at the studio three days ago," Rachel said. "Polite, soft-spoken, Latino, mid-thirties maybe. Said he was looking for you."

Every hair on my body rose.

"He indicated that he knew I knew you," she continued. "He didn't push, didn't pry, didn't ask where you were.

Didn't even threaten or try to intimidate. If anything he was —absurdly polite. But... you know how you just get that feeling about some people. It's unnerving, but you're pretty sure they aren't a serial killer sizing you up for a skin suit?"

Legend's askance look would have been comical at any other time, but right now I was worried about Rach.

"Yes, I do. Are you *alright?*"

"Oh, babe, I'm fine. Seriously. More than fine, but he said he had a message and he wanted to leave it with me in case I spoke to you."

The tension vibrating around the guys stretched even tauter if possible. It was making it hard to take a deeper breath. "In case you spoke to her?" Bones repeated the phrasing in a cool, deliberate voice.

"Yes," Rachel said. "Another reason I hesitated. Felt— targeted considering we've just been talking about setting you up with new headshots and building out your package."

We had.

"Have you talked to anyone about that?" AB asked, no accusation, just straightforward inquiry and he had his tablet up and on.

"Nothing you don't already know about," Rachel said. "But... before you interrupt again. I'm not the only photographer he approached."

Voodoo slid his arms around me. All the warmth of the day had fled and ice seemed to run in my veins. "He said that?"

"Yes, and me being a suspicious bitch, I called a few of them today. He has indeed approached a few photographers, in the U.S., in Italy, and here in France." Rachel huffed out a breath. "Left a message for you with all of them."

"So, fishing expedition." Legend folded his arms.

"I'm not speculating on him or his motives," Rachel continued. "To be clear, he did not ask me if I was in touch with you, did not ask for a number to call you on, or indicate in any way he wanted me to give him your information. All he wanted was for me to give you a message *if* I talked to you and to please only give it to you."

My pulse thudded in my ears.

"What message?" My voice wasn't steady anymore. It cracked at the edges.

Rachel took another breath.

"He gave me a phone number," she said softly. "And told me to give it to you... because it was about Amorette."

The night went silent.

The fire popped. A marshmallow fell off someone's stick into the flames. Goblin whined once, low.

I couldn't breathe.

"What is his name?"

Rachel whispered, like she knew I was breaking apart. "Grace, he just said 'a friend'. When I said that wasn't good enough, he would only give me one name. Matias."

Bones swore under his breath. Voodoo muttered "holy shit" like a prayer. Legend shot to his feet. AB's eyes went sharp—calculating, scanning, already moving through possibilities.

Matias.

That name didn't mean anything to me.

"Grace?" Rachel's voice cracked. "You there?"

I tried to speak and nothing came out. My throat wouldn't move. My eyes burned so violently I had to blink just to see.

Voodoo's arms came around me, steady and warm and unshakable.

"I'm here," I croaked. "I'm... here."

"I don't know what this means," Rachel rushed out. "I don't know if it's real. But if someone had information about someone I loved, even if they turned out to be a quack, I'd want to know. So I'm telling you."

"Thank you," I whispered.

"Want the number?" she asked gently.

The guys drew closer around me like a shield.

AB nodded once and I said, "yes please."

Rachel read the number. He typed it instantly, cross-checking, pulling it apart.

"This could be total bullshit," she said. "Some crazy fan. Or it could be nothing. But it could also be... something."

"If it's something," Bones growled, voice low and lethal. "We'll handle it."

Rachel hesitated. "Grace... are you safe?"

"Yes," I whispered, eyes burning. "I'm safe."

"Good." A shaky exhale. "Love you, girl. Call me after you talk to him?"

"If we talk to him," Legend corrected sharply.

"After whatever happens," she said. "I'm here."

The call disconnected. The world felt too big and too small all at once. I stared at the phone in my hand.

A *friend* named Matias. A number. Information about Am.

It seemed like such precious little information and yet... it was so much at the same time.

It was like the universe had ripped open and handed me a live grenade. I turned slowly toward the guys.

Their faces were a wall of determination, fury, fear, and something so fierce it hurt to look at.

AB spoke first.

"We call only after I verify everything," he said. "We do this smart. We do this together."

Bones nodded. "You're not talking to anyone alone, Dollface."

Legend stepped closer, voice steady. "We move carefully. Deliberately. But we *find out*."

Voodoo pressed his forehead to the back of my head, the loop of his arms around me so damn strong. "Firecracker... breathe for me."

I let out a shaking breath, a half sob, half exhale. Fear, hope, confusion, shock tangled beneath it all. For the first time in a very, very long time...possibilities opened up again.

"Okay," I whispered, throat tight and heart pounding. "Let's find out what he knows."

All four of them answered at once—voices low, sure, unbreakable: "Together."

THE NEXT WEEK blurred into something sharp-edged and breathless.

The vetting process we put "Matías" through was slow, brutal, and methodical—exactly the way the guys needed it to be. AB tore apart every piece of available data he could pull together. Legend cross-checked every document. Bones hunted every possible tail or connection. Voodoo ran the in-person assessments.

And the strangest thing?

Matías didn't resist. Didn't protest. Didn't push.

Running the name against the organizations we'd already dealt with gave us a couple of possibilities but we were loath to push too hard. Still, AB sent Rachel the photos and she identified one of them as the man who came to her studio.

She confirmed it without hesitation.

"That's the guy," she'd said. "That's exactly who came to see me."

After that, we stopped guessing. We played the odds.

Voodoo took the first meeting—alone, but not unobserved. A museum in Madrid, one with metal detectors, cameras, tight entry points, and enough foot traffic that anything suspicious would pop like a flare. Not perfect, but controlled.

Matías arrived alone. Calm. Unarmed. He gave Voodoo five minutes of his time. The gauntlet didn't upset him, but he didn't linger nor give anyone else the message for me.

The guys argued for an hour. I argued for two.

But in the end, we all agreed: If this man truly knew something about Amorette, and I could learn something after all this time, no matter how small, I had to look him in the eyes.

We chose London. Neutral ground, crowded but manageable, a city humming with CCTV we could tap into and maneuver around. Far from anywhere familiar.

We arrived separately, staggered flights, staggered hotels. Layers on layers of counter-surveillance. Then the moment came.

Voodoo walked beside me, but I was the one who stepped forward into the quiet back gallery of the museum we'd chosen. Soft lighting, high ceilings, paintings hung like silent witnesses.

Matías stood at the far end of the room. Over six feet tall, his dark hair had lighter streaks like the sun had dyed it, and his honey-brown skin gleamed the daylight bulbs that illuminated the portrait room. I didn't know him except as a photo. I'd wonder if he would be more familiar when I met him.

He wasn't.

Then his eyes lifted and landed on me. Recognition seemed to strike him like a blow. Recognition followed by relief, that struck a match to the flames of hope inside of me.

I froze.

His breath hitched audibly, his hand gripping the back of a bench for balance. *"Dios mío,"* he whispered. *"Saben... ustedes dos realmente son idénticas."*

God... you two really are identical.

My throat closed. My hands went cold. All the air in my lungs turned thin. I stepped closer, heart hammering so hard it hurt. My voice cracked. "She's alive?" I whispered. "Amorette... is she alive?"

The only answer he gave me was a phone number, then he walked away. The guys offered to go after him, but he'd done everything else. He'd gotten me the number. It had to be enough. We had to let it be enough.

TEN DAYS.

Ten days since I'd stood in that London gallery for a few brief moments before Matías handed me a slip of paper with a phone number on it.

Ten days since I'd called that number and spoke to my sister on the phone. Spoken to her. Heard her voice.

My only regret was I couldn't thank that man. Couldn't thank him for finding a way to get me the information. Because he had, I'd found Am.

The guys were *not* happy about any of this. Not the call. Not Matías. Not the meeting.

They'd argued for hours about the where and when and how. Air-tight logistics. Multiple safe locations. Layers of misdirection. Redundancy inside redundancy.

Honestly? I barely heard any of their negotiations with Am's people. My guys negotiating with hers.

I didn't care where we had to go. Didn't care how long it took to get there. Didn't care how many hoops we jumped through or how many protocols we followed.

I just wanted to see my sister again.

The trembling—the buzzing, electric quiver under my skin—only grew stronger the closer we got.

Until finally...we were there.

An airport. Of all places.

I almost laughed when we walked into the secure wing and I saw the level of overkill the guys had arranged—or negotiated or threatened someone into agreeing with, I wasn't exactly sure. Cameras, personnel, restricted access, sealed doors, more checkpoints than made sense.

Inside the main terminal we'd blended in like regular travelers—handbags, backpacks, the illusion of normalcy. But once we cleared security, everything changed.

A customs officer approached.

"Ms. Degas?" he asked.

I nodded. My legs weren't entirely stable under me.

"If you and your party will follow me."

Bones tensed instantly. Voodoo shifted closer to my right side. Legend slid a hand to my lower back. AB's gaze cut across every angle of approach, Goblin pressed against his leg, alert.

But they trusted their prep. And I trusted them.

So we followed.

Down a corridor. Around another. Through back-access passages and staff-only hallways. A labyrinth of blank walls and humming lights.

My heartbeat was a drumline in my ears. Every step felt both too slow and too fast.

Then the customs officer stopped at a plain door. No window. No markings.

He keyed in a code. The lock clicked. The door swung open.

And my heart stopped.

There she was.

Amorette.

Alive.

Standing in the center of the room with her hands pressed to her mouth, tears already spilling down her cheeks. She was so beautiful, so much fuller than I remembered and—oh my god, so very pregnant—but her face was flushed and full of color. Her eyes were bright, as bright as mine probably were. It was *her*.

It was Am!

My sister.

No wonder they'd wanted us to come to them. It all made sense. A sound ripped out of me—half sob, half laugh —as my knees buckled and I ran toward her.

"Am—" was all I managed before she crashed into me, arms wrapping tight, her entire body shaking against mine.

"Gracie," she cried. "Gracie—oh my God—Gracie—"

I held her like I'd never let go again.

Behind us, Bones exhaled a rough, broken sound. Legend swiped a hand over his face. AB's breath hitched once, sharp. Voodoo murmured something in a voice I'd never heard from him—wet, relieved, reverent.

There were others there, but none of them mattered.

Not in this moment. Because right now, it was me and Am. We were together.

Finally found.

After so long in the dark...the light was almost blinding.

Grab the free bonus scene as the sisters—lost to each other for years and willing to burn the world to find one another—are finally reunited. Thank you for taking this journey with them.

EPILOGUE
ALPHABET

A few months later, everything in our world had somehow settled into a rhythm that made sense —if you squinted, tilted your head, and accepted that "normal" for us now included deck repairs, shared morning coffee, weapons drills, and an internationally recognized model curled up on our laps while we ran surveillance.

Grace had gone back to work in carefully curated, heavily secured, strategically limited bursts. She'd also discovered—much to my suffering and her absolute joy— that she could weaponize my *one* secret against me:

My real name.

Which is how we ended up **here**, in the middle of an op, with her currently holding that damn secret hostage while I monitored from the safe house with Bones, Lunchbox, and Voodoo on the ground.

They had just finished a sweep of the backstage areas when her voice lit up my comms—sweet, playful, and dangerous.

"AB," she sing-songed, "I think you owe me something."

I pinched the bridge of my nose. "Gracie, I thought you promised to *edge* it out of me."

"That's what I'm doing," she chirped.

I choked. Loudly.

"Gracie," I hissed, "you realize we're on comms, right?"

"Yes," she answered cheerfully. "And you're the eyes in the sky. So... watch me."

"Oh, hell," Bones growled.

"Oh, this should be fun," Lunchbox said, far too delighted.

And Voodoo? He didn't say a word.

Of course, he didn't *have* to. Because the second Gracie stepped into the camera frame, he stepped into view right behind her, muttering something that looked a whole lot like *you little menace.*

From my vantage point, I watched her strut through the venue with a confidence that could bring empires to their knees.

People were cheering. Cameras flashing.

A beat later, it hit me: There was a show happening.

A *lingerie* show.

"We talked about this," I groaned into the mic.

"No," she corrected, grinning at one of the girls who winked back, "you talked. I listened. Now, I'm doing whatever I want."

"You're supposed to be the distraction," I muttered, "not the whole damn show..." But that got me nowhere so, I tried, "Gracie, come on. Let's discuss this later."

"Okay," she agreed brightly, but continued to head straight for the side of the stage and reached behind her waist.

To untie her dress.

"Dollface…" Bones warned, murder and devotion mixing in his tone.

Grace kept going.

The hoots and whistles doubled. Models laughed. And Gracie—my sweet, chaotic, beautiful nightmare—shimmied the top half of her dress down.

Thank every deity ever invented that she was wearing the lace set **and** the silk cami we'd insisted on. Still didn't do anything good for my blood pressure.

"Tell her," Bones ordered. "Or I will."

"Nope," Grace said sweetly. "Doesn't count if he doesn't tell me."

Lunchbox snorted. Voodoo rubbed his forehead. Bones muttered a prayer for patience.

Grace looked straight into the nearest camera, like she knew it was *my* camera, one hand on her hip, lips curved, eyes wicked.

And the dress slid a little lower.

God help me.

"Fine," I exhaled. "Fine. But you have to get off the stage first."

"Nope," she chirped. "We tried that last time, and you didn't pay up."

Voodoo was already three steps up the runway, resigned amusement on his face as she prepared to drop the dress the rest of the way.

I cracked.

"*Algernon*," I snapped. "It's Algernon, dammit! My mother loved the sound of it and no one could spell it or pronounce it, so I prefer Alphabet!"

Silence.

Then Grace, dress still barely hanging on, turned,

looked directly into the lens, and smiled like she'd just won the Super Bowl.

Voodoo grimaced. Bones groaned. Lunchbox straight-up wheezed with laughter.

"Gracie wins," Lunchbox announced. "She said she'd get it out of you before the mission was over."

"Wonderful," Bones deadpanned. "Now let's all get back to work—and Dollface? I am going to spank your ass later."

Grace reached for Voodoo's hand, still glowing with triumph as he helped her down from the stage. She turned to let him redo the ties on her dress, but happiness filled her voice as she said, "What did I say about threatening me with a good time?"

"On that note," I cut in, grinning despite every shred of dignity I'd just lost, "looks like we've got movement."

The target stepped into camera range.

Grace straightened, eyes sharpening. Voodoo moved to offer her his arm.

Bones and Lunchbox took position.

And for the first time, the wild, impossible truth hit me with full force: Grace wasn't just part of us. She was *meant* for us.

"Alright, team," I said, steadying myself as adrenaline kicked in and Goblin bumped my thigh with his nose as if reminding me that he was here too. "It's showtime."

AFTERWORD

When I first sat down to write *Burn*, I had no idea just how deep the rabbit hole would go—or how long these characters would take up residence in my head. Now, standing here at the end of the *Blood Brothers* series, it feels a little surreal. These five books represent over three years of living with Grace, Bones, Alphabet, Lunchbox, Voodoo, and Goblin as they grew their chaotic, beautiful, and broke family together.

The seed for this series was planted "many moons ago" during a week-long writing getaway in Seattle with Blake Blessing and our friend Sara. We were wrapping up a *Cardinal Sins* book at the time, and Blake was plotting what would eventually become her *Bastard Brothers of Carnage* series. We were tossing ideas back and forth when I said— half randomly, half instinctively—"I want to write Grace's story." Blake looked at me and said, "Yes."

And just like that, Grace Black found her place.

Grace, of course, is the identical twin sister of Amorette Black, the FMC of *Bastard Brothers of Carnage*. We collaborated on their shared history—their childhood, their trauma, those pivotal flashbacks that connect them—but from the moment the present-day stories begin, their paths run independently. Their worlds intersect, but they don't rely on each other. You can read Grace without reading Amorette, and vice versa. That was important to both of us: making each series accessible on its own, even while rewarding readers who choose to explore every corner of this shared universe.

But even with the planning, nothing quite prepared me for what happened when I finally started writing. The moment my fingers hit the keyboard, the characters took over. Scenes unfolded like they had been waiting, fully formed, just behind a curtain I hadn't drawn back yet. The brothers' bond, Grace's strength, Bones' loyalty, the darkness they all wrestled with—it all came pouring out with a clarity that rarely happens as a writer. Some stories make you fight for every sentence. This one demanded to be told.

Closing the final chapter of the final book feels like closing the door on a home I've lived in for years. Bittersweet, but satisfying. These characters challenged me, broke me open, surprised me, and—more than once—made me cry at my keyboard. I can only hope they gave you even a fraction of that journey in return.

Thank you for reading. Thank you for trusting me with your time, your emotions, and your love for these complicated, flawed, fiercely loyal characters. Thank you for coming all the way to the end.

And if you're not ready to leave this world behind, there are plenty of dark corners and new adventures waiting! Check out What's Next...

For now, though, this is where I leave the Blood Brothers. But trust me—there are always more stories to tell, and I can't wait to share the next one with you.

xoxo
Heather

Website:
heatherlong.net
Reader group:
facebook.com/groups/heatherspack

Blake Blessing's Website:
https://www.blakeblessingbooks.com/
Reader group:
https://www.facebook.com/groups/blakeslustylegion

WHAT'S NEXT?

Thank you for coming with me to the end of this journey. If you're not ready to leave this world behind, you don't have to—there's plenty more waiting for you in the shadows, the safe houses, and the tangled loyalties of the connected series.

If you want more dark, gritty, adrenaline-laced romance in the same universe, explore:

82nd Street Vandals

Violent, obsessive, and fiercely loyal, the Vandals deliver raw edge, feral devotion, and a found-family that bleeds for each other. The Vandals, of course, are Doc's family that the guys came to help. They are also where Alphabet and the guys were first introduced. Start with Savage Vandal.

Bay Ridge Royals

A world of power, corruption, and ruthless men who will burn cities to the ground for the woman they claim. Start with Shamelessly Loyal.

Cardinal Sins

Strategic, dangerous, and sinfully twisted—this series pulls you deeper into the underbelly of the world you've already glimpsed including the characters of Vienna and Cash whom you met earlier in this series. Start with Kill Song.

And if you've been waiting for **Amorette's story**, you don't have to wait any longer:

Bastard Brothers of Carnage by Blake Blessing

This interconnected series follows Amorette and dives into the chaos, brutality, and fierce devotion of life in the cartel and the men who claim Amorette as their own. Start with Addict.

If you're craving more dark romance + psychological suspense, look at:

The Switchboard Duet

While not set directly in this world, it carries the same energy—twisted connections, high tension, and a romance forged in danger. Start with Talk to Me.

Curious about Rachel Manning?

Rachel first appeared in the Untouchable series (which fair warning is a far cry from this one), and she'll be stepping into the spotlight soon. Keep an eye out—she has her own series coming, and she won't be facing her demons alone.

Whether you're hunting mysteries, craving morally gray men, or looking for more broken-but-unbreakable heroines, there's plenty ahead. The world is bigger than ever, and there are so many stories left to tell.

About Heather Long

I *love* books. Not just a little bit, but a lot. Books were my best friends when I was growing up. Books didn't care if I was new to a town or to a class. They were always there, my trustiest of companions. Until they turned on me and said I had to write them.

I can tell you that my own personal happily ever after included writing books. I've always said that an HEA is a work in progress. It's true in my marriage, my friendships, and in my career. I am constantly nurturing my muse as we dive into new tales, new tropes, new characters and more.

After seventeen years in Texas, we relocated to the Pacific Northwest in search of seasons, new experiences, and new geography. I can't wait to discover what life (and my muse) have in store for me.

Maybe writing was always my destiny and romance my fate. After all, my grandmother wasn't a fan of picture books and used to read me her Harlequin Romance novels.

Also by Heather Long

82nd Street Vandals

Savage Vandal

Vicious Rebel

Ruthless Traitor

Dirty Devil

Shamelessly Loyal (Novella)

Brutal Fighter

Dangerous Renegade

Merciless Spy

Reckless Thief

Fierce Dancer

Dirty Dancer

Bay Ridge Royals

Shamelessly Loyal (Novella)

Battle Lines

Deceptive Truce

Wicked Surrender

Violent Chaos

Desperate Victory

BLOOD Brothers

Burn

Lure

Own

Oath

Dare

Blue Ivy Prep

Problem Child

Mad Boys

Party Crashers

Money Shot

Bravo Team Wolf

When Danger Bites

Bitten Under Fire

Cardinal Sins

Kill Song

First Chorus

High Note

Last Word

Chance Monroe

Earth Witches Aren't Easy

Plan Witch from Out of Town

Bad Witch Rising

Fevered Hearts

Marshal of Hel Dorado

Brave are the Lonely

Micah & Mrs. Miller

A Fistful of Dreams

Raising Kane

Wanted: Fevered or Alive

Wild and Fevered

The Quick & The Fevered

A Man Called Wyatt

Going Royal

Some Like it Royal

Some Like it Scandalous

Some Like it Deadly

Some Like it Secret

Some Like it Easy

Heart of the Nebula

Queenmaker

Deal Breaker

Throne Taker

Lone Star Leathernecks

Semper Fi Cowboy

As You Were, Cowboy

Shackled Souls

Succubus Chained

Succubus Unchained

Succubus Blessed

Shackled Souls (Omnibus)

STANDALONES

Kiss of Fate (w/Blake Blessing)

Taste of Karma (w/Blake Blessing)

I'll Be Home... (w/Tate James)

Overexposed (w/Tate James)

Switchboard Duet

Talk to Me

Don't Let Go

Untouchable

Rules and Roses

Changes and Chocolates

Keys and Kisses

Whispers and Wishes

Hangovers and Holidays

Brazen and Breathless

Trials and Tiaras

Graduation and Gifts

Defiance and Dedication

Songs and Sweethearts

Legacy and Lovers

Farewells and Forever

Hellos and Happily Ever Afters

Wolves of Willow Bend

Wolf at Law

Wolf Bite

Caged Wolf

Wolf Claim

Wolf Next Door

Rogue Wolf

Bayou Wolf

Untamed Wolf

Wolf with Benefits

River Wolf

Single Wicked Wolf

Desert Wolf

Snow Wolf

Wolf on Board

Holly Jolly Wolf

Shadow Wolf

His Moonstruck Wolf

Thunder Wolf

Ghost Wolf

Outlaw Wolves

Wolf Unleashed

www.ingramcontent.com/pod-product-compliance
Lightning Source LLC
Chambersburg PA
CBHW020052310726

48970CB00007B/2525